Book Of Answers

R. C. Thom

ISBN Print: 979-8-9861808-0-9
ISBN E book: 979-8-9861808-1-6

Copyright registration:
Case number 1-7249236341, year completed 2014,
copyright certificate number TXu002128817, copyright date 12-22-2018

Many characters, you will meet here, are or were (when living) real people. None of the scenes they appear in were actual. Some places and events did actually happen historically. I played with the timeline a lot. 1960s nerds will see that, but many of the events and people in this volume were real. The details of events, real or not, in this book were entirely invented by me. This work of fiction is not historically accurate. My fictional characters walk through history in Forrest Gump fashion bumping into the icons but I never met them myself and what these characters say is fictional unless quoted otherwise. Mention of TV shows and other common things like household products of the 1950s and 60s are or were real products. When I mix science with fantasy that is where I especially make shit up.

Cover art: Rachel C. Thompson
Book design: Gayle F. Hendricks
Proofreading: Angel Ackerman,
    angel@parisianphoenix.com, Twitter @creativelyangel
Content editing: Lisa Cross

For editing and publishing services:
Parisian Phoenix Publishing Company, angel@parisianphoenix.com
Check out Parisian Publishing: ParisianPhoenix.com, Twitter: ParisBirdBooks

Contact R.C. Thompson by email: Humanrights4all@aol.com
R.C. Thompson's crappy website: rcthom.com or rcthom.net

E-book SRP $3.99 U.S.
Print SRP $11.99 U.S.

"To surrender to ignorance and call it God has always been premature,

and it remains premature today."

— Isaac Asimov

Books by Rachel C. Thompson *aka* R.C. Thom.
Available in print and e-book.

The Aggie Piper series: High school senior Aggie Piper comes of age while discovering the presence of aliens on earth and exposes the Deep State's secret relationship with them. The Deep State will stop at nothing to take or destroy Aggie's alien friends.

SOUL HARVEST:
Print ISBN number: 798-1-7321459-1-7 Also in e-book: 798-1-7321459-0-0

AGGIE IN ORBIT:
Print ISBN number: 798-1-7321459-7-9 Also in e-book: 798-1-7321459-6-2

AGGIE IN SPACE:
Print ISBN number: 798-1-7321459-8-6 Also in e-book: 798-1-7321459-9-3

Dragon Fire: In this epic, the end of the Dragon's Age is at hand. One dragon was to lead dragon-kind away from human entanglements, but treachery makes Mars Hammertail into an outcast who must find his way before all dragons are destroyed.

DRAGON FIRE:
Print ISBN number: 798-1-7321459-2-4 Also in e-book: 798-1-7321459-3-1

Stalking Kilgore Trout: This anthology of 21 short stories presents quirky to controversial idea-based stories inspired by the author's love of Kurt Vonnegut. These stories cross the genres: sci-fi, fantasy, historical and satire and twist them together into new shapes. Thompson promises, "There's something here to offend everybody."

STALKING KILGORE TROUT:
Print ISBN number: 798-1-7321459-4-8
Also in e-book: 798-1-7321459-5-5

Books coming soon:

The Adventures of Tom Conley: An archeological adventure in which Tom seeks the captured goddesses in order to stop the world's destruction.

Anthology II: More of the same but different.

"Intelligence is an accident of evolution, and not necessarily an advantage."
— Isaac Asimov

INTRODUCTION

This novel was 50 years in the making. It started in a dream I had while in college and taking a creative writing class. I woke one morning with this picture in my mind, a vivid picture of a character in a future time and place which was a very unlikely place for this character to be. So, I made up a short story about him and his conflict. My teacher liked the story. The others I wrote sucked. I sent it in to a now gone sci-fi pulp and they paid me in money. After that life got in the way and I didn't have time for creative writing but that character stayed with me.

I had big ideas and a problem: I couldn't type or spell worth a damn. There were huge themes and concepts surrounding this character's unique situation. I knew that if I wanted to do this story justice, I had to learn a lot first. I didn't begin to learn how to write worth half a damn until the late 90s. The story was still in me. By then it had changed, but John Doe, my odd character, had dug in deep.

I finished *Book Of Answers* in 2014, copyrighted it in 2018 and now finally in 2022, it's ready for print. Why did it take so long? I wanted to get it right. I wrote my first books to learn how to write this one. I've spent my writing life sharpening a story knife to cut this book out of my soul. I made strides improving craft but I waited until I felt able to pull together the story I wanted to write and write well. It took me a long time to get my prose together. This end product was not what I wanted to write in 1979. This is much better. I'm glad I waited so long.

After drafting *Book of Answers* (and before editing), I wrote and published other stuff. I have a new novel in the can and more in my head waiting their turns. I have a couple of nonfiction books also stuck in the gray matter. For me, reaching the *Book of Answers'* mountaintop only allowed me to see the next one. It was the start of something beautiful.

One hint for the reader: pay attention to the dates in chapter headings. I jump time in this volume. Some jumps are extreme and in some scenes, time itself is twisted.

I'm happy about how this novel came out. It may not be the great America novel, but it is for me. It represents, among other things, a great American moment in history that meant a lot to me.

Please enjoy. I had a hell of a good time writing it.

PRELUDE

God's Control Room

Near the center of the Milky Way lived beings who were employed by the Intelligent Designer. Her management team, the angel race, didn't create the galaxy, they managed it for Her. One particular spinning ball of contradictions was Her favorite and it wasn't going well. Carl's fuse lit when Earth began to fail.

The Creator herself isn't interested in how management is done like us people who do the work. Her Centerness didn't solve problems. Earth's ongoing issues get worse whenever She puts her nose into it. Carl didn't trust Her judgment. She didn't seem to care. The angels were hired to care.

Carl worked under Larry's direction in Earth's Control Department but Carl kept a step ahead of the boss. Director Larry was the guy pulling quantum strings but he didn't like to work hard. Carl decided to pull the boss's chain… without him knowing it, as usual. Larry was a blockhead. He would use a planet-smasher to nudge an asteroid if Carl let him. *Finesse isn't Larry's talent.* Carl had a mind to use his talent and maybe save Her Centermost's current favorite project without an astral wrecking ball. Larry, Mr. Regulations, was about to do something stupid, or maybe not if Carl's plan worked.

Larry and Carl, lower-upper-managers, agreed to meet in Earth's control room while the shift operators took lunch. Carl knew this station well. He and Larry were the previous Earth Ops control jockeys. Carl arrived in time to check the boards before the boss showed up. He confirmed Earth was in serious trouble. Carl was ready with his first leading question when Larry finished reading meters.

"How do we even know if it failed?" Carl said. "Earth doesn't look that bad."

"Look at the stats, who's in charge down there? What kind of people rule

Earth?" Larry pushed up his glasses, his tone was angry.

Playing by the book, he's not happy. No problem. Bracing for impact.

"Beats me, boss."

"I'll tell you who runs things down there. Are they nice people who care about others? No, it's the scum, the monsters, the reptilian-brained sociopaths run everything, and that sickness is multiplying. We can't have it."

Larry's wings flexed with agitation.

This type of genetic malfunction was understood. Normally there was no hope of abating this order of disease. It was always a big mudslide. He waited as Larry spewed pontifications. *He'll spit out the right answer eventually.* Larry was the kind of guy who must first build justification steam before his take-action whistle could blow. No doubt what was rattling around in Larry's skull were questions like, 'What should I do?' and 'What will She do if I fuck this up?'

Larry can't afford another bad decision but he is good at deflecting responsibility away from himself. Wasting Earth won't be another of Larry's mistakes if Carl took the bullet. There was something about that planet…he didn't know where the idea came from, but Carl's inner voice nagged him to save the Earth. As the boss rattled on Carl worked on his pitch.

"…Earth's leadership poisoned our social structures. Religions' the leg up. Mike and Gabe, don't get me started—they didn't prevent religion—they started one. We drive planets away from religions for a reason, you know. It's too easy for the psychopaths to ruin Her plan—which they did. What we have here is a mad dog. The bad-guys control Earth and…"

Funny how he must tell me everything I already know. Time to turn him.

"Are you saying it's hopeless?" Carl said casting fresh bait.

Larry adjusted his glasses and took a deep breath. "Earth is a mad raptor that must be shot down. That's regulation. What if Earth matures? I'll tell you. It will go forth and conquer, that's what. That's not good for Her other planets, no by wing and feather. She's all about the big picture, you know, and…"

Here we go again. Larry's way of gaining favor was to go by the book. He regularly supplanted his logic with Her examples. Larry tried to play it heartless like Her which seldom worked out. *That's not smart.* Nobody knew what was in that woman's head. Yet Larry always attempts the impossible and tries to impress Her? Higher management must have rubbed off on him. Blue-nosing doesn't work on Her, and he should know that by now. Judging by the look on Larry's face, the boss's heart was already bleeding for Earth. *He loves Earth alright. It's time for another laser shot.* Carl interjected his next pointed question.

"What about the good people, the ones not infected?"

"Genetic contamination-free, you mean. Sure, some naturally resist. More often social structures force gene conversions—not many resist that. Some people aren't affected at all, I'll grant you. The ones that do survive, why…why they're prime seed stock, good results, and don't forget—"

"Innocent people. What do we do for them?" Carl said to get him back on track. Superior seed stock was the best angle to work Larry over with. "Isn't making seeders the point? There must be good ones down there."

Carl kept going with steering questions. Larry's answers were good reasons not to demolish the project. *Larry will walk the right course if led to that path.* Carl kept him talking. *He'll reason it out and think it's his idea. Everybody wins.*

Larry's face turned gray as the implications sunk in. *The boss ain't so hard-nosed, go figure.* Management-wonk Larry was compelled to play a role that wasn't natural. After all, he came up from planet-side operations. Larry had to keep Central Control off his ass like everyone else.

In this situation killing the planet was the by-the-book default procedure. *Killing ain't good for anyone's mental health.* Carl knew Larry well enough to know Larry didn't have the heart to wipe out a nice planet full of decent people just because a handful of monsters took over. Carl raised a wing. Larry shut up.

"Seems like ending the entire race just for a few bad Adams doesn't technically square with Her moral code," Carl said. "You think we should do something about saving it?"

"Maybe, I'm open to suggestions. What have you got Carl? I got nothing."

"What if I accidentally leaned on the reset button?" Carl blew the dust away from the control board and flipped the cover off a special bank of switches.

"Wave release is right next to the volcanic destruct sequence starter. It's easy to get this board confused, I mean, what with so many switches and all. Operators know better, but I'm a Controller now. What do regulations say about accidental Creation Wave release? What's the procedure?"

Larry adjusted his glasses, pushed his wings back, and stuck his skinny chest out. *The guy knows his book.*

"Salvage operation. It's in the manual, by planet!"

"Gee, I wish I had thought of that."

Carl was the low angel in this stack and destined to receive the brunt of repercussions. *I won't get that promotion they're pushing me into—the one I don't want—what a shame.* There were other benefits to taking the heat off Larry. Larry was fun when not stressed out. No worry. Larry will wiggle off the hook, as usual, and cover Her ass doing it. *He's good at politics.* Boss Angel might even get a luncheon out of it. Carl preferred win-win management but he wouldn't ever say that—*it's not in the book.*

The Creation Wave button stuck. Carl leaned into it hard. Alarms rang.

"Oops," Carl said. "I guess you better go tell Control I screwed up."

"Yes, yes I will…stop the recall. Tell Gabe he's promoted, no wait, make Mike higher rank. No that won't work. Make Gabe the top angel but promote Mike, too. Turn that ship around. No, wait, better have someone in Space Transport Operations call the Planet Molder Union shop steward first. Captain Burk is a stickler for protocol."

"You got it, Boss."

"Page Henry and Bob, tell them to get back here right away."

Larry left the control room with vibrating wings and feathers dropping. Boss Angel had nothing to worry about. Carl didn't know why Larry acted so nervous. Then again, Carl never faced God eye to eye himself. And he never will. Of that, he was pretty sure. All he needed to do was keep screwing up and that was easy.

He had disconnected this control room's cameras long ago. The repair order was still outstanding. Nobody had eyes on Carl's real talent: Controlling Controllers. *She'll have to believe Larry.*

Life was good working for the Galactic Control Center and getting better. Carl's promotion will get axed, no doubt. Screwing with Gabe and Mike was just bonus water crystals on a birthday asteroid.

******

Henry and Bob walked the white halls of Center City side-by-side with their Earth-made Oxford shoes slapping and wings fluttering. A messenger had accosted them at lunch after they ignored the pages. They had to go back early but didn't hurry. They returned to Earth-ops in their own good time. Cutting into an angel's lunch break just wasn't done—union rules.

Henry had had a lot of troubles with Earth. Her Centerness's pet projects were never easy. *How did I get myself into this?* Central had control rooms for everything, mundane things like planet creation, star management, and supernova harvesting. He could have gone anywhere. Central managed all of the galaxy's typical business. *But Earth ain't typical.* Sometimes Henry regretted transferring out of the Nebula Department.

The rest of the galaxy practically ran itself. Projects that didn't involve Her sentient being program ran on automatic without issues. When that asteroid killed Earth's dinosaurs, She pitched a holy fit. Over the next 70 million years, She got into making human people more. She had switched focus after Her dinosaurs bit the dust. And now She was back on the dinosaur kick? *Why, because humans are flunking out. That's why She's letting Earth crap out. She's had enough of them already.*

Planet molding was interesting despite the problems. Angels and humans were related but distant cousins. Henry didn't care for dinosaurs. Humans were a pain in the ass, true, but herding primitive people beat the heck out of pushing rocks around space-time. Looking after big lizards was too predictable. *You never can tell what human societies will do next.* He enjoyed dynamic jobs.

"Too bad Earth got canceled," he said.

"Rumor is, Central Control thinks She played Earth out and it ain't worth saving. Then again, Her Centerness was sweet on Her problem child planet for a long time." Bob said.

"For some unknowable reason, way out on the end of Spiral Arm Seven, just beyond outer bum-fuck, there Her favorite human project spins. But not anymore? I don't get it."

Henry and Bob entered their control room and went straight to the boards.

"Why'd She let a Creation Wave Series loose pointed at Earth? What do you think, accident or oversight?" Bob asked while adjusting a tuning knob. "Odd, right?"

"Beats me. She's in charge," Henry said. "Her creation, Her problem."

That's not true. She made this into Henry and Bob's problem and as such, the pressure was on. Henry suspected upper management took pleasure in screwing with operators.

"What a godawful mess," Bob said. "Intelligent designer? And She thinks She is God, what a joke."

They called this workstation, God's Control Room, although She wasn't a god. There were other beings known just like Her also eating the center out of galaxies. Her race builds galaxies and eats them. To lower beings, she may appear godlike. *Nobody knows if there's a God. Some think She's a God. Only She knows.*

Henry didn't care—the question was not his problem. She was supposed to know everything in the Milky Way and clearly, she doesn't. She messed up… again. Gods don't mess up. Henry was convinced She wasn't a god. *If there are gods, they must be smarter than her.*

"Intelligent designer, my ass," Henry said.

"What's that?" Bob said busy with a social tuning knob.

"Forget it," Henry said, "Just thinking out loud. The downside of social construction is fixing mistakes and Earth's a doozy."

"Too many hands in this pie," Bob said.

They confirmed the new directive; Earth is a salvage job. *Do it or forget about retirement.* Henry's people live near the Milky Way's center and close enough to see Heaven, but his race wasn't yet invited. Angels stood ready for transit. But angels had a problem. Angels resemble Earthlings making them useful to Her on Earth-human planets.

"I'm never going to retire at this rate," Henry said twisting a knob.

"She only keeps us around for shit jobs," Bob said in a dismal tone.

"I doubt it," Henry said to keep morale up. "She needs planet molders like us. We're good, the best. She needs us. Can't do without us."

But for how long and to what end? How many more screw-ups can we fix? The others have moved on and we're the last of our type. And this project is a bust, all these resets, why does She bother? These people just aren't going to make it. Seen it before. Cases like this never work out. Salvage? Face facts Lady, angels are the last high humans. Earth version is another washout. She should just let us go to the Center. What's She up to? What's the holdup?

"You know," Bob said, "I run upgrade red. I read your mind just now."

"Oh, shit," Henry said turning on his thought shield.

"She's got a reason," Bob said, "She always has something up her sleeve."

"Yeah, covering Her ass," Henry said. "Earth's nothing but trouble. Right from the start bad seeds mucking up evolution. Who's to blame for that? Only Her."

"She let the bad seeds in, for balance She said: What balance? Earth has no balance; Her best eggs got boiled." Bob said.

"Come on, let's do what we can for them."

They confirmed a series of Creation Waves will overrun Earth. *If only we got word faster, we could do more.* Henry set aside that he was just pissed off about the short lunch. *It's too late to deflect the Waves.* Bob was co-operator on this project and he didn't like Her Centerness's bad planning either. There wasn't time to do anything constructive.

They had just gotten Earth back on track and rolling in the right direction again or, so the theory went. Chances were good that a handful of immortals were still spreading good DNA. He and Bob had received an award for confirming that a pair of immortal seeders remained…but now this.

"She let Master Control reconfigure ahead of schedule and She didn't make provisions to save onsite evolution results?" Bob remarked.

"Yeah, lose those seeds and 100 million years of toil goes out the sewer ejector. No more Earth-type humans—gone forever."

Henry wasn't happy about letting that happen. He would save Earth just to rub it in Her face given half a chance. Once the idea landed, he locked onto it. Angels operated pigheadedly and Henry was no different. Henry just couldn't let those good seeds go. He worked on it too hard.

"It took centuries of DNA correction to get that Peace Generation genetic thread going and it just started blooming," Henry said. "This is bull feathers."

This was personal for Henry. She had to know it would be. Even Henry himself, who thought of himself as Mr. I-don't-care had too many seeds in this beaker.

That bitch hooked me.

"Mike and Gabe were just there and reported bad seeds ruined it," Bob said. "They called in just before jumping out. They lost track of the good ones. They must have all gone bad by now."

"Not all of them," Henry said.

"The masses are OK so far, I agree, but the leadership's infected…not good."

"What're we expected to do with this?" Henry said of the chart scrolling by resembling genetic spaghetti. The salvage contract's collection instructions and conditions followed. Henry didn't see any method restrictions as the contract printed.

"I wish I could stop that Wave series," Bob said.

"We can't save Earth but we can save the DNA," Henry said.

"How'd you figure?" Bob said, "It's too late."

"It's never too late for an active salvage operation. We don't have to just let it sit there devolving until it's gone. Says here to get samples. Nothing about why or how many."

Bob whistled. "Send Gabe back in the middle of demolition?"

"Upstairs didn't check any restrictions," he handed Bob the paper and kicked back into his chair. "I got an idea. Why not…Mike and Gabe can collect DNA as good as any robot. We'll get live samples, too. Hold them in time phase storage and rerelease them on a new planet. She has half a dozen in development. This project doesn't have to end, we can relocate it!"

"You're the boss."

It had never been done before. It should have been all the same to Henry—Work is work was his attitude. Let it rot until it resets. What were ten million years to Her? He was upset about Earth until the contract rolled off the printer and somebody had missed checking the restriction boxes. Henry signed off and released the return order before Control caught on. The monitor chimed, "message received."

Set in stone.

Henry rescanned Earth. "Salvage won't be easy."

"Field operations are going to have to pick spice-mite shit out of pepper," Bob said.

"Mike and Gabe won't get back until after First-Wave hits. Home Office must have sent them ahead to evac Moon Base. Mike will goof off and blow it. He's not exactly motivated. That last intervention was a disaster." Henry said.

"This is a waste of time," Bob said. "Earth's doomed." Bob pushed his glasses up and did a quick estimate on his pocket calculator. "But then again, it doesn't matter what Wave does to the planet. There's enough DNA floating loose to build a Book of Answers. We might get lucky and find the lost immortals: Some were still alive last time I checked—I can't find them now. Waves can't touch them...except for Last Wave."

"Gabe doesn't need to get fancy. Rules are off. Get the stuff and get out." Henry said.

"One decent Book of Answers is all we need to make a new library."

"A solid BOA sure would be nice," Henry said.

"It'll work!" Bob's excitement spilled out. "There is still time, by wing and feather. We are doing this!"

"It'll be close," Henry said grabbing Bob's calculator. "They'll arrive after fast-evolution kicks on. Pre-Wave's already changing psychology. Waves go slow at first." He said thinking out loud. "It won't be too radical. Previous generations will still be usable; gene-carry people aren't affected immediately. The original Peace Bomb is still active."

Henry turned to his board and pushed paradigms around. He read a handful of the possible outcomes and was surprised to see a thread of hope. He could never admit it, but he felt excited and relieved. He had a hard time keeping his wings still.

"The ideal DNA seed sequences fire 1950 local time and before First Wave lands. Ideal humans will be born and remain after Wave effects and long enough to get samples. That's good starter stock. If it weren't for Wave..." Henry's wings flexed.

"Mike and Gabe ain't gonna like it," Bob said showing a lot of teeth. "They had a really bad time. Hate to rub their faces in it. I wonder...should we use that new guy?"

"What guy, that Earth guy?"

"Jesus, the Earthling field ops hire," Bob said. "He's 16% seeder. They shouldn't have put that AI Probe into him. Natural peaknik, too. They regenerated him after that foul-up. He's one of us now. You read the report."

"Artificial immortals aren't good enough. Wave will unravel him." Henry felt a tinge of pride. He was the team's desk anthropologist. Bob always deferred to him on social psychology. "We were going for intervention with Jesus, but it didn't work. He can't resist Wave action in any event."

"We need him here for study anyway," Bob said. "I never saw a host react to a Probe like that."

"I'll tell Gabe's ship to send Jesus on to Central," Henry transmitted the message. "That intervention sure was a bust."

"Salvage or intervention—high failure rates either way," Bob said. "Hate to say it but Mike and Gabe are all we have."

Mike and Gabe weren't exactly stellar operators. Bob's pain showed gray stress lines on his white face. Bob, like himself, would never retreat from a problem.

Field ops had to get in and out before a big Wave creamed salvageable DNA. The Mini Waves in between big ones didn't worry Henry. They had a little time. Earth operations had a few hundred years to get it done. It was a simple job, and if the salvage team fails, Her Centerness will blow a pressure hatch. Mike and Gabe had better produce results. Henry feared that angels will be stuck for another 100 million years waiting for another primitive race to mature.

"A lot's riding on two half-ass Planet Molders." Henry said.

"We aren't going anywhere until someone else takes over Central Control," Bob said.

"Nonhuman types are dead ends. No humanity. Silicone-based life—what was She thinking? No potential as Controllers. Dinosaurs might have made it but that damn asteroid came along."

Henry, speedreading the data, realized why She was so hot on this project. It was mixed with bad seeds, sure, but the seeds worth saving were ablaze with positive DNA. Angels had evolved from that same base stock. Earthlings and angels were closer than he previously realized.

Allowing a chosen people, albeit a primitive version, to vanish because of Her design miscalculations wasn't in Henry's DNA. Mr. I-don't-give-a-shit firmly committed himself to the savage operation's success.

1

Earth Summer 1964

Thirteen-year-old John Lazarus was insane up until now. He and his sister and everyone from his lineage had been born crazy and remained that way until puberty. That fact was told to him before. Today John's mind cleared. For the first time, he was aware of himself.

He looked down at the cat and his tummy hurt. The cat's skin was peeled away. That cat had screamed and screamed but it was dead. No problem. They lived deep in the woods of Eastern Pennsylvania. Only their Negro neighbors were within earshot, and they would never call the sheriff. The cat's cries didn't wake him. What did was the hysterical laughter of a thirteen-year-old boy. His voice. Just yesterday he had opened a mouse like a can of peas same as Margo did to the cat. He remembered looking for something, something inside that animal. *What could be inside a mouse?*

"Hey, we're naked," exploded from his mouth.

It all rushed on him at once, thoughts, understanding, sanity, everything he had been taught up until then. All kinds of things he didn't understand but remembered. All his life, father and mother had taught, and he read. And the information stuck but it didn't mean anything while he was out of his mind.

"Jeepers, this is disconcerting," he said. "Why'd Margo kill Dad's cat?"

He dropped the hatchet, leaped up four steps, ran across the covered porch and into the house slamming the wooden screen door behind.

"Mom, Mom, Mom," John cried. "She killed Hermes."

Mom was up on one of the library walls atop the sliding ladder. The book racks ran ceiling to floor around the living room. Lots of books were stacked everywhere else, too. John had read them all.

Mom turned head and shoulder from her perch. It was the first time he saw her and understood what he was seeing. She was beautiful—long, black hair, deep olive skin—big, green eyes set off by her pink silk blouse which was covered in large black dots. Her calf-length pants matched. She was tall and he was tall for thirteen going on fourteen. His mouth hung open and he didn't drool. *That's nice for a change.*

"I know, dear," she said. "It's alright."

She climbed down with grace. His penis got hard and he felt disgusted. Thoughts and feelings rushed in altogether confusing him until one idea pushed through and formed words.

"Mom, pink pedal-pushers? It's 1964 for Pete's sake. What about Margo?"

He watched her watching him with her Mona Lisa pout. He stared back until the finch on her shoulder flew off. The raven perched on an open windowsill cried, "Nevermore, nevermore."

"Aren't you going to stop her?" He said, "It's wrong."

"You've come awake, and you aren't evil. I'm so glad," she said.

Mom opened the basement door. Mice, bugs, and squirrels scattered around her feet. *No point getting stepped on.* He had cut open many of the same kinds of creatures. *They let me do it. Jeepers!*

She descended into the basement. Downstairs was loaded with books, old books—scrolls—books from Alexandrian and older. *Dad's collection.* He had 'moved them a thousand times in three thousand years.' He said that all the time.

Dad was dark-skinned, short, and fat—a fifteen hundred BC, curly-haired Akkadian Hittite. Mom was older, an archaic Greek. John was told this when it didn't register. Now, an avalanche of knowing weighed on him. His knees went weak, but he wasn't about to let himself fall.

"I'm not a quitter!"

Time slowed. He knew he knew everything all at once and it was too much. He felt the blood drain from his face and into his feet. His jaw quivered. He lost control of his legs and slumped to the floor.

"Jacob, come up, John's awake," drifted from below.

Heavy steps thudded on the stairs. One of the cats popped up first. Cats were always around him. *Dad's cats never bother Mom's wild birds. Holy cow.*

"He's awake, such timing. I'm in the middle of a translation." Dad said entering the common space.

"Why do you bother," Mom said coming up on his heels. "That foolish community college doesn't pay you to translate. Show too much skill and you'll give us away. Don't be a Socrates—you're just like him. I knew him, as you'll recall."

"That's not the point."

"I know all your points, Jacob, now is not the time to debate them. Attend to your son. This is a critical time for him."

"Yes, quite right."

"Dad, aren't you going to stop Margo?" John said picking himself up off the floor.

"No, she must explore, as you did. She'll stop on her own. You'll see, remember I told you that?"

Feelings were mixed in memories. *Dad's looking for his origins.* John was driven like Margo. Only yesterday he was looking for something, too, but it wasn't the same as what Dad was after. Images of small, dismembered creatures crashed into his mind with pictures of his bloody hand on a rusty knife. It didn't seem real. He wasn't allowed a sharp one or else he might hurt himself. He stood there with his head swimming. Realizing he was covered with dirt and old blood; he fell into a Victorian chair swooning with illness.

"She shouldn't hurt living things, it's bad," he said in a rasping voice. "Ask *Buffalo Bob*! *Captain Kangaroo* wouldn't let her, no-siree-bob."

"He has compassion and that is good," Dad said not answering him. "A step forward, indeed. Personality isn't fully formed yet, but he's well onto one. Good so far. I've had doubts regarding Margo."

"Might John be a bringer of love?" Mom asked. "It is predicted, no?"

"Too soon to tell," Dad said. "He's not that bright. Margo might be the one. Maybe there are generations yet to go. We don't know if the old lore is true. The question has been open for 10,000 years."

"Well, I think he's special," she said.

"That's what you said about Jesus, too, and what did he go and do? Ran off with aliens—didn't even take his doves. We immortals are all special but not all useful."

"Jesus wasn't immortal, the aliens revived him."

She turned toward John who was working on understanding his reality. "Come on, you'll need a bath right away. We'll put you in clothes and then I'll make you a nice peanut butter sandwich. I have *Wonder Bread*, your father's favorite."

"What about Margo?" John said.

"Her meal is before her," Dad answered.

Mom led him into the bathroom which had a nice, big, white tub. It was deep and stood on ball-and-claw feet. Black and white floor tiles were the same as on *American Band Stand*. *It's all so clean.* She started the water and adjusted the temperature before opening a fresh cake of *Ivory Soap*. The mirror showed him covered with dirt. He forgot he was naked and covered his private parts.

"After you rinse well, call me and I'll draw more water. It will take extra dunking to get you clean."

"You don't have to. I'm not a baby, golly gee whiz."

"No, I suppose not," she said and left closing the door.

He proceeded with his bath. It took three changes of water before the old dried blood washed out from under his fingernails and he felt clean enough to call himself human. He washed his hair many times using the old white porcelain pot he found on the floor next to the tub. Pouring water on his head over and over washed away layers of confusion with the dirt. He wasn't confused about one thing: *I'll never hurt another living thing again—not if I can help it—no-siree-bob.*

He finished his bath clean as a crackerjack whistle. Mom brought him clothing and sat by while he dressed. Mom talked and talked but he didn't pay her much mind. Blah, blah, blah was mostly what he heard.

"You need to pick a familiar," Mom said. "It's important."

"What the hell is that?"

"Watch your choice of words, please," she said. "It's like a special friend, blah, blah, blah."

Who cares? Isn't everything outside special? He couldn't wait to see the outdoors with clear eyes.

After a bowl of bland creamed wheat, John ran out into the yard. All kinds of little animals followed him where ever he went. They all wanted to be his special friend. There were moles, rabbits, chipmunks, and a fox, but none of them seemed special. The cats and birds ignored him. The salamander under a rock near the springhouse was neat, but the thing's skin was sticky and positively yucky. All he had to do was pick one. *Or is it, one has to pick me?* And soon, too, before he dies, like that's going to happen. They lived in the middle of the woods. *What can happen?* There's nothing but farms and woods around there.

There was so much to see and do and learn. Around the cabin was so pretty with tall, sweet grass, moss in the shade, and ferns edging the forest. *It's all so alive.* It smelled funny around the septic tank but it grew the best grass and cattails too. *Cattails are plants and not tails cut off from cats like poor, dead Hermes. Holy cow.*

Sissy bugged him for a while, but then Margo started digging under the porch. She pulled out the old bones of creatures that didn't make it. After that, she ate a worm! John kicked the bones back under the deck before running off.

He roamed the edge of the property along the woods where he sniffed the trees and hugged a sugar maple. He didn't go far into the woods, but rather, enjoyed standing back taking them in. There were oaks and maples and pines. Dad said, 'one can't see the forest for the trees,' but weren't trees the whole point? He saved climbing one for later. He watched until the smell and sound of water glugging nearby became too much to resist.

He ran to the creek and he liked it a lot, but the dang-gone water bugs and crawdads just wouldn't leave him alone. He didn't want icky bugs for his special friends. *They taste awful.* The turtle was nice, the snakes too, but he didn't want to get his blue jeans dirty. He took off from the creek and left them critters behind sure that he didn't have to decide anything yet.

"What's the hurry anyway?"

The clock in his head went off—time for reruns. *Leave It to Beaver* was coming on.

He ran back into the house, turned on the TV, and flopped down on the rug. The TV warmed up slowly, but he didn't mind. That little dot turned into horizontal bars before fuzzy electronic snow appeared; from that confusion, pictures formed. Every little thing was so interesting. The whole universe lived inside TV snow. Cosmic radio signals made it. He didn't know the psychics well enough and he had questions. All he had to do, to learn and grow, was spin the TV dial and pluck out the answers.

2

Turn Around

Gabe and Mike's dimensional-shift spacecraft dropped out of hyperspace on the edge of Central Control's local space-time just a meteorite's throw from Homestar. Mike was popular and a real card, but Gabe was the shop steward and the memos had to be read. It was Mike's job but he was off the clock so Gabe sat in.

Gabe had come up with that failed plan to keep Earth going. His big idea resulted in an Earth religion even though it was upper management's fault. That AI Probe Control supplied was defective. *They'll demote me anyway.* Gabe wasn't looking forward to reporting in person.

Communications had a sealed message alert blinking 'unread' from Control. Gabe sent it to the printer. It was addressed to Mike. Gabe was the kind of angel that charged ahead while Mike walked away making jokes. *Mike always makes management wait—he takes union shenanigans too seriously.* Gabe tore open the envelope.

In hyper-time, local ship seconds are years or centuries from a project planet's perspective. Time bends in strange ways while traversing the multi-verse. Thankfully, Gabe got the message and not Mike. Had he missed this memo, the salvage job would have been impossible. Gabe had just enough time to forward the order to Captain Burk and launch that Earth guy in a sub-light pod.

Gabe didn't get the logic. After he and Mike left, Control brought in somebody else to clean up the mess. Why send the crap team back? *Is this all by Her design?* No one knows Her ways. Maybe She devised it all or maybe She mucked it up again. Messages ran past Central PO before going out—somebody in authority must be in control. Gabe had doubts. *The good timing's probably dumb luck.* Gabe passed the order to the captain without hope of a good outcome but in time. It could go either way. Gabe confirmed the jump before heading to the bridge.

The ship was on its way back to Earth before Mike knew they had arrived home. Mike sashayed onto the bridge in dress whites with wings spread like a sexed-up peacock ready to disembark. He did have nice wings for a stocky short guy. He even preened. Nobody greeted him. The people, who had faces on the bridge, wore dour expressions. Mike flipped on his station's screen.

"What in the hell is this!" Mike cried pointing at his display. His albino-white skin flushed pink.

"Emergency collection. We're going back." Gabe said. "Salvage operation."

"Can't we send Jesus?" Mike's mouth hung open, breathing hard. "What about vacation?"

"He's gone," Gabe said. "I launched him in a suspension pod. He's on his way to Regions Space Port. We're on our own. Management's call."

"God, I hate management," Mike said.

"That's too bad," Gabe said trying not to laugh. "You've been promoted. You're an Apprentice Controller now. Congratulations."

Mike's jaw went slack then snapped shut with an organic clack followed by a choking sob. He sounded like a sprung space-mite trap. Mike had to swallow his smart-assed remark. He always had one loaded.

Swallowing that impending wisecrack didn't go down easy for Mike judging by the color on his face. That sick green wasn't Mike's happy shade. Managers have to eat a lot of shit. *Get used to it, You're in management now.*

3

On the Road to Find Out

They were going into town tomorrow, and he didn't need one, but Mom said to take a bath today anyway and he didn't complain. On TV, the kids only took a bath on Saturday. John enjoyed baths. Why did *Dennis The Menace* hate them so? John decided to take a long one.

When his fingers wrinkled like raisins, it was time to get out. He didn't notice how or when Mom did it, but there was a pile of fresh clothes and a clean white towel waiting for him on top of the hamper. Standing, he buried his face in that soft, cotton fluff before drying off. It smelled *Borax* fresh. The idea that he knew things like that smell didn't startle him. It was familiar. He felt old and wise and full of things he knew but also, he couldn't make sense out of half of it just like a child. Questions filled him to the brim like a fresh glass of *Ovaltine*.

He put on a blue checked shirt, white undershirt, and blue jeans with cuffs at the ankle showing off a red-checkered flannel lining. His socks were white and thick and his shoes were basketball players' shoes called sneakers. He had missed the underpants and left them on the floor. He liked the feeling of no underwear. *Outside is what matters anyway.* He kicked his *Fruit of the Looms* under the tub.

"Gosh, I've got duds just like *Beaver Cleaver*. I bet I look just like him, too."

Pulling up a stepstool he wiped the steam off the looking glass. He didn't have black hair like his folks, no freckles like Beaver or Wally. His face was pale, cheeks hollow and his blond hair was too long. There was no point in rubbing *Brill Cream* into it. TV said that's what the hip kids do with their hair.

He didn't like the crewcut hair football player Johnny Unitas had. John's hair was wild and reminded him of the animals around the house. It wasn't matted anymore and he liked it better. Mom had brushed it out. It was nice without tangles. Beatniks with long hair were on the TV news. He didn't like the idea of beating on anyone even if Nick asked for it.

More questions poured over him but the panic became less. He had lots of time to sort out everything. It will take time. A lot of time. First things first.

Dad had ignored him and Margo a lot, so it felt like Dad didn't care. *Did they find us in the woods or what?* John exited the bathroom thinking kids should look like their parents. Dark, swarthy Dad was in his *Bark-o-Lounger* easy-chair smoking a pipe that smelled like cherry. A cat rested in his lap, as usual.

"Dad, Dad, don't you love me?"

"Sure, I do, son. I do now at any rate." The cat's ears perched up. "You have to understand. Your mother and I are very, very old. We have had, I don't know, a hundred children perhaps. Most of which didn't make it. No point in putting emotional resources into someone that's just going to die young in some godforsaken asylum."

"They don't do that anymore, dear," Mom called from the kitchen. "I don't have any *Wonder Bread*. I've made fresh."

The smell of baking bread made John's mouth water. He knew that smell from before but didn't know it came from something to eat.

"Yes, they do," Dad said, his voice irritable. "They call them State Mental Hospitals nowadays. It's the same thing—a place where decent people—if you can call them that—put the crazies to die…out of sight, of course. It was better in the old days. They called them demon-possessed, or witches, or whatever religion you didn't like, and killed them fast. That's more humane. Slow death isn't humane. They're delusional if they think—"

"Not now, Jacob," Mom came out from the kitchen wiping her hands on an apron. She wore a pretty pink and lavender flower pattern dress under it. An English starling sat on her shoulder bobbing this way and that. *'Four and twenty blackbirds baked in a pie,'* sang inside John. He read somewhere that the English used to eat them.

"Please, your son needs answers, stay focused. Once he picks a familiar species you won't be giving him permanent memory. He won't need you anymore. Now is foundational. Stop pontificating."

A bake timer went off. She backed into the kitchen eyeballing Dad like he was an idiot.

"Fine then, son it's like this," he pushed the cat out of his lap. "Mother and I are immortals but not every child of ours is or was as well."

"But Dad what's that got to do with anything?"

"Hush, son. I'll tell it my way, see. It's like this. Our kind is born retarded and if we're going to make it, that is live overlong, we become normal first. It's the same for each one, understand?"

"What kind of we are we?" John asked.

"Let him speak," Mom called from the kitchen. "You might not remember, or understand, but listen to your father anyway."

"Damn if I know. I'm on the edge of finding out." Dad said. "My research is going well. I'm close to the answer and—"

"Jacob, stay on track, please," Mom called. "John, pay attention."

"Yes, Mom, jeepers."

Dad lit his pipe. "Everything you learn now and what we forced fed into your subconscious mind while you were insane, goes into Base Memory. You'll have access to that after you die and come back. You won't need a familiar to keep your Base Memory… it's accessible upon your restoration, it's baked in, so to speak, once you activate it. I think memories will come back on their own if you live long enough, how long, I don't know—that's my theory. You'll need a Book of Answers to recover your past lives at any rate. The Book jars origin memories lose as well as reinstituting recently lost lives. For example, when I was a Spartan. I recall every bit—"

"Jacob, will you please stay on track," Mom called.

"Fine, fine, that woman. Anyway, everything between deaths and rebirths, barring First Death, is recorded for you in your familiars. You don't have a species yet, but you'll need one. Why, because when you die you aren't dead, see. You'll, however, forget. This new science of genetics, that I've been reading about, might be the trick. Information is stored in what's called DNA, genetic memory—so to speak—that's my guess. But it's stored in your familiars, at any rate, see?"

"I don't understand," John cried.

"You don't have to understand; didn't you hear what Mother just said? He is dense, did you hear that, Mother?"

"Give him time Jacob; he just woke up yesterday for Pete's sake."

"Fine, fine. Nothing but the basics stick to the surface, language, and the like. When you wake you won't be a baby, you'll talk, walk, shit, and chew gum just fine. Your familiars will have put everything else into your Book and they'll restore your past lives for you when you ask them."

He picked up his cat and talked right into its face. "Isn't that right kitty? You'll remember for me." He put the cat down.

"The key thing is don't die until you find your familiar species because you won't know who you are, or used to be when you wake unless you have access to your Book, see? No familiars and you're screwed. All you'll have are basic functions, base memories, and innate personality traits. See?"

John didn't see at all. Dad's talk was all just blab, blab, blab. 'This is how you retrieve your Book, blab, blab, blab.' *I'm missing Bugs Bunny.*

"Any question?" Dad asked.

"Where's Margo?" John said.

"He's off track," Mom called. "His mind is still too soft."

"Who knows, son. Margo doesn't matter. But she is close to waking and ahead of the usual time. She's early and that's good, shows intelligence. Good, that is, if she doesn't die or worse nearly die before finding a familiar. That is to say, her familiar species and not just one creature."

"First Waking is when your personality is set," Mom called from the kitchen.

"The whole kit and caboodle remember for you." Dad went on. "You must choose a species after insanity but before First Death. Never pick one if you're in a near-death state or insane…"

John understood what crazy was. He felt like that all over. Nothing Dad said made sense. The cooling bread smell made his stomach beg. All he could think about was food and cartoons.

"…Never mention familiars, people will burn you at the stake. It takes years to reconstitute after burning; provided there's anything left to reassemble. Never let them cut off your head. The other important thing…"

John had a partial view of the kitchen table. A big glass of milk with cream on top waited for him. A jar of jam sat there, too. *How long does it take for bread to cool?*

"…If you're a breeder, I doubt it frankly, that's a person who makes more like us. Like Mother and me. You'll want sex all the time. Just like the damn hippies. Free love, my ass…"

John could not stop watching Mom. After cutting the bread, she spread jam on a slice. *What's that, peanut butter on the other slice? Holy cow, that looks yummy.*

"…Not all your babies will have immortal potential. Most will be normal people who have a bit of your stock. Your seed's inside them, see. But if you have a crazy one and they don't snap out of it before, say, fourteen, they never will. It's like I say, most of them don't make it. Now take Jesus, for example, there's an exception. He was Mother's brother's child. I don't know what got into him, but it left a nasty scar. Anyway, he…"

Margo burst through the screen door and ran around the great room kicking animals. She sent an opossum kit flying and grabbed a squirrel by the neck, choking it. It didn't react until she squeezed hard. Then its legs kicked, but it didn't try to escape. None of the animals there ever fought back. She laughed and laughed. John's stomach turned sour. He had done that himself many times. Margo ran outside with her lunch still kicking.

"Any questions," Dad repeated.

He swallowed. "Can I have a sandwich now?" John said, desperate for a drink.

A little vomit had come up into his mouth from Margo's performance. He was still very hungry and that glass of milk would surely remove the bad taste.

"Lunch, come and get it," Mom called.

He ran into the kitchen, plopped down on a big old wooden chair, tucked a cloth napkin into his collared shirt, and gulped milk. His tummy instantly felt better. He dug in thinking that this is living; nice food, warm milk, clean clothes. He felt safe and at the same time, felt like he was on the road to find out a lot of neat stuff.

"Above all else," Dad called from the great room, "you must find yourself when you wake. It'll drive you crazy if you don't…and for crying out loud, don't die yet, it's too soon."

He took another big swallow and licked the cream mustache off. Mom laid a plate of cookies on the table and he knew the rule, 'no desert until you finish your plate.' He devoured the sandwich, even the crust, but took his time counting the raisins in each cookie before deciding which one was best.

Somewhere along the line, Dad had stopped talking. John knew what Dad said was important and he had missed most of it, but John wasn't worried. John felt sure he had all the time in the world.

4

Earth Ten Million A.D.

The mountain's east face blocked the ocean winds thus protecting the west side's outdoor gathering place situated on a wide, mid-mountain plateau. But cold winds came upriver from the south on this Sun's Day. The wide Hudson gave fall's contrary winds a corridor. The Librarian shivered.

"A reading from the Book of Answers," the Librarian called out against a strong wind.

"NO SHIT," the congregation responded as required.

The Priestess took the podium, checked her notes, and read, "it was spring, warm for April in Bucks County."

Of course, no one knew what a Bucks County was, but one did not question the Book. The Book was full of things impossible to understand. *This reading is the first early chapter recorded in centuries.* It was also the first of its kind in the Librarian's long life.

"We were outside in the sun. John, he was called John then, stood outside a log home and it wasn't a crude log cabin. He said, 'Jeepers if this isn't a boss looking *Lincoln Log* cabin, golly, I don't know what is.'" The Prestress signaled and the scribe began recording what she had just said.

"Be-dee, be-dee, be-dee, that's not all folks!" the Prestress cried and fell into a trance.

The congregation stood and said, "That's no bullshit."

No one had ever seen a cabin or knew what it was. It wasn't important. The reading and recordings were all that mattered. Get the message out of mind and into the Book. The people must deliver the Books—should that day ever come.

The Librarian had her doubts that the day will come. There were too few new visions to record of late and that was bad. Needed, true, but this one was disturbing to her. *There isn't much but it is First Life and early.* The Librarian had interviewed this month's visionary before Mass, as usual, and wrote the official notes herself breaking tradition.

The people reclined and the Priestess came back to herself and continued the reading. This wasn't her vision. The Prestress read each installment to the congregation before it is entered into the permanent archives.

"He thought, 'Holy cow. The house is made out of trees.' Margo had Dad's housecat splayed out on the ground. All four paws were fixed to stakes with shoelaces that were taken from his *Converse* sneakers...The cat strained against ropes. The cat was alive, hissing, moaning. The little girl knelt over the creature drooling. She cut into its' gut. 'Dull pocketknife,' he said. 'Girls are so dumb.' A cloud moved in and we were cold. We closed our eyes."

The Prestress stepped back and raised her hands. "That's all folks."

This must be the earliest entry known. The Book had many gaps, many mysteries and the Librarian hoped for a Reading to fill a later gap. She never heard one as old as this read new. It was a big jump backward in time. *What does it mean?* The Librarian mounted the podium to close the ceremony.

"A Reading from the Book of Answers," the Librarian said.

The congregants sang out one of the usual closing responses, "What a crock of shit."

The scribe finished writing and closed the book. The Priestess made the peace sign and touched it. The scribe set it aside—the first blank page of chapter one was filled. Book One's earliest revelations began.

The Librarian's skill was to know where in any one book a vision belongs. That reading opened a new chapter of the oldest unfinished book. The sub heading said 'random visions.' The subtitle was misplaced. This one wasn't random. It was the beginning of the end of Book One.

Helpers ran up and took it away to place it in the correct stack. The congregation filed out.

We will live sane a while longer. But for how long?

If this vision was as old as she thought—the Librarian pushed that idea out of her mind but the pain in her heart remained.

5

Close Shave

Awake three days and John felt hollow again.

The idea of going into town, mentioned at dinner last night, exited him. *Maybe some empty will fill in.* His old muddlehead was coming back making him afraid he will miss out. He already forgot a lot from when he was foggy. *What if I go into town and forget the whole thing?*

Dad had said, 'it's normal, you'll come and go for a while, it will pass.' John still felt like he was walking in mud, everything slippery. Just yesterday, everything on the television had been real to him until Mom shot it down. It was all made up. It's entertainment. The many books he had read while crazy didn't explain it. *Shakespeare isn't history?* That 'Truth in fiction,' idea Mom spoke of didn't make any sense at all. Mud, muddy, muddled.

"I hope like heck the town is real."

Dad called from the basement, "Son, get ready, we are going into town."

Real or pretend, John wanted to know everything. He could meet new people and see a real town. He couldn't wait but it was scary, too. Dad said he won't have to wait long, but John didn't expect it so soon—Saturday morning. He just finished his second milk and wasn't ready. Mom hadn't finished scrubbing Margo yet. *At least Margo shut up screaming, that's good.*

"Golly it's just soap and water for Pete's sake."

Dad came up from the basement wearing a suit, like Joe Friday on *Dragnet*. That detective's suit was something else. Joe's TV dialogue came to mind, 'Just the facts ma'am, just the facts.'

"Son, you washed behind your ears, brushed your teeth, yes?" Dad said.

John had seen people brushing on TV, but he hadn't got the hang of it yet. He huffed on his hand and sniffed it. It didn't stink too bad, nothing like the dead animals under the porch.

"I think so. Hey, *Rocky and Bullwinkle* are on!"

"Good, good," Father said as he disappeared outside. He said that a lot lately, it didn't mean anything as far as John could tell. Dad didn't like cartoons. John got up off the floor and tried to get a better signal. The stupid rabbit-ears antenna was always drooping. He got the signal in as best he could. When he turned around Margo was standing there with clothes on—wearing a party dress for Pete's sake, saddle shoes, and bobby socks. Jeepers she looked ridiculous, like the kids on *Howdy Doody* reruns. Nobody dresses like that on *American Bandstand*.

"What's this, the *Mickey Mouse Club*?" John said.

"She must be presentable while we are visiting town," Mom said coming out of the bathroom with a hairbrush. She turned Margo around and started working out the tangles. John finished the milk he had left in his bowl of *Rice Puffs* and set it aside on the floor.

"Put your bowl in the sink, young man."

"But Ma, do I have to?" John thought he'd try it out although it never worked for *Dennis The Menace* or *Beaver Cleaver* on TV.

"Now, mister," she said. "Hold still, Margo. Dad's bringing the car around."

"We have a car?" John asked returning from the kitchen. He had never seen the inside of the barn. He didn't get that far yet. The woods and the living things within it captured him first.

"Yes, it's a bit of a hotrod," Mom said. "1955 Hudson Hornet, very fast, when we bought it, that is. We need a fast car. It's older now. We'll trade it in soon. We never know when we must run for our lives. The Hornet was, until recently, the best car for that."

"Golly, I hope I don't get stung."

"You won't, animals won't harm us. It's people you should worry about." She said fighting with Margo's hair—yesterday it was matted so bad it looked like a sweater.

"You're getting a haircut today, John."

The porch faced the creek and not the county road which was a mile down their rutted dirt lane. He walked over to the blacktopped highway when he was crazy. He didn't know much about anything then. Only snippets and impressions remained. That the big road was dangerous stuck in his mind.

The car rumbled up to the front porch. John climbed into the car's huge back seat with his insides jumbling. The compartment was nice and clean. A rat, a cottontail rabbit, and two green snakes got in, too. He pushed them out, but a skink and a lizard got between the cushions and he gave up looking for them.

Mom forced Margo into the car's back seat. All in, Dad took off and whipped around the house spinning tires. He gassed it down the lumpy road yelling whoopee. It was fun. But Margo flopped around with her mouth open like a trout spiting a hook.

"Gosh, I hope Margo doesn't snot all on the mole's hair." He knew about moles; the cats had caught many. "How'd they get the hair off some old moles and stuck onto car chairs?"

"It's mohair," Dad said, "doesn't come from animals. It's a manmade upholstery material."

"I don't get it?"

Mom turned around and laughed. "Never mind, it's not important. Knowledge will coalesce in a few days. Once you have your Book of Answers started a lot of common things will become clearer."

"Eat the lizard!" Margo yelled.

"It is good he is asking questions," Mom said turning back forward. "I hope he becomes more intelligent. He doesn't seem very bright so far."

"I'm not dumb, jeepers!"

"His personality is yet to form," Dad said pulling the car onto the blacktop road. "Don't worry, his fundamentals are good. After First Death, he's an open book and we'll be on hand to fill it. I'll form him, make him into a scholar like myself, and you'll give him your best qualities, your understanding of philosophies and the arts. He'll be top-notch after that. Imagine, coordinated input from two immortals—it hasn't been done since..."

An oncoming car caused John to duck. He popped up and saw it going the other way. It was just like the one on the *Andy Griffin Show*, a brand new 1964 Ford police car. After that John became fascinated with everything along the way such as road signs, other cars, houses, and traffic lights. *Just like TV only better.*

Everything was fiction and real at the same time. *Jeepers Margo's missing it.* All she did was bang her head on the front seat's back and babble repeating the word "astrophysics." Whatever that means. *Holy cow, what will the townspeople think?*

Dad parked in front of Roe's Hardware; John read the sign from the back seat. He got out and stood there mesmerized. *This is all real—Holy Moly.*

There were buildings up and down the street, all painted nice. They had brick ones and wood ones, big glass windows all around, and cars everywhere. Town was just like TV's Mayberry, but newer. It wasn't like 'Gritty New York City' from the *True Detective* show. *What would detective Mike Hammer make of this?*

John ogled until Mom closed the car's door and killed the skink. He sensed it die. He shouldn't have cared. It was just another dumb creature but John felt bad for it anyway. He liked reptiles but lizards were best. Skinks weren't as smart. Mom's birds know enough to stay safe up on phone wires. The cat in the store's window acted up jumping around trying to get to Dad. Dad put Margo up on the coin-operated horse ride and put in a dime. John took it all in.

Margo finished the ride. Dad was going up the stoop when the store's big wooden door swung out. Dad was on top of the stoop but the big man came out anyway and blocked the way in. The man bumped Dad sideways and went down the stairs.

"Hey, watch it!" Dad said.

"No, you watch it, Jew boy," the man said. "I'm the white man here." He moved out from under the shadowed overhang and onto the sidewalk. *Boy, he's fat and ugly.* Dad followed and grabbed his arm. The fat man was two heads taller.

"I'm Persian, you idiot," Dad said. "You want I should call the police. You assaulted me."

Fat Man turned and poked Dad's chest with a stiff finger. "Back up, boy, before I arrest you…I'm the sheriff, dumbass."

The lawman didn't look like Sheriff *Andy Griffin* from TV. He wore a flannel shirt, cowboy hat, boots, and jeans, but he had a revolver and handcuffs on his belt, too.

"Why don't you act lawfully then?" Dad said puffing out his chest. Mom shrank like a raisin.

"Whatever I do is the law, numb-nuts. You hippies ought to show respect. Goddamn liberals. What's a Persian, a new kind of New York Jew?"

"He's a Hittite, asshole," Margo blurted out. She did that sometimes; acted like her sane self was bleeding out.

"What have we got here?" The sheriff said. Margo went back to slobbering on the mechanical horse's rear end. "Not bad for a retard. Look at them mosquito bite tits swelling out new and fresh just the way I like em'."

The lawman looked Margo up and down, wet his lips, and made a kissing sound. Mom pulled Margo away from the kiddy ride. Mom's face twisted in horror like the villagers in the Frankenstein movie. Dad put up his fists to fight. The sheriff laughed like *Snidely Whiplash* and pushed past Dad as if Dad were a wet noodle. The policeman crossed the street and into the barbershop without looking back.

"We won't be getting your haircut today," Mom said.

"Wait just a minute; we aren't going to let that blowhard—"

"Please, Jacob. This is a bad time for you to die." Mom said, "Let it go. After John and perhaps Margo has their special friends…then go and do your worst. You can't get into any fights now. I can't afford to have you lying dead or in jail. It took you four weeks to revive last time and much longer for your memory to be restored."

"You saw it. He's trouble. He needs to be put down before he comes after us," Dad said.

"You're not a spearman for Xerces anymore, Jacob. Let's just go home."

They filed into the car. Mom and Dad never argued but back in the car, they went at it like Ralf and Alice on *The Honeymooners*. Dad wouldn't drive until a ceasefire was called. They both shut up quickly. John put a finger in each ear until it blew over. Nothing much made much sense to him but people fighting made no sense at all. He decided peace was better. Peace makes sense. *Maybe I'll be a peacenik like Allen Ginsburg when I grow up.*

6

Ten Million and One A.D.

"A reading from the Book of Answers," the Librarian said with shaky legs.

"Don't give me that shit," The congregation returned quoting scripture.

The Librarian understood their mood. She didn't have a new vision for Mass; such came less and less often. There was nothing else she could do but have the Priestess read an old scripture that the younger ones had not heard, and perhaps, the elders have forgotten. She had pulled an old volume and brought it along for The Reading.

The Librarian handed a thick, dirty, book to the Priestess who blew the dust from it and opened it choosing a page randomly as required under these circumstances. As the pages flipped, the Librarian's stomach churned.

"He lay there under the stars in a desert."

The people caught their breath; there aren't any left on Earth. But everyone knew what a desert was—a fearful, lonely place on flat ground, nothing green. Such had been described and taught in school to all. This early Book was recorded when visions were common but random and out of sync. Such books were written before the timeline was established. The Librarian's innards produced a nervous fart.

The way of the Book traveled deep of late—the Book always chooses, directs a Priestess to the reading. But readings so old indicate a coming danger, too. The Librarian felt the funnel of time tightening, history's hands were squeezing her long neck. She resisted the urge to loosen her cape.

The Priestess became entranced and she read as if it were her vision.

"He's dying. He watches the sky. A gila monster lay dying next to Him. They each suffered a poison bite. He says to his companion. 'Buddy, man, I'm sorry. Shit, man, you shouldn't have gotten underfoot. Damn scorpion, I know you're protecting me, man, but, shit, man, you fucked up.'"

The Priestess swooned, hesitated a moment, and went on.

"He sits up but the sickness is too much. 'Shit. It's OK, man, it's cool.'"

The Priestess lay down the Book and said, "Be-del, be-del, be del, dee That's all folks."

"Don't give me that shit!" The congregation responded.

The Librarian came forward to close the ceremony saying, "Then He lay down and died again."

She paused a moment for reverence's sake and finished with the appropriate closing. "This was a reading from the Book of Answers."

"Damn right," the congregation said as proper for a moment-of-death reading.

The Librarian, unsatisfied, took up the Book and gave it to an assistant. The Priestess had staggered away from the podium leaving it there. Death readings were hard on the reader.

This is an ill omen.

As the congregation dispersed the Librarian felt her hope draining. The people's unhappiness was palatable. Only a new vision could satisfy them and the last thing she wanted was a Book One reading. New readings—early ones, were all that was left. Early visions drew them closer to doom.

7

KKK On the Way

Sheriff Clint Ringo stood by the barbershop's glass door, out of sight, watching the Hornet load. He didn't mind Philly folks. City people spent money in town and left. *But this bunch ain't that, more like cheap New York Jews moving in.* That idea rankled him to no end. How'd them Jews get blonde-haired kids? *Half-blacks adopting white kids, what's the world coming to? Let a few come and the rest flood in like starved rats.*

"Whatcha looking at, Clint?" Billy Major asked.

The barber was sitting on the by-and-by with no haircuts.

"Damn Jew hippies is what," Donnie, another customer sitting there, said. "I saw them coming in. You see the hair on that boy? What kinda parents let a boy go like that?"

Clint smelled barber tonic. Donnie had just been cut and shaved. Clint thought of himself as special with God-given powers of observation. He didn't need to turn around to know the town's mechanic was fresh-cut. Clint kept his eyes glued until the Hudson rounded the corner and out of sight.

"Saving this town for white folks is getting harder every year," Clint muttered.

"Aren't they the ones who bought the Anderson place?" Billy said. "Didn't know they got kids."

"If I'd known them were tarpaper Jews, I wouldn't have let it happen." Sheriff Clint said rolling himself around to the barber's chair: He just about fit. Billy laid down his copy of Guns and Rods and loaded fresh towels into the steamer.

"Anyone out back," Clint asked. He put his official police voice on it.

"No," Billy said, "just us Brothers. What'll it be?"

Billy commenced whipping lather in a mug.

Clint didn't use to be so careful about running the local Klan. Folks didn't use to fool in their business if they weren't invited. The Brotherhood ran this town before JFK got shot, but things were changing fast. Too many damn liberals and Jews and hippies coming and going, and some moving into Bucks County even from dirty Allentown. The Brothers had to be more careful. The old ways were dying, Clint felt it in his bones. So, he set his mind on keeping things the same. Folks elected him for that uphill battle.

The governor and his State Police didn't take kindly to the Klan either. But this was his town and Clint thought it was high time he posted a clear warning.

"What'll you have Sheriff?" Billy asked juggling the towel like hot mashed potatoes. "Close or easy-does-it?"

"What I'll have is a cross burning and maybe a little more, can you do that, Billy?"

"Damn right," Billy said wrapping the first towel around Clint's fat neck. Clint was a proud two-towel shave. He caught Donnie's shit-eating grin reflected in the front window.

Donnie slapped his knee. "Hot damn, Sheriff. I was wondering when we were gonna get busy and that retard girl...we're gonna have us a time. Ain't that, right? Hot dig-it-ty dog!"

"Make it close, Billy, real close," Clint said.

Clint wasn't much for rape. He wasn't into little kids like Donnie. He liked them fourteen—legal age and willing. Donnie was only five-foot tall, kid-sized himself. Clint figured Donnie's tastes made sense. But there was something about that baby hippie girl and the wife, too, that made Clint want it bad.

That woman looked about half Arab and half Jew and he wouldn't touch her for God or country no matter how she made his boner stand tall. Clint had his principles. But that little girl...blond hair and something else. He couldn't pin down what about her made his pecker sing. That boy, too, was blond. *They weren't natural kids to them Jews, no sir.* He figured they must have been adopted out of Saint Ann's Children's Home from up the road. None of them will be missed.

Clint Ringo had a mind for detective work. He had himself amazing powers of observation, by God. He didn't see how he and the brothers would ever be caught. Before his shave was done, Sheriff Ringo decided it was due time for a necktie dinner party with a little cheesecake for dessert.

8

The Long Ride Home

Dad gassed the Hornet and cut the wheel hard at the bend on the end of Main Street. The car pitched and rolled while sliding sideways. Dad had missed the street they came in on. The rear tires screeched and so did Margo because John crashed into her. John burst out laughing as the car fishtailed. Once straight, Dad shifted and it pulled away fast.

"We're taking the long way home, I need to cool off," Dad said, rolling down his window.

"You used to cover your tracks and not make them clearer," Mom said, sounding worried.

The skink was gone but a lizard was still in the car. It clung to the back of Dad's seat the whole time like it was glued there. Its head bobbed up and down when John paid attention to it. This struck John funny and he laughed.

"This beats TV any day," John said.

Mom turned and said, "This isn't funny young man, none of this is funny. That man is evil."

She punched Dad in the arm. "You shouldn't have peeled off like that. We don't need attention."

"Eat the lizard, eat it. Eat it!" Margo yelled with a squeaky voice.

"Peel out is the term. Quiet, both of you," Dad said. "Mother and I are talking. What's your take?"

"He is trouble," Mom said. "My talent informs me that it's time to move on. That man is dangerous. We should leave now, this very day."

"What can he do, kill us?" Dad said. "Let him, then we'll move if we must.

I'm not concerned."

"There's more, Jacob. I sense deep danger. We must be careful. John's First Death hasn't come. We can't let that Philistine upset our son's progress. We must leave before that buffoon acts."

"I have thousands of ancient manuscripts in the basement," Dad said, his voice going higher. "Even from Alexandria. Took me centuries to assemble this collection. It's too much. All that packing. I've nearly worked out exactly what we are, why we exist at all. I'm not budging until my work is done. I'm very close."

"What if you die and must learn yourself all over again? That takes years at our age. You didn't see what I saw. You never do. It is better if we go now, today."

"Forget it, we're staying. That's final."

Dad pushed the car harder. He took a turn and went half off the blacktop. A wayward tire splattered gravel up inside the rear fender-well like hail hitting the house's tin roof.

"Bite the lizard, bite it!"

"Shut up, Margo. You're an idiot," Mom said crossing arms over her chest. She slumped deeper into the seat. "I was referring to you, Jacob."

For several miles nobody said anything. Dad took, "the scenic route." It was all the same to John. The farms, fields, and woods were the same near home but the ride took longer. *How'd different roads go to the same place? How does time work?*

So many questions but nobody spilled the beans. He had funny questions, too, like *Groucho Marx* on that TV game show, but John thought it better not to ask any questions until Dad felt better.

Mom sat up straighter. She got stiff when she figured things out. Mom was a good guesser. John thought he must have something like that too. She got up on her knees and faced the back. Margo stopped picking her nose and watched Mom carefully.

"Father's been distracted lately." Mom softened her voice. She did that sometimes when she talked to them.

"Regarding your education: Father illustrated an important point and one you should heed well before he kills us with this damn car. You may not remember."

She took a deep breath.

"Listen. Like Father you'll forever feel compelled to learn who and what you are. The males of our kind always do. For me, Margo too, someday, it is enough to understand our lives as they are in the present. You have internal drivers that may lead to foolishness, like him. Don't put your obsessions before logic."

Mom pointed at Dad. That funny little lizard jumped off the back of Dad's seat.

"Don't give in to base impulses like he does."

Dad hit the gas. Everybody got jerked around.

"This other male drive is also problematic—the need to procreate. Don't let either malady bring you into bad situations. How do I make you understand? There are so many things you must know before First Death, but Father..."

John was completely confused. It was all gab, gab, gab. *Parents sure are good at making things complicated.* But he had a feeling it was important. He had tingles inside and didn't know why. He tried to focus. She was serious. *I better listen better.*

"…Father thinks it's a kind of program such as computer punch-cards. He thinks it's stored in your genes. He thinks there are tiny molecules inside us. It's what makes you, you, or who you'll become."

"I don't get it," John said. "Aren't I already me?"

"Not quite," she said. "After First Death, your personality will finish its development. Your core personality type will become permanently fixed soon after waking. You'll become who you will be according to environmental influences—do you see? The greater part of your personality will come out of your first rebirth experiences. Oh dear, this is too much. You don't understand."

She turned back around.

"He'll never dig this out. He needs this made simple. Jacob, help me."

"Woman, relax. Nothing's going to happen. We have time. It's like this son: you'll want to screw every girl you meet, and they won't say no. If you wake up and don't know yourself, you won't stop looking until you do. Your familiars will fill you in. After you return, you'll find yourself. Then you'll go and get a girl. It's simple. See?"

"A-OK," John said.

"He's getting it, he sees it," Dad said.

John didn't see it at all. *What the heck's a familiar?* What's First Death anyway? It had to be like on TV's *Gun Smoke* where they get the bad guy, and then next week the same bad guy comes back but he's got a different name. Maybe that cowboy was an outlaw next or a wrangler and then next he's a Mexican bandit or a wild Indian. And every week, the good guy gets a new girl. John didn't know exactly what the good guy did with the girl, but they kissed a bunch. That idea made his weenie stir. Life was just like TV. *Golly, why don't they just say so?*

"That's enough for now," Mom said. "I see you're puzzled. Think it over, will you do that please?"

"A-OK, Mom."

Everybody shut up and the car got quiet. Margo was busy eating her boogers so he got up on his knees and turned around. That little pine lizard was sunning himself on the rear window deck. John wanted to play with it but it froze up when he touched it. All the animals did that. With nobody to play with, he watched out the back window instead.

There was a guy in a Volkswagen Beetle behind them. John liked the TV ads. The Bug wasn't a common car—none in town anyway. What interested him most was the VW's driver. He had long hair like Mom's but he was a man. John ran fingers through his hair. It was long, too, but not that long. He decided he liked it long and was glad he missed the haircut. He guessed that driver was a beatnik like the poet *Ginsburg* he had seen on the *Six O'clock News*.

Jeepers everything is so exciting in the real world. Nothing's exciting around the house, just a dumb old farm, no cows or combines, just a farrow cornfield.

Dad finally pulled off the blacktop and onto their lane and stopped at the porch. "You kids go inside. Everybody out."

John opened his door but Margo rushed over the top of him and spilled them both out onto the grass along the driveway. It was better than landing on the bluestone gravel. Mom went to open the barn for Dad.

Critters were all over the place and more than usual. Margo didn't go after the cat. She didn't stomp on the lizard that was underfoot or eat the grasshopper that landed on her dress. She picked it off and placed it on the ground. Margo wasn't acting right. She never did that before. Her mouth was shut, too. She moved away carefully stepping over the small mud puddle in her path.

"Why'd you go around?" John said coming up to her.

"New *Buster Brown* shoes. What are you some kind of an idiot," she said?

"Hey, you're snapping out of it! Jeepers, Margo."

"Eat the bug, eat it!"

She jumped with both feet into the puddle landing on a patch of milky-pink dead earthworms.

"Oh, that's good dinner," she said.

"Awake? I guess not," John said.

He left Margo and made a bee-line for the TV. It wasn't too late. There were still cartoons on but also *Buck Rogers*, and wrestling. Roller derby didn't even start yet. He had lots to figure out and the answers were waiting for him on the TV set. The sky was clear and windless so why waste time outside? TV got better reception on nice days.

9

Balls in a Vice

Mike was in the spaceship's anthropology office checking the incoming signals while going over the latest data.

"Will you look at that, we're in luck."

None but the ship's AI heard him, but that never stopped Mike from talking before. "Wait 'til Gabe gets a load of this."

The usual procedure was to study the incoming transmissions before dropping into local space-time. Mike had Earth on screen as the ship prepared to enter Earth's real-time. He should have started a week ago. Mike was forced to play catch-up. He didn't know how the Communications Department got signals from Earth's real-time before they entered it. He didn't need to know; it wasn't the anthropologist's responsibility.

"I lost the worm signal. We're breaking into Earth's space-time." He told the bridge.

Mike pushed his chair back. Ship's navigation AI took over everything on reentry. Subroutines sucked up reachable data as the ship slowed. The standard procedure was a big two-way data dump. The Earth agent's data came in. *I'll read that crap later, if ever.* Information sucking programs didn't discriminate, they took it all in, usable or not. The good stuff always got buried.

Things below had changed drastically in the ship-time weeks they were away. A few weeks in null space amounts to eons on Earth. It was the first century A.D. local-time when they left. Now it was 1900-and-fifty something. He and Gabe were labor before and off the hook but promotions had made them directly responsible.

"That Peace Bomb we forgot to set off with Jesus must have disintegrated by now. No reading on it—another layer of screw-up still going strong."

That was management's mistake, not mine. Do they bring field ops back to fix management's bad calls? Never, and we ain't field-ops no more.

"Control's making it easy on themselves. Sure, make field agents into managers—cook the books. Presto-chango, hocus pocus, and now it's our problem. I hate those guys, I really, really hate those guys."

Lights flashed like crazy on a board. Massive amounts of data streamed in as the ship transitioned out of null space and into Earth-time just outside the solar system.

He read the red flags as they scrolled on the alert screen. A big unscheduled DNA bomb just went off on Earth. It wasn't planned or expected. When they were called back, he and Gabe removed their evolution prods, as told.

"Where'd that Prod come from? It ain't mine. What the hell's going on here?" He adjusted a knob. "What good's a Peace Generation now?"

Someone had to have sent a universal genetic shift prod but it wasn't in the files. It was the timed progressive DNA change-maker type but it wasn't them that programmed it. Good timing, too. If he and Gabe return on time, as expected, there'll be plenty of seeds ripe for harvest. They might even save the project in place. The first Mini Wave already hit. Was there a prod inside it?

No, can't be, it doesn't work that way.

"That's shit planet molding, bad engineering. How are we going to do salvage?"

Mini Waves scrambled everything. That incoming Big Wave will corrupt this unexpected paradigm shift making it into garbage. Some stuff will change for the better, but any DNA shift, intentional or not, becomes a wildcard once a Creation Wave series takes off.

"What a can of spaghetti worms! Why should I care? Because those dirty bastards promoted me."

The ship's bell chimed as the ship reentered Earth's space-time. Mike didn't understand space-time travel. He wasn't required as an anthropologist. He knew his subject up and down but was never good at direct species molding. As union labor, Control couldn't do anything about it but now management had him by the feathers.

"This is all on you. Buck up, Mikey." He told himself while rechecking the screens.

"1964, dang. Late again. Thirteen years since that DNA shift. Too bad it didn't spread far."

That Mini Wave had interfered as feared. But there were enough good people unaffected to turn the place around in his view. Mike ran new calculations with rising excitement. Ship's AI was still hogging the processor power so he switched devices to run the numbers. His handheld was old and basic but it crunched enough stats to confirm saving Earth was better than possible. Mike's wings vibrated.

"We can save the Earth! Who knew?"

He switched to the star map. They were still a long way out. He worked out the finer probabilities on his human psychology pocket calculator. The numbers held. Gabe and he had time to turn this thing around. Gabe entered Mike's station and stood behind looking over his shoulder. Mike compressed his wings so Gabe could see better. Mike put the space map up on his big screen.

"At this pace, we'll make planetfall 1970 local time," Mike said.

"I hate slower than light speed," Gabe said.

"We'll land before critical Waves." Mike turned a knob. "The first big one starts June 1970 and completes November third, 1979 local time. We'll make it. We'll save Project Earth. Our lost Peace Bomb must have activated itself." As Gabe read the psychology report Mike's confidence soared. "We can't miss."

"Forget it," Gabe said with a sad tone. Mike spun his chair around. Gabe's wings were slumped low.

"What gives?"

"Control called. They need us on Spiral Arm Six, ASAP. Grays are out there messing up Her new startup world."

"Jesus son of Joseph!" Mike said hitting the dashboard with a fist. "Ouch!"

"He's not here, remember? He's on his way to Homestar. No help anyway. Locals never work out."

"That's not what I mean," Mike said. "If we hurry, we'll save Her project. Doesn't that make sense? Tell Cap to juice it, balls to the wall. We only need a couple of onsite years."

"Get field Ops out of your head, you're in management now. Things don't have to make sense. The salvage order still stands. We're going to Arm Six, that's final."

"Screw Control. Why don't we do this first?"

"Because the big shots called it," Gabe said. "We get samples and get out, that's all. Cheer up, I confirmed there are immortals down there. We'll have plenty of material when we get back."

Gabe must do the job order. Mike understood that. Gabe was the senior middle management monkey on a stick. *And, we can't do shit without Control's direction and they know nothing about what works in the field.*

"This is bull snot," Mike said.

Gabe shrugged his wings. "Whatever, it's not our call."

Gabe's face drooped long. Mike gave him credit for trying to adapt. Gabe even got a haircut, management short. Gabe's hair hardly touched his shoulders. *Screw that, I'm not getting a management haircut.* Short hair on his fat face didn't work. Mike still had his union pride besides. *They got Gabe's nuts in a middle manager juice press.* Mike felt the squeeze, too.

"We gotta fix Earth first," Mike said evenly, serious, he had to try. "She'll love us for it. What's a little detour? What if we…"

"Forget about it. Planet molding is off the table," Gabe said. "Salvage operation, remember? We don't need to beat the Waves. Get over it."

"My balls are in free-fall, here," Mike said grabbing his crotch. "The sooner we get—"

"For-get-it, it's too late. Captain Burk got his orders."

Ship's intercom chimed indicating standby to jump.

Gabe spun and pushed through the hatch. His wings were out and got hung up so he had to stuff himself through. Gabe never could keep his wings folded while angry. *What's he pissed about, leaving Earth or me?* Gabe left feathers on the deck not bothering to pick them up.

"That's bad JU-JU," Mike said about the feathers as he buckled in.

Leaving feathers was bad practice. Standard procedure states 'leave no evidence' so picking up feathers was deeply ingrained.

Gabe's losing his conditioning.

******

I know what Mike's thinking. I'm not a management sellout. Gabe was stuck between opposing forces and Mike had to know it. Gabe turned to the screen a minute before transmuting space-time. No more Earth data after that. Gabe set up a data grab.

The Eye, a special long view monitor provided by Her, was handy for sucking up massive data dumps. It was too advanced for him to understand but his new rank permitted him to use it. Gabe didn't tell Mike the details yet but The Eye had picked up immortals on Earth as the ship coasted inbound. There were two solid readings, plus two marginal ones—one stronger than the other. *Why tell Mike I know where they are and add to his misery?*

Gabe figured the seeders were a family. They were located close together and that was too good to be true. He checked seed status again just before the jump. Readings go crazy during acceleration. The data scrambled mixing past and future. He wasn't sure but he'd swear two or possibly three seeders winked out of existence as he watched.

"That'll complicate salvage operations if true."

Upper management strikes again. We should have gone to Earth first.

Gabe turned off the Eye. There wasn't anything he could do about Earth until they returned. *Maybe I'll get lucky, but if my future is anything like my past, good luck ain't gonna happen.*

Gabe got up and went to his cabin trailing feathers.

10

Burning Crosses

John was watching TV when Dad's turn came up.

"It's time, son."

"Six o'clock already! Golly, do I have to change the channel, ahh, Dad!"

Time for the news. No use arguing. Dad always watches it.

John didn't even ask why. He got up off the floor and turned the dial feeling disappointed. *Merv Griffin* was going to have a rock-n-roll band on. John didn't know much about music but he liked rock-n-roll. Mom had rock music on the radio all the time because it reminded her of tribal music.

John adjusted the rabbit ears and got the Philly News pretty good. A special report was on. *Mr. Mural* was talking to some guy in a dress. John backed up and stood next to Dad's chair. It was something about The Vatican. John tried to pay attention but it was hard to hear because Dad kept yelling at the TV saying stuff like, "'you people don't know your ass from a holy hole in the ground!'"

Margo was watching, too.

John drifted off thinking about the *Beverly Hillbillies* TV show and how much he wanted Ellie May. He daydreamed about what he and Ellie would do although he wasn't exactly sure what that might be. Ellie May made John's private-part stiff.

Dad slapped his back. "See that, son? They don't know Jesus. I knew him. I knew all your mother's cousins. Priests don't have the slightest inkling. Wait until I show them Jesus was married. I got the proof downstairs. That will blow the Pope's cover. The Church screws everything out of shape for a buck. Let me tell you…Blah, blah, blah."

John slid back out of Dad's view and Dad was still rolling when John slipped into the kitchen. Mom was making dinner and had the radio on. *The Beatles* were singing, "'She loves you, yeah, yeah, yeah.'"

He loved the idea of free love and couldn't wait until someone special loved him.

"'...with a love like that, you know you can't be sad.'" He sang along as the song faded.

Mom also sang, while cooking. He took his chair. Lots of cool songs came on over the airwaves. *She sings sweet as birds. Dinner's on soon. It's late, already after seven. No wonder I'm hungry.*

"Set the table, dear. The news is over."

John suffered through a long dinner with lots of talk, talk, talk, and Dad went right back to the TV after eating. John thought about going outside but dinner took too long and it was dark outside.

As he put plates into the dishwater, a car's headlights flashed the kitchen window coming from their lane. The light stayed a moment before winking out. Mom dropped her spoon into the stewpot and rushed to the window. John followed. A bunch of cars were parked on the lane with their lights off. The moon was low but full and he made out one car very well. That *Andy Griffin* Ford police car was first in line.

"Damn, damn, damn, I knew it. He never listens to me."

Mom stomped out of the kitchen. The wood floor thumped as if Mom's *Mary Jane* shoes were angry. John felt something new, fear. His heart pumped wildly as she rushed off. He hesitated then followed.

"Jacob, the sheriff's here with a Mongol horde. We're in trouble."

Dad popped out of his easy chair. "Quick shutter the windows, where's the gun?"

"What about Margo? She's still outside," John cried.

"Forget her, we'll have more."

Dad's voice was squeaky. He sounded like *Mickey Mouse* if Mickey was scared.

"Wife, find that gun! John, secure the windows."

Mom ran around pulling open drawers. Every window had a wooden interior shutter with a cross cut in it like the castle walls from the Middle Ages he had seen in books. This old *Robin Hood* movie got real, he thought. Archer slots were available, but they didn't have any bows and arrows and it wasn't 1060 A.D. John closed the windows facing the county road last and looked through the cross. Ghost figures advanced toward the house.

"Dad, men are outside. They got white sheets on. I'm letting Margo in."

"NO! Don't open that door for anything."

A whole lot more running around the house went on next. Mom found the antique gun but they didn't have much black powder. She loaded it in the kitchen and spilled powder on her nice red checkered table cloth. John recognized the firearm from a book— a cowboy gun—Colt Navy percussion revolver. The ones on *Gun Smoke* were all wrong. They didn't have that many cartridge guns until after the end of the Civil War.

"Only enough for a few shots," she said, handing Dad the gun. "We're out of balls."

A commotion outside started. Men yelling, "come out, Jew" and "we got a necktie for you," while rocks hit the house. Beer bottles crashed loudest. Someone was pounded on the door.

"Goddamn Jews, we'll teach you! This is what you get for killing Jesus!"

The man was right behind the door which didn't feel thick enough to stop him.

Dad's hands shook as he placed tiny percussion caps on the Colt. He dropped the tin and wound up with just enough for each loaded chamber.

"What about John," Mom whispered violently. "I told you, I told you."

"Hush, take him downstairs, out the root cellar. That underground railway tunnel goes into the woods. You hear me, son, hide in the woods. Don't move until it's over, understand me? No matter what, stay hidden."

"They'll see." Mom hissed like a snake.

"Four shots won't stop them. It doesn't matter. It'll distract them. Two minutes. I'll take a shot, another shot a minute later, now go."

Mom rushed him downstairs but didn't turn on the lights. She took his hand. He bumped his way to the cellar's inner door past the book stacks way in the back. She moved in the dark like a cat while he bounced off everything. He had never seen that back door open. It was stuck. She pulled at it like a maniac. The door gave just as a shot fired upstairs. Once opened, she yanked a pull-light string revealing an old wooden hatch high on the outer wall.

"I'll boost you up, hurry. Keep quiet. When you get to the other end, hide. We will find you later."

He couldn't believe that little scuttle hole was the way out. It was too small. She hosted and he scrabbled inside scraping his sides. A couple of old bricks fell in on top of him. She pushed a flashlight through the hole and tapped his feet. He reached behind and took it. No room to turn. The space was coffin-tight.

"I'm breaking the lightbulbs. I can't let them find this escape. Go now." She closed the hatch but it didn't fit tight. Light streaked through the cracks showing him spiderwebs.

The bulb popped and all went dark. He clicked on the flashlight as her steps raced away. The next thing he heard were muffled shouts. He was too scared to move until another gunshot upstairs shook him. *Boy, that Colt's a boomer.* Many more shots from outside followed.

"It's not supposed to be this way. What about peace and love?" He moaned.

Something came crashing through a basement window and John snapped out of it. He crawled down that earthworm smelly tunnel as fast as he could. He didn't mind the root-rot smell, or the mud, or the drips of water and sweat in his eyes. The human bones crunching under his knees were interesting but that didn't speed him along. Spiderwebs wiggling with life was what powered him like a windup doodlebug. Spiders put ants in his pants. *Why does Margo like spiders so much, yuck!*

When he got to the end, he didn't find an escape hole. He should have panicked but for some reason, it was A-OK to be stuck underground. He rested at the end and was fine there until a spider landed on his neck. That started him digging at the roots with bare hands until he disgorged a piece of a skull cap which he used as a shovel. He didn't stop until the moon peeked in and the sound of gunfire became clear. He pushed harder desperate for the open air. He cut his hand but didn't slow until he crawled out breathless and flopped onto the forest floor covered in webs and mulch.

Voices came out of the mists, but it wasn't fog, it was smoke.

"You damn Jews don't know nothing about Jesus," a voice bellowed.

"I know more about him than you…you ignorant fool." Dad's voice was muffled.

"Jeepers creepers, Dad's arguing with outlaws," John said right out loud in surprise.

"The Lord God sent me. I'm his vengeance," a voice called.

"Jesus never spoke of retribution. He's a Jew, you idiot, your god's a Jew!"

"Blasphemer!"

"Your moronic religion is the blasphemy!"

All the men outside started yelling. *Dad got them going.* John had to see it. He rolled onto his belly and crawled a little bit forward under the ferns. Firelight and smoke were thick just ahead. Flickering shadows danced through the woods. He crawled on and got right up to the edge of the yard. There a huge cross burned near the porch. He smelled kerosene. The fire cast crazy shadows on ghostly white sheets. Many had torches. He never saw anything like it on TV, not even on *Ed Sullivan*.

"It's a nightmare circus act," he gasped.

A big man came out from the dark with a black book. He raised his hands. "God the Father is my witness, for the crime of killing Jesus, you must die. The Lord is true! Go on boys, torch them."

That was when Margo showed up still wearing her go-to-town dress. She first appeared like a small ghost drifting out of the woods until she sprang and ran at the house.

"Leave them alone! I hate you, stupid idiots!" Margo screamed.

A guy grabbed her and put a flashlight under her face. "It's the girl, where's the boy? Must have hidden them."

"Kill that light, Clint said no lights."

"Shut up, Bill, he said no names!"

A bunch of them closed on Margo and felt her all over. They lifted her dress. *Gosh if they wanted to see her naked, they can come around anytime.* But it was more than just looking. They were rough. The more she screamed and hit the more they laughed. They weren't nice. John didn't know what was happening but he knew it was wrong. He stood intending to charge in and save her but someone yelled.

"There's the boy."

"All accounted for."

"Quick, put him down."

A bang. John fell over backward. He felt sticky wet ooze crawl all over him but he couldn't move. His heart thumped like crazy; his hearing went fuzzy. *Every-*

thing's hazing over, I'm falling asleep. He fought, resisted it, it wasn't bedtime yet. *They can't make me go to bed.* He was winning, things were clearing, he was not going to die. Opening his eyes, men in sheets stood over him.

"The boy's not dead. Look at that goddamn lizard's sitting on his head."

"If that don't beat all."

"Give that critter some old fashion religion."

At that moment John Lazurus felt this lizard was the most important thing on Earth—the only thing that mattered, his only friend. A pistol came out of the dark and real close.

"Stay with me," John said.

The lizard bobbed up and down. A flash. Everything went black.

11

Ten Million and Thirteen A.D.

The Librarian had concerns. She suspected big things unseen were changing although she could not put a finger on it. She didn't feel it from the Books. Her sense of foreboding usually proved true. She could not tell the others her worries, not yet. Her kind had enough problems such as the threatening mammalian people who bred like tree rats while her people's population diminished. The ones not attending Mass became more animal-like day by day. Mass was the only thing that kept her people intact.

The old Books gave little relief. New visions were rarer and less complete. The earliest—the hardest to understand—were visions of His very beginning. But, also, they were omens of doom and the people did not know it yet. The oldest visions were the only kind of late. The Librarian suspected that the closer they get to The Ancestor's roots the closer they were to finishing his Book, and in doing so, her people will lose the battle for survival. The last act is to deliver the Book and be freed. *Yet John Doe's whereabouts—if he still lives at all—is doubtful.*

"If not Him, then who can receive the Book? How can the Burden be resolved?"

Our people's reason for being is approaching its end. If the congregation knew her thoughts, would they stay for Mass or give up and go wild? Either way, time felt short. More and more she was convinced offloading the Burden was impossible. If He still lives, the way to find him is barred. Should a scout range too far, he did not return. Since the riders stopped coming, hope was cut low. One cannot travel far from the library without a rider and live. Their former partners were recently made enemies.

"Why is it when we need riders most, they abandon us? This feels like a cosmic joke."

A knock on her door came. "It is time. Have you a new reading?"

The Priestess sounded desperate. What could a Librarian do? Yes, there was a new one from the deep past. *One more step closer to attrition*. What choice did she have? Read the new or suffer the inadequacies of the old?

"Yes, just in, it was given me only yesterday," the Librarian said.

The Priestess spoke into the keyhole. "I will call them to Mass."

The Librarian took up an old, worn volume that she had pulled out of the stacks herself. It had room for one last entry. She held it like a baby. Each Book was close to her heart. She knew every one of them. The bell rang. She left her office and trod the Processional Way toting the Book and her notes. *This will finish the volume*. One page left to complete it. A short vision was enough. She shuttered on the thought. The old Books were nearly filled.

It was a typical Sun's Day in the city. Bright and warm with a clear, pretty sky. Since the sky turned blue thirteen years before, every season was warmer. She missed the green sky.

"Why do I feel so cold?"

The bluing of the upper air was an inexplicable marvel, but what did it mean? The trees were sick and falling far and wide but not in her home range? Another bad omen? She put away the clouds residing in her heart. Darleen wrapped her shawl tighter around herself and the Book she carried.

12

The Rape of Margo

Margo woke with the dawn. Orange light broke through a small, filthy glass window. She lay on a dirt floor tasting blood. Memories bleed back into her conscious mind. She was not dead. She did not die—that would have been better. Last night, they thought she had died. The big fat man had tossed her limp body into this nasty toolshed like a sack of feed.

Someone had said, "'Sheriff, I do believe we done fucked that beaver right to death.'"

But he was wrong.

The sun rose higher. Rays filtered in between old wooden slats. She watched the play of light and shadows while remaining as still as death.

This wasn't her home barn. She became fully aware of herself only last night. It was her big wake-up day. Her coming-out party was attended by uninvited men in white hoods. She was in the woods when they arrived shortly after her waking. She understood the horror of it. She should have run from the attack, not toward it. Love drove her forward.

I'll never make that mistake again.

She spat out the ash mixed with blood. They used a burned stick on her—tried to choke her with it after… She kept her wits. Everything Daddy said, years of him going on about this or that was not lost within her terror. She grabbed onto the important things that Daddy had said. That was how she held on. That was how she knew to let death sleep take her and not die.

'If you think you'll die, but you don't want it, fake it. That way you'll keep what you know. That prevents real death.' Daddy had said.

'Our kind can detach, look dead, it's a defense mechanism. Very useful if you want to remember who killed you, or start a religion.' Daddy laughed about it. 'We heal fast. People think it is magic, it's not. It's just the way we are.'

He taught them how to induce the trance and she used it. She didn't want to forget. Had she died, she would have no memories. She had not yet chosen her familiar species. There was no time to pick one so she refused to reset. There was no starting over fresh and innocent as a child full of love and puppy dog dreams for her. She spat at the notion.

"Revenge is better." Her jaw hurt saying it.

Margo sat up and tested her limbs. Her broken arm was fine, her torn private parts were intact, the gash on her forehead was gone although blood had caked in her hair and on her face. The healing was still doing its work. She felt reconstitution's unusual power. Comic book strength coursed in her. Everything was more but it won't last. *Regeneration, just as Daddy said.* Her eyes and ears were more powerful. She reached out and listened.

"Was a hell of a night, Clint, too bad we couldn't keep her. What're we gonna do with the body?" The speaker was out of normal hearing range, but not for her.

"What do you think? We bury her scrawny ass after breakfast. Go get some shovels."

Margo heard his footsteps. She judged the distance and direction. *He's coming, good.*

She took a firemen's ax off a wall peg—blade on one side, pickax on the other. The handle was half her height but light as a pencil under regeneration's power.

"I'm not of this world." She giggled.

She had to move on while she could. She hid behind the shed's door counting his steps. A spider descended from the rafters. She caught it in hand. "You're my special friend. From now on, you will remember for me."

Footsteps closed. She carefully placed the spider on a horizontal 2x4 set between wall studs and raised the ax like a baseball bat. Daddy watched baseball. TV had its lessons.

When the door opened, she stepped out and swung. The spike disappeared into him up to the handle. He spun falling forward into the shed landing on his back. Blood gurgled out of his mouth. He lay gasping. The pick split his sternum. She felt it hit his spine.

"Trouble breathing? That's too bad. I had that same trouble, too, last night."

She knelt beside him.

"Someone put a wiener in my mouth. Here, let me help you."

She shoved a burlap bag into his mouth cutting off his air.

"There you are, feel better?"

With one foot on his chest for leverage, she pulled, but it didn't come out. She wiggled it around until the sound of bone popping stopped—then it came free. She had to work fast; the reconstitution effect was already fading.

She heard no other there except the sheriff. She took her weapon and ran for him. He was inside the hunter's lodge. Smoke from the fieldstone chimney smelled of bacon and watered her dry mouth. A backdoor led into the kitchen. She charged inside with her ax ready.

He stood there shirtless, a blob of wale flesh cooking on a wood-burning stove. He recoiled with surprise, lost balance, and fell back against the sidewall. She followed, swung hard, and chopped his leg below the knee gouging flesh and breaking bone. He collapsed onto the floor smashing a chair under him. He up righted quickly grabbing the wound. A beached leviathan. *He's nothing.*

"Help me! I'll bleed to death! Help me!" He cried. "Tourniquet!"

Touched, she moved in closer, but he lashed out like a striking snake swinging wild fists. She dodged with ease. The flab of his arms jiggled and she squeaked a laugh. *He's the windmill and I'm Sanchez.*

"You don't want help."

"Please, I'm bleeding. I need a tourniquet," he said, pushing more upright.

She crouched at a safe distance to survey him. Making herself small and trustworthy, she waited there out of reach considering her options while her energy drained.

"Please, please." He fell into sobs.

"I'll get help," she said. "You need a grown-up. That nunnery—Tell me which way. I'll get the sisters."

"Down the lane, not far, go half a mile—to the county road, left, go a mile, driveway on the left. Hurry."

He turned death-pale but the blood stopped gushing. He would survive if left alone. *I can't allow that.* A number 12 cast-iron pan sat on the firebox stove boiling pork bellies and enough to feed her family.

"Pig for a pig," she said.

The handle was burning hot but it couldn't burn her yet. She flung the pan with its contents into the fat man's face. Grease boiled his skin away. Rendered fat spilled all over him. He screamed and screamed and she laughed and laughed. He cried until he could cry no more. She waited until he became a whimpering blob. Then, she dumped an oil lamp into his lap.

"Sheriff, I do believe I'll fire you. The charge? Conduct unbecoming of an officer."

She showed him a box of matches. He still had one working eye and it opened cue-ball big. She stuck a stick match and tossed it into his kerosene-soaked crotch. His pants lighted with a whoosh. The pork fat ignited, too. He reached for his privates and set both hands ablaze. She stood by watching until his arm fat caught and burned like two wicks. When he was too horse to scream anymore, she sat on the floor and watched him melt.

"Funny, he doesn't smell like bacon."

She left when the floor caught fire.

Leaving the place burning, Margo set out for the children's home concocting a story on the way. The nuns won't be hard to fool. *They'll take me in.* She didn't need a coherent story.

13

Life at The Morgue

When his lights came on, he didn't know his name.

The room was dark except for a streetlight shining through a high window. That light fell on him. He was naked lying on a stainless-steel table, his head shaved. A mortician's tool kit lay next to him on a rolling steel cart. He understood what those tools were used for but not why he was there.

He untied the tag on his toe and read it, "John Doe."

It was not exactly right but close. Nothing was right. His head felt like a balloon. He didn't know how he knew what a balloon or stainless steel was. Everything was fuzzy, images and facts spun and mashed together like donuts in a cement mixer.

He remembered cold. *Too cold is bad.* He lowered himself off the table and went into the hall in search of clothes. The next door was labeled 'Dressing Room B' and was stocked with cheap suits. Nothing his size and nothing he liked.

He picked up a black suit jacket. "That's no good, needs more color."

He roamed the building and found a janitor's shirt and a pair of dungarees in the maintenance supply closet and put them on. The tennis shoes were dirty and too big, but they seemed to fit his personality and that got him thinking.

"Who the heck am I?"

The sound of his voice echoed off the wood-paneled hallway walls and he didn't recognize it. Panic set in, something was missing. He had to find it.

He ran all through the two-story funeral home looking for what he did not know. He finally burst through a door marked Private Office and skidded to a halt. Another living thing stared at him from inside a big birdcage.

"Holy cow, it's an iguana," he said walking up to the cage.

It bobbed its head as if in response.

"You want to come out, don't you?"

He was oddly taken by the little creature and forgot his predicament for the moment. John Doe opened the cage, took the creature into his hand, and put it on his shoulder. It felt right. He tickled it under the chin.

"You like that don't you?"

He felt better, but soon the place seemed to close in on him. *Get out, get out,* played faintly in the back of his awareness. He realized another problem. *I'm trespassing.* He rushed down the stairs and crashed through the front double doors like *Herman Munster.* He was as fast as a speeding bullet. The doors' deadbolts snapped like toothpicks. An alarm screamed. He ran. The iguana clung to his back. At the end of the driveway, he had turned like Lot's wife. The door's sign said, Philadelphia Coroner.

Spooked, he ran faster than a person can run. He ran a mile down a wide street and crossed a boulevard. The block was dark with closed buildings and no houses, but there was a big well-lit place several blocks onward. Cars were lined up trying to get into the parking lot. He ran on and right past a sign that said "Concert Parking." He finally stopped to breathe deep inside the parking lot.

It's some sort of colosseum, like Rome. Is this for gladiators?

Young people were everywhere. Some were milling around; some were entering the stadium's doors. Boys and girls had long hair and funny clothes and he liked them immediately. The hair, clothes, and hats, all of that culture he inhaled. He touched his head; it was shaved clean before running but now hair fell over his ears. It grew as he combed his hand through it.

"What gives?"

He ducked behind an old school bus and closed his eyes willing his hair to grow faster and it did. He needed to fit in. When bangs brushed his chin, he opened his eyes. The energy, that inner glow was gone. He left his hiding place knowing he looked like them but nothing more. *Defense mechanism.* Echoed in his mind.

A big sign near the road had read, "Chuck Berry" in big letters and "The Warlocks" under that. The lights and activities dazzled him like a sleepwalking dream. *This is magic, but Warlocks aren't real.* He wandered and bumped into a group of hippies passing a cigarette around. The man he crashed into wore a Captain Ahab beard and long straight hair.

"Oh, hey, cool it, man," he said, but he didn't sound angry.

"I'm sorry, mister. I wasn't looking."

"Hey, man, it's cool. Want a hit? Here ya go," he said passing it.

John Doe took the odd cigarette, had a puff, and passed it to a girl with flowers in her hair. He didn't know what else to do. She smelled green like a cornfield.

"Far out," a boy with long blonde hair said. "What's your lizard's name? Nature's cool, I dig it."

John Doe had forgotten it. "It's an iguana. He doesn't have a name, well not yet, anyway."

"Bitchin'."

The blond boy gave him the cigarette. They were all smoking the same one. Everything they did and said registered as good—sharing was far out. A phrase came to mind, *'when in Rome do as the Romans do.'* So, he took another poke and held the smoke doing the same as the others did.

John Doe stayed with the group as freaky stagehands came and went through the gray double doors marked "Employee Entrance." It was dark in there like the morgue so he didn't want to go inside although the music playing there pulled at his heart. Somebody called it the warm-up band, two bands go on before the main act. He fell in love with the sound of it. Everybody was 'grooving.'

He stood between a guy named Jerry and a guy named Pig-Pen. They weren't in the same band but they agreed to play together for this gig. John had fun hanging around with these guys but the fun ended when the stage door swung open with a crash. Bobby, a guitar player, dropped his beer.

"Oh shit, here comes Mountain Girl," Bobby said.

"Can't you hear the fans," she said. "Man, wake up." She slapped Jerry, but not hard.

"It's showtime, you Goofballs."

"Man, give a girl a lick and that's what you get," Jerry said laughing. "People of Further deserve the ride."

He followed her inside.

"That chick sure is rough. I thought the Bus makes ya mellow," a hippie dude said with amusement. "She must be straight."

"Captain Trips will mellow her out, man," a chick wearing pigtails and a headband said.

The door was left open and the crowd inside were yelling and pounding the floor. The band people hanging with John split and went inside. One of the guys stopped at the door and called, "Hey lizard man, come on backstage."

"It's cool, man. I'm good right here."

The kid was young. John guessed fifteen and his same age. John checked himself in a car's mirror. *Yeah, we're the same age.*

The kid didn't give up. "Come on man, we're going on." John waved him off. Bobby shut the door.

People in there were screaming. The dark and the noise were too much. He needed to mellow out and he didn't mind company, but inside was too crazy. The parking lot was full of cars but not many people. Just outside tour bus parking stood a hawker tent next to a VW van. Other booths were there too, but nobody was home. The opened booth had a short, skinny hippie standing behind a table full of T-shirts. His hair was past his shoulders full and nice, but spotty beard. That freak waved for John to come.

"Hey man," the guy said. "I'm tripping my balls off. You look cool. Watch the store for me?"

"Jeepers, can't you?"

"My old lady wants it bad. She's in the van. I never did it tripping. Help a brother out?"

"Sure, I guess."

The guy wandered over to the van, got in, and pulled the split side doors shut. John crawled under the table and explored the tent booth. A cigar box had forty bucks in it and some joints. The front table was stacked with tie-dyed T-shirts. They had a couple of galvanized tubs in the back, boxes of white T-shirts, and a gas-powered washing machine. One box was marked pizza. He didn't know anything about pizza, but he tried it and it was good.

After the show, all the hippies and freaks filed out and bought every finished shirt John had. They were priced at three bucks, but John figured them worth ten so he took down the sign and pushed up the price. John stuffed the cigar box with bills.

Hours after the show, the place became quiet and empty. No customers were left so he stashed the cigar box as not to get ripped off and made a bed of piled white T-shirts. He got himself and his pet stoned before curling up to sleep.

He felt A-OK here—clean and fed…like home? They must have washed him at the…? *Where was I before?* Anyway, he figured he wouldn't mess up the shirts being freshly washed even if he didn't remember how or where he took a bath. He was pretty stoned besides. Nodding off, he felt just like a newborn and fell asleep contented.

14

A Bus Called Further

John Doe woke wrapped in a cocoon of clean, white T-shirts. He didn't mind the *Clorox* smell. Someone yelling was what woke him.

"Hey, man we got ripped off. Man, this sucks! All the stuff's gone."

John rolled out of the pile of shirts and noticed he had very long hair, hair he didn't have yesterday. He had no time to think about it. That skinny hippie guy who had disappeared last night jumped back three feet when John stood up. The man grabbed a maul used to pond tent stakes. He raised it to strike but John sensed he won't let the hammer fall and stepped forward out of the shadow.

"Cool it, man," John said. "Remember last night? You asked me to mind the store. It's me, man."

"Oh right, far out. Man, I fucked up. I tripped my balls off last night. Where'd my stuff go? Weren't you shorter and younger last night? Never mind, man I was way too high. You get robbed?"

"No, man, we sold out," John said. He walked to the back of the tent, pushed a pile of rags off a speaker cabinet, and grabbed the cigar box. John handed it to the skinny guy, "Here you go, man. They bought everything you had ready."

The skinny man opened the box. "Far out! Son, you are stone groovy. Thanks, man, thanks a lot. This is what I'm talking about. This is how it's supposed to be. Peace and love man, sharing, that's what's groovy."

The guy leafed through the bills. John, taller, counted along from behind and over his shoulder. The guy counted about halfway at five hundred bucks before stopping.

"Man, weren't you shorter last night?"

"Naw, you were tripping. You imagined it," John said but wasn't sure.

The freak went back to counting. John touched his hair. Last night was fuzzy. He had smoked a lot of pot but still, he could have sworn he had short hair yesterday. He felt smaller when he crashed, for sure. His hair was past the shoulders and he had a sensation of being shorter. *That was some smoke.* Was it laced with LSD? The band said some prankster was dosing people or was it the Pranksters had dosed the band?

"Cool, man, you bailed me out." He stuffed the money into a paper bag. "More than I ever got. How did you do it?"

"Jacked the price seven bucks."

"Ten dollars? That's not cool. I'm into sharing, man. I give freaks a break. I'm not a rip off. Fuck the Man. Gouging people is so establishment."

"I'm down with that," John said. "But the box was nearly empty and I figured you need the cash. They weren't hippies anyway, just college kids with rich daddies."

"Cool. You put screws to The Man the long way. I dig it. So, man, what's your name anyway?"

He felt a deep pain—a feeling of loss—he didn't know his name. An image of a toe-tag flashed in his mind's eye. They must have thought him dead or something, maybe he ODed? But he got away. But that didn't answer who he was.

"John Doe," rolled out of his mouth.

"I dig it, man. The fuzz is looking for you."

"It's not like that, man. Check it out, I don't remember shit. Too much dope, I guess."

"Get back, look out man!" The guy stagged back and picked up the hammer.

"No, no, it's cool, it's my pet, look." John held out his hand and the iguana climbed on. It went straight up his arm and onto the shoulder where it perched forward-facing.

"Far out, man, natural. Dig it, I love natural. Life is about harmony. We got to live in harmony with every living thing. It's right. It's the way to live, man, the way it's supposed to be. Dig it."

John felt better with his pet close, but there was still something missing, a lot was missing.

"John's not my real name; I don't know what it is. I don't remember. I don't know what happened. I got knocked on the head or something."

He felt loss pile on, the weight of it crushing. He had to sit. He lowered himself onto an unopened box of T-shirts, hung his head, and sobbed.

"Where will I go? I don't know who I am."

"Nobody knows who they are. We all got to find ourselves, man. That's what life's all about." The guy put a hand on John's shoulder. "That's what trips are for. That's how you see—everything's alive, man. Ask Dr. Tim. Hang with us. We're looking for ourselves, too, man."

"Billy," A woman called from outside. "The Pigs want us to move. We ain't got shit for gas money."

A pretty, long-haired girl in a long skirt and a white puff-sleeve blouse swooshed in under the rear tent flap. Her head was crowned with crushed flowers. Backlit, she looked like an angel. He saw right through her skirt's gauze—no underwear. Her boobs loosely flopped within her dance-like movements. Something stirred in his dungarees.

"Hey, Betty, man, this is John. He helped us out last night. We got gas money, plenty."

John stood and held out his hand. She moved toward him to shake but stopped halfway. She stared at him with pouting brows. Her brown nipples, just dash marks behind a thin blouse, pushed out. She licked her plump lips.

"John ran the tent last night, sold everything. We're flush," Billy said.

Betty shook her head yes, and pushed a loose strand of long, straight hair behind one ear. She had a lovely, thin neck. Imagines of swans came to his mind but he had no recollection of where and when he had seen swans. The memory slipped away.

"That's bitch-in, righteous of you," she said. John snapped out of it. "Anything I can do for you, man?" She batted her eyelashes reminding him of *Olive Oil* from the *Popeye* cartoons.

Outside a police car's siren blasted. A megaphone sounded. "Move that truck!"

A truck's motor starting followed. That weirdly painted bus parked behind Billy's tent started, too.

"I guess I better get," John said. "You need to pack and…and anyway—"

"No way, man. What if the fuzz is looking for you? You better come with us. Betty, we'll hide him in the van. Go see if it's clear."

She didn't waste time. She spun on her straw flip-flops and moved out. John guessed they had run from the cops before. Billy started draining the dye tanks into WWII jerrycans. While the old galvanized wash tubs ran, Billy stuffed loose unprocessed shirts into an Army surplus duffel bag. John helped until the VW bus's horn beeped.

"That's the all-clear, man. Get in the van, hang out, we'll roll soon. I got this. After I load the Power Wagon, I'll hook up the tow bar and we'll go. Betty's waiting. Stay low."

Billy gave him a funny wink of the eye.

John hesitated at the tent flap. A cop car was on the far side of the parking lot herding hippies off the land. The van's doors were closed with its curtains drawn.

"Where's your old lady?" John said. "She isn't out here."

"She's in the van. They don't call her Betty Bang-Bang for no reason. Go on, man. Free love, man, free love. It's cool."

John tried not to run but this odd urge drove him. He walked too fast. Lucky the fuzz didn't see him. That stick in his pants didn't make it any easier. The van's side door wasn't locked. He opened it and crawled in. Betty, laying on a profusion of pillows, put a finger to her lips and tapped calling him to her.

"Far out," was all he could say.

A rock and roll AM station played. She touched his face with her fingertips before running her hands through his hair. He swooned. A Bob Dylan song came on and they embraced. It all felt right and natural, harmonious. His worries, his missing answers went blowing in the wind.

"I never done it before," he said. "What'll I do?"

"I'll show you."

They made love and it was beautiful, everything beautiful. Afterward, he lay next to her panting, feeling the hot glow on his face. He cupped one of Betty's boobs in his hand. Her neck and chest radiated heat. Her high cheeks were rosy—her smile lit his world.

"That's the way it's supposed to be. Free love, baby," she said. "You do it groovy."

Noise at the front of the van made John bolt up and scramble into someone's pants. They were Levis and not the pants he had stolen. He couldn't find his.

"Cool it, man," She laughed. "It's just Billy hooking up. We tow the van behind the pickup."

She pulled a peasant blouse over her head, put on a different long skirt, and scooted out the door legs first.

She reopened it, poked her head inside, and said, "Stay here in case the pigs are looking for you. We're pulling out, man."

"I dig," he said.

John hung out under the pillows. He didn't know if the cops were on him or not. Maybe he OD'ed last night and they thought he was dead and brought him to the morgue. That was what he figured. It didn't seem exactly right but close. It had to be that. He thought of flagging the cops down. *Maybe they know who I am.* But then, he would have to trust The Man. Everyone said you can't trust the establishment. That would be a bad scene. Someone said last night, "'Never trust the government,'" and that felt right on. The truck fired up and clunked into gear. Billy rolled. John kept his head down until they were far away.

John parted the front curtains. The van was hooked to an Army surplus one-ton Dodge Power Wagon, a big green monster of a truck with a canvas covered wooden frame built over the pickup bed which carried everything. The Dodge was slow but it didn't stop until it crossed into Delaware.

Billy pulled into a gas station and parked under a sign saying "Trucks Welcome." Farmland all around, the gas station had a tiny general store but the parking lot was huge. John checked out a bunch of freaks that were singing into a megaphone from on top of a *Technicolor* school bus. They had a flying bridge from a cabin cruiser boat bolted to the roof. He didn't have time to hang out. His trouser snake needed relief. He ran off behind the store and pushed out into the cornrows before opening the floodgate.

Coming back, he walked straight into a cloud of pot smoke. Others were parked there and partying with the bus people. He recognized Mountain Girl and a couple of roadies. Billy filled the tanks, hit the store, and parked before John realized it.

Billy ducked into his truck and came back with the carton of cigarettes he and Betty had ripped off.

"Man, 25 cents a gallon, they owe me this," Billy said, waving the carton around.

John didn't smoke tobacco, but the idea of stealing left a bad taste in his mouth. Before long, the parking lot was a regular freak fest and threatened to spread. The joy didn't last. An old-timer in coveralls marched out of the store with a shotgun resting in the crucks of his arm.

"You'll done got your gas, you'll skedaddle now," the old man's eyes bulged seeing the empty carton on the ground. "Goddamn it, you hippies are screwing with ma business. I'm-a telling the sheriff."

"Just a minute, Sir," this older guy Ken said—he was the bus driver's best friend. "We aren't doing anything illegal. Acid is legal, man."

"Don't care if you blow your brains out, you're hurting ma business."

As if on cue, a tractor-trailer slowed down. With no way into the lot, the trucker downshifted and gassed it on down the road leaving black smoke in its wake.

"It's money you love, so it's money you get," Ken said. "I would not advise money's exclusive pursuit for a healthy soul."

Ken reached into his bellbottom pants pocket, pulled out a roll of bills, and peeled off of a couple of tens and twenties.

"Here you are, man."

The old man looked insulted but he stuffed the money into his overall's top pocket. "I'm a fair man. That'll cover the damages but I want you folks gone. Now git. I done called the sheriff. He'll be down here in fifteen minutes."

Nobody from the bus called Further took it seriously but John, feeling the danger, snapped to attention. Billy and Betty registered the message as well and split for the Dodge. John spoke up loud and clear.

"Come on people, the cops will bust your heads. Man, we don't need this shit, we better go."

"Listen to the kid," someone said.

"Everybody's tripping," Ken said, "I'm too stoned. Forget Cassidy, he's gone. I don't drive, Cassidy drives the Bus."

A couple of the Pranksters were freaking out. Billy had pulled out of the lot but stopped at the side of the road. Billy revved the Dodge's motor and called, "You coming with us, man?"

John thought he shouldn't leave Ken and his riders to the cops. They were in no shape to drive and easy marks for pig abuse. He just couldn't leave them there helpless and stoned with the cops. Deep down, he didn't trust the police and he didn't know why but he felt the danger rolling in like a storm. John waved Billy to leave and Billy drove out.

"I'll drive the Bus, man, let's go," John said.

"Groovy. Hey, everybody, get on. Man, you're either on the Bus or off the Bus," Ken said. "Lizard Man's driving. Hey nice iguana, by the way."

Everyone piled on or in. John hadn't driven a car before but it didn't take much to figure it out. Neil Cassidy gave driving pointers and directions in between long speeches on his megaphone about love, peace, and harmony. Ken joined in and talked on and on about finding yourself. John was down with that. They were all seeking the same thing.

"Nothing's more important than going to where you're at, dig?" Cassidy said.

"It's not what they put on you. It's what's in your soul. What Dr. Tim says, 'turn on, tune in, and drop out.'"

John wasn't sure what that meant but by the time they arrived at a commune in Virginia called The Chicken Ranch, he was dialed in. The Merry Pranksters wanted everything he wanted. Peace, love, harmony, lots of free love, and most of all, a way to find himself and make sense of it all.

He didn't go to bed that night—LSD didn't let him sleep—when he passed out in a hayloft the next day he did so as a new follower of Doctor Timothy Leary. Like the two chicks, he made it with that morning, he accepted freedom's way.

John figured his answer would be found on the inner road of self-discovery. One idea burned inside him. *Find yourself, man, you got to find yourself.* The other imperative—getting chicks—took care of itself. That was easy. Dealing with amnesia was harder. Life was a mystical quest but not like religion. He didn't trust religion. He knew its history but didn't know how he knew. All he knew for sure was to trust where his spirit pointed him.

The Man's way ain't the way.

Sex, drugs, and rock-n-roll scared the establishment. There were good reasons why straights were not to be trusted. The establishment was all plastic, fake, and hard, ready for war—not cool.

John Doe didn't know who he was but he was on his way to find out.

15

Margo Converts

Margo had had just enough time to drag the skinny little dead man into the lodge before it collapsed in flames. The last few yards had been hard going. Her rebirth powers went dry before she set out as a skinny, dirty, pathetic little girl.

The candle man lied. He said, 'down the lane,' as if it wasn't very far. It was. Margo walked and walked that rutted dirt track for an hour as the hunter's retreat burned. The inferno blew a smoke fog down her path giving cover. Two miles away the smell of bacon fried man-flesh abated—evidence gone. Her revenge was complete.

"No evidence, leave no evidence," she repeated what someone said last night. The idea cut deep.

She did not know why, did not know who said it, but the idea impressed her. It was logical. The long walk gave her time to think about such things. Where did she get that bit of information? Was it from the stupid TV cop shows her brother watched or the cowboy shows? The idea certainly didn't come from the *Andy Griffin Show*.

"No, it was the fat man himself ordering his men at the cross burning. 'Leave no trace of them damn hippies. They'll never be found', that's what he said."

Margo stopped. She had a brother. Her heart jumped. But they had killed him. They killed them all. No, no point in going back. No point in pining. She didn't know if John was an immortal like her or not. Daddy and Mommy got burnt down to powder so Margo had nobody to ask. She didn't know everything about her kind but she understood Mommy wasn't coming back—nothing left to reconstitute.

What about brother John?

"'Leave no evidence.' They dumped him in the fire. I'm alone."

I am evidence. Her blood-caked rags were a crime scene. *I'll startle the nuns in this condition.*

"They'll call the State Police. I can't have that," she told the big lion spider riding on her shoulder.

A firetruck's alarm sounded in the distance. She stopped to listen. They were on her dirt road and closing. She turned off the path and downhill toward a creek. After the truck passed, she moved downstream and away from the road. She found a little pool and bathed in its cold water dunking her head over and over until the blood washed out.

The little stream was too cold but its fresh water brought fresh focus. The fog of shock washed away but not her fog of war. Her resolve remained. No longer blood-dirty, but wet and worn, she washed her tattered clothes.

A wide spot of grass was nearby where the sun penetrated the canopy. She laid out naked on that sun-warmed turf until her hair dried. Her clothes were damp when she put them back on. *The woods ain't the place for a party dress, that will cover my condition.* In better order, she set out across the hardwood forest while finger-raking the tangles out of her hair.

She arrived at Saint Ann's Children's Home barefoot and briar scratched with torn clothing excuses. The forest explained her condition well.

This is going to be easy.

The children's home's big oak double doors weren't locked. She pushed open the unfixed door assassin-slow entering on mouse toes. The lobby's marble floor was inlaid with mosaics of fish, lambs, and other religious devices. Writing in stone lay under her feet and she knew how to read Latin.

That's handy for impressing the nuns.

"Suffer the little children," she read, whispering.

She needed to make an impression so she knocked the spider off her shoulder and crushed it underfoot. A nun in a black and white habit seated behind the oak reception desk looked up from her book at the sound of a barefoot slap.

"Oh, my dear Jesus. Where did you come from?!"

She pressed a button on the base of a tabletop microphone.

"Sisters, sisters come quickly," echoed in the halls. "We have a walk-in."

Margo collapsed on the floor. Before long, three sisters surrounded her, gathered her up, and whisked her to the infirmary all the while asking questions.

"Who are you?"

Margo couldn't give her real name. She had read Camelot and admired it. A name from mythology popped out. "Morgan, I'm Morgan."

"Where are you from?"

"I don't know."

"How did you get here?"

"My hippie parents left me on a road yesterday. I cut through the woods all night. They're going to California...I think I'm eleven years old. I don't have a last name."

Lies rolled off her tongue as natural facts. She painted a grim picture of her poor hippie parents, who were migrant workers living off the land like hobos. Sadness filled her attendees. The nuns reacted with many an "Oh my," and "poor dear." Worry distorted their kind faces. Concern etched lines around their eye sockets.

It was too easy, they bought everything Morgan sold.

The doctor said she was too thin and malnourished and traumatized, and needed rest. Before the sun went down Morgan had been fed and clothed and led to a small bedroom where a kindly nun tucked her in after a quick Jesus story. Something Daddy had said after reading Edward Barneys' book about propaganda came to mind in her repose.

"'One's self-delusion lends itself to manipulation by others.'"

She knew about nuns and the church and all the horrors of the past. But this place wasn't a workhouse or Magdalen Asylum. Daddy had reasons to hate religion but this place was an exception. Historical context didn't apply. Daddy had suffered many faith systems over his 2500 years and she understood his reservations. These nuns weren't the typical opportunist but rather believers full of deep kindness: Personality types easily manipulated.

"Talk about good luck."

She had read when crazy and all that knowledge spread out on her surface awareness like water bugs over a deep pond. She had no reason to hate this religion, but she will use it anyway. This place and its weak-minded fools were a grand-scale opportunity, an inroad to make the whole world suffer for what was done to her. The Klan didn't come out of a vacuum, it came out of perverting a religion and that wasn't a bad idea.

"Everybody does it."

Hunting down the Klan was too risky. Better to be patient and take down the entire nation. Pay them back for the rape and plunder committed by this and every empire. Possibilities were in plenty. She had time. Long-awaited revenge is sweeter when overripe.

Morgan had feared, in her weakened state, that once relegated to the dormitory, she would become meat on the hook for the Church's cruelty. But they treated her well. The girls were nice. They didn't use children for slaves. Even so, Morgan wouldn't let kindness distract her. She needed a weapon. She picked up the Bible and read it cover to cover that first week.

Twisted words are sharper than swords. This is going to be easy.

The sisters were preconfigured and ready to be pressed onto Morgan's mold. *The last immortal deserves a kingdom.* Other empires never won it all, and the few that tried made mistakes and lost everything. She saw how to gain power slowly and keep it and was determined to do it right this time. Forever gave her time to work out the details.

16

Getting off the Bus Autumn, 1965

He lost track of how many freaks got on and off the Bus over the last year. John didn't know. Ken didn't know. Neil didn't know anything helpful. Nobody knew. It didn't matter. No one scored The Acid Test, least of all the Pranksters. On the Acid Tour, he grew taller and filled out slightly but nothing else changed although everything moved in kaleidoscope-fashion. Up north the colors of fall had dazzled him.

Bobby got on the Bus below San Francisco and they hit it off. John introduced him to Jerry at a café where Jerry was playing bluegrass. The Pranksters didn't hold the guitarist long. Bobby got off the Bus and joined the band pretty quick. John should have gotten off, too. People came and went but John was stuck.

The Pranksters were an irresistible force. The Warlocks played at Ken's place in La Honda on the regular so John saw the band but he couldn't escape the Bus. The pranks never stopped. LSD flowed wherever the Pranksters went. John figured he'd find himself eventually. Blowing his mind didn't get him anywhere so far.

San Francisco was the place to be. When John and the Bus arrived, The Pranksters decided to stay awhile. John, tired of doing nothing, volunteered at the Free Store. By the time the Warlocks changed their name to the Grateful Dead, John was laced into the scene. He loved the place and didn't want to leave but somehow, he wound up back on the Bus when the Pranksters split town.

Nobody told John what he needed to hear. Nobody on the Bus agreed on any answer to any question. When he wanted a haircut, everybody agreed on one thing, "don't cut your hair, man." His hair grew down to the center of his back.

The leather thong he wore to keep it off his face pressed into his forehead but no revelations squeezed out. Everybody was on the same page although what that page is, was debatable.

Further made another loop north and they were heading back. Ken stopped at hotels often spending his *One Flew Over the Cuckoo's Nest* money. He tossed cash around as if dollars were flower peddles at a hippie wedding. Ken preached finding yourself to whoever listened but he never said how it is done. Everywhere they went, every little town, Ken stood on the bus's roof preaching like a guru while Cassidy barked nonsense on his bullhorn.

Cassidy and Kesey taught nothing he didn't know. John didn't find anything out about himself. Love, peace, and harmony were self-evidently the only way to live worth living and he didn't need The Merry Pranksters to tell him that. The Electric Kool-Aid Acid Test shows were groovy—especially when the Dead played—but that scene didn't get him anywhere either.

"Holy cow, I failed the Acid Test," John said slapping his forehead as the bus proceeded south toward California's Hill Country on a four-lane super slab.

Only his pet heard him finally voice what was boiling inside.

Cassidy was driving in two lanes on Interstate 80 and talking shit over the bullhorn as usual. Cars gassed it around the slow-moving bus while Ken's radio blasted a.m. radio top 40 at them from speakers mounted on the roof. Some guy he didn't know was shooting smack in the seat ahead of him. A couple of chicks were tripping and making out on the other side of the aisle. The girl behind him played with his hair cooing.

He spoke his thoughts out loud again just to hear something sensible.

"Why am I cooking my brains? A-OK, it's fun but it's not filling empty slots. What is this all about?"

The chick sitting behind him replied.

"Man, this is all about how to live, see? That's what it's all about, yeah. We got to learn how to do the right thing. This is the right thing."

He turned. She batted her lashes. She had gotten on the Bus in Portland and he ignored her since she got on.

"Want to go back?" She said referring to the love-bunkbed.

"That's OK, man, I'm good."

She's only fifteen.

"Come on, man. Free love's right on," she said. "Sock it to me."

"No, I'm good," he said and turned back around.

What was right came naturally. Love was great but abusing it wasn't cool. Even his iguana showed The Love. One notion finally sunk in—to love is to do for others and The Pranksters didn't do anything constructive. He needed to busy his hands. Work was more and more foremost on his mind.

Further exited the freeway, took a local road, and arrived at a commune called The Farm. John was there before. The Farm was only forty miles above San Francisco.

In no time after landing, The Pranksters dosed everybody living at the commune—wanted or not. When his iguana freaked out from laced drinking water and ran off that was the last straw.

John truly got off the Bus after that. *You don't fuck with Mother Nature.* He stayed out of sight for three days until the Pranksters drove away.

He stood in the middle of the dirt access road with a short white guy named Standing Feather waving goodbye as The Bus motored away at dawn. He and Standing Feather were the only two people not tripping. The commune was up all night but he and Standing Feather weren't.

"I thought they'd never leave," Standing Feather said. "I'm glad they didn't bring the Hell's Angels this time. We'd never get the crops in. You up for farm work?"

"I hope my iguana isn't on the Bus," John said. "I'm cool with farming. First, we better dump whatever The Pranksters touched. Nobody'll be straight for weeks if we don't."

The two men searched the communal kitchen and many unneeded packages had been opened. They made a burn pile and torched bags of flour, sugar, and coffee and dumped opened bottles of wine and milk. John knew the Pranksters' tricks and washed all the dishes and used rubbing alcohol on suspected items.

At a big house party in LA, Cassidy had coated doorknobs with LSD inside this Hollywood Dude's mansion. Even the butler ended up in a dog pile of naked bodies. John cleaned whatever handles the farmhouse had. The kitchen was old-fashioned but had the room and materials for production jar canning. It reminded him of someplace he'd been but he couldn't put a finger on it. His amnesia had gotten worse on the Bus.

Once the house was clean, he and Standing Feather got wheelbarrows out of the shed and went downhill to the vegetable garden. The fruit trees needed attention but had to wait.

He started plucking green beans. Standing Feather two rows over picked peas. Midmorning a few of the others joined but they were still stoned and picked more leaves than crops before wandering off. Around noon Standing Feather called John over to the tomato patch.

"Hey, man. I think I found your lizard."

"Yeah, that's him alright."

It lay on its back under a plant on the ground belly up and stiff as a corpse. John picked it up with great care. It didn't respond. Its eyes faced in the same forward direction and shimmered. His eyes had never lined up that way before.

"I hope he's not damaged, man. Goddamn Pranksters, never trust a Prankster." John said wiping a tear off his cheek with the back of his hand.

"Man, I'd punch Ken in the snot locker if I was you," Standing Feather said. "Maybe use a baseball bat. That might knock some sense into him. You just don't do that to Mother Earth's creatures, jezz-lew-wezz."

"There's no peace in revenge. It only hurts the hater." John said. "Best just to let it go. Look, he's focusing. You're alright, come on little buddy, I'm here."

The lizard seemed to relax a little. John took him uphill to Standing Feather's teepee and put the iguana in his backpack pocket home. The lizard stopped googling so hard once in his home territory.

"Good thing Standing Feather let us stay here. He's a good egg, man."

John had spent three days avoiding the party with Standing Feather's help. He had had enough of the Bus that went everywhere and nowhere at once. He didn't have the guts to get off the Bus, though, until they dosed his iguana. Standing Feather had seen the writing on the wall as the Bus rolled in. John was on the roof and saw Standing Feather cut out so John had followed and they connected like brothers.

"I owe this dude man, right little buddy."

The teepee was out of sight nice and quiet. *Salvation on the hill*. John had left his lizard on Further—huge mistake. Standing Feather shared about the time he was at the *Morningstar Ranch* when the Pranksters dropped in. John had no recollection of it and he was there.

With his buddy secured, John jogged back to the field and finished his wheelbarrow. It took until three to fill each full. A couple of the chicks got up sober and wandered into the kitchen. The veggies were at hand but nobody moved to do anything about it.

He wasn't one to push or complain. Rather, John filled a big pot from the handpump and started it boiling. The stove was an old combination gas and wood-burning *Sears* unit with six gas burners and a firebox. The built-in griddle could cook a dozen eggs together. The place had a big double sink and a pressure cooker. Lots of mason jars filling the shelves with good rubbers and lids. More jars were in unopened cases stacked in a corner.

"This is canning paradise," John said.

He didn't know how he knew, but he knew how to can. Without him saying an encouraging word two chicks started cutting beans. Soon more came in and shucked peas. John and the chicks put cans up into the night. He figured that was why the chicks took to him right off. *People that work together stick together.* After a late dinner of fresh veggies, wild mushrooms, and smoked ham, John didn't know what could be better.

Something he had heard came to mind, "'If this isn't nice, what is?'"

Everyone hung out in the great room after feasting. He kicked back into a beanbag chair with a full belly and sore hands. Someone lit a bowl of homegrown. The pipe was passed. John was glad for the smoke. Except for being worn thin, it was the best day he could remember.

"Man, I'm beat, I don't know how I'm gonna make it up the hill," he said.

"Come sleep with me," Angel said.

Short hair and stature, nice tits. Lovely.

"I saw him first," Linda said.

Round and blonde, killer ass. Wow.

"Hey, I did most of the canning. He should stay with me tonight." Liz said.

Lips like Marilyn Monroe. I can't decide.

"Cool it, man," John said. "Fighting ain't cool. Keep the peace, man. I'll sleep in the barn."

"He's right, girls," Brenda said. "Get it together. My cabin's wall-to-wall mattress. Dave's cool with sharing."

"That's right man," Dave said. "Let's all sleep together."

Brenda sprang up. Her tits were small but they had plenty of bounce. He always wanted to try a black chick. Brenda was a real African Queen in his mind. *Black is beautiful.*

"Far out," John said.

He wasn't up for hanky-panky that night—just too tired—but sometimes chicks won't take no for an answer. It felt like he was back at the Grateful Dead's house. 710 Ashbury had a lot of good loving going on. He didn't know where the energy came from but he did what he could to spread the love.

17

Summer of Love Turning 1967

John fell into a rut working the Farm all last year where he planted, harvested, and tilled the fields, canned veggies, planted hydroponics, made wine, and jarred fruit. He delivered extra food to the Diggers in San Francisco after every harvest and stayed in the city as long as he could. Out of farming season, he stayed longer.

He earned his way and didn't freeload. He did stage labor at Chet Helm's shows for food and board. He even worked straight-ass Bill Graham's gigs when Bill had the Grateful Dead or Airplane. He did trades for his needs, but sometimes he had to take money. He wouldn't spend what little money he had on a flophouse. Last fall, after leaving San Francisco, the Haight filled his spirit. He missed the scene. The bands always stoned him for free. John never asked for roadie money. Everything had been even Stevens.

He hitched a ride into town whenever there was time. This past January's Be-in made it harder to leave. It was beautiful, peaceful, all the town's bands played. Owsley gave the Diggers tabs to handout free. Nobody fought. It was how it is supposed to be…he wanted to stay forever but the Farm needed him.

The change came late spring after another planting. He almost finished aerating the parsley when he made up his mind. The sage took off early. The veggies were in and doing fine. The grapevines were secured. He wouldn't leave them hanging. This time he wasn't coming back.

He started yanking weeds. Maggie pulled worms off green tomatoes. Although pregnant like most of the other chicks on the Farm, she kept up her chores. An unhappy undertone had developed among the dudes. Nobody knew who the fathers were but everyone thought it was John. The dudes didn't like it. *More reason to make tracks.* Brenda had gone off to San Francisco and he missed her.

A song sprung to mind.

"'Hey, hey Maggie May, don't take your love away,'" John sang as he rolled the aerator. He sang poorly, but often.

"Oh John, you're so lame, silly duck!" She batted her eyes at him.

All the chicks did that.

He didn't get why the chicks dug him. He was tall, too thin, and nothing special. He got more action than anyone and nobody minded…at first. Lately, John was the only man working. A bunch of them were up at the barn looking down at him. Even Standing Feather acted pissed.

"This duck needs to fly south." John pushed loose hair off his face. "Maggie, something's missing. I'm lost, man. I can't find myself here. I'm not on this earth plane." He said kicking a clod of dirt.

Maggie lifted her long, homemade skirt, squatted, and peed in the furrow. "I dig it," she said, "but you're a bitching farmer. The Earth loves you. Dirt's your oyster, man. Hang in there, baby."

"I don't know, man. I don't think I'm a farmer." He pulled a grasshopper off a tomato stem and fed it to his iguana.

John liked tilling, but not planting. The pottery shards, arrowheads, and musket balls he uncovered turned him on. He felt like he was always digging for something just out of reach. He had dug into his soul with LSD and came up empty. Lately, he dug into Mother Earth but he still hadn't found what he was looking for.

He stood to straighten his back. Bruce was uphill leaning on a shovel giving John the evil eye. Bruce and Maggie were an item before John arrived.

"I don't know man. I saw the love down in San Fran. Eggheads and gurus on every corner. Man, the Haight's calling. They're playing FM radio, not that square AM shit. Man, oh man even *Herman's Hermits* and the *Stones.* That energy. I need to tune in," he said.

Tune in and drop out of the crosshairs.

"When are you going?" She said with a little tremble in her voice.

"I, I …" He didn't have guilt. He pulled his weight. The Farm was a mess when he arrived. He got them organized. He knew farm stuff they didn't know and he showed them. *Everybody wants freedom but not the responsibility of having it.* He showed them that way, too. They didn't need him anymore.

"When John, answer me. Just don't stand there."

"Soon as I get my shit together."

"Oh man, you'll never get it together." She laughed but Maggie's blue eyes watered.

"Finding it might take forever, Maggie May, but it's got to be somewhere."

John lifted her chin with a dirty finger. Her face was a puzzle of emotions. First, on the edge of crying then smiling, then worried, then angry. It switched back and forth. He had seen this before.

"It's gonna be A-OK, see."

The chicks riding Further wanted him to stay, too. Everyone was cool when he hooked up then. The Farm had lit happy when he mentioned leaving for a break last year. "'Follow your bliss'" was the consensus. That wasn't happening here. He didn't understand why everybody changed—they treated him differently. It was like a cosmic switch had been thrown. The chicks were OK, maybe a little more forceful, but the dudes wanted him gone.

"I feel like I gotta move on."

"Oh, John. Will I never see you again?"

That sexy look came on her just like the others. The pit of his gut hurt. She did him royally and then passed him around. Nobody he knew, not even the bands, got that much free love. *Nothing is truly free.*

"Never is a long time, Maggie." The word 'never' felt like a spike in his chest. *She's hard to leave.* "I'm going. Keep it under your hat, A-OK?"

"You'll be back, right, John?"

"Sure, I will. As soon as I can."

John used that line with every girl: the one in Virginia, LA, that waitress in Oklahoma, and the rest. He meant it, too. But the Bus never goes back—only farther on. He still felt those connections, though. He had loved them all.

"Yeah man, like Dylan said, 'we'll meet again someday along the avenue.'"

He bathed that night in the horse troth and slept alone in a haystack. Got up early, rolled a few joints for the road, put on clean Levi's, a flannel shirt, tied a tight ponytail, and grabbed his old army backpack which he had stuffed with spare clothes.

"Time to hit the road jack and don't come back." He said to the iguana.

When the rooster called, he took off across a misty field on jelly legs. It was a relief crossing over the rise and out of sight. He didn't figure anyone saw. Half of them just got to bed, the others zonked out early last night after too much wine. He didn't say it, but last night was his going away party and he poured a lot of wine. Last year's grapes paid well—no sour grapes.

A few miles on he hit the highway and stuck out his thumb with a feeling that something big was coming. He couldn't sit there on the Farm waiting for it. *Maybe that's what's eating me.* The Haight's fame spread—every hippie passing through talked about how San Fran was The Happening Place.

"I'll find myself if I dig in and stay this time."

The first tractor that whizzed by was driven by a man in a cowboy hat who didn't stop. He slowed and flipped John the bird instead. The next truck that came on locked the brakes and pulled over with its tires skipping and chirping. He got in. The driver was a hot momma, with long blonde hair, big tits, and a pink cowboy hat.

"I never stop," she said. "Just something…I don't know. Where are you heading?"

"Frisco," he said. She reminded him of Mountain Girl. She wasn't as thick-bodied but just as strong and sexy. *Her vibe's groovy.*

"Me too, the Warf, but man, don't say Frisco. Locals hate that. Call it San Francisco on the Warf or they'll freak out on you."

"Cool, I dig it."

It was only forty miles to San Francisco and she had full tanks, but she stopped at a fuel dump anyway. John got to see the inside of her sleeper cab but there wasn't any sleeping going on. It was her idea.

"They say never trust anyone over thirty but that's bullshit," John said. "Mary, you're A-OK for thirty-two."

Mary laughed. "A-O-K, am I? Where'd you get that, Eddie Haskell? Man, that's so square."

This hit John like a hammer. He didn't know where he got it. He didn't know his age either. He didn't know anything. All he knew was he had knowledge he could not explain.

"Yeah man, I'm square alright. But the world's made of octagonal holes."

"What's that?"

"Damned if I know but it sounds funky."

When they arrived at the Warf, Mary backed her rig into one of the many loading docks. He jumped out of the Peterbilt full of excitement loving the smell of fishy salt air. Seals on the pier were barking protests at a docking trawler but to his ear, they sounded jubilant and not angry.

The Longshoremen working on the piers and warehouses didn't look anything like him, more like redneck-straight. He had never been there during work hours. The Longshoremen's Hall was across the drag and Chet Helms did a bitching show there last winter. The Dead, Airplane, and Big Brother played. Everybody blew their minds on Owsley's new concoction, orange sunshine. *What a night.*

A forklift whizzed by to close.

"Get a haircut," the driver yelled.

"You better get out of here," Mary said, "Lunchtime is kick-hippie-ass time around here. I have a load to dump and another to take on."

John took off his *Converse* sneakers and stepped farther out in front of the truck. The gray steel building ran twenty yards to the corner. The pavement was slick with fish slime and seagull shit and he didn't care, it felt good on his feet. It reminded him of cleaning out the chicken coop barefoot at the Farm.

"You got my number, you'll call, right," Mary said in a happy sing-song voice.

He looked at his hand, her number was still there. "Yeah, man. When I get up to Sac, I'll drop a dime."

He turned the warehouse's corner, crossed the street, and proceeded uphill. *Everything's uphill in this town.* But he heard things were going downhill, too.

Late spring every plant was in full bloom. The truck's radio said the coast was too cool and rainy for this time of year. He set out on an overcast day but the noon sun shone between clouds and warmed his back. John's pet made his way out of the backpack's lizard pocket and took up its' regular position on John's shoulder. Lots of flowering shrubs were bent heavy with new life. Every tiny lawn was full of exotic plants. Victorian flower boxes were in style and flush with living colors. He had half a mind to go see Grace Slick's place; he heard she had it painted like a psychedelic orgy.

Every other freak, boy or girl, had flowers in their hair. He picked a carnation and tucked it behind his ear. The usual morning odors of dirt and chicken shit he was accustomed to were replaced with a mix of flowers, car fumes, and grass, the smoking kind.

Asbury Street was busier than ever. Hippies were milling around everywhere in town. Freaks gathered on stoops wherever a guitarist played. Men in business suits walking fast to beat the lunch hour clock shot throughout crowded sidewalks. Busy but not the same—it didn't feel right. Love was still in the air but tainted with sorrows.

"Dig that funky dragon," came from behind as John negotiated the crowded sidewalk.

"It's an iguana man, not a dragon," John said with a chuckle turning to face him.

A group of black men with French hats, like La Bow on *Hogan's Heroes*, were standing on the corner by the Psychedelic Shop passing out leaflets. They all wore aviator shades and stern faces.

"Dig it man, black power, black power." The others said while handing out leaflets.

One dude handed John a flyer and pumped his fist. The vibes were rough. John took the paper.

"Black is beautiful," John said.

"Say what!?" The guy pulled down his shades.

"Black is beautiful."

"Yeah man, good jive, cool man, it's cool. Take off, whitey, I got shit going on."

The man resumed handing out flyers. The other two eyeballed John with that move-along cop look. As he walked away, he heard all three men repeating "Black is beautiful," laced into their barked messages.

He walked on until a young, bean-pole-thin guy chasing a street performer off the sidewalk caught his attention. A television camera crew was there waiting around. They and their equipment blocked the walkway. One open case had a frog and a pig puppet sticking out of it. John picked up the frog and that bean-pole freak came at him all jazzed up.

"Wow, I love it. What's his name?" He pointed at John's pet. John handed over the frog.

"I don't know, never gave him a name," John said. That bad feeling faded. "He's just part of me, I guess. What're your puppets' names?"

The guy pulled up the pig puppet and slipped it under his arm. He put out his hand to shake, "I'm Jim, this is Kermit." Jim said holding the frog up. "The pig doesn't have a name yet."

"You better give Miss Piggy a name. Pigs are smart, smarter than dogs."

"I dig that," Jim said. "Hey, I've got to go. Kermit and the pig are doing a commercial for TV. See you around."

John flinched at the word commercial but moved on. That odd feeling came back dogging his heels. The Black Panthers reminded him…of something…they gave him that same vibe. That feeling like something important was just out of reach. But here on the streets, another feeling pushed down. He imagined a cosmic press forcing love away.

"Man, I got to lay off the acid." *I'm just hungry.*

Arriving at The Digger's Free Food store and looking through the window Tiffany was there—a chunky brunette with white teeth and a nice rack. He made it with her after delivering food last fall. *Runaway trust-fund baby.* She had a house and money to share, and she shared more than that. He grooved with her and her cat at her Victorian house that last visit. She lived only three lots up from The Dead House on Ashbury.

She saw him at the storefront and waved. The bad vibe stayed outside when John entered the Meme Troupe's hangout.

"Hey everybody, it's the lizard man," Tiff announced.

Some Diggers came out from the back. John didn't know the dude upfront sorting a pile of clothes. They gathered around him admiring his pet and passing a joint. Nobody minded that he wasn't there to bring food but to have some.

John filled up on grits and eggs, and fresh-baked bread. It was like Mom used to make. He couldn't see Mom's face, but still, that smell of fresh bread remained. The notion of the loss of his family rushed in knocking him for a loop. He had a remedy for sadness. A worthy distraction always pulled him out of the pit. Busy hands were his best medicine.

"Hey, I left the Farm. You cats need a hand?"

"Does a hippie shit in the park?" Paul said, one of the street actors and the Free Store's cook. John joined him in the kitchen.

"Man, I for one am glad you're here," Paul said. "We do need help. People are pouring in for food. What a bitch keeping up. The streets are mobbed."

"Short on volunteers?" John asked.

"That's right. I don't understand it. Last summer we had to turn help away. Now, good luck. Nobody's pitching in and hungry people are everywhere. Not just hippies and freaks, but conmen, creeps, Panthers, crooks, junkies, homeless, runaways, you name it and they're here and need food—but nobody's doing shit to help them but us. The City's bullshit. They should do something. People are dying, man."

"The cops are busting freaks left and right," Jimmy the guy sorting clothing said, "They're sweeping the streets, scooping up potheads like horse crap after a circus parade. Fuck the City."

"The city wants clear streets. Too many vagabonds. Kids mostly—they should all go home." Paul said. He was older and wiser and more a beatnik than a hippie.

"That's not cool," Tiffany said, "What if they don't have any place to go? We should love unconditionally."

"A lot that will do," Paul said. He acted older than his twenty-five years and looked it, too, with his thick beatnik goatee. "What are we, Jesus on the beach? Pass the fish, Peter."

"Exactly that," she said. "The goal is changing the culture, man. You can't move a mountain from the top down, it happens from the people up."

Paul poked John in the ribs, "Anthropology graduate, minor in comparative religions."

"We should put a Mary-in-the-half-shell up in the front window," John said deadpan referring to the local Catholic Church's landmark statue of St. Mary standing inside half a clamshell.

"At least I'm not a psychology grad, like Paul." She said it with good humor.

Paul and John went to work making and toasting meatballs for the regular spaghetti handout the Diggers hosted in Panhandle Park. Paul talked about his studies with Timothy Leary at Berkeley as they worked. Paul knew Leary before Leary became a big deal. John thought he heard it all regarding Dr. Tim through the Pranksters but he was wrong.

"That guy's a pervert. He drove his wife to off herself—bad scene, man," Paul said. "I didn't drop out as Leary says. I hung tight and got my degree. Leary wigged out. OK, I dropped out of society after graduation. Acting's my passion but I got a solid fallback."

"Leary was establishment before," Tiff said. "He lost interest in rich people's problems. That's not his groove anymore."

She came from money, she should know.

"Follow your bliss, man," John said.

After work, he and Tiff walked back to her place. The sidewalks were mobbed with high school kids with freaks peppered in between. John's heart hurt. He wished he could help each one in need. *Everybody seems so lost.* He was on the street at that age, too. Every time John slowed down, Tiff, yacked his arm to keep them moving to avoid pickpockets. He didn't have anything in his pockets to pick.

"Let them pickpocket my backpack. They can have the iguana crap for free." John stopped. "Look at that."

"We can't stand idle anywhere, the cops will think we're vagrants and hassle us," she said. "Come on."

He walked on but there was a congregation up ahead around a Jesus freak blocking the sidewalk. He heard the preaching from a distance and stopped to listen. Tiff kept going. A lot of street preachers were around, and few made any sense to him, but this guy sounded real.

She doubled back after a minute and grabbed his arm. "Man, that guy's bad news. Can't you feel it?"

"All I feel is his crazy. Man, I can relate. What's his name? He's got some bitchin' chicks hanging with him."

"They're rich kids," she said with a tone of disdain. "Charlie Mason. He's a big fake like all the other mind-fucks in town. Come on."

"No shit." The vibe came on. "He's crazy all right and not in a good way."

It was good she invited him as he didn't have a bed lined up. With so many people in town, the Diggers had set up a crash-pad system, and her place was one of them. A party was going hard around her stoop. Ashbury Street smelled like piss. The house next door rocked hard enough to vibrate plaster of its walls. Tiff's fancy Victorian front door was wide open. Ten people were sprawled on her parlor floor. Freaks snoozed in chairs and on the sofa.

Her pad was the lower half of a Victorian that had been converted into two apartments and wasn't very big stuffed with hippies.

He stopped at the door seeing no clear walkway. Across the room, her bedroom door was padlocked. *She has enough sense to keep people out of her room—idealism has its limits.* Tiff had figured it out. But the place was a wreck. Her nice antique furniture was full of burn holes. Her white loveseat had turned dirt brown. John smelled puke and almost bolted.

"Plenty of cockroaches for you," he said to his lizard as Tiffany glided across the parlor stepping over bodies.

She unlocked her room and waved him over. He took a breath and proceeded to tiptoe through the sleeping bags. The junky shooting smack in a high-back chair didn't bother to look up when John bumped him. John put a hand on her doorknob. A guy grabbed his arm from behind. John spun around.

"Hey, where do you think you're going?"

"Billy! Hey man, what're you doing here? Where's Betty?"

Billy didn't recognize him. Rage covered his face. John never saw Billy mad and he saw the dude a lot last year. Billy was all about the love.

"Billy, it's me, man. It's John Doe. Snap out of it."

"Oh, OK, wow, I freaked out, sorry. I'm just trying to keep the bums off her."

"You're with Tiffany? What about Betty?"

"Betty split," Billy said. "She got knocked up. Gone back to her folks. It wasn't me. I can't make babies. She swore she didn't do anyone but me after you but I'm not buying it. That's fucked up, man. Hate to see that shit happen to Tiff. She's my meal ticket."

"A-OK man, but I'm staying with her," John said. "I don't want to piss you off, but I need a bed tonight."

Billy's expression changed to his old self. "Go on, man, it's these dirtbags I'm worried about. You're cool."

Things were not the way they were supposed to be. Some kind of switch had flipped. *Nobody's acting right.* Billy in a fight, or fighting over a chick? That didn't make any sense. The man was a flower child inside out. John hesitated.

"You're cool, man, for real?" John asked.

"Anyone messes with Tiff, they got to answer to me," Billy said. His face lit with angry fire. The flame winked out just as fast as it started. "Yeah man, it's cool. I trust you but not these lugs."

John was perplexed. How could this scrawny peacenik Billy turn violent so quick, *but not directed at me?* It was too weird. He figured that he couldn't hang at Tiff's place very long. He needed to find other digs.

All summer, people poured into the Haight. Radio called it The Summer of Love. But everything got progressively less lovely. Free concerts and the Happenings were a gas. But, on the other hand, crooks flocked into town, too. The freaks at Janis Joplin's place ripped off everything she had and trashed the house. Janis was forced to split. The Dead and Richie Havens had enough bullshit, too, and moved out of the Haight. The Airplane and everyone with a record deal split for concerts. His old hangouts weren't happening, but the music didn't stop—it escalated and evolved. A new kind of energy swept music forward.

Many of the good freaks John knew had become radicals and rip-offs. A love-eating fog had rolled into San Francisco. Nobody noticed but him. A handful stayed cool, but like Billy, most people sold out. Billy hit Tiff up for money and left a few days after John's stay ended. Billy split to sell T-shirts—twelve bucks a pop. Clean shirts cost him a buck fifty each. *What a rip off.*

The Summer of Love had a lot of good happening and John pitched in. His network of friends worked to save the love. Bands played free so he worked with the bands for free. Love drew him and hope kept him. Music was where the love was at. *Love and music are butter on corn.*

And yet, even as John watched, The Love progressively mattered less while the music mattered more. The scale had tipped.

18

Autumn of Love 1967

John slept under the free stage in Golden Gate Park again. It was too early to get up but he was awake. He had made a nest of leftover blankets from past shows and woke dry despite last night's rain. A real mattress would have been better. Bed bugs never bothered him.

That night with Tiff last April made one thing clear. *Sharing ain't cool no more.* John thought about going back to her place after Billy split but her house was out of control. Tiff's pad had acquired a pecking order and John was the rooster chicks flocked to. That henhouse had too many chicken-hawks clawing for her. He didn't need the hassle.

Under the stage was peaceful and that was what John needed.

Winding up there wasn't unusual. He bounced on the streets all summer sleeping in abandoned houses or the Free Store. The Avalon Ballroom provided food and a backroom bed when they needed him. *Chet's a good egg.* John got to see the bands for free. He did roadie work until they split for greener pastures. With not many options left the summer stage became his home.

When the bus showed up midsummer, he leeched off Ken for a few days like before, but John felt dirty. Ken had rented a house and had room, but Ken was acting like an asshole. The last Acid Test didn't go well, either. The Pranksters had gone too far. Ken predicted the bust saying, "The pigs will stick to it to the Pranksters," and he was right.

The fuzz busted Ken and Mountain Girl smoking pot on a rooftop. Waiting for court, Ken faked his death and took off for Mexico which was a secret only John knew. He helped Ken load the van. Acid wasn't illegal when Ken got nabbed but it didn't stay that way.

Owsley's people had passed out acid last night even though it was illegal. John passed it up. He didn't need money to get high, eat, or make love. Everything was still free, but he felt caged.

"Life's good," he said to Kermit. "But something's missing, man. I should be happier. I'm doing A-OK, but something doesn't jive."

It wasn't the war, or the politics, or the radicals, or the fuzz busting people, or everything together messing with his head. Something he couldn't name pressured him whenever he was straight.

"Can't trust the streets," Kermit bobbed his head as if to agree. "Every day's a surreal circus."

Rolling out from under the stage, a Dead song buzzed in his head. He sang it to Kermit. He often sang or talked to the lizard as if the little creature understood. *Kermit digs music.*

"'One way or another, one way or another, one way or another this darkness got to give.'"

"This darkness is getting darker, man," a nearby freak pissing in the bushes said.

"Dig it. Free shows are more like free-for-alls anymore," John said as the dude buttoned his fly. "You here for the cleanup?" Fewer volunteers came for cleanup lately but John always pitched in. "There's no dishonor in honest work, right."

"This park looks like a trash dump," the hippie said. "I ain't touching that filth."

"People just aren't helping each other anymore," John said hoping the guy would volunteer. "We need more hands around here."

"Too many kids. Too many outsiders in the Haight screwing everything up," the dude said. "I can't walk down the street without tripping over some dumb-ass kid. Thank God the police are mopping them up."

For every teenager, the fuzz took off the street, ten more filled in. There were good intentions behind the roundups, John figured. Sending runaways home to get help was right on and the cops took down crooks in the process, too.

"Shit's crazy anymore." The dude said.

"That's real, man," John said. "Got any dope?"

Weed was scarce but the dude produced a joint, lit up, hit it, and passed it to John saying, "Bands are touring strictly for money anymore. They're not into the revolution. It's all about the money. They all went establishment."

John took a few hits, passed it back. "Hey man, the Dead's keeping the love. They don't all sell out. No fucking way," John's tone showed his irritation. "The Dead had to split—bad vibes drove them out—not chasing money."

"That's bullshit," the freak said. "Man, get with it, it's over. Failed experiment."

"Not the Grateful Dead. Fuck you," John said.

"Fuck me? Watch this," the dude took his joint and walked away.

John was left standing in the mud admitting to himself the scene did indeed fall apart. Speed freaks and junkies stole everything in sight. Last week somebody robbed the Free Store...again.

What the fuck, everything's free.

"Getting high matters more than music for half the cats playing out," John said, "Janis killed at Monterey so you'd think she'd stop drowning her pain."

Killed…she killed…where did that come from?

John stood there until the freak vacated. Cold all summer, now unusually hot…Mother Nature seemed to piss on the hippies. Last night's Happening broke up when the rain came down. Rain season came every fall, but this year the rain had washed Flower Power down the drain. It was safe and dry under the stage, but for how long?

"It's time I get myself out of the rain. Where should we go?" Kermit didn't have an answer.

A chick had invited him to shack-up last night but she sliced her foot on a broken bottle and cut out. He didn't get her address and it was just as well. *It's her home, not mine.* The only place he could call home was under this stage.

John went into the bushes and pissed a bucket. He put Kermit on a shrub to get his breakfast bug. That chick cutting her foot was a bummer so he proceeded with picking up broken glass first. While prying bits of a green *Rolling Rock* bottle out of the muck somebody tapped his shoulder.

"You the lizard man? They tell me you hard worker, ja."

John straightened up. The guy looked OK. He had long hair and a neat mustache, but the slight German accent, and three-piece suit, made John uneasy. *Wow, he's the establishment.*

"I see is true, no," the straight said.

"That Zen master over on Carnie Street says there's no such thing as bad work, just bad workers. I like work, OK? Truck on, man. I'm busy." John turned back to the shards hoping that Square would take his drift and split.

"I don't know him. Sounds like bullshit, ja," the suit said, "is all a con."

Establishment, he ought to know.

John finished the shards and extracted a trampled umbrella out of the mire. The suited man didn't leave. *Gurus are bullshit. Everyone is up to their eyeballs in malarkey.* The Square was right. But the Gurus' message was also right. *Work is good.* Busy hands were groovy.

"You sign for cleanup, did you?" The suit said as John extracted garbage. "Starts at nine. You early."

"No one asked. I saw the need." John spoke facing the mud. "People got to help each other."

John continued piling up garbage. The German followed him. The dude wasn't budging. John figured Mr. Business needed a real answer before he would get lost.

"I like work, OK, man. Keeps my head straight. You dig?"

"I like what I hear. I am stage company," the man stuck out his hand.

John wiped the mud off his hand on his dungarees and took it.

"Phil Barkley, we own stage and rigging, ja. We do the setup, rent it to Helms or Graham, the city, whoever. I need stagehands and riggers. Give it a whirl?"

"You mean a job?"

John never had a check-paying job. He listened to workers talking and knew about it. John learned everything he knew since waking up four years ago by listening. His next question was the universal standard question to ask in this situation as near as he could tell. He didn't care about money but he didn't know what else to say.

"How much does it pay?"

"Ten bucks an hour, no overtime, road expenses except food. On the road most times. Graham's setting up new tours. Helms pays late, but we cover if Graham's slow. Ten's good money, steady work."

It rolled off Phil's tongue like a TV pitchman selling miracles.

"Ten bucks an hour!"

It was an outrageously large sum. A clean flophouse bed was only seven bucks a night. John was too shocked to get his shit together in time to object—it was too much money.

"OK, twelve, Ja. I give two meals; you buy your dope, not me. Agreed?"

John figured he better say something before the guy shot himself in the foot again.

"Far out...er...when do I start?"

Mr. Barkley waved at the stage. "Right now, stage manager's coming." He yelled, "New hire, Paul, right here."

John spun around. Paul from the Diggers—the only Meme Troup actor with talent in John's mind—was coming down the stage's side stair.

Mr. Barkley took off for a hippie stuffing a trash can. The boss didn't seem to mind his high-end snakeskin chukkas getting slathered with baby-poop mud. John felt bad for the snake.

Snakes are groovy, why they gotta do that shit?

"I gotta find my lizard first, "John called after him.

John's backpack was a WWII surplus mobile radio operator's pack with the gear removed. He got it at the Free Store leaving the old one. This satchel was better for Kermit. Kermit's cigar box home fit better. Kermit didn't get squished so easily. John pulled the iguana off a bush and put it inside the knapsack.

"Having a pet is a big responsibility, young man," played in his head but he didn't know who said it. Yet another disjointed memory.

"Too much acid, man," John told Kermit.

Paul had been tip-toeing toward John. Paul's penny loafers were bad in the mud so John, barefoot, headed him off. The mud between John's toes felt as nice as chicken poop.

"Hey, John," Paul said. "Thank God Phil hired you. We need dependable help. The goddamned union won't come out and we don't need them anyway, fuck-em."

"That dude's A-OK." John pointed at Phil. "What're you doing with...Phil, what about the Diggers? What about Tiff? She's your old lady again, right?"

"Tiffany's gone off with some asshole street preacher goes by Jim Jones. Looks like a conman to me. I'm surprised she didn't hitch on with Charlie Manson. Man, Manson's a sicko, but still a chick magnet. Jones is a pervert if you ask me. My psychology degree turned out good for something, right?"

"She's a super freak. But I don't get it," John said. "Why'd she up and leave like that?"

"She found religion. Donated the house."

"How's an anthropology graduate find religion? Isn't that counter-intuitive?" John said, incredulous. He knew some anthropology but not how he knew it. "Tiff always said she knows too much about religion to have one. How'd that go down?"

"Beats me, my man. My degree's shit paper against the fairer sex. I can smell a bum a mile off, but figuring women—forget it. Tiff's preacher man...I know a conman when I see one. People will buy anything. Screw psychology, screw acting, screw living like a dirtbag. I'm blowing this town. Let's make some money."

"Far out," John said. "I'm down with that."

Over the next weeks, the crew didn't travel far. They served shows in Oakland, did three weeks at the Red Dog Saloon in Nevada, and did three shows down south. Nothing was new except he was backstage instead of under it. The tour felt like a whirlwind to John. The bands weren't all locals and he got to see bands he didn't know and others he knew from the radio like the *Love-in Spoonful* and *Donavan*. He saw a lot of warmup bands that weren't Haight headliners. Locally, he set up *The Charlatans*, the *Grateful Dead*, *Big Brother and the Holding Company*, and the latest version of the *Jefferson Airplane* with *Grace Slick*.

He felt like he had come home again.

"Same people, different day, except I get paid." He said to Kermit. "I'd lug speakers for free but getting paid is a grove, too."

And chicks were always around. John dug the job. He told an English guy from a new band backstage, one night, how he felt about rigging, saying "'This ain't working. It's money for nothing and the chicks are free.'" And the dude wrote it down. People respected him and it felt good.

Phil demanded John get a social security number because he got tired of his books not balancing. John didn't have a way to cash his checks and they stacked up. He got a driver's license soon after the bank account and bought a used 1962 Ford Falcon van. He named his little surfer truck, Homestead.

Phil's business blew up fast, and with that, crazy money flooded in. John could well afford his house on wheels and whatever else he needed. It felt good to have a home, respect, and a little bread. His crash pads days were over.

19

Altamont 1969

Back in San Francisco, Phil got the crew together after breaking down last night's show at the Warehouse. He gave them the low down.

"We're expanding," he said. "Going for big acts. The Brits are where the money is at. We have a big gig, we're doing the Stones, ja."

"I'm already stoned," one of the crew said with a laugh.

"No, no, not that. It is Rolling Stones. Big act from London. You will love these guys."

The crew reacted with cheers of far out and groovy. Everybody knew the Stones. They had just rocked the Fillmore but it wasn't one of Phil's shows—the Brits were the hottest tickets in town, and Phil wanted in.

Everyone was up for it, the Brits paid big, but John felt uneasy. Woodstock was a gas, OK, but he didn't like the way Peter Townsend manhandled Abbie Hoffman. Abbie was A-OK in his book. John saw him around and they were tight. Abbie indeed acted stupid on acid. *Shit happens.* But The Who shouldn't have roughed Abbie up. *Where's the love, man?*

"It will be huge; the word is out. People mob Stone's shows. We get a slice of the gate on top of our rate." Phil said wrapping up his pitch.

"What about security?" John asked. "The last show was a bad scene. I spent the night chasing ugly chicks and drunks off the stage. Man, I'm not down with cop work. I'm not doing that anymore."

"Man, you can't hire the fuzz, that's a total freak-out," the new driver said.

Phil stroked his stash. "Good point, Lizard Man. We take a bigger gate-cut if we do security. Hells Angels? Kesey got them cheap, ja?"

"Ken tripped them out at La Honda…I was there, they were OK, to be honest," John said. "I don't know, times have changed."

John didn't feel good about it. The grapevine's undertone about the Angels was ugly.

"Ja, this is good. Stones will pay. I manage it, let them pay. We make money."

"Remember when Chocolate George and Hairy Henry got busted, must have been five thousand hippies protesting at the cop shop," Paul said. "The Angels owe us a favor."

"We should hire off-duty cops, like before," George Barrow, Phil's business manager, said.

"Fuck that. Let's stick it to the Man!" Bob the electrician said.

Phil rubbing his stash meant his wheels were turning. John figured he was counting beans. *Cops ain't cheap. The Angels work for beer. He'll work a deal with the concessionaire, for sure. Phil's slick like that. Buy the beer and pocket the rest.*

Some were for it, some against it. It wasn't John's call. Kermit didn't like it. Sitting on the top of John's backpack Kermit bobbed his head like ringing a bell. Something strange was in the air, John felt it, Kermit, too, but nobody else did. Song lyrics from the radio crossed John's lips.

"'Something's happening here, what it is, nobody's clear.'"

"What's that," Paul asked.

"Nothing man, nothing a Zeppelin can't fix."

John pulled a fat joint out of his top pocket. He wore a new blue checked cowboy shirt with pearl snaps on the pocket flaps. A lot of hippies wore cowboy clothes. *Anything's better than that mod stuff.* Besides, he lost fewer joints with snap pockets.

He took a few hits and blew the smoke at Kermit. His buddy chilled out. Dope always made his and Kermit's unease pass. Feeling better, he sent his fat joint around—the last of his Columbian Gold. He didn't mind—sharing was the way it's supposed to be. Strange that most of the crew didn't share their stash but always partook of his.

This ain't 1965 no more.

Things kept changing and he couldn't put a finger on why.

20

Father Morgan's Secret

He named her Sister Mary Innocent. She was a proud initiate. She stood on the home's green lawn waiting with her mind and heart full of him. She was deemed worthiest of all and on this day, she was to receive his blessing. *I will keep his secret.* She was given his truth. He harbored many more secrets. *He knows everything.* He chose her because she will keep his faith.

Mary was sixteen when The Prophet arrived. He was a girl then. Father Morgan's transfiguration was only one of his blessed abilities. He embodied many. Least of all, he cannot age and will remain eighteen until Jesus returns. Prophets of the Lord receive special gifts as Father demonstrated.

Father Morgan was more than his body. *He is the last prophet who recites lost books.* Books God showed him in visions. Books the Church won't ever allow a nun to read yet he shared them. He told the truth openly. His initiates grew while the Vatican continued to shrink in power. To the Church, Father's way to salvation was heretical.

Father needs followers to pave his road to the Vatican.

God works in mysterious ways. Father Morgan Margo will soon remove the veil, expose the corruption of Rome. Once the Whore of Rome is revealed, he will seize the office. And Mary had a part in his glory. She was an important cog in his wheel of great change. She had reason to celebrate. She was chosen by him to make ready his plan.

'Great things are afoot.' Father had said and she believed.

Standing on the parade line to wish him a speedy trip, she felt sad and weak and nearly dropped her rifle. From orphan to a nun, to doctor of biology, Father

Morgan guided her every step. *My life is his. I owe him everything.* She stood near the end of the parade line and waited with anticipation.

"'The first shall be last.'" She said as he began his inspections on the far end.

He finally came to her. He received and laid down her rifle. Taking Mary's hands in his, he searched her eyes reading her soul. She remembered his love-making and shivered.

"'Mary, Mary, Mary how good it is you are with me.'"

"Yes, Father."

"You must expand your studies. Learn robotics and nanotechnology."

"But Father we are a poor order."

"Not anymore. Use the convent's resources. We have hidden wealth. Sister Margaret will sign. Hear what I tell you."

"Yes, Father."

"I need you educated at any cost. It is your wealth of spirit and intelligence that holds God's value for me and us in this holy cause. We must feed it. My powers combined with your skills will make the Church great again. We will repair what Vatican II corrupted."

He guided her hands to parade rest, patted her shoulder, and moved away from the line. Her gun remained in the grass.

Mary didn't hear what he said to the others. Her heart was too full of his mission to eavesdrop. He had filled each one with God's clear purpose, that she was sure of. *Was it his deeds or words which inspired?* Father planned to change the world over the next hundred years. He cannot die but she herself will be remembered as one of his.

He moved out before the dozen to speak.

"Remember your vows, you all know your jobs. Keep secret everything you do for us. That is all."

"We are revolution," they responded together.

There wasn't a dry eye among them. As he walked to the helicopter, she let tears fall wetting white robes. *I too will be called to Rome someday and that will be a great reward.* Time away from him trenched sadness so deep it could split her bones. Her only recourse was to progress quickly and be ready when he calls.

Saint Ann's Children's Home school bell rang. *I won't be teaching any longer.* She returned to her room. He left an appointment card for City University's admission office on her pillow. He wrote on the card's back, 'biomechanical.' *He thinks of everything.* She changed into street clothes and secured her firearms.

The school's vintage Hudson Hornet automobile had been detailed and polished for this occasion. The driver was waiting in the lot at attention when she opened the home's front door. She hesitated before crossing the threshold. Stepping into his grand generational endeavor awed her.

She reached the Hudson. The driver pushed the spiderwebs out of her away. He had left the rear door open while waiting. *Spiders work fast.* Mary shooed Father's pets off of her seat and entered.

21

Resuming the Job, April 1970

Arriving back at Earth, the team made use of Far Side Moon Base's equipment. The operation was ready to begin within three days. Gabe and Mike boarded a borrowed explorer craft. The old triangle ship had questionable stealth capabilities. It wasn't built for angels either. There was no room to spread wings. Gabe requested a bigger cabined ship but he didn't get it. *Why? The cheapo bean counters, as usual.*

"There's a nice new shuttle parked in hangar two," Mike said blowing the dust off his seat.

"Moon Admin claims it isn't operational," Gabe said smacking the engine start button that was stuck. "That's a lie. It runs. The problem is nobody's qualified to operate it. Central conveniently forgot to send a union bus driver."

Hardware nobody can use and Moon's local fleet is outdated trash, typical.

"Admin said make do," Mike said. "Engineering told me, and I quote, 'You may find she's a little temperamental.'"

"No shit," Gabe said retiring the motor that wouldn't start. Mike was busy with his systems' problems.

"Moon's equipment is crap. What, they don't have funds for a bus pilot?" Mike said. "Different budget, I guess."

"That's a crock of space mite truds," Gabe said. He planted his feet and pushed on the engine start safety switch with both hands. It flipped over and the first motor finally started but the starter wouldn't stop staring.

Rumor had it Moon's personnel were getting pulled off the job which made sense to Gabe. When America landed a primitive spacecraft on the moon Control cut the budget—standard procedure. *Apollo something?* Gabe got the starter to stop.

"Hey Mike, wasn't Apollo a Planet Molder back in the Hellenistic period," Gabe asked but Mike was busy and didn't answer. "Everybody's dropping hot satellites and I got to keep mine in orbit. What's one bus driver cost anyway?"

"Control won't spend support money on a salvage job," Mike said like a management wonk. "That's the procedure."

Both motors running, Gabe squeezed into the other pilot's seat. The dash was dusty and half the indicator lights were out. He punched the board and one light came on.

"Ship's motors are taking forever," Mike remarked.

"I don't get it. How can the Designer of All not see how bad Control manages?" Gabe didn't care if Moon's AI heard him. "Central Control sucks Astro dust."

I hope they fire me for a bad attitude. One of the few working dash lights winked out. He pounded on the console ignoring the warning sticker which read, "Do not harm the equipment." He hit it again. The light came back on.

"I swear this must be some kind of a cosmic joke."

"What's that?" Mike asked still focused on checkout.

"For-get-ta-bout-it."

Gabe didn't know why he felt so pissy. This situation wasn't anything unusual. *Maybe I hate management more than I thought.* He hated going back to Earth to be sure.

"We wouldn't have failed the first time if Central Control had provided decent equipment," Gabe muttered.

Gabe was so mad his vibrating wings unsteadied his hands. "I gotta relax. You take the stick."

"Where to, Boss?" Mike said.

Every time Mike called him 'boss' a tinge of heartburn clawed up Gabe's throat. Mike's devil-may-care tone and his impish, mocking grin didn't make Gabe feel any better about being the boss. He and Mike were promoted to yet higher positions while in flight which increased Gabe's responsibility and paranoia.

Management was getting to him. *I just ain't myself anymore.* Why did Mike stay the same? Control moved Mike up, too. Gabe's higher rank was given only because of seniority, but Mike's better suited for this.

Why did She have to hand me the hot asteroid?

Gabe's hot potato was, in reality, lukewarm. They had all the time in the world. Salvage contracts are open-ended but Gabe still felt like time was short. He used to trust his feelings and they used to prove right until that thing with Jesus happened—but, that was Control's fault. But lately, he wasn't so sure. *I could have done better.*

His intuition had since gotten infested with management training. They were required to take management courses in flight. Gabe didn't believe his mandatory in-flight education was helpful. He couldn't decide what was right anymore.

Upper management confused the feathers off him.

"Mike to Gabe, respond please."

"Funny. Take us to the last place where seeders were recorded. If we find them or trace evidence to track them with, we'll pick them up fast and get the flock out of here."

"What's your hurry?" Mike said.

"I don't know. I just want it over with. I hate train wrecks."

The navigation AI zeroed in on a hot spot. Mike landed on an old farmstead in Pennsylvania not far from Philadelphia. They were safe enough. Not much development around there, and it was just after sunrise. Gabe didn't need to worry about their cloaking device crapping out. They landed and un-shoehorned themselves out of the triangle-craft and stood side-by-side on the ramp for an overview.

"Mike, run the detectors."

Gabe watched as Mike worked his hand-held. Seeders had been there alright, at least two, maybe more. They were here and now long gone. History meter said they had lived there for fourteen years.

"Where'd they go? Immortals don't like to relocate." Mike said.

"We need a closer look," Gabe said walking down the ramp.

"When we flew by 1964 local time, before jumping, I picked them up on the scanner," Mike said following. "They were here. I've got ghost signals. They left right after us. Had we landed, like I said…you know…" Mike spread his wings.

"Screw it. It doesn't matter. I don't care. We'll find them. Let's look for trace elements. Must be clues to their whereabouts here," Gabe said.

Gabe pressed the door's remote control. The hatch didn't move. He hit the button hard.

"Damn it! Fucking batteries, I hate batteries."

"Testy, aren't we?" Mike said. "Try unlocking it first."

Gabe tossed the door controller inside and proceeded. The ground was covered with dense tufts of grass and tall weeds. The lawn hadn't been mowed in a decade. Saplings and brush encroached. If this was a live operation, Gabe would have a botanist come down. A growth-rate examination would show when this place was last occupied. No need. This job wasn't about recording seeder progress. Flora testing costs money. His salvage budget didn't allow it. *I hate thinking like a manager.*

"Run your handheld bio scan. We need more data," Gabe said. "Let's figure this out."

"Interesting puzzle." Mike agreed.

Nobody lived there and that was all the team needed to know. They both proceeded with Field Ops protocols anyway. Management training didn't kill Gabe's field agent habits. Like Earth itself, this property was decaying. The barn had caved in years before. The springhouse had a small tree growing through its roof.

"Spread out, look around. I'll take the woods," Gabe said.

Mike had the better handheld device and he soon called Gabe.

"Hey, oh man, take a look at this."

Gabe walked over. "Big hole in the ground, so what?"

The hole was half-filled with water and rubble. The stone masonry basement walls had collapsed. The cellar also contained burnt black and rotting wood. Crispy wooden structural beams stuck up like mammoth ribs melting out of the permafrost. The hole didn't stink half as bad.

"It was a log house," Mike said, "Strong readings. Immortal residue lingers for centuries. This is where they lived."

"No shit," Gabe said. But he had a strange feeling. Gabe took the device, adjusted it, and took new readings.

"Lots of dead cat and bird trace, familiars I'd guess. There are bones piled up under there." Gabe pointed. Mike tore the grass back. Gabe waved the device over the spot. "It was a porch. Bones under planks. They had kids."

"Scroll back," Mike said. "I think we found our seeders—their remains anyway."

Gabe checked. "Crispy bodies in the basement, charred bad. They'll take a thousand years to reconstitute."

"It might not be possible. They're pretty far gone," Mike said and he wasn't smiling. Mike thinks everything is funny.

"Fine, we take them and go home. It's all we need," Gabe said.

"Wait a minute, Skipper." Mike had taken to calling everyone above his rank, Skippy or Skipper. "If, and, it's a big if, if they come back what good are they to Her without familiars?"

"Yeah but…"

"Familiars have all the important stuff—see any hanging around? No, there aren't any. She can't know how Her seeder evolved without the Book. Important stuff…What's the Planet Modeling Department going to without history?"

"It doesn't matter." Gabe's wings dropped so low they touched the ground. "Stop thinking like Field Ops. This is a salvage operation, remember? That's the job—"

"Man, don't be a dick," Mike's wings bristled. He pushed his barreled chest out. "What is wrong with you? They said no rules so why are you enforcing them? We got an opportunity here."

"Forget it. Call transport. Get these bodies picked up."

Gabe walked away toward the woods. Mike's idea of opportunity was always about rattling Control's cage. It used to be funny. It still would be funny if Gabe wasn't stuck in middle management's crossfire. He had two choices, either go full-on management mind or act like a human being and get fired with dishonor. Eyes down, an oddity became evident at the edge of the woods. There was an odd but faded outline of a human figure drawn under the weeds. *That's not natural.*

"Mike, take a gander at this."

Mike came over and used his scanner. "It's an outline. Police outline where bodies are found. They used lime to mark position. Lime killed the plants." He bent lower scanning for bio-sign. "It was a child. That was their kid."

Mike adjusted his device. "Blood trace…it was an immortal, alright. They had a kid. That's what I saw just before the jump. I didn't believe the signal—they had a kid, holy shit."

"Or two," Gabe said, remembering the blips he saw before jumping into hyperspace.

He rechecked reports while on the moon and compared them to new Eye readings. It looked questionable before, but now they had solid evidence. But then again, it was old.

"The Eye didn't show any when I checked last night," Gabe said. "They must have been wiped out of existence."

"Or dormant, still in stasis." Mike's voice went up an octave. "Maybe the kids are still in sleep mode, or maybe they don't have familiars?"

"I don't like where this is going," Gabe said. "Them immortals in the hole are burned too badly. Headless, don't come back at all. That's a lot of blood trace. Looks like the kid lost his head to me. Recovery's a dead-end anyway. The Eye's got nothing. Why are you laughing?"

Gabe didn't see anything funny. The important thing was to find a seeder. Salvage will be a tough, long, boring process without one. The only way to get this done fast was to recover an immortal and that wasn't happening. The hard way was the only way open. They will have to spend decades gathering. And every time a Mini-Wave hits, DNA screws out of shape. The good stuff becomes harder to find. *Busy work ain't funny and Mike's laughing like an idiot.*

"There's only one way to gather massive amounts of DNA fast," Gabe said. "And, I'm not gonna hire those Gray alien parasites. Good collectors, but no thanks. They make my skin crawl."

He and Mike had just run a fleet of them off Spiral Six. Grays weren't trustworthy but they had the art of kidnapping down cold. Gabe was sure Mike would never consider using Grays. Mike's shit-eating grin indicated he had another idea in mind. Mike's vibrating wings flashed in the rising sun. *He must have cooked up a zinger.*

"Go ahead, shoot," Gabe said.

"Look, Skippy, there might be more seeders. We should look. Control wants good samples not trash, right? The next big Wave isn't due for ten years. The Peace Bomb fired, Mini-Wave hit in '67, but the social matrix held. A lot was still good after 1969 and that one hit hard. Lots of good material survived. I'd say 30 percent. We don't know if the burned ones will come back or not. The kids, if we can find them, are resistant to Wave action, see, and—"

"What's the payoff, Mike?"

Mike was on a justification roll. He will get to the point eventually. Mike would talk forever if allowed. Gabe opened his ears for a way in but Mike got to his point faster than usual.

"This'll be a big-ass win for Her," Mike's teeth shining in the morning sun could have blinded a Trod. "No time limits, right? Screw the Grays. We do this in-house, old school. It's an open contract, right. The longer we stay out, the more we get paid. And if Control doesn't like it, tough shit, they released it this way—not our fault."

"But, but I—"

"What, you don't like overtime pay? Besides, it's the right thing. They'll get what they want. We'll pull a rabbit out of this hat. It'll be big points with Her Centerness and we get to stick it to Control once more, for old times' sake, right?"

"'I hate when labor is right,'" Gabe said, quoting an old middle management mantra.

This ain't gonna work.

Mike laughed so hard feathers shook off and he didn't bother picking them up. The leave-no-trace rule wasn't in force. But Gabe wasn't feeling it. He had a hard time breaking tradition.

I should take the bodies, hope for the best, and just go home.

Gabe's idea was to get it done fast and Control might give them a better assignment next time but Mike was way off Control's rail. As stomach acid came up, Gabe gulped it back down.

Mike's right about one thing; if we go back without good samples—

"It'll take a hundred years before the lab even knows if the remains are any good." Mike said. "We should stay."

"The Big Wave isn't even on scope yet." Gabe mused.

"I'm telling you, Gabe, there's got to be a living seeder around here someplace. I can't prove it, the data was fuzzy, but the scope read four."

Small Waves weren't usually critical. Gabe wished he could detect and read the outcomes of smaller Waves in advance. Control wouldn't argue the logic of waiting it out for better data. *If a new seeder gets born and pops up, we'll be heroes.*

"What if the immortal doesn't go online?" Gabe said. "Sometimes they don't. Who's going to tell him or her what they are? Finding an offline seeder, or one that never went online, is damn near impossible."

Mike pressed his door opening device and the landing craft's hatch opened on the first try.

"We could be stuck here forever."

"You say that like it's a bad thing," Mike flexed and cracked his wing joints.

"Maybe it is and maybe it isn't."

Only time could tell and they had it in spades. But why did Gabe feel that pinch between his wings? Something wasn't right. His inner need to get it done fast slipped away and got replaced with a sense of standing on a cliff's edge. It was exhilarating but also dangerous for a guy with clipped management wings.

Management training didn't cover intuition. 'Go with it' pressed into Gabe's mind. His union-bred feelings felt right. He had that same flutter new agents get on their first job. No worries or cares just do your job and collect the money. Project control was then management's problem and not his.

Gabe didn't feel like management material since he got back to Earth. For the first time in a long time, he thought things might swing his way. He carried that hope halfway up the ship's ramp.

"Hold up, Gabe, look at that."

Something destructive was hauling ass and plowing down overgrowth where the entry road had been. Hidden by tall vegetation, only a car can knock down small trees and cattails that fast. The wave headed right for them.

"Shit! They'll see the ship!" Mike activated cloaking but the ship didn't cooperate.

A new white Cadillac broke into the clearing, turned hard, and skidded sideways to a stop. Two Earthmen in pajamas and bathrobes got out leaving the doors open and motor running. The Earthlings marched straight for the ship, which finally went into holo becoming invisible to Earthing's eyes. The Earthmen marched on anyway.

"Gabe, do you think—"

"Shut up," Gabe hissed, "they'll hear us."

A short, dark-skinned Earthman with a hippie hairdo wearing thick glasses walked right up to them. Gabe held his breath.

"It's about time, what took you so long? Code EB Field Ops."

That was the right contact code, but Gabe was flummoxed and couldn't think of the correct return phrase and rather spit out, "You see me, what gives?"

"Wrong response," the other man said, he was taller, white, and fatter. "Whatever. Where the hell have you been? You landed on the moon days ago."

"The bastards almost left us," the short man said. "Of course, we see you. We're local Field Ops, where do you think your anthropology reports came from?"

"They're not very smart. They must be in management," the taller one said.

Gabe bristled his feathers coming down the ramp. The Earth-side team had to know who he and Mike were. Communications with Moon Base were two-way. Mike and he were famous in Field Ops. *Or are we infamous?*

"Nobody told us—"

"You're right. They aren't very bright," Shorty said.

"Watch your mouth," Gabe said.

They didn't back off. Mike laughed until Gabe shot him the evil eye. Gabe had to assert his position and repeated the question forcefully.

"How is it you see us?"

"Don't know shit about biology, do you?" The shorter one said. "We carry immortal's genes, but don't get excited, we're artificials. They upgraded us when you were pulled off. We don't have enough seeder stock in us. We took over after you two clowns left with Jesus."

"But I didn't pick you up on ship's sensors," Mike said waving the handheld at them. It beeped the employee code.

"Shit, they're for real." Mike waved it at Gabe. "Scanners ignore local crew. It doesn't track people already logged."

"Captain Burk's ship is ten thousand years old." The tall one said holding up a fancy handheld. "Your technology is crap compared to this. And no, you can't use our equipment. We signed for it and nobody's touching it until it's turned in. Union rules. Besides, Wave interferes with your antique ship's long-range sensors. You should know that."

"But, but, we need it..." Gabe stammered.

"You aren't getting our gear."

"He's right," Mike said with a toothy grin. "We can't touch their stuff. It's off-limits until Central inspects it for reissue." Mike spread his hands wide and put on a fake sad face.

"You're enjoying this aren't you," Gabe said.

"You should have used that on Jesus," the tall guy said pointing at Gabe's handheld. "You might not have put a Probe in him. He's a high percentage immortal genes-carry mortal, ya know. IGM's the reason he went nuts."

"I see why they got promoted," Shorty said.

"Holy shit," Gabe's wings dropped to the ground.

It was the biggest screw-up of his career and he didn't even know it.

He tasted vomit and swallowed. That a primitive local told him his mistake only made it worse. His wingtips could crawl under a rock. Rule one: Never put a Probe into a highly-developed human. Gabe had not scanned Jesus before inserting the AI-7.

"Any-who, you're late," Shorty continued. "The first Mini Waves already hit. Our contract is over. Get us out of here. We're susceptible to big hits and First Wave will be here by 1980. Sixty-nine's Wave was iffy for us. Get us out of here."

"Now I'm a taxi driver?"

Gabe's wings dropped to maximum low. *Promoted as a punishment confirmed and why.* It was another heart-stab and just when he was beginning to think he had been upgraded as a reward for good service. He had no reason to push this operation out fast. *Mike is right, it's time to milk the cash cow.*

Gabe had a license to print credits but he still felt lower than trog poop.

"Cheer up, Buck-o," the short guy said. "It's all over. Read my contract. You guys have to take us off-world. It's in the large print section."

Gabe didn't like his attitude, but then again, he had the same attitude when he was labor. He knew one way to shut them down.

"I'll set up a pod for you. That'll get you to Galactic Center in a few hundred years and you'll—"

"Put us in a pod, you crazy?" The tall guy said. "From that junk ship? Read my contract—I'm not going third-class."

"Suspended animation, you'll be fine. AI will keep you safe," Gabe said.

"Artificial intelligence, huh? Like that number seven you guys installed in Jesus, I don't think so. We'll stay on the moon until you clowns are finished or a real transport shows up."

"Yeah but—"

"Forget it, Gabe, you can't win," Mike said through that damnable grin. "I'll call Moon Base and tell them to get the Earthman shuttle out of mothballs."

"Fine," Gabe said. "Be here tomorrow at dawn, a shuttle will pick you up. Moon has an old Earth-sider in drydock. It should run."

"Damn well better," the short guy said. "I'm not getting in a triangle. They leak air."

The Earth humans marched back to their car. Gabe and Mike stuffed themselves back into their landing craft and took off. On the way up, Mike chattered away in a good mood. Gabe didn't hear a word. He was too busy silently beating himself up.

How did I miss scanning Jesus?

He had to fix his screwup and had no idea how.

Getting good samples became Gabe's only path to redemption and that road was full of pit traps. Uncertainties twisted around inside him. But he was sure of one thing: Screwing this up will kill his career.

21

John in Business 1975

21

John in Business 1975

The Philadelphia Spectrum was a good venue from John's perspective. They had good equipment. The house system's tie-in was easy but problems with people weren't so easy. The union hated John's methods.

John had finishing touches to do on the rigging for the Dead show when Phil arrived. John was high up on the scaffolding adjusting a laser when Phil called from the floor. The rest of John's crew had gone. John was the last company man in the house.

"Lizard Man, you come down, ja!"

John monkey-swung his way around and down. Phil didn't like John's methods either, but the union riggers hated John's act flat out. He didn't use a safety harness or follow any of the other rules. John's safety equipment amounted to a pair of cheap sneakers, a tool belt, cutoff shorts, and knee pads. He wore a shirt sometimes, too. They made Phil wear a hard hat. John never wore one.

John jumped the last eight feet and landed on stage with a thump.

"What's happening man? K pasta."

Phil got older and more worry-riddled every year as the company grew. Even his balding head had stress cracks. The dude used to have nice thick hair. *Phil needs to chill.* The carefree way of doing business in the 60s had morphed into serious shit. Phil lately handled giant shows that cost a million bucks to set up.

"I must boot you," Phil said. "The fucking union walked. The split shop deal is off. These guys are killing me."

Phil pointed at a guy on the floor in a pinstriped suit fifty aisles out from the stage who was yelling at Jerry and Phil Lesh.

"Union Rep's a ball-buster." Phil said. "Jerry's telling him off. The band says they won't play unless you do the sound check adjustments, fucking Jerry."

Phil popped an antacid into his mouth.

"Wow, not cool, man. Union doesn't know how to do this shit right…The band digs my work. I got it down."

"Nobody does it like you," Phil agreed. "But that's not our problem, ja?"

John called it. The permanent stage crew didn't have the right experience and the union riggers didn't have a clue. The Dead were perfectionists with music, sound, and light. Bands hired Phil because they wanted the Lizard Man running setup. Kermit was practically the industry's mascot. Everyone inside knew it, too.

"What do you want me to do?" John asked coming closer. "The guys need me, man. I gotta go back up. We aren't ready."

"They won't budge. Nobody's giving an inch. Cancel the show over bullshit?"

"They let you in man, what if you go up and finish?" John said, thinking back to the old days.

Phil used to climb just to flip off the unions. But he was overweight and out of shape. Having Phil go up was a bad idea. Phil's face turned pale on the suggestion.

"Forget that, man. Why'd they let you rig before?" John said.

"I'm the owner. They can't stop me. I'm…wait a minute. That is an idea. I don't have heirs. Why the hell not?"

Phil closed his eyes and thought for a minute like he always did to clear his head. John figured Phil should never have given up pot. If the boss got back into smoking dope, he wouldn't be so freaked out all the time. *Screw meditation, man, grass rules.*

Phil pulled a legal pad out of his case, wrote something on it, and stamped it with his notary seal.

"John, sign this, right here," Phil pointed to the spot, John signed, then Phil signed it. "I'll send you a copy, after my lawyer files. Welcome, partner."

"What're you talking about, man?"

"I just made you an owner, 49 percent interest. They can't do shit now."

Phil headed for the argument, waving his notepad.

John called, "Hey man, is that legal?"

"Of course, it is. I was a lawyer before this business. I keep my license up."

"Far out, man."

Phil waded into the argument. John couldn't hear what they said, but Jerry fell out laughing. Phil Lesh was all teeth. The union rep turned and ran out like he had the shits. The boss gave John a thumbs up and left waving his notepad, singing opera in German.

"Far out, man."

Kermit had finally made his way to the lower scaffolding and was hanging upside down by the tail when John retook the stage.

"Sorry, Kermit, I'm going back up."

John grabbed the lowest bar and climbed. His lizard followed in comparative slow-motion.

A union electrician yelled, "Where you going, scab!"

"I'm checking my equipment. A man has a right to look after his shit, right?"

The higher John climbed, the higher he felt. He never wanted to be an owner. Phil was a good egg and always treating people right, but the dude was in over his head with the unions.

Yeah, but the show must go on.

John didn't care about the money. He figured he might help Phil unload a shit-box full of stress. It was the only way a man like Phil, one that never asked for help, would accept it. For Phil, it wasn't just business but he would never say that. John only wanted to help his friend.

John thought about the organization. He organized the Farm. Everybody will do their jobs as always. *Paul runs the stage. I'll look after the rigging.* Nothing will change, but he made one decision. *Everybody gets a union card.* In so doing the union monkey gets pulled off Phil's back.

Take it out of my pay.

Union cards weren't cheap. Phil would never flip that bill. John had no plans for his money. He didn't do hard drugs. Mary Jane was cheap or free. His van's mattress was stuffed with cash making it hard to sleep.

John's idea worked out, but his hope of saving Phil Barkly didn't. Phil had a massive heart attack six months later and died, leaving John holding the responsibility bag and the majority of company shares.

23

One Million and Twenty-Seven A.D.

A special meeting of the Library Council was called. The scribe apprentice's lover had a vision unlike any before it. It was an early one but so strange there was no accounting for it. The Council had to decide whether to exclude it from Mass or stash it with the other inexplicable notebooks. Should this be written into the Book of Answers at all was the question which beguiled the Librarian.

"As you all know, Shelly had a bad trip," the Librarian said, addressing the Council seated around her living room. "Some of you have heard the Book entry. There is nothing new under the sun, but this is. We must continue the Book. But I hesitate to add this chapter."

"Let's hear it again," the Priestess said. "It'll suck balls if we leave it in a note-book unused. What if He shows up and wants that page? It'll get lost or rot. We need fresh material."

"Yes, yes, let her speak it," one oldster said and the other five agreed.

"Go ahead, Shelly," the Librarian said. "Speak it."

Shelly stood wringing her hands together.

"It's very confusing," she said. "It isn't like that time some kind of drug got into the recorder and like messed it up all weird and stuff, ya know?"

Shelly stopped. Her jaw quivered and her crown feathers stood tall. She wasn't a speaker, just a simple, young girl with not a tenth of the experience the other women had. She would have run out the door if the Librarian let her.

"I don't know, I'm not sure…"

"Please continue, Shelly." The Librarian projected kindness within her voice.

Shelly brushed away a tear.

"OK, so like there were lights, see, blinding. Was like looking at the sun, but lots of lights in colors, and it was hot, really hot. Some asshole stuffed me, not me, you know, stuffed Kermit inside a giant beachball. That's what they called it. Wait. It's all jumbled. I was up really, really high, like flying you know, and I looked down and there were like millions of human people all like dancing and swaying and so much pot smoke and it was loud, like an avalanche but it was music. I don't know how to say it right. They didn't have tails, either. I think…I think it was at the Grateful Dead, the actual Prophets. I know this sounds crazy. Anyway, the Prophets were real."

"That's fine, Shelly, you need only give us the gist of it. When you sit with a scribe after services, he'll help clarify your words and fill in details for the archives. Scribes are skilled in that."

We do need a new liturgy and this will work. The Librarian took notes again, although she had most of it from the previous interview.

"Please go on dear." One of the oldsters said.

"OK, so like I was inside this huge ball. It's not real clear but I can see outside it. The man that put us…er me…inside said something like, 'goddamn scabs, I'll show you.' Then I was in the crowd boom, boom, crazy music. The ball was flying around, getting punched and stuff, rolling all over on top of people. It was so weird. Is this making sense? The Ancestor was nowhere in sight but poor Kermit was scared shitless."

"That's fine Shelly, I think we heard enough." The Librarian said. "Go see the lector and he'll get you organized for a live reading. Be sure to check in an hour before Mass starts. You may go."

The seven remained quiet until Shelly had gone. By the look on the faces around her, no reservations were showing. The Trustee spoke up. She had an eye to see between lines.

"We must use it. There is nothing else fresh. I'd rather not do rejected verses. Using too many Red Books threatens cohesion. This one says nothing, this one is safe, it can't be understood."

The group quickly agreed. It didn't need to be understood, only recorded and recited so it can be delivered…someday. The only alternative was to glean through stacks and stacks of notebooks until a verse was found that was previously unread. The process must continue.

Why not *'take the easy road,'* the old saying crossed her mind. No one knew what roads were but that verse fit. Whatever keeps the people another season is good. But a lie cannot work. She realized after the group departed that they have a filler for an unfinished chapter that she had almost forgotten.

"A new Reading to keep us—lucky break."

But how long can our luck hold?

24

Lizard Productions 1989

John walked from the bus stop to his office every day. Public transportation in Woodbridge, N.J., wasn't bad. He could afford a car or a taxi but he liked the smell of the bus exhaust and enjoyed the walk to his office from the depo. It was a fine summer morning until he got to his building and had an LSD flashback.

A hot office chick sashayed up the block at this hour and she was due. John wanted to ask her out. Instead of girl-watching, his attention was drawn across the road. Two pale-faced dudes in blue overalls and white angel wings were standing on the sidewalk. *Actors? Street preachers? The ghosts of Laurel and Hardy?* Nobody passing by paid them any mind.

"Man, I did too much acid in the 60s." He said to the doorman. He tapped his temple with the heel of his hand. No good, they were still there. "Far out."

One of the angels stuck a knitting needle into a passerby's ass and removed it fast as a cobra. The guy acted like he was bit by a mosquito. John rubbed his eyes. *Yeah, still there.*

"Hey, Spike, you see that?" John said.

"Yeah, that's what I call a babe," Spike said. "Suzy Creamcheese." John gave Spike a playful push. Spike pretended to be hurt. He was shaped more like a wall than a doorman. "She can ride my bagel anytime."

"No, no, the two dudes," John pointed but they were gone. "Never mind, man, see ya later."

He handed Spike the usual twenty. John had a lot of money and no matter how fast he gave it away, more always showed up. He wasn't comfortable having so much bread.

In the elevator, he thought that he had imagined them same two angel-dudes before with the same white wings, long hair, and blue coveralls. They were either actors or circulating handbills for the Broadway show *Jesus Christ Superstar*. He figured, and not for the first time, he had done too much acid back in San Francisco. But then again, no one ever proved acid caused brain damage. Still, he wondered if he was losing his mind.

They look so real.

John blew past the staff and straight into his office. He needed to get his head together. He plopped into his leather office chair, slipped off his sneakers, and lit up. Kicking back, feet on the desk, he smoked furiously hot-boxing the joint. He used the ashtray often not wanting to drop an ember and burn his antique oak desk. He respected old furniture. His office set had belonged to the governor of Rhode Island, circa 1850. He had paid a lot for it. Anything old and historical turned him on.

Snuffing out the joint, one of his spells came on. He had seen a place like his before. Kermit was in an antique birdcage. He had rescued Kermit from an office with nice old furniture. Death-smell and chemicals were in the air. As soon as he put half a finger on it, the memory was gone.

"Wow, day-zah-voooo-do, man. I need a drink."

He clinked the intercom. "Marge, do me a favor. Call downstairs. Send Spike for beer. Don't give him too much bread, thanks, man."

Spike retired from the Hells Angels but his old habits didn't retire. If given enough cash to buy drinks all around, Spike wouldn't come back. John had cause for celebrations. He had signed a deal to rig and run sound at the *Garden State Arts Center*. Too bad it was a tight-ass venue. State Troopers cover all those shows but that was not a problem. What was, was John needed better-paying work for his people and not more low-end gigs. He supported his family. His thing was doing for his people like the Grateful Dead did for their crew.

Times of weed and no money were not better than times of money and no weed contrary to the *Fabulous Furry Freak Brothers* comix book. *Fleetwood Mac's* management tipped him off. It paid to know people. The business was one big family and he was all about family. It was on him to take care of his people— *that's the way it's supposed to be.* Share what you have. Too bad his competitors didn't agree.

The intercom chimed, "Hey, John, guess who just walked in."

"Jerry, Phil?"

John touched the photo of Pigpen on his desk. He still missed the Dead's dead pianist after all this time. People thought Pig drank himself to death, but that wasn't it. He drank, but his medical problems were what killed him.

"They aren't due until two," Marge said. "Nope, it's Abbie Hoffman."

"No shit! Send him in."

John expected Abbie to storm in flooding the room with piss and vinegar. That guy had more energy than three protesters combined. Protesting was how John met Abbie. Back in Chicago, John fixed his megaphone. That 1968 gig was huge. It had been twenty years since they hung out much. After the launch of Abbie's book, *Steal This Book*, he saw Abbie less and less. John had paid for his copy.

Abbie shuffled in old-man-slow. He was only fifty-something but passed for sixty-five going on a hundred. Abbie was puffy, worry-lined, and unkempt. The plastic surgery didn't make him any younger. His eyes were ringed red. Scratching his bearded, dismayed face, Abbie lowed himself into a chair like it was an endangered species. He waved a greeting at Kermit who rested on top of his cage behind John. Abbie redirected his squinting eyelids at John.

"Say, you haven't aged at all, man. You pass for thirty. Shit, thirty. I miss thirty," Abbie said. "You sure you're you? You could be the Lizard Man's kid. That dude fucked his way to the top, man, to-the-top."

Abbie stopped and checked around as if suspecting an attack. He even looked under the desk with an effort. He came up short of breath.

"They let birth control out just to stop the Lizard Man." Abbie laughed but his face turned sour. "The Feds man, things are fucked. They killed JFK, man. I can prove it. I got paper on it."

John wasn't sure how to take it. Abbie radiated both wild-eyed nuts and somber. Like Abbie's joke wasn't a joke. Abbie's crazy wasn't Charlie Manson crazy, but some other kind John hadn't seen before.

"Are you the real you, man?" Abbie asked.

"Yeah, it's me man, that's Kermit, for sure," John reached over the desk handing Abbie an unlit joint.

"Bobby Weir turned me on to good health practices. I do natural foods and yoga and shit. Look how young Bobby looks."

Abbie was right. John didn't age and not aging bothered him. *Man, I'm a real freak, I ain't right.* So far, only Abbie noticed.

"I don't know, man, you could be a plant." Abbie lit the joint.

"Remember my backpack? You busted my balls in Chicago because of its military surplus. Remember Kermit lives in it? It's right here."

John pointed at the standing coat rack in the corner. Abbie squinted and smiled like *Gomez Addams.* "Far out, man." Abbie said, "Damn, you look good. What the fuck?"

"Wish I knew. So, how's it hanging man?"

"Man, it's not hanging. I'm useless, my youth is gone. I'm worthless without it. They don't listen. The Feds are on me, man, they stomp on everything I say, whatever I do. I know too much, too much man. Life's too much."

"Oh, OK, so what brings you? Need help? Put you up, or something? I got lots of bread. Money to burn," John said.

Abbie sat there quiet with his mouth twisting, watching something in the distance that wasn't there.

This wasn't the first time an old hippie came begging. John always helped. But Abbie wasn't the usual commune refugee or a down-on-his-luck rock musician. To production companies, Abbie was the asshole who took the microphone and stopped the show with pissed-off speeches. Woodstock had ruined Hoffman's reputation. But John remained his friend. John figured the guy was crying for help back then same as now.

"Hey, are you OK, man?" John asked.

"NO, I'M NOT! You're the one guy I thought would never sell out. Look at you, man, rolling in dough." Abbie scratched his beard like it was on fire. He pushed back, relaxed a little, and leaned forward. "Sorry, man. I got to tell someone I trust. They won't let me publish, man. We're so fucked."

Getting called a sell-out struck John hard.

"I don't get you, man. I take care of my people. They get top money. A-OK, I'm doing all right too, but—"

Abbie bolted out of his chair.

"You don't see it? Everything changed. People think Reagan's a fucking hero! He's the biggest crook of the 20th century. Man, I'm not kidding. Something big happened, it's still happening. We're devolving man. The spirit of '66 was murdered. The Man is a real monster. The Complex makes the 1960s' cops look like play time. Man, shit is going down. I'm telling you the world is in big trouble. We're all gonna die. Hopeless man, it's hopeless."

"What're you saying?"

"Aliens are fucking this world. The government is controlled by aliens. What else can it be?"

Abbie fell back into his chair out of breath. He took a big hit off the joint and blew it toward Kermit. Abbie picked at his beard. John wondered if he had lice.

"Hey man, I'm sorry," Abbie said, his voice lower. "Things are changing radically, but not everybody. You're the same. I'm the same. Jerry's cool. But a lot of people sold out. Specter, Graham, Turner, sold out before it started. Corporatism took over rock music, for sure, but why? Why'd the love die, man? Why'd the love generation turn into shit? I know why."

John didn't have an answer. He had not thought of his flower-child days in years or why he left the Haight. Abbie's questions bored holes in him. *Things did turn.* And John let himself down. Nothing was more important back then than finding himself, getting to his roots, and living the pure, free life. He started out digging for his truth and wound up a big-shit stage producer.

John lived a no-freedom responsible life. He hated that idea bank in the 60s. Having responsibility for so many people trapped him—that's what happened. *This ain't aliens.* Abbie was tripping, but he was right for the wrong reason. Shit was turning bad all around.

"I don't know, Abbie, I lost myself...somewhere...you never did."

"I, I had to tell someone and say goodbye. I'm retiring man, I'm done. The bad guys won. Someone should know that the oligarchs' control everything. It's a sickness that can't be fixed...I saw it, man, I see it...Nobody cares...Time to check out. You're one of the good eggs that never cracked."

"Come on man, you still got something to give—"

"You don't get it, man, we lost. The revolution is over."

Abbie took the joint and hit it hard. The color drained out of his red face as he blew the smoke out. He took a big breath of smoky air.

"Eisenhower wasn't fucking around," Abbie said, a new light in his eyes. "The men behind the curtain—goddamn Iron Curtin is right—but it isn't between us and Russia, see, never was. It's right here, it's everywhere."

Abbie spread his arms out like Jesus on the mountain but his hands were shaking.

"Abbie, can I get you something, want a soda or anything?"

"The elites' control everything. It's all a big game. But who controls them? Look at Reagan, he got away with murder. Contra operation, illegal as hell. All that damage down in South America, Cuba, Palestine, we caused it, man. The CIA's behind it all. Reagan's just the latest puppet. This Reaganomics bullshit is all Milton Freidman's wet dream. IMF, World Bank all tools, and it's working—I'm telling you we are fucked. There's nothing anyone can do. The fix is in. I'm finished."

"Abbie, that's bullshit…not coming out of you. You always fight, always work for change…"

John's words and encouragement dropped off. They both knew Abbie was finished. *Nobody pays attention to him anymore.* Too much cash flowed against Abbie's stream of thought. John saw the shadows, too, but with less clarity until Abbie dropped in.

"Where have all the hippies gone?" John said. "We got to turn them on. Save America."

Abbie waved dismissively. "You can't save it, man. America's dead. The experiment failed. This isn't democracy. This is plutocracy—it's fucking hopeless."

Abbie hung his head. His bald spot shone in the fluorescent light. John waited.

"My life's work, all my efforts were wasted. If I were young again, oh man, I'd make them see." Abbie sobbed.

John saw some of it. Whatever it was, it wasn't aliens. The worst people were always in charge. *It's always been the same in history.* But things did feel like somebody flipped a switch. Historical changes were happening hard and fast. John couldn't wrap his head around Reagan's election. *What can I do? I'm not an activist.*

The best he could do was take care of his tribe. *Crosby, Stills, and Nash's* lyrics, 'love the one you're with' flashed in his head. Chicks were especially groovy but he loved all people. His employees were family. He made his little world right.

"I see it, Abbie. I'm with you, man."

Abbie's head came up with heavy eyelids. "That's all man, I'm going. I got shit to do…I might make one more big statement. Go out big." Abbie got up.

John pressed the intercom. "Marge, give Abbie whatever he needs."

Abbie turned and shuffled out. By the time John got his head together and realized that there was more to Abbie's talk than just his regular rant, it was too late. Abbie had gone.

He pressed the intercom, "Marge gets Pete Barnyard in here."

"Who's that?"

"My personnel lawyer."

"You have a lawyer?"

"He's in the Rolodex under friends."

"Everybody in your roller is labeled friend."

Abbie reminded John of something he had to do but put off too many times.

Marge entered his office waving Pete's roller deck card.

"Abbie's gone off the deep end, for sure," she said. "I tried to hand him money and a bag of weed but he ignored me.

"He lost his shit, man," John said. "He never turns down a free-be."

"He wouldn't take a dime," she said. "He grabbed a joint and left with it dangling from his lips, dragging ass. That's a bust-me neon light. If the cops get him, I hope they take him to a mental hospital."

The phone rang. John picked it up, Mick Fleetwood's stage manager. The *Tango in the Night* tour needed rigging. Back to business. Abbie was soon forgotten.

Word came a few weeks later. Abbie had killed himself. Serendipity, the sad news came on the day John arranged a big company meeting. John never imagined Abbie could do that, the idea of suicide was radically counter to John's concepts of life. John thought something bad might go down, like an overdose, crack-up, or bust, but never that. John could relate to Abbie. John had felt hopeless after *Kent State*, but he didn't harbor it long.

Abbie's despair had hung on too long.

Pete had started the papers before Abbie kicked the bucket. *I decided because of Abbie. It is time I find myself.* Abbie had provided the push.

Staff gathered in the conference room. A fresh case of beer was cracked open, joints were lit and passed around. Someone had coke, but John turned it down. Word got out about the big show. That was not why John called them in.

"What are we celebrating," Paul, now aged but still sharp asked.

John couldn't have found a better general manager than that old Mine Troupe actor.

"Fleetwood Mac is a lock. That's not this. What are you up to?" Paul asked.

John stood up and raised an imported beer.

"First a toast to life, and the life of my friend Abbie."

Moans and other sounds of grief were followed by clicking bottles. *How funny it is, everyone thought Abbie was an asshole, but they appreciate what he did.*

"Anyway, yes we have the contract," John said and waited until the murmurs subsided. "There's more. I need to take a walkabout, like that alligator guy in the movie." John took a swig of beer.

"I gotta go find something…I'm leaving the company."

The group of twenty reacted as expected with pleads of "don't go" mixed with "what will we do?" His ex-lovers shed tears.

"It's cool man. My lawyer, Pete Barnyard here, best legal guy ever set it up." John tipped his drink at Pete.

"He did the papers. You're all the owners now. Spike, too, the company is yours. I made Marge CEO and Paul President. They get more money, but it's all yours. You're a worker's co-op now. Dig it."

A couple of folks jumped out of their seats. Someone dropped a beer. The mailroom chick chanted a Hindu celebration prayer. Imagines of the *Morningstar Ranch* flashed in his mind. That time Ginsburg chanted with the *Morningstar Tribe* droned behind his ears. The rest started jabbering all at once. Pete stood up to calm everyone after a few minutes and he went on to go over the details. With everyone's eyes on Pete, John said he had to take a leak and slipped out. The conference room had a door into his office.

He grabbed his old backpack off the coat tree, Kermit was already inside. It felt good in his hand. He stuffed a big bag of weed into an outside pocket, dug out the two rolls of cash he had in his desk, and left by the side door. No one noticed. Downstairs, the other doorman, Bob, opened the exit for him.

Shit, I forgot about hooking up Bob.

"Taking Kermit out," Bob said. "It's cold today, be careful."

"That's no shit, man."

Bob held out his hand. John always tipped well. *Bob's a good egg.* He cared about the iguana and the environment.

John knew Bob from his Haight days and made sure the building's management hired him. John was the biggest renter in the building. Bob, Spike, and he protested together, front-line, at the police station after Chocolate George got busted. Hippies and Hell's Angels marched hand in hand. That was his favorite memory; a time when peace came first. Having money was too establishment. It felt dirty. More reason to bail.

John pulled out his two rolls of bills to peel some twenties off for Bob. One roll was small bills, the other large bills. The money weighed a million pounds. He stopped pealing twenties and tossed the roll of hundreds to Bob, turned and split before Bob could react.

For the first time in years, he was free.

25

Ten Million and Forty-Eight A.D.

The Librarian gave her the sign. *This one is near to his birth.*

The Priestess sang the chant, "Make love not war, make love…," as she proceeded to the podium. Her clear, high voice bounced off piles of cement rubble and bluestone slabs for a mile in every direction. Her song reached distant Broadway. The congregation put their heads down when she stopped.

"Amen."

"A reading from the Book of Answers," the Librarian said with jubilance. There were far more in the house than usual.

"No shit," the people responded.

The Priestess took the lectern and read from her notes, "'Man, I ain't never seen nothing like it.' That was said to him," she interjected before continuing to quote. "'Them fucking pigs just swooped in, busting heads, man bad scene.'"

The congregation stirred. The Remembered One's words, which the Priestess conveyed by changing the tone of her voice, displayed deep fear. Of course, no one knew what a pig was, but it must have been fearful. The Librarian thought the word was a metaphor.

"'What the fuck?' He said, 'Where's everyone going?'"

The Priestess fell deep into a trance. She ignored her notes and recited live from her vision as it reemerged.

"'The Pigs got Chocolate George. They busted Flower Cheeks. They knocked Spike off his Harley, man. We're protesting the Pig Shop, you coming?'"

"'Fuck-in-A right,'" The Priestess said in John Doe's voice. She snapped out of it and closed her notebook.

"A reading for the Book of Answers." The Librarian said, stepping forward.

"Fuck-in-A right," the congregation responded.

The Priestess placed her notes on a stack of books next to the podium. The people filed out. Those books were recently topped off. No more blank pages but nobody stored them yet. The pile was unruly and soon to topple.

Who has the heart to file them?

Finding blank pages became difficult, as did finding volunteers to file completed books. Book One, which the scribe had opened today, only had a few pages left. Blank pages filled faster and faster of late. To think she used to worry about blank pages. She used to worry there weren't enough visions. She spent a hundred years sorting and locating unfished books and there were many pages unfilled back then, not so anymore.

No new books will be started. The spread is covered but if He is still alive... there was no indication that He was. The youngest dated books recorded took place tens of thousands of years ago. *Is He still sleeping?* They can only record His waking times. She put that hope of Him yet living away long ago. The gap was too wide. He never lived this long in one life before.

"Truly, He must be dead," the Librarian whispered. "True death."

A breeze blew the notes off the pile. The new vision, representing one less blank page in the last Book, fluttered to the ground.

How much longer can we dig at roots?

She didn't like the answer. Book One, His life before His first rebirth, was rapidly filling.

26

Homeless in NYC 1999

Nobody paid attention. In dark and dirty places, people don't see each other. Under the grime, he looked and felt twenty-something and that was impossible. His last ten years were hard, but it didn't show. Scrub off the dirt and nobody would guess he was going on fifty.

He lived in an unused subway car service bay, formerly a subway tunnel. Steam pipes there were hot all winter. Someone named John had scratched his name into a rock wall there. John hadn't thought of his real name in a long time. The other hole-dwellers called him Larry the Lizard Man. Larry had gotten good at locating warm places. Kermit didn't ask for this cold life. New York City winters kill reptiles.

Burt, Ernie, and Darla followed him into his current hiding place the last few nights. He had unwanted neighbors. He knew them. Sometimes, out on the street, they shared food. They weren't so bad. He always shared what he had, like it was supposed to be. The reason they tracked him, they claimed, is they like his lizard.

They'd eat Kermit if he was the only meal around.

Larry ate well for a homeless person. Why was simple—despite word on the street that he had magic—magic wasn't required: He kept his eyes and ears open. He found lost money and other things that people walked by. He was always looking, looking for something just out of reach, always digging and seeking it.

"Yeah, I'm fucking crazy, right Kermit?" He whispered.

Long ago he had heard workmen talking about the deeper levels and so he searched and found them. His fellows thought him lucky. He didn't have luck.

He had sobriety. He didn't like hard drugs or whiskey. Pot made him think too much. He gave up thinking because it made his brain hurt.

The others that slept around him were A-OK at the moment. He could find a deeper tunnel and lose them, or maybe give up. *Why not just cash out like Abbie?* That went around in his head often but he hated giving up this good spot. All he wanted was to be left alone.

Dragging my sleep bundle farther into the tunnels won't be fun. But one more time was necessary. He had escaped the crowd for a while but others will soon come once word gets around.

It's time to split.

Lizard Man Larry, quiet as death, laid his effects on his bedroll. His bed consisted of dirty blankets layered thick. He used a long leather belt to keep the bundle together. He peeled it off the fattest dead junky he had ever seen. The dead man's wallet was empty. Larry didn't mind.

That dead junky gave him an idea. *It's the new year after all.* A quote from a movie he liked back in the day came to mind, "'Today is a good day to die.'" He muttered to Kermit. The Indian in that movie had kept trying to die but never got there.

"I'd have done better," he whispered.

"Lazarus, hey, mon, where you go?" Darla said from the pile of rags she lived inside. "Don't be take-in me Kermit away! Eases me, good friend."

She wore all her clothes at once year-round. She didn't have a satchel. Everybody stole from everyone else so it wasn't crazy. It was self-preservation.

Abbie would have done the same.

Normally, Larry would get nasty, that's how he survived, but he never had the heart to play hard-guy on her. Darla had been clocked in the head with a piece of rebar in Central Park during a rip-off gone bad. *She's never been right since.* She was a high-pay imported Jamaican nanny before that. She had just gotten her citizenship, too, when it happened.

If there is a god, he's pretty fucked up.

"Hey, now Lazarus where you be go-in."

"It's Larry, not Lazarus," John said. He regretted saying it so harshly. His name is, or was, John. Did it matter? She didn't know the difference. *Keep the peace, man.*

"Ya don't fool me now. Suit yourself, mon, but don't take me home lizard away. Woe to me. He talks to me."

"I never heard him do that, but A-OK. Darla, stop picking, will you."

That crease on the side of her head constantly oozed pus where her dreadlocks got permanently parted. She scratched at it all the time so it never healed. She was like a child and reminded him of the flower children in the 1960s: A simple, free soul. She wasn't old enough to have been there. She was too crazy to help herself and not crazy enough to get locked up.

John liked her and did what he could for her. She loved Kermit. *Maybe Kermit is the kind of lizard that lives on her island.*

"I got something for you. I won't need it anymore." John said on a whim, but it felt right.

He made sure Burt and Ernie were still out cold. They drank a fifth of 96-proof grain last night. It should have killed them, but when he checked, they were still breathing. John/Larry reached deep into his battered Army coat. The lining was full of holes, and in one he stashed his money. He peeled out half and put them into her hand closing her dirty fingers around a short stack of filthy dollar bills.

"Get a good meal. I'll bring Kermit back soon. We're just taking a little trip."

"AO-K, mon, say it to me, AO-K, now."

"A-OK man," he said but he didn't feel that way.

He hated lying to Darla with her so full of goodwill—that was why the *Muppet* Brothers tagged along, to take advantage of her and him. He never got those two bums' real names. Maybe it was Ernie and Bert.

"Don't let them know you have money, A-OK?" He pointed at the sleeping drunks.

"What you say I do."

"Promise me."

"Me no lie, no take me for no lie. AO-K, Laz."

John knew her well enough to think she will be fine for a while. *Kermit will take care of her.* He backed up and slung the bedroll over his back like Santa's sack of goodies. He set out to go deeper into the maze and he relaxed once he got past the steam relief valve that often popped. Steam would block the view of anyone on the other side.

He didn't have to look. Darla followed as usual and that was how he wanted it. Nobody could tell her to come or stay without her getting mad.

He reached the new spot he had scoped out and laid the bedding out upon a concrete platform four feet above unused tracks. *High and dry.* Not too much mud around. The niche was cut deep into the bedrock putting it well out of the tunnel's service lights. It had been a shed in the 19th century. *The Muppet Brothers won't see it.* They never go past the steam manifolds. *She'll have a warm place now, her place.* He set Kermit on the bed.

"You stay," John told his pet. "Wait for Darla, she needs a friend."

The iguana bobbed its head. John pulled a small flashlight out of his pocket, turned it on, and set it next to Kermit.

"She'll see the light. She won't leave you, Kermit…take care of her for me, OK."

John left and made his way into an unlit abandoned branch tunnel. Darla was never far behind. He waited on the deadline near the hatchway he wanted and opened his ears. Soon her voice echoed.

"Oh, dare you are, me lizard friend. Me and you, we keep things nice until Lazarus comes home. Now here come to me, baby…"

Satisfied, John climbed the ladder. He had been here before; it was one of his escape routes. He had many. *She can't find me if she doesn't know where to look.* He was sure she wouldn't follow. The bottom rung was too high on the wall. He got off the riser at the next level and snaked his way from point to point until emerging in a subway workmen's passage off Grand Central.

He entered the breakroom where he regularly got coffee and donuts. He was about to snatch breakfast when footsteps approached. He hid in the closet just in time, the door swung open and two hardhats blew in. They put a fresh pot on.

That's good, two guys can't drink the whole thing.

"Where're you going tonight?"

"Where else? Times Square. It's New Year's fuck-in eve 99. If the world ends, I'll be passed out under the ball waiting."

"Too many tourists."

"Who cares, it's a free-for-all. Man, booze flows like an open sewer all night."

The men chattered fifteen minutes and left. The coffee was still hot and there was milk in the mini-refrigerator. He couldn't help but think of Abbie Hoffman. Abbie would have thought John's free food routine was ideal. But Abbie offed himself in the end.

John held his cup high. 'I Luv Daddy,' was written on the mug.

"To you Abbie, this Earth ain't made for freaks like us." He drank. "You knew who you were, man. Wish I could say that."

The dirty wall clock over the coffee counter said 9:20 a.m. It was time to get a substantial meal. He didn't bother the workmen's lunch, that would bring eyes on the place. It was better to steal food nobody wanted. He made it to Santo's Pizza's backdoor just as the prep guys arrived.

"Hey, Larry, nice job cleaning the ally," Tony the dough man said. "I'll send out a little some-thin, some-thin for ya."

"Thanks, man. It's cool, I dig the work."

Tony smiled like he meant it and went inside. The night crew doesn't wash the cases so the morning guys had to toss the leftover pies. John got whole pizzas that never saw the inside of a dumpster.

"Help out people and people help you," he said to Kermit, but Kermit wasn't there. He felt a pang of hurt. "I hope iguanas go to Heaven."

He talked to it a lot like it was a tape recorder. *OK, I am a little crazy.* Missing Kermit, he almost turned back. He took one step toward the street but saw those two angels again and this time they were waving magic wands around.

"That tears it. I'm not crazy, I am fucking crazy, no shit, man."

Tony stuck his big head out a tiny, high window. "Got something good for you, don't take off. I'm heating it, alright."

Folks were decent. People shared if you let them. *That's how it's supposed to be.* The Man was who kept free people down, not the worker bees. Not all workers. New York cops were freedom-eating monsters…no justice at dirt level.

It's a good thing Darla lays low.

John smelled the pie as the flat steel door swung open. Tony Zinno's shitty younger brother came out with the pie—that was the Zinno John wanted to see. The kid delt heroin.

"Tony warmed it up, here you go."

John took the pie. "Hey man, don't split. I need a little something—smack and works, what do you say?"

"Get the fuck out of here, you got no money."

John produced a wad of bills.

"Fifty smackers, man. I need three dimes and a needle. Can you do that?" John was willing to overpay.

"Man, I got fat dimes. One's a party for two. You sharing it Lizard Man?"

A good dealer doesn't kill the customer. Dead junkies don't come back. He had never got anything from this guy before but he seemed A-OK. Dealers weren't the brightest bulbs on the Christmas tree but this one was smart enough to sell clean dope.

"You want it or not?"

"Yeah, for sure, my family's having a party. Can you do it or not? There's a guy down at—"

"I got ya. I'll be right back."

The kid ducked inside and came out with the stuff in a flash. He kept it in the utility closet near the backdoor. John looked it over pretending to care. It was more than enough to overdose. The boy gave John a dirty spoon, a syringe, and a half spent lighter for free. John decided to tie off with the dead junkie's belt he had brought along. He didn't need a bedroll anymore. He paid the kid. The kid counted the money and had to see the extra cash but he didn't say it and went back inside.

"Happy fucking new year," John said to the closed door.

He took his warm pie and grabbed a bench across the street in the little park. His angel delusion had moved on. He ate but had too much food. He surveyed until he spotted her. He got up, went over, and gave the pie to Bertha, the old lady who slept in the park. She was down the block picking trash cans looking for food when he gifted her.

She opened the box and dug in without cleaning her filthy hands.

"Thanks, Larry, you're a good egg. If I didn't have crabs, I'd fuck ya."

"Anything for the ladies."

That night, John situated himself into a deep entryway of a closed building close to Times Square. It was a quiet, private space that nobody had pissed in. It wasn't in sight of the party. John cooked his dope and filled the syringe. He had seen it done a million times although he never shot up himself. He had left the belt somewhere and didn't have anything to tie off with.

"Fuck it."

The people started counting down in one jubilant voice. He jammed the needle into his neck and plunged out the contents in one thrust. He felt himself age instantly.

He planned to shoot up then go and see the ball drop. That was the plan. He wanted to make a statement and show New York their inhumanity. He had planned to die in the street before the revelers but his liver-spotted hand had no time to release the syringe.

His death made the news anyway.

27

Ten Million and Forty-Nine A.D.

The Priestess raised her hands. The congregation below were many. The overflow waited amongst rubble piles. She opened the ceremony.

"A remembering for the Book of Answers."

The congregation responded, "No shit, Sherlock."

The Librarian had opened a massive volume and set it on the scribe's table in preparation. She didn't need notes. The scribe signaled ready to write and dipped his quill into an inkwell. The Priestess yielded the altar. It had been a long time since the last live reading. The congregation fidgeted as she took the podium.

They need this. John Doe will want to know.

The Librarian had had a vision herself—a rare event. She hadn't had one in fifty years. It had not been realized that Book Two was incomplete. A prelude was required. She saw it as a reprieve.

"So came the day they laid him into a stone box. It was his second death. Rock stars, record producers, and a certain T-shirt mogul named Billy gathered outside the crypt's door. 'Thanks for helping me pay for his funeral. I'm glad we're all here to send him off,' Billy told the gathering."

"Finely dressed, they stood in the snow. His body is within the crypt. They put him in 'a thousand-dollar suit.' Some asshole spouted off but nobody listened. 'Dis de way he wanted it,' the crazy Jamaican girl said."

The Librarian lowered her arms to address the congregation directly. "Darla said part of this, some of this is her thinking, as I tell it. She spoke it to half-frozen Kermit. My vision is mixed. I see parts. I'll leave the interpretation up to you."

The Librarian resumed and slipped into a trance.

"'They were too drunk or stoned to care about the cold. It's the way he would have wanted it. Darla said 'he aged in death,' but none responded. His hair was gray. His face was rutted. The mourners see what they expect. The famous people left.'"

The Priestess stood for a clarifying remark. "They did not know, once the way was clear, he would revive and leave." She retook her seat.

The Librarian worked herself deeper into trance to better express what she saw. In this way, she recalled her experiences as they happened, and as one that was there encapsulating the events. Old habits informed her speech but her mind was not all her own. Ideas poured in spurts. Her voice changed with who spoke through her. Visions were usually processed before presented at Mass due to this confusion, but the Librarian choose to share it raw. The people needed it.

"The crazy girl and Kermit go back to the grave often, that's how Darla is noticed… The cops pick her up next spring…Pete Barnyard, the city defense counselor, is assigned to her…She reads the charges to Kermit. Trespassing on John's grave. Pete recognized Kermit…he looked into her. Pete becomes her guardian. She wins a lawsuit… Pete cares for her and Kermit., Whenever Kermit escapes, he goes to John's grave."

The Librarian dropped her arms and head.

The Priestess came forward. "From what we've seen in other books, his friends died long before he revived. Grave robbers won't break into the mausoleum for many years and long after Kermit's vigil."

The Librarian raised her head opening eyes. Her mouth was dry. The scribe put down his quill. *It's a good one, answers a question.* He had been alive forty-eight years. *I'll drag up more details later.*

"A moment of silence," the Priestess proclaimed.

Visions take time to sink in. The Librarian wondered if that tiny new moon or the sky's new blue color affected genetic dreaming. Of course, none understood what any vision meant in its entirety. They did not need to understand it to record it.

Jerry forbids, it makes sense to me.

The Priestess raised her hands and said, "What's up Doc?"

And the congregation said, "That's all folks."

After the crowd filed out an apprentice scribe asked the library hostess, "What's a defense lawyer? I don't get it. What's all that supposed to mean?"

The hostess looked stricken and did not reply. Many words can't be understood. The word 'grave' was used in a new context. The Librarian overheard and answered the scribe's question as only one can. Visions were seldom understood—never are they questioned.

"Ours is not to ask, ours is only to write what we see and feel. Get your shit together, don't be an asshole." The Librarian said.

Her remark was too harsh.

"Sorry, I'm getting pissy. New Sky is making people crazy, even me."

The scribe waddled away with his tail between his legs, which made it very hard to walk. Apology accepted, even so, the Librarian was proud of her hostess.

That one has respect for scripture, successor potential, she knows the rules.

The young lady could be a librarian herself one day if only the people live long enough to pass the Burden on. It was a weak hope but the Librarian and her people lived in hope nonetheless.

28

Going to Calico

The police found him in New York City walking around barefoot in a fine but out-of-date business suit. He was incoherent. The homeless people living in the graveyard pointed him out to the police. They claimed he rose from the dead. They had a crazy story about breaking into a crypt but no one admitted they had done it. He heard them talking to the cops and everyone else around for a mile and all at once. It seemed like his talent faded a little more every minute.

"That guy's a spook or something, he ain't right," a bum told one patrol officer while pointing in his direction.

"Too many vampire movies," one cop said to the other.

"Stop drinking Mad Dog. That stuff melts brains," the cop said to the homeless man. "Looks like another John Doe."

After the cops were done with the witnesses, they marched John Doe over to a big tree. He liked that tree. It had pretty colored leaves. *Maybe it's fall?* It was peaceful there.

"What's your name?" The cop said.

"I like peace."

The cops ran a few tests and made John Doe touch his finger to his nose. They wanted to see if he was drunk, he wasn't. Or stoned. He wished. When they asked what the date was, he said 1999. They said it was 2030. He imagined that was when the cop's internal lightbulb flashed *"not my problem."* He didn't trust cops and he didn't know why. He didn't know why he thought that: They were nice to him.

"Tell you what, how's about a nice free ride to Bellevue?" The chunky cop said.

"Cool, far out. I'm starving, man, I dig the Belview dinner."

"Far out pretty much covers it," the skinny cop said.

At the hospital, they named him John Doe because no one knew who he was and frankly, he didn't know either. But he liked the name. It seemed right and he decided to keep it, even if they did figure out who he was. *Amnesia's a bitch.*

He looked like a rich white guy so they spent a lot of time and effort and public money figuring him out at the looney bin. It took two years to prove he wasn't nuts. He grew out his hair. He liked it long. They shaved his head at intake, lice prevention. They did it to everybody.

The nut farmers never did discover his identity but the institution learned much. They told him he was intelligent, educated, well-read, and there was no record of him anywhere. Nothing showed up in fingerprint files. The government had no choice but to assign him a personality and send him on his way.

Sitting in the Social Services office, waiting for job placement test results gave John time to read fresh magazines. The Daily Times and Newsweek Review were there with others too, all full of ads and crazy prices. *You could buy a hardcover for what magazines cost. And they think I'm nuts? Who pays for crummy ads?* The essays read like propaganda because they were. The waiting room TV had nothing but crap on it. *But wow, what a great picture.*

Digging deep in therapy, all he got were fleeting glimpses of a farm, a concert, a few faces, none of it clicked in. The copy of City Gossip Today on the end table had his face on the cover. The headline said, "Who is This Man!"

"Good question," John said tossing the old issue aside. He rubbed his head glad his hair had grown fast. That bald guy on the cover was him but it wasn't him.

John wanted to work. He needed something to do. Anything to keep his mind off himself and that hollow feeling. Everyone agreed he was somebody but nobody knew who. The clothes they found him in were vintage designer and popular lately. He had to have been somebody important.

The secretary said, "You're up, Mr. Doe."

"Cool, thanks, man."

"I'm a woman." She batted her eyelashes at him "Right down the hall, first door."

His regular counselor, Elmer Stone, was there. *Nice guy.* He was big around and tall but gentle and soft-spoken and always in an unshakably good mood even though America was a mess. The career counselor girl was there, too, a short, skinny Jewish chick, 50 years old, and a bitch. He should have made it with her when she came on to him.

She does have nice tits.

"So, what's the word, man?" John said taking a chair.

"I'll take it, Ova," Elmer said.

After banter, Elmer gave him the low-down reading from the files on his computer screen.

"Near as we can tell, due to your extensive knowledge in history, anthropology, and related fields, we think you were in academics or research. You obtained a higher education. You may have come from another country, a researcher perhaps, but we don't have access to foreign records, things being as they are. INS came up empty. Without paperwork proving your education, placing you in a job is tough."

"Don't worry, Johnny boy. I have something for you." Ova said with a sneer.

I should have fucked her. She was begging for it.

"That's fine, thanks, Ova. What we have for you is a job offer at Calico." The man said forcing a tight smile.

"It's an archeology site in California. My nephew volunteers there and says the director is retiring. I hope you don't mind me telling them about you. It's a non-profit, not much money in it, but it's steady and they provide accommodations. It's a little bit of a tourist thing but they do science as well. It's a controversial thing. What's it called, dig site? It's an ongoing dig site. Doctor Leaky was there a hundred years ago. They need a supervisor to oversee operations and work with students and volunteers."

"I know about Calico," John said. "I read about it, interesting shit, man. I dig digging."

"You'll go then?" Elmer said.

"I don't know, man." He said thinking of his lover.

Ova twisted a smile of spite. She had been aiming to get rid of him for a while. Elmer's big goofy face flashed his dental bleached white choppers. *No telltale there.* John knew how it worked. Take the job or wind up on the street. *The cops stick homeless in for-profit jails.* Mistrust of cops came to him naturally. The regular Wall Street protesters were busted a lot but that wasn't the reason why he feared the police. Busting peace protesters wasn't the only example of modernity that bothered him.

He didn't trust the establishment and he didn't know why. There was something about the concept he just couldn't dig out or shake off. But the establishment was nice to him so far, but for how long? *They offered me a job.* The Northern California desert was as far away from the establishment as he could get.

"I'll take it, man, but how do I get there?"

Ova sneered at him.

"A-OK, I'll hitch-hike, it's cool."

"Hitchhike? Hitchhike...Oh, I see, no, no, that won't be necessary. The Calico Trust will fly you." Elmer said.

"Groovy, man."

"Groovy?"

"I told you he came from another planet," Ova said.

The arrangements were made. He had two weeks before his flight. Because he was not deemed a threat to himself or others, Bellevue's low-security ward allowed him to go out unsupervised. John wandered around Manhattan and beyond for a few days and recognized a lot of places. He felt like he had seen it all before but everything felt older and worn thinner. The subway felt good and he didn't mind the smell.

He had spent most of his time at the New York City Public Library reading periodicals on day trips before they granted him freedom. He had gotten to know the place and the people there well. What he had read was good stuff but most interpretations seemed off to him. He felt a deep connection to the place for no reason he saw.

A cute librarian, Mary Cook, had shown him how to use a computer and a whole new world unfolded before him. She was good in bed, too. With so much information, so many things to learn, he forgot about searching for himself which was why he got started in the first place. The past had captured his heart.

Feels like I'm made for this Calico gig.

The leaving-on-a-jet-plane morning finally came, he got up and dressed before Mary woke. He sat on the side of her bed stroking her hair. She woke, smiling.

"It's time, Mary, the car's coming soon. I should go down and wait. I don't want to miss my flight."

He felt the airline ticket in his jacket's top pocket. He wore the suit they found him in, someone had had it cleaned while he was in the ward. One headline said it was a two-thousand-dollar suit.

"I'm going to miss you, you're one fine babe."

Mary looked hurt and happy at the same time. She wore a strangely familiar expression that he could not place. He had seen that look before…but he had no idea where or why.

"I know, I know, you must go, commitments and all. You'll come back and see me, won't you?" Mary said fighting tears.

"You know it, Momma. As soon as I get up some cash and figure a few things out."

As she rolled out of bed, he picked up that old Army backpack he had found in a thrift shop. It seemed familiar and he felt an odd attraction to it. The few things he owned were already inside it. He kissed her on the forehead and left.

He had every intention of going back and seeing her again. But in the back of his mind, he thought it might not happen. This all seemed like it had happened before.

"Daz-za-voodoo, man."

He took that odd feeling as a sign that his memory was coming back.

29

Leaving Calico 2057

"He's nuts," Jenny Carter said.

She and Rodriguez were above the fan up on the catwalk overlooking dig pit 17. In the distance, the new professor was striding toward a flatland called Lake Manx on foot. That ancient lake had drained off catastrophically about 18,000 BP. Geologists had determined that Manx had filled and drained, off and on, for 500,000 years as the ice ages progressed and retreated. That dry lake was not the place to go looking for older human artifacts.

"He's wasting grant money."

"Could be some Paleo-Indian stuff out there, bone fish hooks, spear tips, but it's been surveyed lots," Rod said. Everyone called him Rod. "If he's anything like his old man, he'll find something."

Jenny wasn't so sure. She student-volunteered a long time there and was there when John Doe, Sr., took off. He offered her the dig manager's job, but she didn't want it, not with all the craziness going on in the world.

Never work for a fuck buddy.

There was more to it than that. He had to know it, too. Why would anyone want an isolated job in No Man's Land while the whole world goes to hell? She didn't believe in archeology or anything else anymore.

What's the point? The Earth is dying.

Jenny needed to be with her family when everything collapses.

The old man had sent for his son before leaving. Three days later, the spitting image of Professor Doe, *uncanny really*, showed up. The old man didn't look that old and his son didn't look young enough. One stark difference was the hair.

Professor Doe had long gray hair and a wild beard. John Jr. wore his mouse-brown hair military-style. She quickly got the hots for Jr., too, but decided not to sleep with him.

Way too weird even for me.

"The old man had the knack," Rod said leaning on the railing. "Nobody found as many eoliths, and that biface; evidence indisputable. Somebody had to have lived here 130 thousand years ago."

"Whatever, who gives a…never mind."

She couldn't keep the bitterness out of her voice so she bit her tongue. Old John did more than find hard-to-find evidence. As her lover, he pushed her into new realms and not just sex, he helped her publish. He gave her all the credit, too.

Thanks a lot. The Church hates me.

She, the old man, and a couple of shovel bums found things that should have changed world history but nobody had listened.

Her paper in *Nature* got trashed. Universities wouldn't hire her because of that. Institutions wouldn't touch their evidence with a ten-foot pole. The older the layer the more advanced were the tools and the more her career possibilities sank. Nothing like this was ever before seen in the Americas—*unless they were found and covered up.* Bucking the establishment killed her career.

Thanks, John.

The *Smithsonian* actively snuffed her paper. The *Journal of Archeology* wouldn't even respond to her letters. *Now, this man comes along and wants to dig older deposits and fuck me on the side too?* Jr's come-on was the last straw. *Horn dog, just like his old man.*

"I give up," Jenny said thinking of all the issues she had to deal with along with the hole in her heart that Professor John Sr. put there. "I've had enough of this shit."

"There are other opportunities," Rod said, "Chinese took over Middle East archeology. It's exploding over there. Tons of jobs." Rod had been talking about going for a long time.

"Yeah right, all they care about is gold. Archeology is dead. I'm taking that cashier job at All-Store. It's safer than walking in minefields for Sumerian coins."

"Looks like the car is charged," Rod said.

The rooftop indicator light was lit green.

"You sure we'll make it to Barstow in that?"

"Ye of little faith, fresh batteries, wind and break generators, juice to spare," Rod said.

Rod didn't hide his pride. He was good with power management. She missed gas cars and wished China would sell more oil. Only the rich, the Church, and governments ran fossil fuel anymore. Professor John had the foresight to buy a tanker truck full of fuel before the war. *The Powers won't waste oil going to war anymore.* There was no beating China anyway. *Who fights their landlord?* Even so, the government won't sell fuel to the public. *Old John was smart to stock up.*

"I still think you should have added more solar," she said picking up her bag. "Let's go, I'm ready."

Although it was late morning in May, they had no worries. Desert temperatures wouldn't return for another month. Climate change did strange things. Ice-melts 10,000 miles away ran new rivers into the region and created cloud cover and cooled the desert. The aquifers were filling, too. John Jr. wanted to dig the lakebed before it refilled. *Crazy, just crazy*. Water was coming and nothing would stop it.

She and Rod got into their homemade electric car and started out. Looking back, the mountains of dirt and rubble piled from years of digging gleamed in the sun. The heaps were so high they hid the catwalks. All that work had been for nothing. A few interesting dino bones didn't justify it. She was happy to be moving on.

John waved at them just before they drove into and out of the new running creek. Jenny didn't wave back.

***

"There they go, groovy."

John said talking to his new little lizard friend, *Dipsosaurus dorsalis*, a local desert iguana he caught yesterday, or maybe it was the other way around.

"We'll get a fresh start. Whoever comes here next won't know the old me."

He had dumped his old pet after splitting to change his identity. He would never convince anybody he wasn't him if he had that same pet. Zebra-tailed lizards were too fast and wild. Z-man wasn't trainable but John had trained him anyway.

"'One way or another, this darkness got to give…'" He sang the old Grateful Dead tune to his new pet as he hiked. He had forbidden 1960s music deep inside his head with no idea how it got there.

Nobody caught on to his other odd attributes, either, like he didn't age. Dying his hair worked for a time but he couldn't figure out how to age his skin. The beard was his only option. Bleaching his hair white had made his scalp itch. The beard sucked anyway, and bleaching it made it worse. Shaving it all was his rebirth solution. He hated cutting his hair but didn't miss the whiskers.

He had a picture in his mind of a 1960s football player named Johnny Unitas. Doe copied Unitas' hairdo. He didn't know why he knew a football dude from eighty years ago. He shouldn't have known. When he focused, the memory slipped away.

"I can't believe my ruse worked. Belief, maybe I should take up the habit."

He thought himself the only nonbeliever left in America. He hated the idea of having a religion. The New Inquisition law put a warning spike in his heart. *How did the Catholics pull it off?* The Church alone was reason enough to stay in Calico.

America had turned into shit. Institutions came crashing down. Only the Catholics stayed together after the war. When China bombed the Temple Mount nothing happened as the Pope predicted. Jesus didn't return. Evangelicals joined The Church in droves. The Pope had used that cashed alien spaceship discovered on Phobos to flip the public's directional switch but it gave John ideas, too.

"That's some shit, right, little guy?" He scratched the lizard under its chin. "Mars, man. Somebody was on Mars half a million years ago. We must go deeper and older. You dig it, man?"

He laughed at his joke and his pet store iguana bobbed its head. *Weird it ain't that hot.* The lizard didn't need to cool off. The lizard's white feet inspired a name.

"How's about Bobby? Bobby Socks the lizard, not bad, right?"

He set the iguana down and it took off like a shot. Desert iguanas move fast. It got up on hind legs and hauled ass. She went fifty yards and stopped, came back, and repeated.

"'You trying to tell me something, Girl? Maybe I'll call you Lassie? Naw doesn't fit."

The sound of him speaking caused a flash of memory and another of his spells seized him. A vision came. He was sitting on someone's knee; a Middle Eastern man and they were reading a book together. He saw the book's cover, *Lassie Come Home*. In memory, he read a line out loud and repeated it.

"'You trying to tell me something, Girl?' That's what Timmy asked Lassie, far out."

The vision faded. It felt real. He wanted to believe he had read it, but he was a scientist and belief is not data. Of the many books he had read in New York and since then, a children's book wasn't one of them.

"It's a trick of the mind. Too many peyote buds, man. I'll fix that." He had a pack of All-Store joints in his top pocket and pulled one.

He lit up walking toward Bobby Socks and felt it right away: Not the weed but what was hidden underground. He discovered a trick when he first came to Calico. He couldn't explain it. It was like divining only he didn't need wishbone sticks. It had to do with quantum mechanics, but that wasn't his thing and he didn't have the background to figure it out. Something old was there and he marked the spot on his GPS watch before turning for home.

The bunkhouse was empty but food stores were full. He had plenty of diesel for the generator. The place had everything except diggers. He had room and food to host seventy-five guests. Two seasons back there was a waiting list. But since the U.S. military disbanded, nobody cared. Nobody believed in the mission of science anymore. Reality lost footing to the Church's miracles which were plastered all over the media.

John Doe didn't mind being alone. It was better. He cooked a big meal, drank too much beer, and planned to crash early.

"I'll dig that new spot tomorrow," he said to Bobby Socks. John didn't remember letting the lizard back inside. He did let it out. I should have been outside hunting; it was a night-hunter.

"Dude, why are you here?"

Bobby Socks didn't respond but it remained focused on John as if it were listening. John didn't mind the company.

30

Digging Deeper 2069

An old Joe Walsh tune came to John's lips, "'Everybody's so different, I haven't changed.'"

Rock music was still illegal on the radio but John remembered the lyrics. He knew songs he didn't remember hearing. He often sang or talked shit although only Bobby Socks heard him. Talking to a lizard seemed less crazy than talking to himself.

Half a lifetime had passed since the shovel bums stopped coming. Meanwhile, John had dug a pit two yards deep by fifty foot-wide by hand himself. He didn't waste fuel running the backhoe out to the lake. That was wise. He figured he would need the fuel for more important things later and later had come.

He had discovered a settlement of geodomes. He had to be sure of its staggering old age. Inside each hut were human-sized furniture made of plastic—the former occupants had left behind particle-beam guns. It was a high civilization camp and one beyond the technology of the present. He guessed they were anthropologists observing whoever made the eoliths 250 thousand years ago which he found scattered about and inside the dwellings. He could not escape the evidence. These advanced campers were homo sapiens.

"We rose and killed ourselves off, wow, man. That's far out."

He had sent his photos, samples, and reports to New York and Washington and waited and waited. They never called back. So, he called the director of the *Museum of Natural History* this morning. He talked to various people until landing on a big shot in Washington.

"What do you mean I faked it? I have proof just come out and—"

"Look, Mr. Doe, I don't have time for this. The Mars Mission has our attention and resources. I'm not leaving here to chase windmills. Try the Met, Johnson over there has a soft spot for oddities or a soft head, I should say. Nonetheless Calico is off our pallet. Good day, sir."

"He hung up, goddamn it, Bobby, he fucking hung up on me. Bunch of shit. If Mohamed won't go to the mountain…I do have a tanker truck of diesel. Hitch up the travel trailer Bobby Socks, we're going to New York City."

That night John loaded the best artifacts and copies of all his meticulous records, a lesson learned from Lewis Leaky, Calico's founder. Only overwhelming evidence can persuade entrenched bureaucrats. He had video, soil samples, small in situ artifacts that he had removed and did so keeping its concretion matrix intact. *Let the lab boys have at it.*

Earth had risen high and collapsed before, and it was happening again. He had undeniable proof of concept.

They'll accept it. Somebody has got to do something to save us.

31

Local Help

Gabe and Mike worked the boardwalk in Seaside Heights, New Jersey for weeks. The new boardwalk brought a concentration of people. This was the fourth one rebuilt in thirty years. The ocean lapped under the boardwalk's pilings but still, people came unsafe as it was. Gabe felt the dock flex with each wave. *Old habits never die even when swamped by ocean water.*

The stupidity of rebuilding in the same spot was an aspect of the Wave Effect. People were stupider. Beliefs and traditions overrode logic like never before on Earth and that worked for and against Gabe. Good samples were harder to find. Devolution was taking its toll.

Mike's idea of stretching the job ain't working out.

Any crowded place worked for collecting. Mike got that much right. Just a quick jab with a DNA extractor was all it took. If the dumbass noticed the jab, he blamed it on the guy behind him which sometimes resulted in fights. Mike never got tired of it. People fought over the smallest things anymore. For anthropologist Mike, direct observation of devolution in progress was the cat's ass. Gabe only saw the practical side.

It got harder to move unnoticed. They couldn't be seen in holo, normally, but they were heard and felt. Total stealth wasn't possible. Waves had screwed the holo projectors.

What bothered Gabe was the lack of good samples as expected. After years of collection and thousands of bad samples, finding seeder DNA got serious. Overtime pay had piled up but demerit points began to whittle it away. If they didn't get a better result rate, they will owe the company credits.

"This ain't getting us anywhere," Gabe said. "There should be more, what was he doing, hiding out in a monastery?

Gabe was in line at the Wildfire roller coaster when his communicator chimed. The guy in front of him scratched the mosquito bite Gabe just gave him with the extractor. Malaria was on the rise or the guy wouldn't have noticed.

Gabe stepped out of line and joined Mike. Mike was scanning people from the ruins of the kiddy-ride pier. Gabe's wings were twitching. Mike pointed at them.

"What's going on? Why are you so frazzled?" Mike said.

"Control called," Gabe said. "Will you take it, or shall I?" Nobody in Planet Molding ever wanted to talk to Control, least of all Gabe.

"No way, Skippy," Mike said. "You're the boss."

Delegation of responsibility wasn't working. Gabe opened the communicator and checked the screen. *Not a two-way call, thank goodness.* It was canned instructions and the response to his last progress report.

"Control directives," Gabe said. "I'll put it on speaker."

Mike closed in. Gabe fast-forwarded past the ID stuff and pressed play.

"…samples and rate of delivery are unsatisfactory according to your onboard artificial intelligence…"

Mike yelled stop. The recording paused. A little kid turned and looked at Mike and pointed directly at them. Mike shut up until the kid's mother yanked him around the other away and left.

That kid saw us.

"That's bull," Mike said. "They got balls trusting the AI report before our stuff. We're living beings, that thing's a piece of crap…"

While Mike ranted about union rules, which didn't apply, Gabe ignored him and scrolled through the text for the important stuff.

"Mike, will you please shut up a minute. We got bigger problems than bad samples. Given enough time, it might be enough, but time is the problem."

Gabe hit play.

"…The next scheduled Wave has picked up energy and it is not authorized to do so. It has been radicalized. Wave impact is estimated to arrive early. It will arrive three years after receipt of this message…"

"Stop playback. So, what?" Mike's tone was crabby.

Three people walking by looked at each other. Mike stood there with his mouth open, waiting for them to pass. The people moved on. Gabe didn't let Mike resume.

"Stick a feather in it, will you? Listen for once." Gabe said hitting the play button.

"…Estimate sample collection rate inadequate volume before impact…"

Fast forward. "…team must abandon planet side operations before impact as field operatives must be shielded…" Fast forward. "…a rogue Wave status warning has been issued."

"I don't get it, what's that mean?" Mike asked.

Mike didn't know shit about Wave Physics, that was Gabe's area.

"It means we're screwed. Simple astrophysics. Rogue Waves carry sub-frequency pulses that will disrupt our DNA. We can't stay. We don't have time to get adequate samples. It's over, Mike."

"What about the missing seeder! It's confirmed. There's one around here somewhere."

"This Wave likely won't affect him. Only the End Wave can do that. But that's just a theory," Gabe said feeling hopeless. "But survivors, the resisters of Wave action that we need…There won't be hardly any left. There aren't many left now."

"We haven't found them yet, that's all. His offspring got to be someplace."

"What if he didn't make a lot of babies?" Gabe said.

Mike's wings stopped buzzing and dropped, his mouth opened and snapped shut.

"Shit, we got nothing."

Mike figured it out, how nice.

Gabe lowered himself onto the hood of an old aluminum bumper car. His wings felt like lead. All this effort was wasted. The two bodies they picked up weren't regenerating fast enough or well enough. Moon doesn't have the right technology to do better. Failing felt like the only thing he was good at. His former so-called bright ideas always turned bad.

"That's it. We're done here."

"We can fix this," Mike said. "Don't puss out on me."

"How?"

"I got it. We hire the Grays. They've sucked on Earth people for thousands of years. We'll make a deal, see? They can tap 10,000 a day. DNA extractors are cheap. Let them get the material for us, you'll see, that'll work."

Gabe's back went straight involuntarily. Mike was on to something, but Grays, Gabe wouldn't abide. *Too creepy.* Besides, they didn't have spare extractors or the budget to make more.

"Too expensive," Gabe said. "If they know what we want they'll jack up the price. They ain't after the material we want so how can we not tip our hand? They're parasites. They'll back-stab us. Forget it."

It was Mike's turn to feel crushed. *Good, let him taste my defeat.* Mike fell back onto a pile of bulkhead timbers and got creosote on his wings.

"You have the right concept," Gabe said slowly. "We need volume and a way to get samples fast. If we can entice the type of people who are most likely to have the right DNA to come to us, that'll do it. We get them to volunteer. No more chasing weak signals. We make them come to us."

"How the hell are we going to do that?" Mike sat up pulling his wings around. He smelled the black goop on his plumage and made a sour face.

"I just had them cleaned."

"How? Religion." Gabe said, pulling Mike's leg. "It's perfect."

Mike jumped up with his face twisting and wings bristling. He paced the boardwalk with hands behind his back. It was his usual way of thinking hard.

What's knocking around inside Mike's union-breed noggin?

Gabe was joking but it sure got Mike jazzed up.

Religion was always a bad idea. He and Mike were union-trained anti-religion planet molders. That screw-up with Jesus still tasted bad. Starting a religion was against Her policy and everything they ever did for the company. Professional planet molders don't make religions. A field agent's purpose was to aid evolution and not detract from it. The task was to push emerging sentient beings away from fantasy and into reality. In no other way could an advancing race join Galactic Center; Rule one: Stop Religions.

This will rub Mike's union roots thin. Then again, Mike never stopped quoting the no-rules salvage contract. On the other hand, any opportunity to poke Control in the eye was always taken. Mike stopped pacing. His lips turned down.

"How, how're we going to pull it off?" Mike said. "We stop religions. We don't make them. Only three years? I hope the big portable hologram still works."

Mike flopped back onto the woodpile ignoring the tar.

"What about the Church? They got a lock on that." Gabe said, keeping a straight face.

Gabe enjoyed screwing with Mike for a change. Mike was the anthropologist. He should know this can't work. Maybe they promoted Gabe for a reason. Maybe his occasional decent idea got upper management's attention. Gabe didn't mind recycling one of his big mistakes to poke fun at Mike.

He can't take this seriously.

"Local help. We get us a Prophet of the Lord," Gabe said to egg Mike on. "Think about it. We had the right idea with Jesus, just the wrong guy."

It wasn't a bad thought experiment. Gabe did a paper on it his freshmen year of tech school. Nobody in planet molding ever started a religion intentionally before. *Ridiculous notion.* Mike jumped up.

"You're crazy, look what happen with Jesus. Crap, Gabe, it all blew up in our faces."

Got him by the short feathers.

"Exactly, and our mistake is still going strong. Religion must have been baked in, a genetic flaw, and we missed it. That's a flaw we can use." Gabe said with an artificially straight face.

"Starting a religion is easy, controlling one, that's the bugger." Mike went back to pacing.

The original love-and-duty gene was released bent out of shape and later integrated into the play-need and ritual-need genes. That was the twist which doomed Earth. *There it is and ready to be taken advantage of.*

That was why She sent evolution Waves, Gabe thought. DNA had gotten too tangled. Too much good spliced into bad. Control regularly parted out such failed projects. They bust them up, take the good, and trash the rest. Her logic made practical sense. Nobody can fix a root design error.

If that's what this is.

He waited for Mike to come up with a plan that can't work. Gabe needed a good laugh.

"I don't know how to do this, this is crazy," Mike finally spit out.

"Make something up, you're the anthropologist," Gabe said.

Mike resumed pacing but not for long.

"I got it," Mike said. "We go get that homeless guy, that guy who can see us.

Lots of kids see us but not grownups." Mike pointed north. "He's right over there in New York, remember?"

"Good plan," Gabe said. "Prophets always come out of humble beginnings. He's on the street. He kind of looked like Jesus. We'll coach him in real-time. Stand right there behind him telling him what to say. That'll work."

You always pull my chain so why shouldn't I jerk back? That homeless guy was fifty years ago.

The plan grew as they walked back to their transport. Gabe's objections weren't strong. It was a simple plan. Have an Earth guy talk special people into visiting a special temple. They'll use portable interdimensional holding tanks. Make it look like a Catholic Confessional Center. *Everybody's a Catholic.* Make the new religion an offshoot of the dominant system.

They could collect thousands. Make people inclined toward peace the requirement. Put them into suspended time chambers and haul them back to the Center. *Let the genetic manipulation boys deconstruct it.* Plus, the subjects get moved out of the Wave Zone. They won't devolve further. Patch them up and use them to restock the next Earth. It was brilliant, unique. It all made sense…on paper. Nobody ever did it before.

What a dumb idea. Gabe's intuition kicked the back of his head. He ignored it; intuition was for labor. Bad ideas were standard procedure but he didn't feel like management. The concept didn't sit right. Gabe worked to figure it out. Mike completed his circle and stated over.

"What if we can't find him?" Mike said.

"Who, oh, that homeless guy? He's dead by now." Mike looked dejected. "Cheer up. It's New York. There must be good seeders there." Gabe said. "Denser population gives us better odds. We could just keep collecting anyway. We might get enough by the deadline."

Shit, did I just say that?

Gabe's joke morphed into possible. For the first time in a long time, Gabe felt good. Salvage wasn't working so they may as well ride it out and have fun. New York still had a big population. Prospects were thinning in New Jersey anyway. With luck, he might find a local Guru worth hiring. *The plan can't work, too outrageous, but why not try? It'll look good on the pay sheets.*

Whatever happened, it was a great way to jerk Mike around. Gabe's plan was put into operation with no hope of pulling it off.

32

Vegas to NYC

The first leg went easy with nothing much between Yermo and Vegas—the green desert and abandoned pitstops were empty. Interstate Forty was the most direct way to go back east. But after such a long time in isolation he deserved some action. The idea of hot chicks and beer had inspired him to take the scenic route.

"The scenic route, where did I hear that term?"

He rolled into a little town called Jean twenty miles south of the Strip. No traffic, not even wagons. A couple of horses were tied to rusted parking meters. They were eating the turquoise grass on Main Street in front of the Confession Center. A hot chick in short-shorts and cowboy boots exited the Center. The name Elli May Clamp-it popped into his head and he had no idea where that came from. He stopped the truck in the middle of the road and got out. The wet grass felt nice on his bare feet.

"You must be Jean," he said. "Nice town you have here."

"Very funny, I've heard that joke a million times. What do you want?"

John flinched. Whenever he talked nice to a chick, said funny things, gave a girl a nice smile, the chicks dug him. This one got pissed. *Too bad.* She was showgirl pretty.

"I better cool it," he whispered to Bobby Socks. "I'm on my way to Vegas," he said addressing the girl.

"No shit, Sherlock."

"Could you direct me to where a man might find a bed, and maybe a little more."

"Where you been? Gambling and whoring ain't legal no more. Church shut the Strip down years ago, praise the Pope." She crossed herself.

"You know a fast way to 40?"

"Forget going north. Hoover Dam Road's closed. Back the way you came, 15 miles take 164 east, 95 south, then 163 east. Better git before Archie shoots you. We don't cotton to government people around here."

"But, but I'm not—"

She strode off like a military momma. John drove up the block, pulled into the All-Store, and looped around. He headed out and didn't stop driving until he reached New Mexico.

Everywhere he went it was the same. Chicks were hostile. There weren't many people and he only had seen a few kids. Nobody wanted to make love anymore. The chicks used to love him but now they acted like he had the crabs. Nobody wanted to party. Nobody liked him. Because he was driving, people thought he was with the government and that brought him nothing but grief.

"Never trust The Man, how'd I become The Man?

He made it to North New Jersey in a week and was glad to see cars on the road. Canada Gas Inc had carved out a dirty-gas market. He attempted to park in Newark and take the train before dragging all his shit into the city, but the trains had stopped running.

Traffic was dead so he took his tank truck and house trailer through the Lincoln Tunnel. He parked his traveling sideshow in the bus drop-off zone in front of the Metropolitan Museum's archeology building. The two guys wearing angel wings eating pizza on the corner were a little weird. *That's New York City for you.* Still, they looked familiar. John exited the truck and climbed the tall stairs to the top of the stoop.

A security man stopped him at the door. "What's your business?"

"I'm here to see Johnson."

"Who sent cha?"

"Washington D.C."

"Good enough, pass."

John walked half the building before he found Johnson's office. He stopped at the door. Levi Johnson looked up from his desk, a crumpled old man with sharp eyes and thin hair. His office was littered with stacks of old paper books. They belonged together like Siamese twins. Johnson's paperweight was the biggest megalodon tooth John had ever seen and he might not have noticed it in this menagerie but Johnson picked it up and waved it at him.

"Don't bother me, I'm busy."

"The Smith said I should see you. I came from Calico, I've got—"

"Calico! I know you. Yes, they told me about you, but I didn't pay much heed. They can't tell me how to run my department. This isn't the Catholic Church. Come in. Sit down, young man."

John took a chair, the only one not stacked with books, and pulled it up to the gray metal desk.

"I was told you handle anomalies in archeology. I have stuff that'll blow your mind."

"Think so, do you, young man? You have no idea. What do you think we do around here? Generation after generation, we find unusual material just to bury it. Let me guess, Geodome people or the Cart-rut people who weren't only on Malta and Crete you know. What about Knossos, ha!"

"Cart ruts, I didn't see any," John said. "Domes."

The old man laughed and slapped his knee. "Old news, old. Not to you, surprising, yes?"

John's heart missed a beat. All kinds of facts about the past flash-flooded John's mind. He spent years working on the question of how Summer and others had advanced so fast out of the neolithic. His answer was, they didn't spring out of the ether: They were resurrected from an older advanced civilization. *And they know all about Geodomes!*

John stood back up but on unsteady legs. "I guess I'm wasting your time, I'll just—"

"Look, young man, there is nothing new under the sun. Neither is what's about to happen. Sit."

John slunk back into that hard chair. "What's happening, man, que pasa?"

"Nothing here. Let me be clear, I'm not crazy." Johnson said. "We are protected by alien technology. It's a force shield the same as the Pope has. That's the reason why Vatican City hasn't ended whereas all the other religious institutions have. The Pope has the same toys we have."

"I don't get it, man."

"I'll tell you a few things as it doesn't matter now. Another cosmic wave is inbound. Vatican's astronomy department, still operational, knows this, too. It may well be that it kills us all. Nobody knows."

Johnson rubbed his head like he had been dipped in fiberglass insulation. Johnson's dandruff snowed but got lost in the dust.

"I've penned this up too long."

Levi explained the secrets of church and state. They both possessed advanced technology. Most of it was not understood. What they had was seldom used. They tried things in the past which failed. 9/11 was the biggest blunder. They employed an alien wave projector tuned to disappear the Tower's criminal paperwork but scaling proved to be a disaster. Their understanding of that tech was lacking. For the people's good, it was covered up.

"Security institutions do whatever is necessary to uphold the state's power," Levi said. "For the people's good, my ass. I'll tell you what we were really up to."

Johnson gave examples and named names. The fat cats behind everything never let on what they had. John received the unspoken message. 'Keep your mouth shut or they will shut it for you.' Johnson also admitted there weren't many mouth-shutting agents left. Johnson felt free to talk, he said, given that in three years nothing will matter.

"What if I blab?"

"Nobody will believe you," Levi said.

"What about my stuff? My travel trailer's full of evidence."

"Security took care of it right after you parked. We can use a smart guy like you. Want to work for the Met? We'd like to stop the effect. Cosmic waves don't affect everyone. One in 10,000 don't get infected. You appear to be one of them."

"I'll need to think about it."

John left reeling and dejected. He wasn't the regular employee type. If the world ends in three years, why waste time working? Levi said the next wave won't take out the shield. John thought otherwise.

Outside, his tank truck, lizard, and travel trailer were still there, but not his samples and reports. He went around the corner, grabbed a couple of hotdogs, went back, and sat on top of the museum's wide stairway in front of the main entry. He ate and watched the street.

Electric and gas cars zipped by. People walked past. Nobody came up the steps. Those two guys dressed in wings were still across the street poking people with a short metal stick. People didn't notice. *That's crazy.* Years back he read in *Anthropology Today* about yuppies who dressed up in animal pajamas to get their kicks.

"Whatever floats your boat, man. Wings must be the new thing."

John spoke to his pet but he had left Bobby in the truck.

33

Hiring Local

Gabe and Mike were in dilapidated old New York City sticking sample-pullers into people's asses randomly in hope of finding decent seeder genes, or anyone that saw them despite holo. With so much life around and prior Wave actions, their old hand-held scanners weren't working right. The AI agreed there must be descendants of seeders in New York. *Maybe this isn't a waste of time.* They didn't yet have enough trace material to reconstruct a seed program, but it was possible although time was short.

Gabe hailed Moon Base with a device replicating an Earth cellphone. The retired Earthling agent picked up Gabe's call. Gabe didn't like him but he was better than nothing.

What's-his-name's a real pain in the ass but I need the help.

"Where are we at?" Gabe said. He had the Earthmen working with the Eye. The Eye spotted good regions but couldn't zero in.

"New York City, Butthead. I have you on screen. You better shake a leg. In twenty-nine months, the big Mama-Jama touches down."

"That's not what I mean. I know where I am. Where are we at with samples?"

Mike poked Gabe in the ribs. "Hey look at that."

Gabe pushed him away. "Not now, I'm on the horn."

"But Gabe, I think…"

"Shut up Mike, just shut up."

"Oh, aren't we testy today? What, you got sand in your wings?"

Angels weren't good at that Earthman expression known as 'if-looks-could-kill,' but Gabe did his best to convey that message. Mike came back with a big grin. Meanwhile, the Earth guy talked and Gabe missed it.

"Sorry, please repeat."

"I said, you guys got a long way to go. You'll never get enough in time at this rate. I don't know why you haven't used the finder. How'd you think we located the farm?"

"Finder? What finder?" Gabe said. He put it on speaker.

"You guys are thick. Superior race my ass. Your sample-pullers, the ones I lent you, against company rules, by the way, have built-in finders. It's only local. The range is a hundred yards. You can zero candidates in that radius. It's tuned for seed carriers. Don't you read the tech reports?"

"Our equipment doesn't have that," Mike said. "That's why I—"

"Shut up. No, not you, Base. OK, Base, you're telling me the sample-pullers we have with us are equipped with built-in finders?"

"You got it, Skeezix."

"Why didn't you tell me?"

"You didn't ask."

Mike fell out laughing. Gabe felt sick. Of course, labor never tells management anything voluntarily. *I should have known better.* Gabe couldn't wait to get back to the moon so he could grill them two like ballpark franks.

"Keep me informed of any new updates, Gabe out."

Mike stood by with a half-cocked grin. Gabe used to think this stuff was funny, too. But the pressure was on. Mini Waves kept coming. Every passing day made it harder to find what they needed.

"Don't say a word, Mike, let me think."

Early Waves didn't affect minor seeders at first. But as Waves got stronger, seeders faded out, and Gabe's problems increased. The only people left undamaged were the rare dominant seeders, and few if any were left. He gave up the idea of finding one. Gabe went after numbers. *Like gold dust, sift enough dirt and get a bag full.* Immortals born after they leave can't survive. End Wave takes everything. Gabe's knees felt like soup.

"I gotta sit down," Gabe said lowing himself onto a park bench someone had dragged out of the park and onto the sidewalk.

Gabe's wings skewed sitting down. *I should preen.* Mike fooled around with his borrowed DNA puller while Gabe picked at his wings.

Mike figured out how to activate the finder and pointed it across the street.

"I knew it, I fucking knew it," Mike said. "See that guy over there?" Mike pointed. "Solid trace."

Gabe turned to look. The bench faced perpendicular to the street making his movement obvious. The Earth guy over there looked away when Gabe faced him directly.

"That guy sees us. I tried to tell you." Mike said.

"I'll be damned," Gabe said. "You're right. Think he's an immortal? Jesus, we'll scoop him up and get the hell out of here."

Great, now I'm thinking like management.

"He does look a lot like Jesus..."

"Hold on, Skippy," Mike said. "This finder is tuned for trace, not immortals.

Second, don't forget some seeders can see us. Remember that shaman in Brazil? Even so, I bet that guy's prime stock. We should talk to him."

Mike dipped a wingtip in the guy's direction. The guy flinched.

"That's just great, the best ones are the ones we can't jab," Gabe said, stomach acid rising. "They go bananas. He must think we're a couple of end-times nut-bags. 'Oh, excuse me, sir, let me stick this needle in your ass.' That guy in Brazil came at us with a machete."

"You been in management too long," Mike said. "Where's your imagination? Let's talk to him. Maybe we'll use him. You already approved the local hire idea. He might be Prophet material."

"I did?" Gabe hated talking to Earth people. They were stupid.

"You did. I have it on record," Mike said with his fake concerned face. "You saw the latest Eye scan. Looks like there are a lot of carriers in the Middle East. We know that from the burnt farm people. If we hire him, we can fly out and cover the other hot spot."

Mike pointed at him with his DNA puller.

"Think Gabe. With us covered here, we can go. Palestine, or what's left of it, looks good. What if he ain't profit material? He can still jab people."

Gabe twisted around fast. The guy looked away. *Yeah, he sees us.* Using another local didn't sit well with him. Every time he hired one, he got the wrong guy. Besides, scabs were against his union DNA. He previously broke that rule and suffered bad results. Giving field-op jobs to scabs just wasn't smart business.

"Think, Gabe. That guy might be our ticket off this rock."

Talking and planning for local hires, back in Seaside, was only a game for pulling Mike's chain. Gabe thought they had agreed to drop the idea as unwork-able. *Now Mike takes it seriously?*

"That's my problem. I am thinking about it," Gabe said.

Everyone knew how Gabe's Satan Probe failed. But, the two Earth-hire jok-ers up on the moon, not his hires, did a decent job. Gabe hated to admit it, but Mike was right. That Jesus-looking guy didn't look insane. *How bad can he be?*

"Look at him, he's got hair like an angel," Mike said.

Gabe swallowed the bile rising in his gullet.

"What the hell. Fine. Good. Come on, let's talk to him," Gabe said without enthusiasm.

They walked straight across and directly to where the guy sat eating. He didn't look like much as he stood. His long hair was orderly and a sign of sanity. His ragged appearance reminded Gabe of Jesus but his clothes were clean. Everyone on Earth were disheveled anymore. Quality textile production was a thing of the past.

"No way, man!" The Earth guy said. "I knew you dudes were real. I've seen you before…I think. Weren't you in New York back in…shit? I forget when. Maybe it was New Jersey."

"Hello, sir," Gabe said. "Please, don't get the wrong idea. We're not preachers. I'd like to—"

"Yeah, I know man. You're aliens. Religion's bullshit," He took a hit off a joint. "I was up there with the government. They know about aliens." He pointed a thumb over his shoulder. "They have been tracking you fuckers for years. The space science dude told me about the cosmic wave, bummer man."

"You win the booby prize," Mike said.

"Boobies rock, man. I love tits." The guy said. "Too bad chicks ain't sharing them anymore."

Gabe slapped himself in the forehead. Great, they found a gene carrier but one already Wave-affected and half-crazy. *What the hell, I got nothing to lose.* They had two finders. *Use the guy. Mike's right, it's time to pull the stops.* A girl passed by below on the sidewalk.

"Check out her ass. That's one fine chick, groovy man."

"You got that right," Mike said, bumping fists with the Earthman. "I'm Mike, that's Gabe, glad to meet you."

"Cool, I'm John Doe. I knew I wasn't crazy. OK, maybe a little. What're you two cats up to?"

"Glad you asked," Gabe said.

Gabe gave him the whole spiel, about the Wave, the time left, the seeder genes. He explained that the Planet Molders were there to save humanity by gathering the best genes to bring to a new planet and start over. Gabe used copious white lies—he didn't know what Center planned to do with this Book—*it'll probably get mothballed.* He didn't tell details, only what might convince Doe to join them.

John listened and smoked and lit another joint before Gabe finished. With Mike's prompting the conversation turned toward Mike's on the fly plan.

"I dig it, man," John said. "I'm with you. But how the hell are you going to do it? Getting the right people together ain't easy. Ever live in a commune? It's a trip."

"Religion," Mike chimed in.

"I'm not down with that," John said. "Religion doesn't save anybody. Look what the Church did to America, nothing but bad shit, man."

"I could tell you stories," Mike said and went on with examples.

Gabe almost kicked Mike. The Emergency Procedures booklet said: "'If you can't beat them, join them.'" The master rule book also prohibited using religions along with stricter prohibitions against allowing clients to know Control's business. At this point, they weren't doing anything by the book. Gabe had to use whatever might work.

"See, religion is a tool," Mike finished with. "It's always been a tool."

"I don't know, man. Religion is pretty fucked up."

"No, no, it's not like that," Gabe said.

He took a breath and relaxed his wings. They rose high whenever he got excited. Spread wings were intimidating. John didn't seem to mind it.

"We don't believe in that god stuff either," Gabe said. "Here's the thing. We must gather living people with the right genes, of course, for transport. We'll put them in stasis and take them over to another world. Religion, our design, will draw in the right kind of people. We promote ideas tuned for the type we need, people inclined toward peace and love."

"I dig that, man. Peace is where it's at."

Mike's wings buzzed. He had figured out Gabe's on-the-fly plan. Gabe wasn't flying blind—they had talked about this—but he couldn't believe what came out of his mouth either. He and Mike had bounced around a lot of weird hypothetical ideas for entertainment but they were ideas and not plans, not really. Mike's excitement sucked Gabe in.

We're doing this.

"Yeah, see, we put satellites out and run a reaction wave signal," Mike said. "People with the gene receive an impulse. They'll react to keywords. So, you preach the message and the right types will respond. They'll do what you say. I'll write your script. We weed out the pretenders at the transport gate. It's simple. No genes, no pass. Get it? It's beautiful."

A cop walked up. He looked John up and down. John handed him the joint. "Good shit man, look at me, I'm talking with invisible people."

The cop took a hit and walked away with the joint.

"Typical fuzz, man."

Mike pointed his device at the cop, "Bad reading."

"We'll set up a temple. It's not a real one, it'll be a transport center, a multi-dimensional portal. Looks like a church building but it'll hold a million people." Gabe said.

"Far out, like *Dr. Who*."

"Right," Mike said. "I love that show, funny as hell. So, you go around and send them on a pilgrimage. You won't even need a finder. Where do you want us to set up the transport system?"

"I'll convince our Earthmen crew to run the temple," Gabe said thinking out loud. The plan jelled. "I can pull my Earth guys off the moon."

They'll be pissed. Gabe didn't mind spreading a little payback icing on this job cake.

"Hey man, I'd like to help. People got to help each other. But how do I know you aren't a bad acid trip? This is a lot of shit to take in. I'm into doing the right thing, for sure man, but I got to get my shit together. I got to think, man."

"Tell you what," Gabe said. "Come to the moon. Meet the others. Stay awhile. Mike's the anthropologist, he'll work out the script. It'll take time to set up the temple anyway."

He's thin. Food doesn't come easy on Earth.

"We have Earth food. Pizza, hamburgers, you name it."

"Got any weed up there?"

"Only the best," Mike said, and that was no lie.

The two retired Earth agents had hydroponic weed farms on Moon Base. All Earth plants and animals were already stored in their data bank. The lee side of the moon can't suffer Wave effects because it doesn't face the right way. The retired Earth team didn't have anything to do but play with the Eye and grow food and smoke. Why do high seed-count people love hemp? He made a note to ask the biology lab.

"Moon pot is the best in this part of the galaxy," Gabe said.

"Far out, man. Count me in."

The three entered the overgrown park and proceeded deeper in pushing thick foliage aside. They trampled on to the lander. Hiding it wasn't necessary with the ship in holo but Mike had parked it in seclusion by habit. John crashed into it hurting his knee. *That'll convince him.*

The door opened and broke holo, Mike and Gabe escorted John on board before he had time to think.

Three weeks on the moon were fruitful. John Doe wasn't as dumb as he looked. He learned the routine fast for a pothead.

Back on Earth, John got right to it. Gabe and Mike saw John doing well, so they took off for the Middle East. The Chinese were done killing for this season. Dead seeders weren't any help. The oil war was predicted to overrun Palestine when hostilities resumed. Gabe and Mike didn't stay in New York long.

34

Becoming Pope

Cardinal Morgan Margo was ready to become Pope. The fix was in. Her inner circle, those few who knew she played the part of an old man, were called before her. She sought confirmation of their loyalty. She only ran the alien cosmic shield when a wave was imminent but wave effects lingered. She saved that protective device for her inner circle.

The wave made people harder to control. She protected her men to better use them. She didn't trust them. They also knew how the Church hoarded and hid alien artifacts. To what extent only she knew. To them, she was a living miracle, alien hardware aside.

Her old men understood she can't age. She hid, as the Vatican Archivist, in deep caves. Sub-basement vaults and time had given Morgan opportunities. She had saved the holo projector's batteries for rare appearances. The time had come for a special projection. Only her men saw her without her electronic disguise.

The stupid Church has had alien technology stashed for centuries and they never explored it. What a bunch of douchebags.

She was on a mission for God. God gave her the resources and know-how, she claimed. They believed. Her men spread her propaganda. They paid the bribes. *So far, so good.* The twelve waiting on her within deep chambers knew many unspoken things but they didn't know what she had in mind next. She called them to the gates of her secret laboratories to tell them and test them.

"Gentlemen," she began, "I'm glad you all could make it."

She liked that cliché, even after a hundred years.

"Make yourselves at home."

Her office had rock walls, a metal desk, folding chairs, and little else. The riches she had stolen weren't evident. She had spent that treasure years ago. The two doors behind her desk, one leading into the robotics lab, and the other into the biology lab were flat gray. She had calculated her office's effect to make wondering believers think Morgan was a pious devotee.

"Don't just stand there, gawwd. Sit already, gezze."

Watching twelve old men unscramble cheap metal chairs was funny, but she didn't crack up. She didn't even wink at her grandson who danced among them. Her serious countenance did not change while musical chairs played in her mind. She shorted the number of chairs on purpose.

"Sir, we are ready to hear your wisdom," her secretary said.

Dispensing with Church titles, her Initiates were programmed to call her 'sir.' The secretary was a dependable man so she renamed him Able. Too bad she had to kill Able's father. They were soon to meet a pair of followers who also bucked her. *Nothing like an example to make things clear.*

"OK, here's the plan. After I become Pope, we launch an attack on the United States."

"How, why?" Howard said. "Nobody wants to fight. All the armies have dispersed except China and they don't care either. Not since the last Great Change. How're we going to form and motivate an army?"

"I'll tell you how. I'll keep why to myself for now," she said. "After the election, when I take the balcony to greet the people, I'll transmute and tell them who I am. It's time to shake the tree. I'll produce magic and power that'll blow their shit away. They'll get in line. New converts and old are gonna worship me."

"What if they don't?" Father Bush said.

She wanted to laugh but didn't.

"The same tried and true techniques that governments and churches have always used still work. Fear never fails. I've something special planned."

"This better be good," Father Zinno said.

"Oh, it's better than good," she said.

"What about an army?" Monsignor Clinton asked. "Since the Great Change… who will fight?"

"I was hoping you'd ask," she said squeaking out a little laugh.

She snapped her fingers. The robotics lab doors swung out. Two abominations walked in.

The first being was the dead upper body of Father Bain laced onto a headless ostrich body with legs. Father Bain was a bit of a muckraker. Shirtless, he had four budging hearts of different sizes pumping just under his chest and abdomen's skin. He was covered in slashes closed by exposed staples. The black AK-47 slung on his shoulder contrasted sickly with its death-white skin. The other abomination was the missing Swiss Guard Sergeant Borne, another trouble maker. He was likewise constructed but his human torso was sewn onto the back half of a zebra. Born had to keep moving with tinny tap-steps to maintain balance.

I must work on that. I'll try a brown bear or an orangutan next.

Several of the seated fell backward off their chairs. Two of them turned and vomited. All were pale as washed-up corpses excepting one, Able laughed like Snidely Whiplash. Zinno held his lunch down with tight lips.

"See, I have fighters. It just so happens they generate massive fear as well. Handy, right. I'm geared up to build an army. I won't need a lot of them."

"What are they?" Someone choked out.

"In life, they were critical thinking agitators," she said. "Tell them who you are now."

The dead father turned his head like it was on a post and answered in a rasping voice.

"We are Guardsmen, guards of the highest, Pope Joan."

"Oh shit," Bush said.

"Biological robots," she said. "I learned a few tricks from the Gray aliens' archive. You didn't hear that. Pretty neat, right? They make them out of cows. Cows, I don't need no stinking cows."

She laughed. No one else got the joke.

"This is more effective. Don't you think?"

Everyone mumbled in agreement. She watched them carefully. They were with her. Her point well taken. Disagreeing with her was dangerous. Borne and Father Bain had found that out the hard way. Having had her fun, she proceeded with business and worked out a production plan to build an army of monstrosities.

35

Morgan's Big Day

Three days after assassinating the former Pope, she met with her twelve and instructed them on final preparations. She took her private elevator to her office inside Saint Peter's Basilica to get dressed. Her men knew the drill. She expected no trouble with them. She waited for the call with confidence.

"My turn to take the pointy hat." She said to the spider in her hand.

Her main reason for attacking America wasn't for the needs of the masses. America had acquired a new religious hero and that was justification enough to satisfy the faithful's questions. She had pushed the idea for a hundred years: There mustn't be any usurpers or Jesus won't return. That was her scam. But she had other unstated reasons.

"America's subversive hippie religion stands in God's way." She held the spider in her palm up to eye level.

That wasn't her core issue. Revenge drove her. She guessed but her spies had confirmed it. Hacking the U.S. government had told her the rest.

"First, we kill brother John, then we attack the Smithsonian and grab whatever alien tech they have." She put the spider on her desk. "My long-lost brother let those pigs rape me. America keeps pigs in power and for that sin, they must pay."

It would take an army and only the Pope could raise one. People in America defended him, even Church leaders. Her faithful won't kill and John Doe takes advantage. The alien's shield over the Vatican was wearing out. Her well-controlled staff was wavering and turning peaceful. The clock was ticking but time was with her. Her robots had no aversion to bloody murder.

The secretary came. It was done.

She dressed for her entrance wearing an old man's priestly robes. She jacked into a hidden remote control and called two Guardsmen to her. Activating the holo let her walk the halls disguised. The secretary proceeded in front, the Guardsmen behind like fuzzy apparitions inside the shield. The priests and Swiss soldiers lining the way fell on their faces trembling. She pressed on leaving a wake of dread, vomit, and piss behind her.

This is working so far.

Entering the balcony anteroom, the Guardsmen stayed back in the shadows. She shut the door locking out the Church's high officials. For the first time in history, the new Pope will take the balcony alone. The holo device worked perfectly. *They'll get what they expect, I'm just an old man clothed in finery.* TV still worked, on and off, and it still captivated but cheap tricks didn't work. It had to seem real. She had that covered.

After ten minutes of waving to the crowd, she stepped back and raised her hands. A bomb blew the balusters and rails off St. Peter's balcony. Stone posts and pickets cascaded down onto the lawn with mushy thumps. It could have been better, more dramatic. The earthquake of 2035 destroyed the paving stones below and replacements were impossible to find. The caretakers had planted grass instead.

"Your Highness, are you well? The rails are gone!" Howard yelled into her earbuds. He monitored the proceeding from the CCTV system's control room.

"That'll give them a clear view," she said into her headset. "TV camera's still rolling?"

"All eyes are on you, my Lord."

"Give it a minute. Get the live feeds going. *CNN* is going to eat this shit up," she said.

The crowd went crazy. The Swiss Guard wasted no time and moved into the crowd beating them back away from the lawn below her. She moved forward through the smoke with hands up. The people stopped dead. She clicked on the microphone. Thinking ahead, she had it bolted down for this occasion.

"The Lord has given me a gift, the gift of youth, but the devil fights me for my body. Behold." Her voice was feeble but clear.

Her robes dropped off. A naked old man stood before the world. She had rigged the holo to melt on voice command.

"Behold the Lord's gift!"

The hologram cascaded bright, multi-colored light from her head down like a Fourth of July sparkler. As the spark-fire descended her true self was revealed. A pretty, thin, small-chested teen girl emerged. The crowd was outraged. People whelped. Others cried. Most called out "fake, fake," in Italian and every other tongue. She had anticipated this reaction.

"The devil attacks me, who will save me?" Margo's original voice boomed all over Rome.

The crowd booed. The eyes of millions watching TV and the multitude there before the jumbo-screens saw everything.

Her belly swelled as she moaned while aging to a woman of thirty. In seconds she became late-with-child. Then her gut exploded with bloody water issuing. A red, horned child with a forked tail emerged and stood smoking as blood ran from its mouth. Disguised by holo, her great-granddaughter, a toddler, became the devil.

Onscreen, the holo stalked around her like a wolf while the real baby, drugged, lay dazed and still.

"Lord, Lord, send me angels! Provide Holy Guardsmen! Come cherubim, come cherubim!"

Two Guardsmen rushed out wearing flowing robes which hid some of the horrors of them. Her monstrosities stomped all over the living child while the holo created smoke. Morgan could not fake a dead body so she used a real child. The Guards pitched the corpse into the crowd. It flew a hundred yards with arms and legs spread star-shaped and spinning like a *Frisbee* before splatting down among a group of nuns.

Good aim, you guys.

"It has no tail, no horns," a commentator's voice came over the jumbo.

Reruns of the devil's appearance flashed. A camera view zoomed in on the corpse. On the big split-screen, the devil child flew out a monster but landed a perfectly normal, although mutilated, dead toddler.

Good work with the cameras, I have to give kudos to Howard.

"Look," she said, "I have saved my child's soul! Evil cannot defeat me! I am the Lord's gift. His power is my power!"

She stood naked, a fourteen-year-old girl, on the edge of the ruined balcony. The Guardsmen, plastered in blood, rested on either side of her but a little behind. The tradition was that the Pope took a new name. She used this occasion.

She raised her hands. The crowd stilled.

"Behold Pope Joan Innocent."

The crowd went wild. Margo withdrew with her robots following.

"You impressed them, my Lord," Howard said in the hallway still wearing his headset.

"Just wait until they see my dragons," Pope Joan said. "That's what I would call impressive. Real mythological creatures."

The moment she left the balcony, the masses rioted. The Swiss Guard lost control. The riots lasted three days and many died. The news everywhere hailed a new world leader. She didn't pay attention to the news. She was busy with robot production. She had a lot of freshly dead bodies to convert—too many had died. The spare body parts were not a problem. Her dragons needed the food.

36

Pope on the Ropes

Pope Joan Innocent wasn't pleased. She sat on her throne twisting a lock of dyed-black hair around her pinky pondering her quandary. Many small cosmic waves had come and gone since becoming Pope three years ago. Each made the people stranger and the big wave hadn't come yet, but it was coming soon.

"I'm running out of time."

The U.S. military shut down its satellites and the alien's orbiters weren't hackable. She couldn't tell what was happening in America. Communication by short wave radio with her troops wasn't working any longer. Tech support had filtered away. The shield failed and The Vatican became a ghost town.

The only remaining clergy were her relatives, generations of people she spawned by implanting her eggs into church mothers. Cosmic radiation didn't bother them as much as other people. No effect on her at all. She was sure her brother was the same. He had fucked his way through the music business 100 years ago. Given the nature of that industry, he didn't have many descendants. Abortion was the music industry's answer to pregnancy.

That's in my favor.

She wanted to wipe out every part of him, even his heirs. On the plus side, she had far fewer of his heirs to kill than she had anticipated. America's birth rate faltered long before. Things were leaning hard her way.

"We live in hope," she laughed. "I can't miss. I have all the advantages."

The last report, before world communications ended, spoke of her Guardsmen floundering. Deadly yes, slow and stupid, yes again. Computers laced into living human brains created internal conflicts. However, the kill command worked flawlessly. Even so, her Guards couldn't kill a man they couldn't find.

The hundreds of Guardsmen she had sent disappeared one after the other. Some wandered off mindless. Others got killed or burned out. Most of them, ineffectively, killed anything that moved and were forever running out of bullets. There weren't many AK-47 rounds left to be had. The U.S. military had destroyed their stocks before she invaded.

"Tracking targets without reliable intelligence sucks. Dead people don't answer questions." She told the spider on her shoulder. "My best robots are by now low on munitions. I'll fix that."

She touched her headset. "Howard, come to me."

Young Howard came wearing jeans and a white wife-beater T-shirt. Warming made Rome hot as hell. He was the son of her great-grandson or something like that. She didn't care. Screw nepotism but the man was not a slobbering peacenik. He was one of the few that didn't evolve after the wave, and, as such, he was still corruptible.

"We still haven't got that bastard and we may never get him at this rate," Joan said as Howard entered the throne room. "What have we got for ships? I've gotta go to America myself to see that it gets done."

"Lord, I would not trust the ships. There are only two troopships left and both leak…Steam engine drive. They aren't reliable. I might find a sailing vessel?"

She threw her scepter at the wall and chipped an Old Master's fresco.

"Idiot, you know anyone that knows how to sail? Don't even say airplane. It'll take years to get one flying. I need to get over there now."

"I could program a robot crew to sail," Howard said.

"Screw that. What else you got?"

Howard's face lightened. "The dragons are far advanced. Many are of mature age, remarkable. True nonhuman intelligence. Thinking dinosaurs. I once thought it impossible…birds and lizards. The big one is fully sentient and without cosmic wave brain melding. It's beautiful, I—"

Joan slashed a hand across her throat to shut him up, he would have gone on a long time otherwise.

"Yeah, I've talked with it. I got the rest of them with us already. How's the flying going?"

"They fly like angels. Very good for prolonged flight. They stay aloft well, gilding, they—"

"Howard, let me ask you this, do you think one can cross the ocean?"

"I'm sure of it, Lord. The big one. I do think—"

"Do the Bilbo Baggins routine," she said.

"Sir?"

"Send one there and back again. Have it fly to American taking 120 pounds both ways—Come back when it's done. Oh, and time it. You're in the observatory. How long until the next cosmic wave?"

"Pre-wave is 6 weeks out. Big wave a few weeks later. A very big one, indeed."

"I want that sucker airborne in the morning and back here in one week, no excuses, get lost. No wait, get all the ships together. Fill them with bullets and whatever Guards we still have. Send them to America. Send the dragons, too, all of them."

"But Lord, I don't think they'll make it. Maybe one steamer or a sailing ship, but it'll take weeks to land…if I can find one seaworthy, but—"

"Howard, I don't care what you think. Send everything that floats. One or two will make it. Do it, get busy."

Howard backed out bowing. The only way she was going to get it done was to do it herself. The Guardsmen were falling apart. She had a fresh weapon, a better one, one that will carry her to America and scare the shit out of her opposition. All she needed to do was show up and take control.

People will scatter. He likes reptiles. He'll come to me.

"This will be easy."

A new attack gelled. A handful of fresh robots were to proceed ahead of her and gather the others for making ready the trap. They had time to regroup ahead of her. She felt sure enough of them would make it.

This is gonna work.

37

A Dragon Holds the Road

John was in Scranton when Gabe's lander appeared in the distance lining up for a touchdown.

This city was the same as most—abandoned but canned food was still there in collapsing stores. Few people hung around dead cities. The handheld worked for finding food when it worked. He stopped in the middle of an overgrown street in front of a six-story imitation Victorian building called The Cannery. It was an office complex before.

He followed the shuttle's progress until it landed up the street crushing a stand of saplings. Frick and Frack exited the hatch. He let them come to him.

"Man! Where the hell you been!?" John said flinching at his pissy tone.

Mike and Gabe were gone a year this time and the Wave was due soon. The batteries in his communicator had given up. He didn't think they'd be able to find him up in the Poconos. It was a long walk to Springfield, Connecticut, from Scranton but doable. *What if I don't make it?*

John kicked himself in the ass. It was his idea to land the temple on the grounds of the old Indian Motorcycle Museum. John liked old bikes. *Dumb idea.* At least Scranton wasn't that far. He figured on walking it and picking up as many believers as he could on the way…if he had time. He didn't know how much time he had.

"Man, it's almost September. Reagan Wave Two's almost here," John said. "I thought you forget me."

"Reagan Wave?" Gabe asked.

"Yeah, that's when the first big one hit right? I'm not stupid. I figured it out.

You guys haven't been straight with me. This handheld computer is shit. I had to go to a library, man. I cut myself pulling boards off the windows."

"Take it easy. It's cool," Mike said.

John liked Mike better than Gabe. Mike reminded him of Earnest Borgnine but with a sense of humor. Gabe was more the science nerd type and pretty square.

"Tell him," Gabe said.

"We got two weeks. We're going there now." Mike said. "We gotta start the temple's engines, finalize everything. We got room for you, you coming?"

Mike pointed at the little flying saucer. John had time to walk from Scranton with a few days left over like before unless he needed to go around too many Guardsmen. They hunted him but they were stupid and mostly out of bullets. People, not Tribe people, knocked off Guardsmen whenever possible. There weren't many left.

"I'll walk," John said. "I sent tons of initiates up the highways but you know how they dick around, walk slow, party camps. I'll put a fire under their asses."

"That's not a good idea," Gabe said. "We think we have enough DNA samples and adding a few dozen more colonists isn't going to make a difference. We can leave at any time. Sooner is better."

"Fuck the samples, there are good people still outside," John said. "We can't leave them. What will the next Wave do? Nothing good. You won't even stay. It's dangerous. Man, I got to help my people."

"If you're late," Mike said, "We can't wait. The Wave will trash our files. The people in stasis won't be protected. When it's launch time, we're gone."

"No shit."

John moved his latest iguana off his shoulder and put it down to feed. The damn thing was too big to carry around.

"I'm going for it. I'm for the people, man."

"Suit yourself," Gabe said. "Don't be late. Once we secure the lander, we can't take it out again. You've got to be inside the transport."

Mike handed him batteries for the communicator/scanner. John didn't need the computer. Everyone knew the Prophet. He was all over the news before TV went out. Good people followed him. Bad ones ran. John wondered if his buddies shut the TV satellites down themselves. *That'd be an easy way to screw up the Church's army*. John loaded the communicator's powerpack. It still didn't work. John handed it back to Mike.

"I'm not lugging this shit around anymore. Look, it's broke."

"He's right," Mike said. "This equipment sucks."

The aliens boarded their ship. They didn't bother with holo anymore. More people can see them anyway. Mini Waves had messed up everything. Running holos made it harder for the handheld to spot good DNA. The aliens didn't need to hide. People who saw their wings became instant believers. How people acted was the only reliable indicator anymore. John mock saluted as the ship took off.

"Iggy Pop! Come on boy, where are you, damn lizard."

The lizard came crashing out of the underbrush with a bird in its mouth. It ran up and wagged its tail. It struck John what a weird creature it was. It had long legs, a track of fur running down its back, and the temperament of a Golden Retriever. Of course, dogs were extinct but when did lizards become dog-like?

Shit's getting too strange on this planet.

Iggy took off with a looping run. His pet usually came back when called, but not this time. John was about to make tracks, and cover a lot of ground in a hurry, but he wouldn't leave Iggy behind. He followed.

Iggy had treed something and was grunting and howling up ahead. *Weird that the lizard won't climb.* John pushed through the brush and found Iggy below an old monkey-bars playground structure shaped like a geodesic dome. Sitting on top of it was a hot chick and one of the elected according to her lack of clothes.

"Iggy, come!" The lizard backed off wagging its tail hard. "He won't hurt you. He just wants to play."

"I know, I know, he's cool," she said. "It's just that he reminds me of the dragon."

"Dragon?"

She climbed down. Her tits jiggled nice. *Defiantly hot, nice round butt, and rocking C-cups.* Nothing much hid her goodies. Her cutoff short-shorts were rags. The loose men's suit vest she wore didn't cover much. For sure, a barefoot natural blonde. The name Ellie May Clam Pit flashed in his mind, but he couldn't put a finger on where he'd seen a girl by that name.

"I finally found you," she said. "I'm Bertha of the Atlantic City Tribe. They sent me to find you. We need the Prophet's help."

"Have we made love?" John asked.

She looked familiar. *Raquel Welsh* was long dead, but they could have been sisters.

"No, but I was there when you preached in Rehoboth Beach. I came with my Tribe. We were on our way to Springfield until we got stuck."

"Stuck, that sucks. K-pasta, what do you want from me? I got shit to do. Come with me."

"I can't. You'll see. Come back with me and I'll fuck your brains out."

She batted her eyelashes.

"Nobody sent you to screw with me, right? You want me for real. I dig that. Let's do it right here."

She screwed up her face in frustration and blasted off.

"Look, OK I came on my own. The goddamn men won't budge. We found a bunker full of canned food and they won't leave unless you tell them, stubborn assholes. Besides, there's a roadblock. They won't leave the blessed trail and go around. They'll listen to you."

"I don't see how I—"

"You're the one that said we have to go to Springfield, that road too, and it's blocked. It's on you."

"No shit."

Yeah, it was on him. And, he wanted more people onboard. *What the hell, I got a look after my Tribe, right.*

"OK sister, tell me more."

She explained the situation. John was so enamored with her boobs he only caught half of it. She said something about a dragon upon the highway catching travelers on their way to Temple. The creature ate people and blocked the route. It had Guardsmen working with it.

It's not that hard to get around them. All he had to do was send her back to tell them to take the alternate route. The chick also talked shit saying he had to kill the dragon, or whatever it was.

That ain't happening.

Still, he figured he'd go along. Their camp wasn't far from The Way. *Why not get laid?*

"I'll tell them assholes to wake up, lead on Bertha."

She'll make love to me, for sure.

All the chicks wanted him since he became the Prophet. How could he refuse such a boner bonus? She was too hot to pass up. He would lose a day. *Not a bad trade for a sweet piece of tail.*

She set out at a good pace with her long legs churning butter. He dug her more and more as he watched her butt swing down the trail like a ringing bell.

38

Meeting the Tribe

The lady's hotness distracted him. He had a hard time deciding what he liked better, her ass or tits? Her rear was winning, but he should have paid closer attention to his surroundings.

"Hey, what's your name, man?"

"Bertha. I already told you. Men are so dense."

Walking ahead going fast, she crossed wild-country. Occasionally, she picked their way through crumbled, briar-infested towns while pushing directly northeast seeking the derelict Tappan Zee bridge.

Once over the bridge and onto the thruway, they would hit Springfield in no time flat—if there was still enough bridge left to cross. The last time he crossed there wasn't much left of it.

Climbing down the palisades would suck. Crossing the Hudson River was tricky. The river was shallow and shoaled in with deep mud and dangerous. The crossing would be more a slog than a swim. He didn't trust the crocodiles, either. They never bothered him but Tribe people were on the crocodilian menu.

"The bridge is the most direct way," he said.

"No shit," she said.

The roads were overgrown with asphalt-loving tall weeds, wild hemp, and young trees. It all had grown over the last three years. It was easier to travel inside old-growth forests. In open land, parting overhead weed stalks showed movement at a distance. Roads made it easy to detect Guardsmen but roads also make it harder to hide from them.

After a day's march and a night's rest, they reached a well-used deer path.

"This is it," she said, "goes up to an old National Guard compound."

"Cool man, so your people aren't far from the Tappan Zee."

"Not far, but Church-bots are all over the place. We better go quietly."

"I dig it, man. Good land here, not many ruins, where are we?"

"This was a game reserve or some such thing. I don't see any place to play games, whatever. We're under the east-west Parkway extension on the south side. That's what Grandpa Faithful says it was called. He's totally old. He was around when the government in Washing Machine declared marcher law."

"Marshall law."

"Whatever. Shut up, OK? The woods are safer but not that safe."

Midday they came to an open field two miles across and twice as long. Their path ran dead center. Many seed-bearers had gone this way. The compound wasn't visible but in the distance past the tree-line, spires of the old bridge shimmered in the warm sun. He made out cables. That was a good sign. Bertha wanted to go around way wide using the surrounding forest. But the clock inside his head was ticking down. It took a long while to convince her to go for it.

They set out at a fast clip. Halfway across, Guards moved toward them from opposite edges of the field. John increased speed and lost sight of them when the ground dipped lower. They couldn't see the weeds parting until they reached higher ground. The Guards were closing fast.

"Look at that," John said breathing hard. "If we went that way, we'd have gotten creamed."

"You're wrong. Fucking men. I didn't plan on walking the field's edge," she said launching forward.

"Once more Jerry was right," he said.

"Who Jerry? Saint Jerry?" She asked not even a little breathless while picking up the pace.

"I'm not sure. Somebody who's Gratefully Dead. He sang, 'Women are smarter, that's right, women are smarter, smarter than men in every way.' That's stuck in my head, man."

"It's Saint Jerry, alright. Finally, a man with a brain. Rare. Anyway, keep on trucking." She didn't slow as the terrain got rougher.

That Momma's a bulldozer.

The Guards were still closing. John felt doomed until Bertha hit a well-worn deer path. They jogged on at a faster pace. Guards weren't able to run well but they were coming from three directions. The sound of metal on metal and rattling ammo belts, like ironclad pit vipers, freaked him out. His jog turned into a flat-out run.

"We gotta get off the path," Bertha turned a 90 and plunged back into the reeds.

The field had narrowed, the woods were closer north and south on the east end. They arrived at the edge of the forest but John was wiped out. His chest felt like a hot bong hit. She wasn't even breathing hard.

She'll burn me out like a toasted bong screen in bed.

"Man, I got to rest."

"We're almost there."

"I can't, just can't," John's chest-blaze added lightning bolts.

She picked him up like a sack of corn and ran. Deep in the forest, she flopped him down into a depression thick with foliage behind a raised tuft of mossy grass.

They lay side-by-side on their stomachs under the ferns. He opened his mouth but she jabbed him in the ribs. The smell of the forest, the Earth's goodness, filled him with the peace of green air. He enjoyed Earth's smells, but by lying next to her he also breathed in her pheromones…his nature didn't call, it begged. He was about to cop a feel when two Guardsmen crashed through the forest nearby.

He stilled his heart. He had done it years before while hovering on death's edge after a nasty fall. It was like magic. He had risen out of his body and looked around like he was tripping without the acid and it was happening again. *I'll ask Mike and Gabe how this works.* He saw the Guardsmen but he couldn't hear anything.

There were two of them, brand spanking new and sharp, unlike the broken-down Church-bots he had seen before. They talked and checked their guns. They had many bullets draped on them. If the Guardsmen had looked down, they would have seen the trampled brush leading to his hideout. They stopped ten feet away, turned, and went back the way they had come. He followed until they were out of his roving-eye range.

"Hey wake up, wake up, don't tell me you're dead."

He snapped out of it.

"Far out…hey they're fresh, they got ammo and everything."

She popped up, grabbed his hand, and jerked him to his feet like some kind of Mountain Girl.

"You didn't hear a word I said. I told you about them. I've been telling you all along. Goddamn men never listen to me."

She ignored the path and he didn't argue. They zigzagged until she decided they were there and she took off out of the forest running hard. He ran after. It was a 100-yard sprint from the woods' edge across open grassland to a stockade gate which was made out of flimsy-looking corrugated galvanized sheets.

A cry went up. He ran like hell and caught up. The gate swung open ten yards before arrival. Bullets flew ringing the sheet metal. He and Bertha tumbled inside. The gate clanged shut. He rolled to his feet laughing.

"Them assholes can't hit the side of a barn. They ain't crack shots after all. Go figure."

Nobody else was laughing. The bullets that had hit the gate went through her first. She stood, one leg up, holding onto a rusted chain-link fence while the other leg bled. Blood also issued from a hole in her shoulder. The through-shot in her calf was the lesser wound but it had to hurt bad. Three good-looking young men rushed forward, put her on a stretcher, and hauled her off to a galvanized hut. Before he could shut his gaping mouth, Bertha was gone.

Getting laid ain't happening.

People gathered around him. Old people, a few kids, and many young men with exposed rippling muscles. Why so many dudes were there figured. *Bertha is stud-bait.* John felt like the dumbest rat in this trap. One dude looked like Dr. Kildare. John remembered that legendary chick magnet doctor. Kildare's face was in memory but not where or when he had seen it.

"Chicks always fall for the doctor." He said to Iggy but Iggy wasn't there. "Hey, wait a minute, this ain't a campsite. It's a fort."

The cement food bunker was intact, but the rest of the buildings were in shambles. They had stripped off the galvanized roof sheets and roped them together into a fifteen-foot-high barricade. They strapped metal sheets onto an existing chain link fence. The old rations center was also fortified with scaffolding inside the perimeter. Lookouts had clear shots. *These assholes aren't going anywhere.*

"What's with the walls?" He asked the nearest dude.

"It's for defense. We only have shotguns and twenty-two caliber rifles."

This Tribe had held on with hope, duct tape, and spit. *Guardsmen with fresh guns can shoot the shit out of this place.* What was this Tribe waiting for? It didn't add up. Time was too short. They can fix Bertha up later. He had to get them moving.

"Hey man, nice hangout, and all," John said, "but we got to boogie. We'll need to carry Bertha. The Temple calls. Get your shit together. We'll have to go around the long way."

An old man hobbled forward and the rest gave him room.

"Son, I'm afraid that's not possible. We must wait here, here is where we received the true Word of God."

"Hey man, I'm the Prophet. You sent Bertha for me, right. You dudes gotta go where I—"

"The Lord has spoken. We heard Her voice. It came from the forest. It came from the sky. Our redemption is beyond where the dragon waits. It is the only way. The sacrifice was made. The dragon will yield or die only by the Prophet's hand. That is God's promise."

"What the fuck?" John said.

Another old-timer perked up.

"It was ordained, to save us you must kill the dragon. It's what God requires."

"Man, I can't do that. I'm all about peace, OK. Guardsmen aren't living so it's cool to blast them, but man, kill a living animal. It's not a robot, right? Man, killing's not my thing."

"We may not leave this place until the dragon is dead. The Lord spoke it. You must sacrifice it."

"Dude, there is no lord. The Guards have a megaphone or something. This is bullshit."

"What is a megaphone," the first old man asked.

John couldn't remember. Sounded like the right answer. Mike could tell them. *I got to call the ship.* John reached for it, but he had given the communicator back to Mike. John's internal clock screamed. *Cross that bridge today or never.*

"OK, tell you what," John said, "I'll get you to the bridge. But you got to cover me, dig it? Keep the Guards off my ass. Saddle up cowboys, it's time to ride."

"The Guards never go east of this camp. The Dragon's abode is in that direction." The old man said pointing at the Tappan Zee. "The Church fears the dragon as we do. God says the Prophet must kill it."

The elders gave him few details beyond that the dragon lives on this side of the Hudson a mile from the bridge. John explained alternative ways to beat it. He shared how they could go around it, and get back on the road. Or go under it and climb down the cliffs.

"We don't need the Parkway to get to the bridge," John said. "We can climb down and cross." He pitched many ideas but this Tribe wasn't buying.

John got no affirmations. He had no time to screw around. He got along with reptiles. No kind of animal ever messed with him unless he stepped on it. He decided to go see the critter and figure something out. Kill it, no way. John didn't know a whole lot but he knew if he didn't get across the Hudson soon, he would miss his ride.

"A-OK, I'll go and talk to the dude. Get ready to roll. We got to get to the temple fast. Take Bertha on a stretcher."

On the word 'temple,' the Tribe's people shuffled their feet and looked at their toes. *They aren't up for it.*

"OK, fine, I'll kill the dragon already." He lied. "Get it together and come after me."

The oldest codger said, "The Prophet has spoken."

John took time to eat. He smoked a fatty while they told him the way. Nobody made road-going preparations. *They don't need much, it's only a couple of days walking.* Less makes better speed. He crossed the compound to the back gate with two dozen people following him, hot chicks among them, but not Bertha. They said the dragon talks.

Talk, hell yes. Kill it, hell no. I'll convince it to back off.

Reptiles always obeyed him. If anything, he would see his way clear and beat it on down the road. *If talking doesn't work, tough shit, this Tribe's on its own.* There was nothing for it but to keep on trucking.

39

Dragon Guard

John bugged out the back gate alone. He figured some of them would follow, at least a little distance, but that didn't happen. They pointed out a path through the woods going to the Garden State Parkway. He didn't go fifty feet before they shut the gate.

These bunker-assholes aren't moving.

A half-mile out, the woods gave way to a raised road. He climbed a grassy bank and stopped to look around thinking he might spot Iggy. There wasn't much left of the road although it was well-tread. For sure a lot of people had been on it. From the roadbed, he caught glimpses of movement on either side.

"Shit, them fuckers lied to me. Guardsmen both sides."

His idea to turn off the road and split wasn't happening. Going back was no use. They had him funneled in.

He picked up the pace and aimed straight for the dragon's hole, as the Tribe called it. Coming over a slight rise where the pavement had been pushed up, he saw why they called it a hole. The beast had a pit spanning two lanes filled with human bones—some with dried flesh clinging on. The monster lounged on top of a bone pile leaning against a light pole. I picked his teeth with a piece of re-bar. Gabe had said a lot of invited people didn't make it lately and John saw the reason.

The breeze blew and a stench smacked him. He fell to his knees and nearly lost his free lunch. Gaining control, he got back up on weak legs like a swaying drunk.

The dragon saw him. It raised itself, opened, and stretched its weird wings but it didn't fly. *Bat wings with feathers?*

It had humanlike arms and hands besides wings. Its body size was that of a big skinny draft horse with undersized hunches. It could pass for a museum dinosaur. The Smithsonian jumped to mind but he couldn't remember if they had bones. His memory was foggy but still, there had never been any such dinosaur recorded as that one. He had never heard of a velociraptor chicken with human arms and eyes.

"Dino chicken to the rescue! Buck, a buck, a buck." He laughed and laughed. Laughing blew away his fear.

"Ridiculous. A couple of well-placed bullets will take care of it."

That concept iced John's amusement. The idea of shooting it chilled his soul. Tribes don't have killing ability. The chosen were chosen because they weren't killers and he should have known. *Making me do their dirty work is a cop-out.* Killing it wasn't the answer. The damn thing was chained up. Anyone could walk right past it.

Where did it get people to eat?

"Come to me," the dragon called in a musical tone of voice.

"You're shitting me, right? Why would I do that?"

"Aren't you the sacrifice?" The dragon said.

It retracted and sat back. The sound of bones crunching gave John goosebumps.

"Oh, hell no, why would you think that?"

"Come closer and we'll discuss it."

"Get the hell out of here. You come here. You aren't my boss," John said.

The beast needed compliance. The light pole it was chained to was solid aluminum and cemented into the ground. If someone didn't feed it, it would starve to death.

It's a prisoner.

"You didn't catch them…dead people, did you?"

"They were sent. Frankly, I don't much care for the taste. But one must eat. I rather like sheep better. An occasional rabbit is nice. Duck is very good. However, what I crave at the moment are apples, I smell them. A balanced diet, don't you know, is best."

"Far out, man. I dig that."

The dragon moved off the pile of bones to the end of its chain and sat like a dog with its tail behind. There wasn't anything ferocious about it. John felt bad for it. The dude felt like a kindred spirit. The poor thing didn't know shit. John moved closer and sat cross-legged before it on the edge of the bone pile. It didn't reach for him.

"You know, you are the first American I've seen alive," the dragon said. "They always bring me dead ones. Back in Italy, I fended for myself. She let me roam as I pleased. Coming to America isn't working out. She lied to me."

"I see," John said. "How'd you get here, man? Why'd you come if you had it so good?"

"She talked me into it. I made a mistake, an error. I should not have trusted her."

"Her?" John asked.

"Pope Joan, she's looking for some religious leader. Someone whom she feels is causing the Church grief. I'm afraid I don't understand what the problem is. She locked me down here and, well you see how that is. Not to complain, but I don't care for it."

"If I let you go, are you going to eat me?" John asked but he didn't think it would. "Sorry man. Stupid question."

"Of course not. I smell apples, why would I eat you? It is fall is it not?"

"Dig it, man, that's right."

John unslung his pack. He had a set of lockpicks. Somebody named Abbie showed him how to pick locks a long, long time ago but he couldn't remember the face or the place. Picking locks became second nature after breaking into so many food lockers.

"A-OK, I'll set you free, man. First, promise you'll leave people alone. Maybe do me a solid and go get Bertha from the compound and ride her over to Springfield for me. She's wounded, can't walk. You cool with that?"

"Do this for me and I'll be forever indebted to you."

"Far out. The trick is; announce yourself like a god or something. But hey, if they shoot, take off. Forget it. There's no need to get your ass shot off. If you'd fly over at least, then they'll see you leaving. That'd be groovy."

"I will gladly deliver your message."

"It's a deal."

John moved to the hind leg and went to work. It was an old lock but a complicated one. The shackle was blacksmith made. Figuring out the mechanism took time. While John worked, he gave the dragon the low-down on the state of the world. The dragon was so new and young, he didn't know much but he was smart. John told him about how the Pope screwed America and dragons, too. The dragon got progressively pissed off. He wasn't mad at John or the Tribe people he was forced to eat. The Church was what got under his scales.

John got an earful in return. The Pope had engineered dozens of dragons like him. She made a new species out of dinosaur DNA, lizards and birds. Before the dragon was freed, they both had gotten an education. John felt the love. Cracking the lock took two informative hours. John and the dragon spilling their guts together made them fast friends.

Finally, the lock sprung. John pulled it out of the hasp and tossed it into the bones.

"There ya go, man," John said backing up to give him room.

The dragon stood, stretched his wings, and shook his stiff legs one at a time. The beast shed a tear.

"I don't know how to repay your kindness," the dragon said.

"Hey, it's cool man. Friends help friends, right? That's how it is supposed to be. Are we buddies for life or what?"

"Will you fly with me?"

"No, that's OK, man. I got shit to do. Besides, I don't like flying."

John lied. He loved flying but that chick needed an airlift. *They can fix her up on the moon for sure.*

"If you'd take Bertha that'd be a groove. But run if they shoot, OK."

"My kin and I will honor you always and until the very end of time!" It sprang into the air and climbed.

John called after it. "I'm holding you to that, man!"

The creature dipped a wing and flew off toward the camp. After it was out of sight, John gathered his tools and loaded them into his backpack.

"Time to get the flock out of here myself."

"You should have taken the dragon's offer."

John spun around. A skinny girl in blue jeans and a green poncho stood on the rise. A pair of Guardsmen wearing camouflage overcoats made tracks toward her from the woods and she didn't run. They stopped on either side of her. Even without the robes and funny hats, he recognized her.

"Pope Joan, goddamn it."

"Take him, boys. I want him alive."

One of the Guardsmen moved toward him. Its high weirdness froze John's feet. It had the lower half of a bear and walked oddly but with power. John snapped out of it and swiveled looking to run, but an ostrich-legged Guardsmen was on the other side of the hole. *Those bird-legged suckers can outrun anything in a straight line.* A zebra-legs dude moved along the woods blocking that way. That kind was fast, too.

"I'm fucked."

All three Guards were fresh, well-armed, and ready for war.

40

The Pope

The Pope's monsters took him southeast cross country toward the palisades and well away from the stench of rotting bodies. The Parkway wasn't in sight when they arrived.

At least the Tribe can split now. The way is clear.

The Guards lead him to a hole beneath a giant two-story-tall boulder. The Guards had recently ripped it out of the ground and pushed it uphill leaving a ten-foot-deep crater about twenty yards around beneath where that massive boulder had been. They stood him on the edge of the excavation.

The hole being new had no plants growing in it. The bottom was gravel, dirt, and dead leaves. The only shelter was a little cave under the boulder. An upright pole with wood piled around it had been placed at the center. A coiled rope lay there, too.

"Wow man, torch me and push the boulder onto my ashes. That's what I call overkill."

Joan put a hand on his shoulder from behind like an old friend.

"I hope you'll find your final resting place acceptable, big brother."

She pushed. He teetered on the edge.

"Brother? What the fu—"

John fell but landed well. He rolled and came up spitting leaves and dirt. His hair was full of crap. She stood on the edge looking down at him with her hands on boney hips.

"There can only be one Church—my Church."

He mustered his courage; it was that or shit his britches.

"Hey, man, this ain't necessary. My church is over, it's done, we're going... disbanding. Leaving altogether."

He almost spilled it. What would she do if she knew about the spaceship? Nothing good. He figured he had better delay her and give them time. The only weapon he had was his mouth. It worked on nice people, maybe she will listen, too. *Keep her talking.*

"I'll take the rest of your church out next, dear brother," she said.

"Hey, what's this brother shit? I don't get it? You're gonna have to explain that one."

"You don't remember Margo, your sister? How many times have you been dead? I've never died, but you left me for dead, you let them rape me. You abandoned me. Remember?"

"You're one crazy-ass bitch, man. I never had any sister, no way, but I, I..."

John flopped down on the ground with his mind worming madly. He had a bad case of I-can't-remember-shit. He had no memory before Calico except tiny bits and pieces just out of reach. The name Margo stuck in his throat.

"Sorry man, I can't remember. All I know is the cops picked me up in New York fifty years ago. I had amnesia."

This seemed to interest her. Her eyes opened wider and she put two fingers to her lower lip and pulled it down. She had perfect teeth. She fell out laughing.

"Oh, that is rich. You don't know, do you? You forgot our parents. You never chose your special friend. All that time ignorant. You don't know. You simply wandered around like a blank chalkboard for 150 years. Let me fill you in. We are siblings and you are an immortal."

"Get the fuck out of here, that's crazy!"

But in the back of his mind, it rang true. He was at Calico for two lifetimes and was forced to fake aging. A headache came on.

"How old were you when they found you, thirty maybe? How long ago? My records show you at Calico in the 2000s that's over seventy years. You know anyone else that doesn't age?"

Pieces clicked into place, snatches of memories he couldn't explain—things without context often played in his mind but rarely made sense. *And how do I know so many things without knowing how I learned them?* He had recited every song from the 1960s while preaching and right off the top of his head. *I can't be that old. That generation is a hundred years gone.*

Maybe she was right. His life span wasn't normal for sure, but why? Why did the aliens hire him and not somebody else? She had the puzzle pieces of his life in her hand. But she wasn't trustworthy. He wanted to keep her talking and not for the Tribe but himself. His need to find himself kicked in hard. Calico was all he knew of his past. The aliens said they would help him figure himself out. *So far, they haven't done shit.* This was the opportunity to untangle his life. Like at Bellevue, his livelihood depended on a crazy-ass chick.

He looked up squinting eyes at the sun. There was a family resemblance. His gut guggled. *Keep her talking, don't ask the wrong questions.*

"OK, dig it. If I'm immortal, how are you going to take me out? Keep me locked up forever in a hole? I could dig myself out with a toothpick in time."

Her childlike lips twisted like a snake.

Shit, wrong question.

"You don't know, do you? Too bad. I planned on making you suffer. Rubbing in every mistake you made but you can't know them. I haven't seen your book-keeper. You don't have one. You can't retrieve lost memories. They're lost. This is pointless."

"What in the hell are you talking about?"

"Mine are small," She held out her hand. It was crawling with spiders. She moved her hand close to her face, cooing to herself, watching the spiders. She turned to a Guardsmen.

"He hasn't got a familiar species. Look at him. He's ruined my fun. Is he not pathetic? Is he worth our valuable time, no? I am right, of course." She turned her back to the pit.

"I thought I did too much acid. Holy cow. What're you on? Lady, you're tripping."

She spun around like an unpracticed ballerina.

"You will die just as our parents died. Only two things can kill us, which are getting burned to a crisp or beheading. There's no point delaying it."

She backed away from the edge and he lost sight of her. He scrambled for a way out. The sides were loose but had enough roots for handholds. The big rock was climbable too. As soon as it got dark, he'd climb out and cross the river. He smelled water. The river was close. He could still make liftoff if he went like hell. The pit couldn't hold him for long.

"Take a leg."

Shots fired. One hit his leg, the same as they did to Bertha. He fell and rolled over. A bullet went through his calf. Not a death blow but walking anywhere wasn't happening.

"Good shooting." She said standing between two Guardsmen. One beast had a gun trained on him. Speaking to the Guardsmen she said, "I suppose we should shoot more holes in him, but don't kill him yet. He can't leave. We'll burn him alive tomorrow."

"Your wish is my pleasure," it said.

John didn't wait. He rolled under the overhanging rock and pressed himself as far back as possible into that shallow cave. Shots rang again. This time hitting the ground which kicked wet dirt into his face. John peeked when the zebra man stopped to reload. Two Guardsmen soon resumed fire. She encouraged them while squealing with glee like a demented Pop Warner cheerleader.

"That's enough. He's not leaving. Save the munitions. We still have plenty of… what do they call themselves? 'Saints of the Tribes.' We have many more heretics yet to kill."

Their shadows lay on the ground in front of him, elongated, bizarre figures. He dared not move. With flashing speed, a shadow overwhelmed the pit followed by a sickening thunk. The air roared. Clods of dirt and leaves flew in every direction.

A human head rolled toward him and stopped just outside his shelter. It may have been the Pope's head but he wasn't sure. He shimmied forward for a better look. Guns fired. Dirt kicked up.

She's trying to trick me.

He retreated. Furious thrashing sounded; guns fired. A war raged out of his sight.

A voice boomed, "I'll show you! Chain my brother, will you?!"

The sound of a sledgehammer hitting a side of beef came from the rocks above. His hiding place shook with the impact. Flesh sailed on a torrent of wind before him. John imagined a twister in a hamburger factory. The wind increased and he was forced to shut his eyes while he got pelted with dirt and wet gore. As sudden as it had come, the wind left.

"What the fuck!"

All went still. John lay there wiping crap away from his eyes. The first thing he saw was the women's head staring at him. He recited a calming mantra inside his mind not wanting to speak and give himself away.

He pressed in deeper and picked the dirt and leaves out of his beard. He was too afraid to do anything else. An hour of silence passed before he risked a peek. No sign of life. He rolled out of the cave. Daylight was nearly spent.

Shreds of dead Guardsmen were in the trees. Red flesh strips, arms, legs, torsos, human and not, hung like Christmas tree tinsel. John barfed. He heard tapping on the stone wall behind. The ass-end quarter of a zebra was wedged in a clef and still kicking—giant claws had raked open its flank exposing wires.

He spun around dazed searching, ignoring the pain of his wound. Nothing was left of the Guardsmen except fleshy pieces twisted with wires—red licorice and phone cables.

In the distant sky, several winged dinosaurs flew north. One with Joan's mangled body dangling from its talons. He looked away and down, horrified, and saw her severed head again. It wasn't a fake.

"Man, I'm gonna have a hell of a time making the rendezvous."

John found a spot on the rear wall he figured he could climb. He still had time to make it. He grabbed a root to climb with and it was well fixed. A shot fired.

John Doe fell over dead.

41

Ten Million and Ninety-Seven A.D.

"A reading from the Book of Answer's supplement."

The congregation said, "No shit."

Someone yawned. A few people laughed. Nobody took supplements seriously. The origins of these books were in question and likely did not come directly from the Ancestor's familiar, or so it was thought. The Red Books came from old mystics of the deep past before the people were properly civilized when writing was young.

The Librarian called for quiet. She opened Red Book number one; a book recorded before her generation.

This addition was a copy of a copy of a copy of a dragon's diary going back many generations before the Mass was codified and organized, and before the danger was understood. This one had an oral history long before it was written. The narrator was long dead, and whoever recorded this first was also unknown. Was it from a later narrator speaking vision, or was it an associate of the Ancestor recalled from the narrator's genetic memory? This book may have been written by a dragon that knew him. The idea was staggering.

Red Book readings were a fill-in tradition. Something must be read. Old books came out when new readings weren't available. The gathered whispered in disapproval; nobody wanted the old anymore.

"'I should have looked for him. He was my friend,'" the Librarian read the first line and handed the old, tattered book over to the Priestess.

A collective groan went up. The elders shushed the younger ones. Muddied, old, unqualified material was disappointing for the young. Youth requires the newest but the Librarian had nothing new. *What better reminder that our time is short?*

Once the people quieted the Priestess resumed.

She read, "'I should have known he was there. I kept the promise yet I failed him. Later, after my mission, I returned and dropped Joan's body on that pile of bleached bones from on high. I thought let the remains of the dead who sustained me received her. I winged forth into the world seeking more of the others of my kind. She insisted I call her Joan to make her a friend of mine. However, she was no friend of dragons. I paid her in kind for her hospitality. I went for John's girl and left her within walking distance of the temple before returning to despoil the body. Saving Bertha was the one promise I was able to keep.'"

"This was a reading from the Book of Answers supplement." The Priestess stepped back from the podium.

"You got that right, Skippy." The congregation said.

That was an odd response. The response was always spontaneous and never planned. In all of her 1100 years of service, the Librarian had not heard that line used in response. It was in the Book, she was sure of it, but here, like the reading itself, the Reading was out of context.

"'Strange times, indeed, honey,'" She whispered a John Lennon quote as the people exited.

The Librarian closed Red Book One and sat on a rock until the congregation had gone. This book was worn and needed to be copied again, but there weren't many scribes and they were behind.

"If things remain as they are, there won't be another reading from Red Book One." The Priestess said.

"Even so, in the morning, I will assign a scribe to rewrite it."

The Tradition must go on until the very end. She and her people sensed the cosmic wind changing. The Librarian felt sure this was the last Easter reading. The young ones won't mind, but if she was right, they will soon not have enough mind left to mind with.

42

The Last Guardsmen

He woke face down in a bed of dry leaves. Rolling over, the sun felt warm on his beaded face, and the air was pleasantly cool. *This feels like fall.* He sat up blinking. Big trees were overhead, red, gold, and orange blobs of color. He smelled the life inside them.

"Old trees don't forget old habits."

The younger ones were still green. The foliage reminded him of a word, Halloween, but he didn't know what it meant. A stream of memories rushed in but he could not hold them.

"What happened to summertime?"

His internal clock warned the temperature wasn't right. It was too warm. Halloween was a cold-weather word and it wasn't cold outside. He didn't know anything about where he was or how he got there but a million images and ideas flashed in his mind. The show slowed when a policeman accosted him inside his mind by saying, *'Nothing to see here move along, damn hippies.'* Then it was all gone.

"Far out, man. What a rush."

"You're back. It is nice to see you again John Doe." A rasping, whispering voice said.

John couldn't tell where the voice came from. His sight was still blurry but his ears were sharp.

"I killed you enough. Isn't it funny how I lost my desire for it?"

"What time is it?" John said wiping dirt and leaves off his face. He pulled a twig out of his hair. "Do I have to go to school Mom? Yes, Beaver, now drink your milk."

"It's November, late," the voice said. "You would have frozen years ago. It's warmer now. Funny how the trees don't know. Evolution is a slow thing but not always. Sometimes it's sudden. I know, I have witnessed it. It comes in waves you know."

Finally, his vision cleared and what he saw made no sense. A man was sitting on a rock above. His chest was naked with four blue bulges pulsing. His lower half was a zebra's rear quarter. John looked away. Another zebra leg, just bone, and hide, hung on the rock wall behind him. Nearby laid a bleached human skull nestled in blonde hair and leaves.

"Funny how clear I'm able to think. I was in a dream recently. It was myself a walking nightmare." The half-man laughed with deep wheezing. "Looking at myself, I must say, I am a living nightmare."

"What are you, holy cow?" John crawled backward.

"Hey, don't go. I won't kill you again. It doesn't work anyway. I'm lonely."

He dropped the rifle.

"Please come up. I saw things I want to speak of. I know many things. You should hear me."

John's curiosity heightened. This seemed familiar but why? He feared the hole more than the wounded creature. He felt a power within, stood, and jumped. He sailed twenty yards landing on the edge of the pit. The creature before him was horrible. It smelled of death. John stood shaking with fear despite the power that was on him. Yet he felt sorry for it.

"Hey man, if you know so much, who am I?"

"Why, John Doe, of course, prophet and wizard. And I, I am Doctor Zinno, or I was. Church astrophysics department. She didn't like my observations. I was right about the cosmic waves. For punishment, well…look at me. She sent me to kill you, you know, but that doesn't matter anymore. The cosmos changed me. I have my mind back for a little while."

"Far out, man. Whatever you're smoking can I have a hit?"

"That dragon came back and dumped her body which is moot. I don't think it saw you. Everything has changed. But I don't believe it changed the dragons. It's the wave, you know."

Zinno's perch sat near the lip of the hole under the shade of a tree. John took a few steps closer.

The creature was in very bad shape. Its remaining lower half was rutted with puss and rot. Where the animal leg had been torn away worms mingled. The upper human half was full of oozing sores. Wires and a rib bone poked through Zinno's skin where a claw had raked his side. How he was alive at all was a total freak-out. Ugly as Zinno was, John felt compassion for him.

"Shit, man. Can I get you something, water, food? Tell me where it is and I'll hook you up."

"That's not necessary. I'm, well, as far as I can tell, I run on fuel. I rather you sit with me. My end is at hand."

"No shit, man. I'll hang, but dog-gone, you got some stink going."

"That is kind of you. I don't know why she wanted you dead. You are a nice young man. I was not aware of that until recently. I suspect my brain was used as a control device. It is funny how I remember myself before she made me into this. There was a cosmic wave event, waves of energy we haven't seen before. I told her it will cause great harm. Radiation has all sorts of harmful effects. She didn't listen."

"Bummer, man."

John wanted to ask about himself. He didn't remember shit. But Zinno was dying and he deserved to have his last say. John figured it was better to shut up and let him talk.

"Cool, go on, man."

"I wanted to come back to America, and see Harvard once more but not like this. Harvard had been closed. Everything closed. Not enough population. There was a pestilence when I was human. It wiped out the urge to procreate for many… so many. Good people were never born."

The creature's head dropped to its chest and it rested awhile. John waited and watched it breathe. Zinno sounded hollow. John moved upwind and sat on the ground cross-legged. It didn't stink as bad there.

"Oh damn, will you look at that? The ape heart stopped," Zinno said. "Her lab put that one in for strength, all these hearts serve different functions. But you know what, that's a lie. She wanted abominations. Fear motivates like nothing else." He laughed with an echoing rasp. "I don't think that's true anymore. I have no fear, no fear of sleep, it's… it's beautiful. Angels know."

"Shit, man, cool. I think I saw angels once."

"They're out there…" He pointed at the sky.

Zinno straighten and watched something in the distance that wasn't there. John followed Zinno's line of sight and saw nothing but colorful trees and blue-green sky. Nothing moved except distant birds in flight. John didn't know anything about angels other than from old books. He knew about birds the same way. What he saw flying wasn't birds.

"Dang look at that, what are they?" John turned back to Zinno, but Zinno was dead.

John closed Zinno's eyes and laid the zebra-man on the ground and covered him with rocks. Bleached bones were scatted all around. *There must have been a terrible fight here.* He ignored those remains. He found a backpack that felt right, put it on and it fit. In a side pocket, he found a bag of pot that was loaded with seeds. The half-humans had carried packs too but they were filled with bullets. He managed to scrounge some canned food and a few other useful things. The animal people must have carried supplies for regular people.

It was late by the time he got his shit together, but John wanted to get away from the stink. North the woods had weird, tall, and thick trees. He went east until reaching a wide river below hundred-foot cliffs. He climbed down and hiked south along the riverbank.

A long-legged lizard knee-high, with black rings around its eyes like Egyptian mascara, joined John's march. It had black lines running down the sides of its mouth and under its eyes. John was glad for its company and named it *Alice Cooper* for no particular reason.

They followed the river on and on. Once it got too muddy, he went by way of an inland deer path. He traveled south until the cliffs disappeared and a wide river delta laced with marshlands spread out. He knew it was called Meadowlands; he didn't know why. There was no easy way around the marsh.

Clams and crabs the size of watermelons scurried everywhere in between flightless ducks and walking catfish. They didn't retreat when he approached. *Meals everywhere.* He made camp in the woods on high ground just off the edge of the wetlands and stayed a hundred years. It was an excellent place to grow weed.

Alice brought back whatever it caught like the lizard needed permission. *That's some lucky shit.* Alice loved playing fetch.

Things were going great, nice and quiet until village people out fishing found him and started regular visits. He didn't mind. The village called South Orange had some hot chicks although they had a weird name for a place without any fruit trees. The girls were juicy, and willing, for sure. People traded him stuff for singing songs. The songs were cool but he didn't write them. Someone named Jerry wrote them. Whatever he remembered about Jerry, he shared and they scratched the songs of Jerry into the trees.

Life was easy but something was missing. No matter how much dope he smoked, or how many mushroom trips he took, he just couldn't remember anything about himself.

One day John Doe packed up and headed west zig-zagging north and south on a mission to locate a mystical place called San Francisco. He traveled as the spirit moved him. He thought to find San Fran, but *California Dreaming* didn't work out. The word "further" popped into his head often on the road. But the farther west he went the less he learned. In a place called Jane, the jungle got too thick to go on. Thus, after one hundred and thirty years he turned around and headed back the way he had come.

43

Five Thousand A.D.

Chief Bongwater sat upon his wicker throne. The seat had been woven out of magic weed taken from the Meadowlands. He stole this weed behind the Seer's back. What made his chair special was that the hemp it was made from had not been given, rather, he absconded it. That Bongwater was able to accomplish this without the Seer's knowing was a feat worth praise and that was why the Tribe voted him Big Chief Mucky Muck in the first place. Bongwater's position wasn't secure.

He had heard his Great-Great's saying, 'people don't vote on facts, they vote their emotions.' Where Great-Great got that from, was anyone's guess, but it sounded right. It could have been tree-written. Other such sayings came directly from the Seer quoting his ancestors.

Stealing that weed was far out. The chicks dug it.

"That was no chin off my nose."

Flower Face, the Head Momma, was a shoo-in. She should have been elected. *She is wise.* She grew the most righteous weed. Her weed was what got the Seer to move into E-Orange in the first place.

Singlehitter, Bongwater's son, approached. Bongwater had set his chair out in front of his love shack. The thatch got old and stunk up the place. Bongwater was too lazy to fix it, but as the Mucky Muck, he could get others to do it. The women were always looking for something constructive to do. *They'll form a committee. Lord Jerry knows why.*

"Oh, hey Daddy-o," Singlehitter said walking up.

"Son, I'm the Mucky Muck. Man, knock that shit off. Address me right."

"Screw that. Anyway, Flower Face got an impeachment committee together. They're going Nixon on your ass. And they're right behind me."

Singlehitter pointed a thumb over his shoulder.

"There're in the tee-pee smoking up. You better toke while you can."

Bongwater, taking that good advice, stood to get a pipe out of his jean's pocket. Over his son's shoulder, vapers poured out of the smokehouse. Before he could pull his peace pipe, the tent's door flap opened, and out came Flower Face followed by a bunch of her fuck buddies. They had been doing more than smoking. Flower Face was naked except for face paint. She marched right up to the Seat of Weed.

"Bongwater, you're an A-hole and everyone knows it," she said as her crew of men and women gathered around. "Stealing from The Seer Man is cool, ya know, but that doesn't make you any good. Men suck at leadership. We got to move south. You don't have the balls to get it going. We should have left already. That's no bullshit."

"So, what?" Bongwater said. "It doesn't get that cold here. There's plenty of food all winter. Why should we leave?"

"Man, are you shitting me? We need veggies. You want cricket legs?"

"That's an old wife tale. Besides, old wives aren't that smart. I say it's better to stay and I say I'm smarter than you. So, we do what I want. Can you dig it? The smart one, that's me, gets to choose. I'm the Great Decider. Let me think a minute, will ya."

The small crowd of Flower's supporters shifted uneasy leg to leg. Many were clothed for travel. Bertha even had her tits covered. It was getting cold. Pretty soon they'd have to wear a lot more to stay warm. He thought wearing clothes was better than walking down to Mary's Land. Bongwater liked fancy clams but he didn't like them enough to walk a hundred miles.

Flower didn't wait long and spoke up, "Your plan sucks. Besides, I'm smarter than you. I can prove it."

"Bull poop, go ahead. I stole His weeds, right? That takes brains. I got the smarts for that. I got the smarts to decide and I say we stay this winter."

Flower Face called out to Mary Prankster, who stood by the smokehouse. "Go on let him out."

Mary beckoned to someone inside. The Seer himself stepped out and he was wasted. *They must have gotten him to smoke Silly-Head.* He staggered and danced and twirled around no doubt hearing music inside his head. In the way-back, there used to be music concerts. It was said that The Seer can hear the ghosts of The Dead playing.

Everyone gave him room to let him dance himself out.

Bongwater wasn't sure if he was The Seer or not. Nobody of Bong's old Tribe had seen him in years. *Maybe this ain't phony baloney, but maybe it is.* The man was tall, too tall. He had a long beard, long hair, and was skinny. *He's got Levis and a flannel shirt.* All anyone ever found were scraps of clothes. Bongwater's cutoffs-of-power were passed down for 300 years and they looked it. The tall guy's clothes were fresh.

"Mary, walk him over here before he falls off the cliff," Flower called.

The Seer danced his way over with Mary pushing him. He gyrated before the new mayor in a trance. Nobody else got that high on purple buds and this guy was tripping his balls off.

Bongwater was caught. He had no choice but to hear the Prophet. No time to set up a protest march. The rest of the Tribe closed in. The Seer, already blitzed, was ready to pontificate.

"How's it hanging man?"

"It's hanging," Bongwater responded as was proper, but his tone was dour.

"So, man, what's happening? K-pasta."

All the ladies shouted out the big question together.

"Who's smarter, men or women?"

The Seer gyrated and danced. His fly was open and his big weenie flapped. Everyone formed a circle. Somebody beat the drum. Another lady hit a tambourine. Everyone clapped in and out of time until it all came together in one beat. The Seer's dancing and whirling stopped. Then he sang from the Book of the Grate Dead.

"'That's right women are smarter, that's right women are smarter, that's right women are smarter, smarter than men in every way...'" He continued singing Dead Songs for quite some time.

The Seer finally finished his songs and grabbed his junk. "Hey man, I gotta take a piss." He wandered off.

"Shouldn't someone keep an eye on him?" Mary Prankster said. "Remember last time he got drunk? He almost jumped off a cliff."

Bongwater wasn't with this Tribe back then. His people hadn't seen The Seer in a lizard's age but these chicks said The Seer visited them all the time. That was why Bong relocated in the first place. The Seer was all about the best weed and Bong wanted some.

"I should follow him." Mary Prankster said.

"Naw," Mary Jane replied. "He's The Seer, right. He doesn't like followers. He knows his shit. Let's get on with the pow-wow."

The Seer staggered off into the woods.

"He must have drunk a shit-ton of go-go juice on top of that bud," Bongwater said.

The impeachment continued. There wasn't much to debate. Bongwater had no defense. Everyone heard what The Seer said. There had been men in charge lots of times before, but this came off like a major pronouncement. In the back of Bongwater's mind, he agreed with The Seer mostly because he didn't have time to get high before the proceedings. He would have put up a better fight had he been stoned.

The writing was already on the tree trunk, as the saying goes. Men did make shitty leaders. It didn't take long before he conceded. Bongwater removed the Tribe's only pair of cutoff denim shorts and handed them over to Flower Face.

Flower Face held the Cutoffs-of-Power high and cried, "Far out man!"

Everyone responded as was proper, even Bongwater. He got caught up in the moment, too. They cried together as one. "No shit!"

The next day everyone was busy packing to truck south. Nobody had much because that was the way of The Way. Material objects weren't cool. The Tribe will hit the road as soon as everyone had their shit together.

Bongwater had time so he made up a package of blue bud wrapped it in banana leaves for The Seer. He went to where The Seer was sleeping it off in a ravine under a cliff. He stuffed it into the sleeping Prophet's top pocket.

"Dumbass fell off the cliff again."

The Prophet looked dead but that was a crazy idea. The Prophet can't die and everyone knew it. His head was bloody. *Shit happens. He'll get over it.*

"That go-go juice must have been pretty far out."

Flower said they were going to Floor-a-dope this year and maybe they weren't coming back to E-Orange anyway even if they did come back north. She said the food was doper in South Jersey Land.

The Seer was out cold and Bongwater felt bad that nobody would be around when he woke. It was a good thing that The Seer wasn't alone. His pet, a daddy long legs lizard called Longlegs Peach Fuzz, and a big land turtle were hanging tight. *The Seer's got protection.* Leaving was cool.

"You can't remember shit after drinking like that. Sucks for him." Bongwater said to the lizard. "I think somebody needs to do something."

He rejected the thought. He didn't have to think.

"I ain't the Mucky Muck no more. No hair on my knee."

He carved a message into a living tree's bark addressed to John Doe to tell him where they were going. Writing on trees with knives was an old tradition. Nobody gave writers shit about it. Defacing Mother Nature was a sin but this wasn't that. Trees absorbed words; they eat them. Words sunk in after a while and disappeared.

The sky was clear of clouds and not a dragon anywhere. And the sky's regular pink hue had a touch of mint green in it today, and that was a good sign. The sun felt warm. Flower was right. It was a glorious day to start trucking south.

44

Five Million A.D.

He tried to stay out. Every time he felt The Waking coming on, he forced himself back into the comfort of his abyss where he watched snippets of memories and tried to make sense of them. Always in his head, a little voice implored, "you got to find yourself, man." He was sick of it.

Only in his dreams did he have a chance of knowing himself. Only there, did he escape the longing.

This time, half-awake, he heard something: A girl humming *Smoke on the Water*. Her voice gave him a woody. He let one eye open anticipating casual sex with the chicks at the Farm. But the Farm faded...*lost it*.

Maybe the chick is real. My pecker sure is. He sat up.

He was covered in dust. Pushing back his hair made crud fall into his eyes. By the time he cleared it off, she was gone. The vault's door was left open a crack. He had light but his sight was fuzzy. *Normal vision takes a while.* He laid his head back closing his eyes.

He wanted to see that chick, or was she a dream? *Maybe not.* It had to be another dream. *But you can't smell anything in dreams.* He sat up again. After a lot of blinking fresh flowers appeared out of the fog all around his bed.

"Wow, that's rad, man. Somebody cares. Flower Power."

He had recently woken to find flowers. But he thought it wasn't real at the time and rolled over. This time it wasn't a dream. Just before waking, he was backstage at a concert, and *Smoke on the Water* wasn't playing. He squinted trying to recapture that show but it was gone.

He opened his eyes with clear vision.

"Oh fuck, reality. What a drag, man."

This wasn't a subway concert. It was his suicide crypt. He had made it himself under an old collapsed onramp of the Garden State Parkway. He forgot which exit. Things were still fuzzy. Things he knew just before he died weren't slipping away as fast as before.

"I wasn't dead this time."

Just before this sleep-death period, there was a feast with lots of chicks. He screwed his brains out, smoked a ton of pot. Everybody said goodbye. He didn't hear his name. He didn't know their names. Who were they? Come to think of it, he didn't know who he was, either.

"This is bullshit, man."

He swung his legs out of bed with a puff of dust. His final resting place was a pile of furs on a raised platform. His bedside end table held fresh flowers. He opened the table's drawer. There was a joint there and a Zippo lighter. The lighter was a WWII relic he knew but he didn't know how he knew it. He levitated the joint with a thought, lit it with a finger, and took a deep hit.

"Wake and bake, man. Groovy."

He sat on the bed's edge smoking and getting his bearings. The raised scallop trim on the table's edge rang a bell. Sliding a finger over the trim made a memory flash go off. He blew some of the dust off the table for a better look.

"Wow, man. Philadelphia Federal period game table. For sure."

Black and gray dust coated everything so he didn't know what everything was. A ray of light lit another table's chrome leg below a cover. There was stuff piled on it under a tarp. Stiff, he hobbled over there doing his best to avoid stepping on his beard. His sight improved by the second.

"Man, I'm stoned. That was good shit." He lifted the cover a little. "Formica kitchen table, circa 1950, far out."

The image of a woman making a peanut butter sandwich on *Wonder Bread* flashed in his mind.

"Man, I've got the munchies."

Yanking the canvas off that table sent up a big cloud. A pile of scrolls and books appeared as the dust resettled. He couldn't read their dirty covers. He wiped off the topmost book. It was a composition notebook such as school kids used. He didn't know how he knew that—was it something from his dreams? He moved into better light and opened it. Pages cracked off at the edges. Whoever wrote it knew to only write in the middle where paper lasted longer. The hand-writing was faint but familiar. He read.

Hey man, if you are reading this you aren't dead. I tried again but it didn't work. You are me and all this other shit in here you wrote, too. I'm your book of answers. You don't know who you are, right man? You are John Doe.

"Dude, no way! Dreams aren't real. Wow, I must have done a fuck load of acid. Chill out, man. The Pranksters doused everybody again. It's cool, your cool..."

He hobbled toward the light's source. Cracks in a barn door were what lit the place. He pulled the door open. The outside wasn't familiar. He sat on the nearest stump. The place was on a patch of high, dry ground in the middle of a wide marsh.

A road came up out of a lake a mile to his right. South, no sign of that road. A wide raised footpath led west into a dense forest.

Foggy conditions screwed up his perspective and he couldn't tell how far the woods were. His nose worked better. He smelled salt. An ocean was nearby. He turned back toward the ocean and his door.

Two carved log totem poles, badly weatherworn, were on either side of his rough-plank door. Above the entry, a sign read, Grand Wizard. The totem poles had sculptures of lizards, snakes, and birds with depictions of him in between. Each section had him in various states of hair and beard. Lower, there were no carvings. Top to bottom each successive carving was progressively cruder. No two logs of this stacked barrel column were from the same hand or tree…or time.

"How the hell did they do that?"

He went back inside to find out, but first, he opened the interior's window shutters. The windows were pieces of concrete sewer pipe penetrating the earthen sides of the structure and were stuffed with leaves, vines, and dirt. He pushed that crap out with big heaves. He was as strong as a bulldozer.

The roof and one side were cement; the remains of an overpass. He didn't know how he knew that. The rest was rammed earth mixed with tires and logs except the front was made of rough wood planks. It only took a short time to open things up and shovel out the dirt as he had *Superman* strength. He worked at high speed until his power faded.

"Not one spiderweb anywhere, good."

He hated spiders and they hated him: That much he remembered, and wildlife didn't mess with him. Before long small lizards and a couple of cat-like lizard things and flightless skin-birds were clamoring underfoot. He liked them but they were a hassle. He shooed them all out except one small lizard with google-eyes.

He picked it up and said, "Man's best friend."

The little creature bobbed its whole body up and down.

"Wow man, you're from New Jersey. The Pine Barrens. How'd you get here?"

He placed it on a table.

"Where is here? I wish I could remember better. I was there once, I think."

Names and places popped into and out of his head without context and faster than he could grasp.

"Man's best friend? Pine Barrens? What's a New Jersey anyway?"

He took a book off the pile. The cover said "Wake Up Instructions by John Doe." On the first page, he told himself to check the time. There was a special hourglass under the bed sitting on a wooden track just off the floor. He pushed the flowers away and found the clock.

The notebook said the sand count of each glass spans five hundred years. It still had sand on top. He had slept 300 years. On closer look, there were places on the rail where it had been before. The dust was deeper on the far end. Somebody turned it over a shit load of times moving it from one end to the other each time they turned it over. He counted the places. That timer had been moved dozens of times.

"No shit, that ain't real. I need to get high."

There wasn't any more pot there. He had smoked the only joint. He yanked flowers off the plant in the big bowl and sniffed. More of the same plants were in a tall, skinny stone jar. The stuff in the bowl smelled like weed, alright, but it didn't look like any pot he had seen before. He took a deeper sniff. *It's pot alright.* He ate a bud. It tasted right.

"Skunk, man, that chick set me up righteous."

His bong was where he wrote he left it. There wasn't any water in it. The lake was nearby but he wasn't up for walking after his power burned out. He smoked it dry. He didn't have an urge to hurry. Time didn't matter. He smoked and leafed through the pile of books between hits. Mostly it was just bits of his dreams. But they ended or began weirdly like the guy was working something out. The dumbass didn't explain much. *Like why write this shit down?* An idea struck him like ringing a bell.

"Man, you're looking for yourself. You got to find yourself."

What he had written was bits of his past. But none of it made sense compared to what he saw. He knew Bucks Country was a real place but that place didn't exist anymore. *How'd I even figure out I'm millions of years old anyway?* That's what the book said. It said a lot of bullshit.

"I must've been tripping my balls off when I wrote this shit." He picked up the lizard. "Hey little dude, was I tripping or what?"

That wasn't the answer. Books don't get covered in dust overnight. Smoking and searching his mind, he knew all kinds of things about archeology, the city of Troy, King Tut, Nazca, and Calico. He was there once. But that was old shit and not in this time.

Where is my time?

"I got nothing, man. What do you say, little dude?"

The lizard didn't answer. He didn't know why he expected it to.

"I'm a dumbass."

John Doe lit a *Colman* lamp and took the reclining chair. There he read deteriorated books late into the night until falling asleep. He had a night of regular sleep and not a dead sleep.

***

"The Ancestor has awakened," Mother said waiting at her tent flap. Her man-servant backed away, as was proper.

Mother thought He might soon wake; the signs were ripe. Sunshine was elected The Sacrifice this month. She was prepared for sex like all the generations before her, but the teaching didn't take with her. She did the required and brought fresh flowers, smokables, and she had worn flowers laced into her hair. It was her vigil and her job to look sharp. She rolled the joint herself. But when she saw him stir, she lost her mind and ran.

The young don't believe in the legends. They question tradition as youth will.

"Oh, they will believe now."

Sunshine hadn't paid attention at catty-kiss-him school. She wasn't the right type for this. *Sunshine is not what's needed.* She failed to study. Mother did study and it paid well. She eventually became the keeper of stories. She was elected Executor of His Will for good reason.

Sunshine ran back to camp singing the reptile antidote. Everyone hated that song, but it was better than getting eaten by gators. Mother Momma Cass Elephant had heard Sunshine coming a mile off. Sun entered the forest's edge screaming the song. Mother was at her flap waiting when Sunshine ran up with her tits heaving and threw herself at Momma Cass's feet. The child confessed all she had seen.

"And why did you not wash him, welcome him. Did he have a woody?" Mother asked.

"Yes, but, but Mother, it's huge! And he's a dead man! Dirty, too. And so strange."

"Not anymore child. Go and tell the people. We must make ready and greet him with honor. He is the founder of our race."

"But he's a man?"

"Nonetheless, he is a special one. He is not like Jeeves. He has a good stoner brain. Now go."

Sunshine ran off like her hair was on fire as the old saying goes. But there was no reason to hurry. It was written: When he wakes, he wakes slow. The stories say he was useful. He keeps the dragons and gators away. He can control them with his magic voice. He will remove bad reptiles when treated well. Give him girls to fuck and weeds to smoke and he will conjure things out of the past for his Tribe, strange things, things like what was inside his chapel. He had desirable things.

"Meet his needs and he will share his boon."

All well and good if true but Mother did not know. Old stories were just that whereas only facts mattered. A woman must be logical. The best way to learn the truth was by way of a welcoming committee. Mother was required to provide him with a party.

"'Food, dance, and weed,' that's not it. 'Sex, drugs, and rock and roll.' Something like that."

Her man grunted.

There was more to that old saying. She was missing a phrase. *I'm remiss in my studies.* Most of the lore was kept in the old hippie language. Many words taught to students weren't understood by them.

"Party hardy. Yes, that is it."

The quote was one part of the incantation. But there was more. Something to do with 'Peace, love, and understanding.' It came from the *Fifth Dimension Album*, whatever that was. Grandmother Bongmaker would have known but she had died too soon. Mother never did get the whole story.

The greater part of the people went up-tree many generations ago. The masses who lived in the canopy took the best stories with them. Mother's group was the last Watcher's Clan and she wished to be free of the vigil. Retirement to Bricktown was but a dream. She and her group were in constant danger on the ground.

The Tribes won't visit here. Mother had not seen her sister in forty years.

Until the Holy Hippie releases us, an exodus isn't possible. She went inside to ponder it and find a way.

A man-servant came at dinner time with leaves, fruit, and a roasted bird. Even he, as dumb as a mushroom, knew something was afoot judging by his service behavior. Having eaten, Mother sent him to call on each house with a message.

"Go and tell each house we will go to chapel in the morning. Make ready." It was a simple message. "Please don't screw it up." She pinched his ass.

Men were not smart but without them, there would be no children. *Perhaps that's the Prophet's main function.*

Mother didn't know his true purpose. All the lore said the same thing about John Doe: He loved sex far more than what was natural. He was said to be non-seasonal. There will be no need to ply him with a strong drink.

It was said that John Doe is a good egg. His offspring, going back thousands and thousands of years, were groovy. Few of his direct descendants lived but Mother's Tribe was still connected. Her Tribe was known as the grooviest.

John Doe had spawned her peace-loving Tribe. But, she of his line didn't accept mindless peace. Peace depended on security. Survival was her top priority. *What good is a dead Tribe?* To her, peace was conditional, and the conditions weren't good.

She bent her mind on finding a way out.

45

Morning Sunshine

John Doe woke in the morning clearheaded although he had read books half the night. He forgot what he had remembered before he woke. He did learn a lot by reading, though.

"I'll have to check it all out, confirm it." He said to his little lizard. "I wish *Linda Lovelace* was here man, this shit's hard to swallow." He had a picture in his mind of a girl giving oral, but he had no idea where that came from.

The book said he could resurrect things from the past. It had to do with transmuting himself out of time, grabbing stuff from the past, and coming back. He couldn't stay in the past. He never did find his past in the past. But it was an easy way to get what he needed. He had written how he found buried places. He had gotten his bong out of a head-shop down south in Toms River.

He set aside the book in his lap.

"Book of Answers, my ass. I must have been tripping when I wrote this crap."

He was hungry and decided to try it anyway. He walked around with his hands out until sensing something. He sat cross-legged on the spot and chanted, "om, om, om." Like the book said.

He appeared in a Jersey Mike's sub shop and ordered a twelve-inch meatball with a bag of chips. The chick there was hot and she dug him. He reached for the sandwich while checking her out and woke with something hot in his lap. He expected a woody but had a sandwich instead.

"That tears it, this ain't real. Too much acid, man."

The lizard bobbed in agreement.

"I'll call you Owsley."

The food tasted real. He ate and watched as a procession of people march slowly toward him from the west. The road was full of puddles and reptiles. As they got closer, he heard them singing *Smoke on the Water*. Big alligators, little frogs, and a snake the size of a Volkswagen slithered out of their path. He didn't blame them critters. *That song sucks.* He always hated it.

"At least it ain't *Free Bird*."

He swallowed the last bite as they closed in. There were thirteen women wearing body paint which was more like mud than paint. Two men holding fans made from big leaves shaded the two old mommas. Everybody was wearing dreadlocks. He liked the look of them until they got close.

"Wow, man a bearded lady?" He called before they got too close. "I'm going back to bed. Come back later!"

John shooed them away with hand gestures. The group left. He picked up a lizard and held it in his hand.

"Man, they got some ugly ass chick around here. I still smell them."

He turned around, went inside, climbed into his easy chair, smoked a joint, and drank way too much beer. His place was right on top of a 19th-century pub. He took a snooze and dreamed about that time he made it with this super hairy Italian chick in the back of a technicolor school bus.

46

Meeting the Ancestor

The women gathered around the fire. The men stood behind.

John Doe's reaction was not unexpected. He had rejected Mother's predecessors upon first contact in the past but later accepted them. Mother Momma Cass Elephant Flower Sky, etc., etc., was a woman of long lineage, and as such, she was Head Momma. She gathered the Tribe together, eleven sacrifice women, a couple of spare old-farts such as herself, and two breeder studs.

"Let us meditate, prepare your hearts." Mother said.

It was Mother's duty to keep the Sleeping Ancestor's abode in order. One hundred years she waited for his full awakening. She used to think it would be exciting. Old age told her the risks of ground-living outweighed her duty.

The Ancestor had revived briefly several times before Mother's enlistment. On each occasion, he had smoked the magic weed, had sex with the sacrifice, and went right back to bed. Mother herself was a product of this. The rest of them there were more distant relatives. Her line had provided for the Ancestor from time out of mind.

"He never blew us off with such distaste in all of recorded history." The Second Momma said after a short silence.

"A sex slave must be provided, I get that. But what about the dragon captive?" The senior fuck-bunny asked.

"With John Doe up the gators will stay away from our village. John Doe is said to draw reptiles to him like death draws vultures." Mother said.

That doesn't solve the dragon problem.

With the Ancestor around her predator deterrent won't be needed. Keeping it alive took a lot of work. She had no choice. She had to kill the dragon. Dragons don't die easily. *First things first.*

"You have heard what this month's Top Chick saw. Do you know its meaning?" Mother said.

The young women were a new batch and not yet fully instructed. The older sacrificial chicks had served and retired. No one answered.

"Anyone, anyone, have a clue what this means?"

"No Momma," they said.

The old breeder, an excitable male spoke out of turn.

"He's gonna fuck the shit out of you chicks!"

"Watch yourself, Ringo," the Second Momma said.

Moon Face was in charge of the men. Mother wasn't one to micromanage. *Let Moon do her thing.* Ringo Rock Hudson wasn't done pontificating.

"Hey, I'm not stupid. I know what gives. I'm as smart as you bitches are."

He was wrong, but men were getting smarter. Moon started building up rage by slapping herself in the head but Mother had no time for emotional bullshit. She put the ka-bosh on it and stood raising her long arms.

"This isn't the time for a protest rally. Let us sing a saying of the Great Dreadful Dead."

Sayings of the Dead were the traditional start for meetings. Mother chose a tune that put men in their place and soothed the chicks. She started singing. Everyone knew it. The chicks joined in.

"'That's right women are smarter, that's right women are smarter, that's right women are smarter, smarter than men in every way.'"

Ringo backed up scratching his ass. Of course, he smelled his fingers. *That's what men do.* The other male, Bob Dill-hand, smelled Ringo's fingers, too. After the song, the women sat.

"There is no easy way to say this. You chicks haven't finished orientation yet." Mother said. "The Ancestor wakes for sure. He will not sleep again for generations. One of you must be his sex slave until you get knocked up. I know this is strange."

The girls swigged their asses and started talking all at once. Everyone liked sex, in season, but they didn't know what they were getting into. John Doe had a huge dick and he will use it all the time. Mother skipped over that part. *I'll walk that branch later if necessary.* The chatter quelled.

"We have a big problem," Mother said.

Everyone became still.

"Our ground-based weed crops have failed, as you know. There isn't much left. There's no time to go up to treetop and resupply. He is going to be pissed when we run out of weed."

Mother let that sink in. The girls grumbled. Pissing off a man wasn't a concern normally. Nothing normal counted. The crocks were dangerous but avoidable. A huge pissed-off hippie with a big swinging dick could become a reoccurring nightmare. But nobody knew how he would react as the weed never failed before. Lore stated the only thing John Doe liked more than pussy was weed.

"The dragon prisoner must be killed. The Ancestor will keep the reptiles off us instead." Mother said. "We won't need dragon-stink anymore. The dragon cannot be let go. It will bring back others. They'll take revenge. Dragons don't let shit slide."

This set off a wave of chatter. People feared the ground, but they feared dragons more. Only John Doe's relatives could live on the ground and tolerate dragon-stink. John Doe's Tribe was braver, smarter, and more adaptable than other clans. It was the Mime Tribe who discovered dragon-piss repels predators.

The new-bees didn't yet learn of the perplexing issue: John Doe loves reptiles—the people's natural enemy. *And he hates violence.* What must be done won't be cool with him.

"Once he learns we have an intelligent reptile chained, all hell will break loose. He's a peacenik. He'll be outraged." She shuddered thinking of it. Stuffing down important information made it worse.

"Are you OK, Momma?" Flower Paddy asked.

"Fine, just a chill," She made a show of wrapping her hemp shawl tighter. "Now quiet please, girls. I must think on who will be the sacrificial fuck-bunny."

The girl on duty won't do. It's time to break with tradition. What's worse? Breaking dogma or letting one of my girls get fucked to death?

She didn't know what he might do without weed. Nobody knew. Legend, history, and rumor had blended into myth. The rule book gave only one way out.

Ask him to release us? It has never been done before.

Killing the dragon was an awful prospect. *If John Doe releases us we can leave it to starve.* She assumed he will stay home until the dope runs out and that gives them time to climb.

This idea Mother dared not share. Another idea came. The young ones didn't yet know hippie language other than a few words. She and Moon had not taught them much of it yet. The chicks only understood basic hippie-speak.

I'll use that.

"Betty Bang-Bang, you will go first. Make yourself ready. Tomorrow we go back for a second try. Tomorrow we sing the wake-up song. Pray the tree he's in a good mood. Ladies, go about your business."

The girls went to their huts and cookfires. There were chores to do. The dragon needed to be fed as well. Moon momma stayed with Mother until no ears were upon them.

"I see your mind," Moon said. "I am of it. The ground oppresses. We must go to tree else we lose our humanity."

"Then you will not tell. He may be the Ancestor, but he is a man and men are controllable. I will convince him to let us go."

Moon laughed. "They don't know hippie-speak. The young will not hear our sleight-of-hand."

"Or why Betty is chosen. Her tail stub has grown quite long."

Both women laughed.

Mother Momma Cass hated tails. Intelligent women knew them as a disgusting primitive feature. Cutting off one's tail was instituted by John Doe himself long before she was born. Mother Cass supported that old tradition. But then again, she didn't mind using a failure of tradition to get her way. Very few women were able to regrow their tails and the least able to regrow were his relatives.

Betty was the one in a million exception Mother needed.

Mother had stepped in shit with Betty Bang-Bang. Home Tree was no longer so far away.

47

The Dark Ages

He didn't deep-sleep last night, rather he fell into a light dream-state whereby his mind poured over ideas as his body rested. He considered what he had read. The book's titles were foremost on his mind. As dawn broke, he blew the dust off another volume.

The book had a message carved deeply into its wooden cover saying, "*IMPORTANT SHIT! Everything I know so far.*" Below the heading was a line that said, "*Don't fuck this up.*" He picked it up and read.

The book said it took a few thousand years for him to figure out how to deep-sleep. It wasn't normal human sleep, more a shift in dimension. Something Margo said had tipped him off, he read, but the writer didn't say who Margo was. He had come from a place called the Haight but what that was, was fuzzy. *Real or not?* It was a place of teachers.

He had recorded recurring visions of a dude named Allen Ginsburg who talked about inner space at the Be-In. That fleeting memory had given his older self a concept that started him meditating.

The book said all the pieces of his life were somewhere inside him but he had doubts.

Old-self had followed the inner light which pulled him out of time. In that state, he saw places and histories, and books he had read. He had relived snatches of many lives that way. Some he recognized but most he didn't. He never got to his beginning. None of his written visions depicted his current reality. Sleep-state, where he got puzzle pieces, didn't fit anything. He was working on the puzzle when the Tribe returned.

Music slapped him out of concentration. They were singing outside like nothing he heard before. It was more like a bunch of monkeys chanting than music, but he knew the song. A young mop-top monkey called Davy Jones popped into memory. Davey wasn't a zoo monkey. *Day Dream Believer* played in his mind's ear. The inner music came with visions of bright, crudely drawn flowers in primary colors.

He imagined painted words. Love and peace were spelled out in vivid, wild colors as Davey sang. He wanted to get back into it but the noise outside distracted him and Davey Jones vanished.

"I got to write this shit down, man."

He pushed out of his Bark-o-Lounger with the compulsion to write. Other than his hair reaching the floor, everything else was tidy thanks to yesterday's whirlwind, but he couldn't find a pencil. He had chopped his beard off and half the length of his hair last night but didn't remember doing it.

"Man, my head's Swiss cheese. CRS man, can't remember shit."

One idea did come back as he topknotted his locks. *I'm the Wizard of this Tribe.* Not a god. There are no gods. He had trained them to watch over him while he slept and not to wake him except for an emergency. The pieces were falling in. They never bothered him. He always woke on his own but that singing outside could wake the dead. It was terrible.

He stopped at his door. The counting marks on the wooden wall were many. Hash strikes covered the old planks from top to bottom.

"Wow, that ain't bullshit. Far out."

The books didn't go back to his beginning. The oldest ones were on the bottom and had turned into termite shit.

The song outside changed. The natives were just beyond his door singing fast like a bunch of meth-heads. All he made out was, "Oh, hairy kiss ya. Oh, hairy kiss ya. Oh, hairy kiss-ya."

"What the fuck?" He called to them, "You dudes got the wrong words! What a bunch of shit-heads. I'm John, not Harry."

The chanting stopped. The door was shut but windows lit his place. He needed a pick-me-up before facing them. The bowl of weed the Tribe had provided seemed empty. His bong had water he didn't recall getting. He checked the bowl confirming his disappointment, nothing was left but stems and seeds.

"Hey man, where's the dope?" He said between cracks in the door planks. "Didn't I tell you to keep me stocked?"

No answer came from outside. Just a lot of chatter he couldn't make out.

"I'll use my reserve. I'm not doing nothing until I get high."

The end table drawl next to the lounger was where he had kept his stash box. It was where the book said it was. He had a nice little teak box with mother-of-pearl inlays. He had filled it with joints before checking out. The rolling papers had crumbled but the weed was good. He found a pencil as well. He stuffed the dry weed into his bong and took several big hits.

Things left near him while sleeping stayed fresh. The kitchen table was far away so those older books went bad. The Tribe's bowl of dope was new. He felt bad for thinking they let him down. The Levies and flannel shirt he woke up in was dusty but whole. His *Converse* sneakers didn't last as he had kicked them off before bed. Only the souls remained.

"*Rubber Soul*? Wasn't that the Beatles? I got to write that down." He took another hit. But the music started again. "I better go see what the Tribe wants."

He didn't know what he had seen the other day. He was too cloudy.

"Well here goes nothing."

Bong in hand, he swung the door in. Leather hinges creaked. Outside stood a contingent of short people, shaped like people anyway. A dozen half-naked chicks in body paint, long dreads, and feathers took a step back as he stepped out. What clothes they had were loose. Tits flopped out every which way.

A couple of old farts were covered up and that was cool. He didn't want to see old ladies naked. The only two dudes, holding fan branches over the old ladies, wore nothing but jockstraps and way too much body hair.

"Hey, weren't you different yesterday?"

Everybody talked at once like TV pitchmen on crack. He couldn't make it out. He took a bong hit and waited for them to chill. The head woman's furry face seemed grave as she came forward. The rest stayed back.

"What gives Big Momma? What's up, K-pasta?"

A young chick ran up and fell to her knees. *Hairy, but not too bad. Still doable.* She looked up trembling. The old lady moved closer to speak.

"I am your great, great-grandniece, oh Wizard of—"

"Dude, take it down, man, chill. Talk slower. Go easy, OK?"

She bowed. "The magic plants you love have failed. A fundamental change has passed over the land. Everything good is in the trees for the trees suck Mother Earth's tits."

"Bummer, man. That shit did taste stale. It's cool. I'll figure something out. What else…Wait a minute."

His perspective had cleared. The marsh was miles across like he thought but the tree line…the trees were redwood size but taller. He judged they averaged a thousand feet high.

"That's a mind-blower. No farmland, bummer. Go with hydroponics. I'll show you how."

The old lady turned to the people and spoke a fast rap he didn't understand. The women looked relieved. The girl kneeling bowed lower. She put her hands way out in front like a yoga stretch. The girl's tail stub stood up. He reacted like he had eaten a bad taco.

"What's going down? You came for something. What do you want?" His mood matched his stomach.

"Before we ask, here is our gift as tradition provides. I present Betty, a girl for your leisure. Fuck her as you please."

The girl stood and spun around. All the others did as well. She exposed her bush by splitting back her skirt, tits were already out, really nice ones, too. He knew the routine from the book. He was supposed to make a show of looking her over. He wished he hadn't started that tradition. Besides the tail, not a long one but a tail nonetheless, she was hairy as hell.

"Talk about jungle love."

Her dreadlocks are cool. Only two tits but four nipples? When did they start growing tails? That chick ain't fuck-able.

"How long was I out?" He asked with a dry mouth.

He considered drinking the bong water. The head woman unrolled a scroll.

"The wall count got stopped when space ran out. We continued as tradition demands. You slept ten thousand years."

"No shit! You're fucking with me. That's gotta be a new record."

It came back in a flash. There was a huge village, lots of people, larger people. A couple of dudes had had tales. He had gotten upset. They asked why. He told them he didn't like tails so they cut them off which disturbed him more. Only a few dudes had tails back then.

These people were shorter, hair covered, and had longer arms. *That ain't a birth defect.* There was no sign of normal people. The distant smoke was fog and not industry. The environment had changed radically.

"I'm all fucked up here," John said. "Where are my people? Where'd they go?"

"We are yours. Most of us live in the trees. Only we, your descendants, come here…with fear and loathing. We preserved you for a day when your powers are required. That day has come," she said.

It sounded like a lie to him.

"We bring payment." The old lady pointed at the little monkey girl.

"You figure just give me a chick to bang and I'll jump into action. Is that it? Exactly what is it you want from me?"

"Kill a dragon," she said. "It is evil. Dragons eat us, take our young, smoke your dope."

"Oh no, fuck that. I'm not killing anybody. I faced a killer dragon once and you know how I beat his ass? I talked to him. I made peace with him. That fucker did me a big favor. Ever try grooving with dragons?"

The head woman looked down at her hairy toes. He followed. Her toenails were too long. *These people aren't people, they're something else.*

The book said dragons were cool. He guessed they never once tried extending a hand to the other sentient race. The idea that they even asked him to kill somebody pissed him off big time.

"Man, you got to make peace with dragons. Peace is where it's at."

"They are dangerous," someone said. "They eat people."

"That's bullshit. Look, you guys are distant relatives right. Dragons and I go way back. You go see that fucker and tell him I sent you. Tell him John Doe said it's cool. You guys have the dragon connection. If he doesn't want to make friends come back and let me know. You dig?"

"We will," the old woman said. "Will you accept Betty-Bang-Bang? Will you give us another child of your line?"

John looked at the girl and his skin crawled. The idea of making it with a nonhuman chick didn't gel. Maybe they were his relatives, but evolution had left him behind. They weren't his people anymore.

It's time to cut this yo-yo string.

He had to be harsh, that was the only way to get a monkey off your back. The last thing he wanted was sex with a monkey chick.

"Sorry, no thanks. Tell her to get lost."

"Please you must fuck her."

"No fucking way. I'm done. You're fired. This is my last word. Make friends of dragons. Some of you have it in you. If you can't do that, then go climb a tree."

"We must kill it if you won't. It's the law. We must unless you give us leave," the old momma said.

Her eyes shifted around. Her tight lips reminded him of politicians. He didn't need to fake getting mad to get this monkey off his back. Momma wanted him to do her dirty work and that pushed his disdain over the top.

"You're off the hook. Get the fuck out of here and don't come back. Don't you dare hurt any dragons, not no more! You hear me!"

The kneeling girl shot up and fell backward.

"You release us?" The old woman said. "You eject us?"

Her eyes bulged. Her hairy face became all teeth. *She has fangs, Jesus!* He didn't know what her showing her teeth meant. Monkey-smiling could mean anything. John loved nature but that bitch was a freak show.

"Are we free to go?"

"Fuckin' A-right. If you do like I say. You're my peeps. Here's your inheritance. Go and make peace with dragons. That's your mission. Just do it."

The procession went back the way they had come singing *Louie, Louie* and they had it right. He had resurrected that road called the Processional Way. It used to be called something else. The book didn't know what the name was. He felt empty as the tree-people withdrew but he didn't long for their company. Talking monkeys was too big a freak-out.

He had a pet lizard yesterday but it split. The music scared it off and all the rest of the critters. He had to find another one and he didn't know why. He thought he should go talk to the dragon. The book said dragons were intelligent people. But he wanted a mindless companion for company and not a debate.

"They ain't pets, that's for sure."

Back inside he rolled a fresh joint and dusted off a fishing pole. It still worked. He could have reached into the past and snatched something to eat but he had enough unreality for one day. Besides fast food didn't satisfy. He headed for that big lake in the distance thinking about a fish fry hoping fish hadn't grown arms and legs yet.

48

Up Tree

Waking up was a pain in the ass according to his books and he concurred. Things were scrambled. He remembered recent stuff but the farther back in time he searched, the less he recalled. He had a shit-ton of catching up to do.

Getting acclimated, figuring out location, and re-remembering what happened before was a massive chore. Most of the books he wrote to himself were trashed. The pages in the middle were A-OK, but the edges were gone, so they didn't make a lot of sense. The books said he had remembered bits of the deep, recorded it, and tried over and over to pull it all together, but he never could. *No context, man.* He thought to resurrect his older books but he needed a bowl of motivation first.

The one thing he confirmed about himself: Nothing gets done without weed and he didn't have much left. He had sent his dealer packing.

"I better go and patch things up," he said to the nearest lizard. "Thank Jerry I saved the seeds."

He dropped the seed bottle into an empty backpack and grabbed a couple of the apples he had picked out of the past and headed west down Route Nine, or Route Seventy, he wasn't sure. The marsh spread all around the raised road like a levy and that reminded him of a song.

"By, by Miss America Pride, drove a heavy with my Chevy and the bitch was dry…"

He sang sure the tune was right but not the words. He had Dead songs down cold. Others of that time played in his head, too, but the words were scrambled. His memory had massive holes in it but the Dead songs stuck. Frustrated, he clammed up and hummed the tune instead.

The landscape was more a cranberry bog than a salt marsh. The salty smell came from a nearby ocean. This wetland was freshwater. All kinds of reptiles and birds were around. As he walked, he lost count of how many animals and plants he spied that weren't normal yet still familiar.

"Evolution happens, man. I was out cold ten thousand years, holy cow."

After an hour's march, the trees were closer and the road improved with reed-woven mats. The village had maintained that end. No smoke ahead, no sign of people. He walked faster. It took another twenty minutes to reach dry land. The foliage changed from tall weeds and tuffs to low bushes and giant ferns. The trees were still farther on and so tall they disappeared into the clouds.

"You could carve a condo into one of them suckers and you'd only be scratching the surface." He said to the little lizard hanging on a fern.

The paths of this treeless zone were well worn under the twenty-foot-tall ferns. He slowed down not wanting to scare the natives. They had freaked out the other day and he didn't want to be a dick. He took the widest trail.

The village entrance had an arch made of twisted saplings, thorns, and vines. He stopped at the gate and tested the air. No smell of cooking or weed. No sign or sound of people.

"Bummer man."

The gate was left open so he walked right in. There wasn't much there, a dozen low, round bowl-shaped huts made from bent branches covered in tree bark was it. The enclosure had pointy-top wooden poles stuck upright in the ground around the perimeter. The fence was laced with long, thorny vines. They were keeping something nasty out. Why was the gate left ajar? They must have left the door open for him.

"OK you guys, ha, ha, ha, very funny come on out."

Silence, no response.

"Hey you guys," he called louder. "Come on, man, give me a break. I'm fucking hungry."

Still nothing. He ripped open the nearest hovel's woven reed flap, nobody inside. He went from hut to hut tearing open the flaps finding next to nothing. Realizing they had left; he lost it and pulled a floormate outside and jumped up and down on it screaming curses until he ran out of steam. He flopped onto the mat cross-legged, head in hands, and sobbed for a long while.

"Man, I got to chill. I'm freaked out," he said, lighting one of the few joints he had.

Smoking and thinking didn't make him feel any better. He was the one that told them to leave. He made them go. They didn't abandon him. The village had bugged out on his word. He couldn't believe they split because he refused to murder a dragon.

"This is so bogus, man."

He knew a dragon once. He didn't remember exactly when or where but that dragon was cool. That positive impression stayed with him. The book said dragons were A-OK. He was right not to hurt the village dragon. Screwing over a harmless creature didn't jive with his inner being. He had the proof these people weren't his people but any people were better than no people.

"What was so bad about this Tribe anyway? They weren't that bad." He said, feeling alone. "This is what I get for talking shit. HEY, WHERE ARE YOU!?"

He didn't expect an answer, but a gargled voice answered. He never could walk away from anyone in need. *Maybe they left granny behind.*

He see-sawed up and strolled out the gate. Back among the tree trunks and taller ferns he found a woven thicket jail enclosure. It was cave-dark deep inside. A pair of green reptilian eyes glowed from the shadows.

"Have you come to finish me, Wizard?" His voice was low and raspy. "The ladies said you would come and kill me. They didn't have the stomach for it, did they?"

"Oh, hell no," John said. "Man, I'm not killing nobody. That's bullshit. Dude, I'm into life."

"You will help me?"

"Shit, yeah, can you move? Come out into the light and I'll do what I can."

The creature crawled out from its shelter. It had a broken wing. A bunch of pointed sticks stuck out of its body. *Them fuckers stabbed him.* John was glad he told them to get lost. This pissed him off big time.

"How could they do that?"

This dragon wasn't as big as the one he dreamed about. That sucker was huge. This one was only the size of a pony. It had the same double folded wings, long arms, and human hands as in his dream. Memory or dream he didn't know.

"Shit, man. You're a mess. What happened?"

"I hit a tree and busted my wing. I came here looking for help. They attacked and chained me here."

"What a bunch of assholes," John said.

He could hardly believe anyone could be so cruel.

"Let me look. I need to pull out the spears. Dress the wounds. You cool with that?"

"If you would be so kind as to lend assistance. I'll repay you."

"You don't have to do nothing for me, man. People should help each other, that's how it's supposed to be."

John broke the lock using stones from the village firepit. It was a piece-of-shit lock. *Thank Jerry.* He led Barry the dragon back to the enclosure. John rooted around until he found a cache of medical stuff inside a hollow log. Further investigation yielded food in a buried stone jar and clean water in a gourd jug. He found a gallon skin bag filled with moonshine in another log thanks to Barry's nose.

The spears came out easy, just sharpened sticks without barbs. The wounds didn't bleed much. He used the moonshine as an antiseptic between sharing swings. He packed the holes with a blowout patch made of bee's wax. John also found a big woven-fiber bag full of smokables after figuring out their storage method.

Who keeps their shit inside trees?

Those monkey assholes were supposed to bring him food, weed, and booze. *Holding out on me.* But they fucked Barry over and split instead. Once the dressing was done and some water drunk, John sat with Barry and rolled a fresh joint. He hit it a few times and passed it. Barry took a couple of big hits. Barry didn't exhale fire.

"That's the good smoke," Barry said. "We call it Tree Top. It grows wild in the canopy."

"Far out. Dragon dudes are stoners. I dig it, man."

"Too bad human people aren't so wise as to indulge in weed's wisdom. Smoke opens the mind, you see. They have gotten a bit too self-righteous if you ask me."

"Why'd they fuck with you? You're a cool dude," John took the joint and hit it.

"My scales and feathers are earth tones while non-sentient types are green and smaller. You know the universal law, red means poison. Crocks won't come near me, as to them, my color and scent are poisonous. But I'm not toxic to humans. Someone should tell them to stop shooting arrows at us. My theory is they are confused."

"You dudes need to get together, call a truce. Like when Kesey met with Hells Angels."

"I don't see how that is possible. I tried to reason with them. You see what they did."

"No shit. Angels were hard asses, too but…Lost it, man. I had something. It went right out of my head. Anyway, the point is people need to reach out. Nothing happens if you don't try. Can you dig it?"

"I see your point. It is worth a shot. If we can make amends, I see there are mutual benefits to be had."

"Them dudes that were here, find them. They were my people. There has got to be some peace lovers in that troupe…*Mime Troupe*. That reminds me of something. Can't put my finger on it. Man, I need to find myself."

"I won't forget their odors," Barry said. He took a sniff. "You have the same pheromones. But yours are not sour."

John sniffed his armpits.

"Right on. Smells like onions."

John spent the next few weeks with Barry Man-O-Low. John sewed his wings like new blue jeans and the repair took.

Barry was a good egg. He looked dangerous but he had a heart of gold. Barry was a miner for a heart of gold. *'I want to live, I want to give, I am a…'* lost it again.

Barry said he was on a *magical mystery tour* to find something or someone, but he didn't know what it was or what drove him to seek it. John could relate to that. He had something to do, too. But something was missing, something bigger than himself. Bits and pieces flashed into his head and disappeared all the time but he didn't have the time or material to take notes.

I'll write it after Barry splits. I'll figure everything out eventually.

The day Barry was to take flight they hiked out to the beach house. John had resurrected it one day while looking for clams at the ocean. Barry, in reasonable health, carried the food, towels, and dope in the sling John had made.

"This ain't a beach house, it's a shit-shack," John said laughing. "I don't know this beach's name. Point Pleasant is south. I smell roasting peanuts, and dead fish coming up the coast."

Barry put his nose into the air, "I don't smell food, only saltwater. I need room to take off. I'm still weak. This open sky and strong wind will do nicely."

"Let's do the dune beach after lunch. There's a good wind coming off the sea."

The undergrowth was still thick a little way east of the shack. Barry hopped over most of it but John had to bushwhack his way to the dunes. Arriving, posts were sticking up out of the sand piles. John couldn't tell if they were petrified trees or pilings but it seemed familiar.

Barry found a clear dune and climbed up. The wind came out of the east. It was an ideal place to take off but John didn't know how or why he knew that. His memory scrambled more every day.

"We part here my friend," Barry said, "I will keep your wisdom and seek your relatives. Perhaps a meeting of ways is possible."

"You sure you don't want a hit off this?" John had a lit joint cupped in his hands.

"No, thank you, I am flying."

"I dig it," John wrapped his arms around the dragon and patted him on the back. Barry's feathers tickled John's nose. "I'm glad I got to know you, man. Better get going before I start crying."

"As you wish."

Barry Man-O-Low took several long looping strides downhill into the wind and opened his wings. He shot up like a runaway kite, twisted midair, and rose in wide circles until he became a dot on the edge of sight. John lost Barry in the clouds and turned for home.

Arriving back at the book house John's heart sunk. Words to a tune came to mind. *'Nobody left alive in here, nobody but me in here,'* rang inside his head. Alone again, he flicked away the roach burning his fingertips and cried out.

"I got nobody but me. Anyone there, anyone? Somebody tell me who I am!"

Nobody answered. But a dozen lizards all different sizes came running. The bravest one hung on the side of his open door bobbing its head. John reached out and the little fellow jumped onto his palm. John looked it over. It was shaped like Barry but tiny. Many lizards around had Barry's body style—feathers, wings, and scales in weird combinations.

"Hey, little guy, you're my friend any-who. A man needs a pet, right. I don't want a soccer ball. A living thing is better. *Tom Hanks* missed that boat. *Tom Hanks*, I better write that down."

John put the lizard on his shoulder. Many of the others followed them inside. He decided to write down that latest flash memory, but he also decided to get high first. He then forgot what he was supposed to put down. *Something about a ball named Wilson.* He wasn't a sports fan so he blew it off.

A few thousand years later, or thereabout—he didn't know exactly—he remembered that he had forgotten Barry. A flash of memory about that dragon came to him. What sparked the idea was what he thought he saw.

He looked into the sun and had imagined a monkey riding a giant flying lizard way up in the sky. That was when a dragon named Barry Man-O-Low popped into his head. John Doe couldn't decide if Barry was a dream, an acid trip, bad mushrooms, or a good memory. Searching his oldest books, he didn't find anything out about Barry.

"Maybe I wrote over it?"

Nothing was ever straight in his head. He saw what he saw but he decided not to record it. He often saw flying saucers too. Making hemp paper was hard work and he didn't waste it on nonsense.

"Monkeys don't ride dragons, that's impossible."

He figured it was another flashback. He chalked it up to too much acid in the 1960s and then he forgot the 1960s again.

Gabe's Screw Up

Gabe was in his office diddling around. He didn't have much to do. Bored, he launched into the paperwork. It took months, ship-time, to reach the drop-off zone where he could hand off the DNA samples and breeder stock to another Planet Molder crew. The thing he hated most about management was paperwork. To make less work for himself, he had put everyone on that detail to get it over with. *Management has its perks.* He sucked at data review and he knew it. Report building wasn't his cup of isotopes.

Central upgrading me was stupid. I'm not an office guy.

Lacking administration skills didn't impede Gabe's technical perspective. Things weren't right in the seeder collection. Early reports showed they were short on stock.

Oh, so that's why Earth failed after the megafauna reset.

If they didn't acquire the right combination of seed samples and live shoots the new Earth needed, this version will fail, too. Reseeding the new place was iffy according to the data Gabe reviewed. He had assumed they will reseed but he didn't have orders for it.

If I screw this up, I won't get to retire for another ten thousand years.

More stock would have been better. It was good John had sent people at the last minute. It could make up for the shortage. Gabe didn't like the guy but he grew on Gabe after they had left.

"Poor John Doe. May he rest in peace."

John was long dead. Two years ship-time is ten million years Earth time. They were just under a year outbound when Gabe got around to doing his paperwork.

His door chimed. One of the local Earth hires was at his door. He buzzed the guy in.

"Jeez- Louise, will you turn it down."

"Oh sorry, I forgot," Gabe said.

He had his office lights at normal for his planet which was blinding for an Earthman. He adjusted the lights. The rest of the ship was set for the Earth guests. Gabe was so bored even a visit from What's-His-Name was better than pushing papers.

"What can I do for you?" Gabe said.

"Got something to show you, Chief. Take a look at this."

The Earthman laid an old newspaper clipping on his desk. Gabe turned up the desk light. He had assigned the Earthmen to search archives for seeder evidence. The newspaper clipping had come from the San Francisco Chronicle circa 1966.

Gabe read the headline out loud, "'*Jim Henson* films a TV spot on Haight Street.' So, what?"

"Look at the picture."

"Looks like John Doe." Gabe pointed at one of the background figures. "So, what, hippies all look the same. Poor bastard. I wish he had made the deadline."

Gabe thought John did a good job even if he was an Earth local. He could have used John's sample, too. He had forgotten to prick him.

That guy was good seed stock material.

"I blew up the picture and did an analysis. What was John Doe's e-meter reading?"

"High, just over 10 percent," Gabe said. "The highest sample I've seen on my handheld."

"That's what I figured."

The Earthman anthropologist shoved an enhanced picture under Gabe's desk lamp.

"He's a dead ringer for John Doe, so what?" Gabe said.

"He's more than that dumbass. He is our guy."

Gabe didn't buy it. Maybe the man in the photo and John Doe were distant relatives. Maybe this Earth guy was plucking Gabe's wings. No way the pictured Earthman and Doe could be the same guy. Anyone from the 1960s was long dead by the time they took off. An unease parched his mouth but he had to ask.

"How do you know this?" Gabe said.

"I was in biology before I switched to anthropology," The Earthman said. "Inactivated immortals read 11.2 percent seeder genes or better on e-meters. I ran calibrations. Your meter was way off. John Doe comes in at a twelve on my meter. He's a nonactivated-familiar immortal."

"Wait, no. How can that be!"

"Do you guys ever connect the dots? It's basic seeder biology. How do you think we ran into you at the farm? We were tracking immortals. You found the remains of the burnt ones. They had two kids, not one. You knew that, right?"

That info refused to register in Gabe's mind, too shocking to grasp. The Earth guy had to be wrong. No way Gabe screwed up, no way, not again, not this bad.

Two kids, we only saw one child's body.

"Seeder biology, you got it wrong," Gabe spit out. "Seeders show over 15.5. It's in the textbooks."

Gabe stood up and leaned over the Earthman. The Earthman, two heads shorter, didn't flinch.

"Yeah, after they activate. But only after a seeder consciously accepts a memory-familiar species. How would he know about that if no one was around to tell him? Dead parents, remember? If he died First Death before he knew about familiars, well…there you go."

"Shit, shit, shit!" Gabe fell back into his chair.

John Doe had a pet. Activated familiars follow immortals but what if Doe didn't know he activated them? *That's not in the book.* Pets were the giveaway and Gabe missed it. Familiars follow seeders like St. Patrick leading the snakes out of Ireland. Snakes, reptiles, the guy in the picture had an iguana on his shoulder.

"OK, OK, what happens if he doesn't choose a species? What if he did and doesn't know it?" Gabe blurted out.

"Bookkeepers will follow him. We aren't sure how that works. The species records him anyway. All of them passively and one directly. They won't stop recording his Book until they deliver it."

"I don't understand, this can't be right."

"He must have indicated a favorite as a child which he never recognized. Come to think of it, I bet John Doe doesn't know he's an immortal either."

"No shit," Gabe said miserably.

How can I be so stupid? It was right there. I'm too dumb for field ops, I'm management material alright. If I got to be in management forever, go big. I might as well screw up all the way.

For once he decided to go according to what he wanted and felt, no rules, no nod to book-procedures as before, no consideration for the union. This was all on him and he had nothing left to lose.

"Whatcha gonna do?" What's-His-Name said with a shrug.

It was a rhetorical question. Gabe said the same often enough when management did something stupid.

"I'll show you." Gabe pressed the intercom. "Mike, this is Gabe. Tell the captain to turn the ship around. We're going back to Earth."

The Earth guy's smirk turned down as Mike's voice came over the speaker.

"Are you nuts? By the time we get back…Jesus…you know we're in null space, right? It'll be ten million years later Earth-time when we get back there. Nothing will be recognizable. Evolution's playing out. What possible reason can you have?"

"We left a prime seeder behind."

"Whoa, wait, what!?"

"John Doe. He's an immortal."

The sound of Mike falling backward out of his chair came over the com.

"Well, all righty then," the Earth guy said as he left.

Gabe pulled out his pocket calculator. He was good at multidimensional astrological calculus. If all went well, they will make it back just before End Wave. After End Wave, nothing will be left, not even an immortal. End Wave recreates everything. Only basic species that were programmed by Mini Waves for evolution survive and humans weren't listed.

"If John Doe is still alive, we'll find him," Gabe said.

He flipped on the bridge's video. Mike was picking himself up off the floor. Gabe didn't laugh.

Although immortals were hard to kill, they can and do die. The odds were slim of recovering John Doe. No Prime Seeder ever lived that long before. The crew will have little time to find him before End Wave. It wasn't worth the cost. Accounting will scream. Gabe's career was over anyway.

"Are you sure?" Mike said once back in his chair.

"No, but do it anyway."

"You heard him, Captain," Mike said.

Gabe owed John Doe this attempt. Win or lose, Gabe could still get unemployment and with a clear conscience. *Getting canned beats another promotion.* Weirdly, Gabe felt better. No field operative in his or her right mind would ever reverse course with such low odds. Gabe didn't ask for this job. Control put him in charge. They gave him the ball. They were who declared Earth a salvage operation, not him. *No rules.*

"Upper management screwed up. They shouldn't have trusted me."

"No shit Skippy," Mike said.

Gabe ended the call. Lower management had its advantages. The guys upstairs never expected much from a newly upgraded office wonk. It made no sense to Gabe for Control to place a field-ops trained guy like him in the office but they did it anyway.

Salvage operations were supposed to be no-brainers—that explained it. Control didn't expect much from him. Gabe came through on that account.

What are they going to do, fire me?

He hoped like hell they would.

50

Ten Million and Ninety-Nine A.D.

A tamed red-faced blackbird roosted nearby. Lonely, mister Jaybird Blue spoke to it often.

He had not left Home Range in a year. He stayed away from Bricktown having been humiliated at the Community Stump. Village people scorned his theories. He had hinted at bigger, worse things he didn't say directly. *That's what you get for not speaking outright.* He decided not to return to public speaking until he had something solid. He wanted Gram's official approval first, but she didn't understand his motives.

Gram's power had long been subjugated, so to others, her ideas didn't count for much. But he trusted her. She didn't agree with his perspective on his artifacts though she did understand his found objects were of great age. She thought his proposal was too dangerous. Revolutionary ideas don't fly even for a former dragon rider such as Gram.

On his last visit Gram had said, "Don't caste seeds at ravens. They will eat their fill and curse the giver.'"

What's that supposed to mean? Fine, Gram won't help. She won't stop me either. I'll tell villagers the truth. Let Gram chew her sour bugs.

Jay had jumped on the stump last year saying he had a thing of metal which he had found inside a conveyor knot. It had come up from deep roots and was very old.

The people had come in closer to see it. Commonly accepted, conveyor knots transported things up from the tree's roots inside itself and such things were strange: Be they rocks or bones or whatever else infected a tree. Irritants were ejected through surface knots.

The ground, being taboo, was a popular morbid curiosity. People feared the lower world which attracted interest. He should not have mentioned roots right off the last time he stumped.

Jay didn't share the people's fears. He thought the lower regions were more than fodder for myths. Jay considered The Down-Low a depository of history.

'This thing could not have been dragon-made.' He had said like a fool at last year's stump.

People don't care for history. They had chased him off the stage. He dropped that metal object and lost it between the cracks.

What he discovered since was better. It was unidentifiable like most objects. It was made of a finer metal. In his view, it was woman-made but not by his people. *Why will they not see this?*

The dozen who had gathered around Town Hall Stump last year debated the meaning of the rusted object he had presented. They were curious but none had touched it or looked closely before deciding to reject his idea. Jay had thought his presentation might get them thinking. His hope collapsed when one old woman ended the discourse.

'It is dragon-make,' she had declared. 'It is old dragon-make from when dragons lived on lower branches and nothing more. Perhaps it fell when dragons were young. It is nothing.'

She spoke and turned away. It was the final word. The crowd had backed out leaving him alone at the podium. More and more anything dragon-make was taboo.

"That bitch was just like Gram, stubborn and all-knowing." The bird made no response.

That lady was an irritant to him just as Gram was to the mayor. Jay was tired of arguments. He was tired of holding his tongue with Gram and the other smartass females. Against tradition, he had called that female out as the stump-jumpers dispersed.

One taboo begets another.

He had yelled at her. 'It is human-make you fool, a thing of the way-back. Can't you understand we were more advanced? We worked metal and stone before dragons. We are from the ground!'

One doesn't treat an old female like that. His idea was ridiculous on its face and he made it worse. They laughed him off the stump before the old lady had time to get mad. The ground had been taboo for eons. The idea that people had once lived on the Down-Low was beyond tolerance.

Jaybird Blue had gone home dejected but determined to turn their leaf.

His treehouse was on the Jersey side across from Manhattan. North Forest contained the longest-lived and thus tallest trees. Few ventured into his home region anymore. The great trees were falling one or two every year. It had started in Springfield before he was born when the sky had changed color.

Living here is crazy. Jay made his home in the shunned zone for good reasons. The oldest trees pushed up the most interesting knots.

His raft was as close to the top of the canopy as he dared. Large treehouses were more stable lower down. The top branches were too thin. It was a fine location for hammock living, but not for a conventional raft home. Jay gambled and it paid. Nobody ever visited. His finds were many.

He had worktables and tools and the things he collected. He talked to the blackbird as he worked but it didn't understand. He named what he saw as he opened a large knot with his crude and dull metal dragon-made knife.

"My research is important. If they ever see they will know we too can do what dragons do. Why not make things for ourselves? Is that not smart, little bird friend?"

'What does it matter?' Gram's words resurfaced in his mind.

He ignored Gram-Mother's advice although she was usually right. There wasn't any need for material things. People weren't inclined to hold possessions like certain birds and flying lizards do. The new social movement was counter-progressive. People were for eating raw meat and leaf and foregoing firepots. Bobbing a person's tail recently became more than out of fashion. It bordered taboo. 'Tail bobbing's unnatural,' the Mayor often proclaimed and the people believed him.

"Naturalism is the enemy of progress," Jay said feeling disagreeable as he sliced another layer of bark away.

Jaybird's family line did not usually grow tails and those who did grow one—males for the most part—once cut off it did not regrow. Some had spine-buds which did not blossom. But females of his particular family tree didn't bud. Gram was the last female of her bud-less kind.

Finally, Jay reached the softer bark layer.

"This knot's insides resemble bug-pulp pudding. Interesting."

He wiped the knife off on his petal-pusher pants. The object was made of glass whole and unbroken and not in shards as he often found. It was not ceramic, either.

"By the branch of plenty, what are you?"

Its color was soft green and the same shade as the skin under his fur.

"Unusual, indeed."

He reached with hands weakened by excitement. He tingled as he pulled it free. Fearful of dropping it, he set it on the table and lowered himself into a woven vine chair to examine it. His eyes never moved away from this wonder. He thought if he blinked it might fly back into the past.

For a long time, he watched it. The bark slime ran off making it fully visible. The goop had finished dripping off the table by the time he touched it. One end of it was open and the other flat. Gaining courage, he carefully stood it on its base: A glass cylinder, ten inches long, with a metal stem such as a tree pole angled for sunshine. On the end of the stem was a tiny metal bowl.

"So finely made, but how? What is it?" Jay chanted, "Om, Om, Om…"

Jay had a secret. Images and words would flash out of deep memories that were not his own. His dreams were not the Dragon's Vision that Gram spoke of but similar. Dragons understood it as deep memories and trusted them as truth. He trusted his visions, too. Only his line had them. A word rang his heart.

"Bong, it's a bong. For smoking. How am I to prove that?"

It was for smoking but it was nothing like what people used. Gram had long stem dragon pipes on her raft with other dragon artifacts. She was the last person to have ridden a dragon or to have had an association with them. Jay wasn't sure of the make. *If it is not a dragon device, it proves evolution.* Whoever smoked it was not a dragon.

"We have been makers of such things. If we made this, we can be makers again, by the tree!"

His excitement turned bitter like old honey. There was a logical step he must take before he revealed this, his greatest of all his discoveries. He must know: Is this dragon-made or not. Gram was the only living person who could answer his question and Jay had had enough of her critiques.

"But if she blesses this, the old ladies will support me."

He pulled leaves from the ceiling and wrapped his prize with care. He used a piece of bird net to hold the padding and added vines for strapping it to his belt or back. With Gram's blessing, the old ladies must accept the truth. Gram had rejected his spoon with anger when he showed her. But this was different and more convincing.

"She's going to dislike this even more. But, can she deny it? No. 'There's no way under this branch,' as the old saying goes."

If he had to go down to Bricktown without her blessing he would. Jay stowed the bong under his table. He felt for the new spoon, still safe inside his waist sack where he stowed it. This one was not rusted and indefinable.

"If this spoon doesn't convince Bricktown, I'll lug the bong down to Atlantic City."

Gram often said, 'Feed a starved person small bite first. This makes her ready for a big meal.' It was a good strategy but didn't take. Jay had tried it. He showed them small, debatable things for years, such as pottery, glass, and rusted metal. Jay felt it was time to jump the snark-bird.

Gram's not right about everything.

It was known that an electric snake will make a person lose grip. He planned to shock Bricktown into letting go of orthodoxy upon his next stump.

Dragons don't use spoons. This bong can't be used by them either.

"Let them refute it. This will be one for the books."

Jay thought he had them against the bark. Even so, he still had to go and see Gram first. Women's Wisdom still mattered...or at least it did to him. Her blessing carries weight.

51

Gram's Raft

The call had been sent. She sat motionless listening. So thin, old, and gnarled, like the main branch she lived on, made her naturally camouflaged. Her meal was on its way.

Her skin, after two hundred years, had become dark green and splotched in forest colors. Only thin patches of her silver fur remained. She had only a little body hair to begin with and most of it had gone. She resembled the lichen which covered the vines and branches supporting her simple raft.

Sophie's raft was higher than any other. The sun shone on her vine and plank platform between shadows. She did not grow a leaf roof, rather, she slung hammocks under her tightly woven living floor. Her home wasn't on the main tree but rather on one of its branches. Few trees were as immense or as old.

Only the oldest home trees pushed conveyor knots from its trunk into its branches. Her isolation had better reasons in past times. Dragon riders long ago flew from tip-tops. She chose this spot, not for that tradition, but because this branch had a good hollow. It was well hidden and far from Mr. Mayor's foolishness.

She loved her life of solitude in hiding but not the necessity of it.

Sophie had regrets. One smoldered before her. The iron cookpot she and Jaybird dug out of the hollow of this very branch when he was a child.

Her impossible iron cookpot had started Jaybird down his unstable branch. The boy became obsessed with what was inside conveyor knots. Knots also conveyed dangerous ideas.

"Such found things are better kept under branch."

She hummed the call again. The response came. Her meat bug was close. She listened for it on her haunches ready to spring. She heard everything including a distant person. She bent her neck. It was Jaybird. *He is no woods walker.* The eco of swishing vines proceeded him.

"Thank the tree no one follows after him."

He took air across an open, snatched a vine, and swung dropping onto her raft with two feet and not gracefully or quiet, but a solid landing nonetheless. She wished his skills were better.

"Hi, Sophie," he said.

"Don't call me my dragon's name, it's dangerous. Get that out of your mind."

"Who can hear?"

"Don't test me. What brings you Gram-kid?"

"Your wisdom," he answered.

The beard of his forehead wrinkled. She did not need to know what was in his belt sack to know what he was after. He desired permission, support, and vindication but giving it was bad for him. She did not have it in her to lie, either. Riders don't lie. Least of all to kin.

"Show me."

He reached into his sack and produced a shiny metal object and gave it over. She turned it over and over in her hand feeling its smoothness with bony fingertips. It was finely made and not smashed into a shape such as dragon-made items were. It could be a scraper. It certainly was not dragon-make. *He must know that.*

"What does your heart say?"

"Spoon," he said.

One doesn't question the naming. *He knows the old wisdom.* She taught him it.

There are memories hidden within one's body. One can be taught to recall them as dragons do. It was practiced in her youth but became a cause for distrust. Few had natural civilized intuitions anymore and if one did, the others would 'kill it before it grows,' as the old Slow-Hand saying proclaimed.

"The mayor thinks the old ways are evil. Goodly it is that you have sense enough to keep intuitions to yourself."

Gram-kid walks a wet branch.

"I should bring this to stump. My idea is provable. We are not as advanced as we think. Here goes the proof. A dragon could not have made this."

"The old argument." She breathed out.

The meat bug zoomed in and hovered above them confused by the lack of a mate. The lobster bug was prized for its meaty tail. The rest was junk food. This one was big enough to feed two.

She had in hand a thin sharpened green stick used for cooking. Lightning bug-fast, she skewed the lobster mid-air and set it down to roast on her firepot.

"It is said, lobster bugs once lived in the sea," she said.

Reaching into the hollow she pulled out a crock filled with tree-butter. It was a recent dragon-make ceramic which was a thing the authorities would persecute. Trade with dragons was illegal. Jaybird was used to her items. Taboos didn't work on dragon-line people. He harbored heresies of his own and ignored hers.

"You come for wisdom. I will tell you. Don't show that around." She pointed.

"But this will save the people, force them to think, move forward—"

"No, it will get you and me killed."

"I don't get it. If I show them that we were once more advanced, it will sire ideas, advancements, wonder. Maybe bring back Women's Rule."

"Quiet, let me cook in peace."

She turned the spit. Bugs cook fast, unlike mammals and birds. She listened for the interior to sizzle. Its wings burned off as it boiled inside its shell. Hot bug juice seeped from its shell segments and dripped onto the coals sending up a fine aroma. She waited for the juice to run out so it would sear.

How to make him understand?

This backward fall Jay identified was not a concern in Bricktown. They were of it. She and a few elders, Jay's dead mother and him included, weren't bothered by the great sky change but all the others were. Jaybird was the only male not made stupid since the sky turned blue and that before he was born. Odd how one so concerned with the deep past will not see recent history. Did the new sky cook his brains too?

"You climb a rotten vine," she said moving the bug off the heat. "The old traditions, you don't abide. The new traditions, you stand in opposition. You won't accept either and I agree by half. All the more reason why you must stay away from Bricktown."

Jay's light green face flushed ugly purple.

Oh, he does not care for that advice.

Had his tail not been cut, he would be whipping it. Not cutting his tail upon coming of age would have made his life better. No tail, no respect since skychange. Males with the longest tails were topmost in Bricktown.

"I don't get it! Jeepers."

"You don't fit in. You never will. You are of the dragon rider's tribe," she said. They were harsh and true words which needed to be said. "You are a man now. Chew leaves of truth."

She cracked open the bug, tore a piece out, dipped the meat in butter, and handed it to him. He put it in his mouth and chewed. *He can't talk nonsense with full cheeks.* But he did manage to spit out one question.

"Why?"

"A change has come and it is fundamental. The dragons have not succumbed to it, but the people have. Why not dragons? That is the question you should answer."

She dipped meat and ate and made another for him.

"What changes? I don't understand?"

"There is no respect for women anymore and especially lacking for a dragon rider. The women have lost control. This new social order. Boys coming of age not bobbing their tails! Men embrace animal ways. My forbearers would go purple with embarrassment. Men have become horny monkeys. Their swelled balls are so large they can't walk the plank. I see darkness ahead. The people have taken a whole step backward and all at once."

"That's what I want to fix! I have better things. If I show them this spoon—"

"You walk a thin branch. The mayor is not a friend. He seeks power. In my youth, I would never have suspected Bricktown's rejection of our allies. It was a good arrangement. Together we hunted large game. It was good. The dragon gave us stone and metal and fish. Everyone cooked food. The mayor will soon make cooking taboo just like he made dragons our enemy."

She saw the frustration on his face and quieted. The same words have been said between them before. Why let him hear it all again? She changed plank and made her voice softer.

"The people were radicalized. We are not now what we once were. The new ones are not human. Men, women, even you have forgotten, women are smarter in every way. The sayings of the Grateful Dead are ignored. You can't fix this. No one can fix stupid."

He took the spit, ripped the lobster off, and flung the arachnid's shell away. He stood ready to leap but did not.

Had he been a village male, hooting and a head-slapping display would have followed. Such foolishness was considered disgraceful within the Rider Tribe. Jaybird swallowed his anger as a human being should. She felt hope in his frustrations. *He is not like the others.* An idea she had been chewing lately came to mind.

"You must go to the dragon's mountain and become a dragon rider. Apprentice there. Tap into them, hear old wisdom. Then you will know I am right."

"'No fucking way,'" he said quoting a dragon saying he learned from her. "I'm not going anywhere near them. It's off-limits. The grapevines say dragons aren't trustworthy anymore, they eat people and even worse."

She hoped for better. As a youth, he had an interest in dragons although he rejected dragon religion as was proper. Her line had a natural aversion for it 'If you believe in things you don't understand, you will suffer.' Jaybird took that old saying to heart.

Why does he now believe anti-dragon propaganda?

He was not afraid of the sky or the ground. That talent made leaving the canopy by air or by a ground crossing possible. No other could reach Manhattan. Jay embraced the Down-Low and if people knew, it will be the death of him.

"One such as you, rarely suited to go below, should never speak of it and you want to stump," she said.

Sophie felt the weight of her age pressing her toward the ground. It was said, 'All dead things go to ground.' Not everything at ground level was dead. Earthbound creatures were thought deadly. A smart tree person could live among them. For him the ground was salvation.

"I will say it once again and no more." Her tone was hard. Her wisdom carried authority. A flick of the tongue wet her thin, dry lips.

"Go to the dragons and if they will not take you, go far away. If not the north, go to California. Go anywhere. Live on the ground. Stay away from Bricktown."

Jay leaped straight up with eyes as round as the moon. His bad speech would come next but Sophie wouldn't suffer his arguments again.

"Go," she said, "Leave me. Go home."

Jaybird turned and leaped from her raft. He missed the nearest vine in his haste but caught a branch and swung on. She watched until he disappeared into the green.

"The last of the dragon rider line, the last visionary, travels like an ape."

But he was not a primitive. The free air was what made him swing she thought. The genetic memory of dragon flight was in him. That was good and bad, bad if Mr. Mayor catches on. Good if he uses his talent.

Sophie placed more fuel in the firepot. She sat on her hunches and began 'singing for her supper,' as the saying goes. She wanted dessert. Roasted honeybug always mended her upset inside. She sang loudly. Her heart's healing required a great many sweet bugs.

52

Dragon Mass

Her finely polished cave-home, located just above Vision Rock, was called a cave but it was dragon-made. Old New York had provided the building materials. A flit of the wings will bring her to the pulpit.

Darleen wasn't the only dragon on Manhattan Mountain feeling the strain. The ruins she lived among were more than a mile above flat earth. She looked down upon New Jersey's treetops. The western forests added to her tension. No human, other than dragon riders, had ever visited Manhattan.

That will change.

Main Trees couldn't grow on Manhattan's slopes. Yet smaller trees of a new kind were on the island's shore and threatening to create a path for humans. Humans had become more aggressive in recent years but they won't leave the canopy.

What will we do when the trees came to us?

She had more pressing issues to deal with. Carla was there making preparations. The Librarian had little time to dress for Mass as the congregation came early. This Mass was not the usual. The calendar called for High Mass.

"The last one. We are out of material."

Darleen turned her back on the distant forest and went inside. *If we don't unload the Burden soon, we are finished.* The humans will attack. But where can dragons fly to? The Librarian didn't know how they would survive. Vision Keepers can't leave Manhattan. Forgo the Book of Answers and dragons will degenerate.

"Carla, bring me my robes, please," Darleen said speaking kindly to hide the fear in her.

Carla was new, a young dragon who was born after humans and dragons parted ways. Darleen hoped Carla would never suffer the Burden, but it was a vain hope. The Burden comes with age and Carla was maturing.

Stay and die at the hands of savages or abandon Mass and become an unthinking animal? What was worse? *Carla may not have a choice.* Since sky-change, trees have progressed upslope at an alarming rate while visions faltered. The oldest trees were falling and how long before one bridges the Hudson?

"Do you have my sash?"

"Yes, Librarian, got it right here."

Carla helped Darleen get the robes over her wings. The librarian cloth was long and white and tradition demanded it stayed clean. The holes for wings were small slits. It took time to wiggle her long feathery wings through them. It was always difficult.

"Dragons weren't meant to wear clothes," Darleen said although she liked clothing herself.

"The humans wear less and less clothing all the time," Carla said. "Who is more animalistic now?" She picked up the hourglass. "Five minutes flat, that's my new record."

Darleen stepped outside and spread her wings. The robe was fitted well. "Carla, close my door before you follow."

"Yes, Librarian."

She took off and glided down the mountain's eastward face, pulled up smartly, and landed light as a sparrow on the flatland. *Legend calls it a parking garage deck.* Jimmy Hendrix had already lit the incense which her wings blew out. Jimmy relit them.

Below her, on the flat called Giant Stadium, thirty dragons who were once plagued with visions waited on their hunches. Each person represented ten others not there. Only three hundred of them were left altogether, a record low population of Seers. Carla landed. Two helpers picked up Darleen's robe tails and together they moved to the edge of Vision Rock. Carla Santanis and Jimmy Hendrix flanked Darleen.

"A vision for the Book of John," the Librarian said with her arms raised looking down upon the representatives.

No priestess today, this was High Mass, thus the Librarian herself presented instead. It was her vision and not one of the congregates. Librarian visions were rare.

Strange timing, indeed.

"Make ready your hearts," she said.

"No shit," they said together.

Scribes on either side of the alter signaled ready.

"Let us meditate. Ready your minds," the Librarian said, lowering her arms and closing her flight lids. "This is for Book One."

"Far out," the congregation returned.

Books were arranged according to epoch. The timeline wasn't certain. Educated guesswork was applied. Much was seen but not understood. No matter its meaning, the practice gave relief to all. Dragons suffered maddening visions and nightmares whenever Mass was ignored.

Ignoring Mass was tried and each time Darleen's race sickened. Many had died insane. The people of Manhattan were the last. They remained close to his homelands out of hope for delivery. John Doe had lived and died many times in this region and his essence was heavy there.

"If any can add or correct you will be heard," the Librarian sang out after a short time of silence.

"Far out," they said all at once. "Sock it to me, sock it to me."

"What does that mean?" Carla whispered.

Darleen ignored her. Carla was too young for visions. *Strange words will soon fill her dreams.* John Doe's common phrases were made liturgy.

Writing inside trees and on artifacts, was not His doing. He did not write; they wrote for him. Trees held books of saints but dragons cared not. Tree-script, already written, did not concern them.

"I see him," Darleen cried." The reliving of her vision came fast and hard.

"No shit!" The gathering said.

The speaker was not a dragon, but rather the essence of John Doe's life pouring out. The narrator becomes His familiar of that time. The speaker waxes between the observing mind and her mind. Darleen was one of the few who was able to make comments while reliving the experience. A change of voice denoted different speakers.

"'Are you ready? We're to go to town,' Mom said. Dad replied. 'Do you think he'll handle himself alright? He just woke up for Christ's sake.'"

"The little female is there and slobber runs from her mouth," Darleen said in her voice. "John looks at her. 'Jeepers, she's got crazy eyes.' He's embarrassed. 'Does she have to come, too?'"

The congregation repeated the word "jeepers." *New taglines won't root.* The new reading was too close to John's first death.

"They get into a magic vehicle, a car. It's on the ground, the flat ground! They drive to a town…dwellings. Go to a store. John's excited, he has never been to town before. There's an animal made of carved inert material called the Carousel Horse Ride. The girl got on it. 'I'll put a dime in it, it rocks back and forth.'"

Darleen lowered her long neck. Her impressions had mixed with his. The scribe will sort it out later. She dropped her arms.

"That's all folks," The Librarian said.

"That's all folks." They repeated.

"Anyone got anything to add?" Darleen asked. Hight Mass was an open forum.

Paul Lennon raised his head from the pavement and spoke.

"I saw them outside the store. John was given a piece of candy. He did not know what it was. Dad said 'it's OK.' I saw a larger man, who said he was the sheriff. John didn't like him. Words were exchanged. I missed it. We were on the car's windowsill. That's all folks."

"Anyone else?"

Nobody moved, everyone's head was down. Darleen waited. When the scribes stopped writing, she raised her head and said the words which dismiss the gathering.

"This meeting of the Library Council is now over. Peace out!"

"No shit!" The congregation said, and other sayings such as, "that's no bullshit," and "holy cow."

Everyone filed off the big flat area. Some took to the air. Others walked toward their homes to get ready for the evening's party.

Bullshit is right.

Paul Lennon's contribution wasn't enough for a proper recording but it filled a gap in hers. Early visions were the least comprehensible. But this one, Paul's and hers together, had a sharp point. His First Death was closing in. They had better deliver His book and soon. Reaching the bottom meant no more visions and no more relief. *Insanity will take us all yet.* One or two more readings and the Book of Answers will be full.

"Carla, gather some of your fellow young folks. Go to the library and see if you can find anything we have not read before. Look for post Mass notes, anything will do."

"Yes, Librarian!"

Carla flew off Vision Rock like an excited child chasing a hawk. Carla didn't see the large bright light descending over West Island behind her. It was not a meteorite, too slow. It was not a dragon, too bright. *Is it another sign of doom?* It reminded Darleen of the spaceship John Doe saw in Red Book One. But spaceships have come and gone before often enough.

Perhaps the aliens have come to watch us die.

"The last dragon rider will know. Her lore runs deep."

Should I bring Sophie here? It was forbidden by her people. Mr. Mayor will kill her if she is seen flying. Darleen turned for home with the Book of Answers on her mind, a book which held no answers for her.

53

Jaybird at Stump

Jaybird went home to pack for Bricktown. His home and lab were not near to one another as a hedge of safety. He had too many illegal things in the lab. His home wasn't much better. His house was a respectable treehouse although situated in an old-growth canopy. Old-growth was where the best conveyor knots were.

He had hung his place far away from the nearest village inside the dead tree zone. It was a good place to indulge his taboo curiosities. The phrase 'historical research' had come to him in a vision there. If people knew of his unnatural dragon-like talent—He didn't want to think about the repercussions.

I'm relatively safe.

People hated old-grow hoods. Trees fell too often and their leaves were hard chewing. The hood had been abandoned since sky-change times. Manhattan was within sight which also dissuaded visitors.

"Gram says sky-change triggered hate of dragons but I don't hate them?" Jay spoke to his bird as usual. "But don't things change all the time?"

His platform was made of boards scraped flat and smooth, unlike Gram's live floor. He had deadwood tables and chairs, but also, traditional constructions such as a living leaf roof. Trees supported many useful parasites which he didn't mind using.

His prized possession was a flat board table although it was less practical than his dragon-make stone cooking hearth. Should any townie visit, they would be leery of his polished plank floor for its bad toe grip. Jay's fancy dragon-made firepot was an outrage although still legal. Forced to toss one item over the side, he'd sacrifice the dragon hearth.

"If the authorities find Gram's raft with her dragon stuff, they'll chop her tree down with her in it," Jay said with a little laugh.

"Down will go many heretical objects. What do they expect from the last dragon rider of old? No wonder she remains hidden."

Gram's safety was not Jaybird's immediate concern. He had bigger bugs to bake. Gram and he disagreed. But he had many ideas in common with her, he hated the new politics and desired the truth.

"Speaking truth will set them free." He hesitated on the edge of his raft. "Defying Gram may be bold and a little wrong, but science truth must be allowed to speak."

He almost leaped but withdrew half a step instead while pitting his logic against morality.

There is no other way. He had to try and save them. Rider Tribe was for peace. He couldn't turn ass to people in trouble. The people were diminishing and he had the key to change declining minds. The evidence was in his belt sack.

"It's the right thing to do—time for show-n-tells."

He felt the shiny metal thing. It was still secure in his sack. Bricktown was a long swing south. He stepped forward again and stood wavering on the edge.

As a child, he had seen a tree go down. The open space it had created was clear to the ground a mile below. The view had captured him. Others looked away but not him. Others ran from the edge in fear, not him. Of course, now it was branched over. Space fills fast. Vine travel is safest. He can't fall far unlike his people who were falling backward ever faster.

"For the good of the people."

He jumped, grabbed a vine, and swung southwest.

Jaybird wasn't a skilled wood walker but he was good with vines. Thus, he swung when he could. Jump-ready, he tiptoed thin branches of the upper canopy swiftly and always with the next vine in sight. Vines were many lower down but he was careful never to go too low. If anyone saw him do that, they would curse him as a ground lover.

Gram's words surfaced in his mind while he traveled. 'Keep sunlight paths or the predators of deepness will get you.' He took her advice on that but not in all things.

He made the Parkway without incident. Not one cat or giant constrictor blocked his way. The Parkway although neglected was still walk-ready. He tested the deck with both hands on a good vine. The woven floor held. He smelled no leaf-rot. The canopy above still let in light. As far as he could see and smell, it was the same as last year. He walked on with one eye always on the next vine.

Two days later in the late afternoon, he reached a well-worn exit. He took the plank up-tree a few hundred feet and stopped at the tollbooth. A younger male sat inside chewing skunk weed. Jay smelled the drug before he reached the toll-taker's window.

"What exit, what're you looking for?" The sentry asked.

Green juice dribbled down the toll man's furry chin. The man's tail swished intimidation. Jay touched his tail stump.

Words will have to do.

"Bricktown," Jay said. "I'm going to the Public Stump."

"You got the right exit. You're a Bumpkin. Today is Sun-dee. Stump is closed. Go to the common tree. Left plank and up, right at the fork, ten home-trees on."

The sentry stuffed more skunk-weed into his mouth and put out his hand. His nails were claws. The man was stoned off his ass. Jay handed him an iron-wood trinket. The bribe-taker accepted it and motioned Jay to move on. *Just another worm in the bark.* He had heard the mayor's men can do no wrong and that grapevine held its weight.

He reached the guest tree where many hang-nests were strung from poles embedded in the trunk of a giant iron oak. Some people were already sleeping. A few travelers gathered on the public platform around an un-lit ironwood firepot as daylight receded.

The women sat on their haunches smoking black wool. He had not smelled it since Gram smoked it. They noticed him looking down. One stood, lifted her skirt, and showed him her ass.

No tail, that's cool.

A tail wasn't expected. These were old women come to stump. They don't share smokeable plants with young males. Gram smoked him up but he knew better than to ask them. The Rider Tribe had its rules, too. He resumed climbing the rope ladder, found a clean hammock, and slipped in.

A nice fist-size zoom-bug landed on his bed mast in easy reach. It would have made a decent meal and he was hungry, but not hungry enough to eat it raw as the villagers did. He liked his food civilized which meant cooked.

Beg use of the Common Raft's firepot? Surely Gram-like sour faces will appear on each philosopher. The nesters above might rain filth down for making smoke at bed time. *Cooking isn't worth it.*

It was still dark when morning birdsong woke him. Women get up with the sun. The women's guest berth was on high with the birds and got first light. Women slept less and did more. The old Grateful Dead saying was true.

"'Women are smarter, that's right.'"

Jaybird sang as he made his way low, took a leak, and climbed back up to the walkway intersection. After a quick bite of leaves, he stopped a man and asked, "Where's Big Stump?"

Jay had lost track of where he was.

"All paths lead to Big Stump," the man said walking away.

Jay followed. The main trunk was called Center Village same as in every big town. He arrived late. Old men and young women were listening to a momma while others huddled on a bench waiting their turn. *It's too dark here, the canopy isn't trimmed. Tailless old men milled about.* A good sign. The speaker was in the middle of her rant.

"Mister Mayor is failing us, I tell you..."

She's an old one, but still half Gram's age.

"He is not caring for Main-Tree properly. Look around, too many leaves overhead. It is quarter sun and still dark. Look at this deck. When's the last time new vines were cultivated?"

Her tone was bitter. Platform care was the responsibility of young males.

The two-dozen people there followed where she pointed.

This place is going to shit.

A matriarch wouldn't let this happen. The oldsters were tailless, like him, but born before the sky turned when it was common. Jay was the only young one stumping and young without a tail.

"Where are the young?" Jay whispered to a nearby stumper.

"Up the mayor's ass," The old man said pointing at Main-Tree.

The trunk was several hundred feet around and housed a massive hollow. The mayor had made it into his office. *People just didn't use trunks like that.* Two young men with spears stood at the mayor's door with knives in their belts and swishing tails. The sentries made angry eyes at the stump with ears tall.

Jay felt like a wingless bird. Fifty years before when he first made the trip as a child, the old people stumped and the young bent their necks for every word. What happened? *I will have my say and change things for the better.*

The next old one hopped up onto the stump.

"What of the alien spacecraft," she said. "Mayor has made it off-limits. No one can go to look at it. He says if any go and talk with them, she will be vine-tied and hung for a spider's meal. What man has a right to do that? It is Women's Rule broken. This cannot be allowed."

He had heard about the alien craft. A flying machine had landed on the far side of Manhattan. Will the dragons attack it? Such things were seen in every generation but never had one landed. This one was different and not the common pie flyer, but rather a glowing ball. Jay didn't care about aliens. Such things weren't his interest but the grapevine had recently been heavy with this topic.

"Who will stop Mister Mayor!" Someone shouted.

"Is it right to tie up the duly elected?" Another said rebuking the challenge.

The reciting of philosophy went on a long time with no resolve. What was the answer to such a vexing problem? The mayor abusing his authority was only a small part of a bigger issue to Jay's mind. Jay waited his turn and said nothing.

Science and politics don't mix.

"It is a free canopy. No human being can restrict another," an old man said voicing the consensus.

Jay slid down the bench as each speaker finished while he considered how to say it. The raised platform, a large vertical branch cut flat, was carved with intricate designs on its vertical faces. Dragons were carved on it from the olden days but the riders were gouged out. The carvings were made when women flew dragons over the You-Us-of-A.

Big Stump hadn't changed except for the vandalism. People came to learn and teach and grow as usual. Jay felt the timing right as debates quieted. He signaled for the stump and was given the platform.

He began, "The mayor is only one bud in a tree sprouting many new leaves. The bud doesn't define the tree. Some buds are good. Some will flower and some will rot."

It was a good beginning. The people murmured approval. Old people respect old wisdom. He needed them in a willing mood to give his report. He waited until the murmur subsided.

"I'm from Bergen County, old-grow, the oldest, not far from Manhattan. I search conveyor knots. I have found many things. I want to tell you what I have found and what I think it means."

This caused a wave of chatter. It had been long accepted that knots come from the ground. People feared them as was natural and right, but that didn't stop them from looking and spouting speculations regarding the Down-Low. Knots held unusual bones made of strange flint rocks and such items were useful thus acceptable. But most finds were mere curiosities.

"I know a very rich knot field. The first of its kind. But I only keep what is most unusual and what is proof of my idea. I have come to show and tell."

"No more of your shit," an old man said.

"You going to show us rock bones?" A woman asked.

"I've seen enough of your dragon-stock," the women that jeered him last year said.

"Pass it around, don't Bogart," an old lady said.

Jay pawed at his waist sack. He had to spit out what he came to say or forever hold his peace. Once an artifact is produced for sharing all the attention will go on it and not on his ideas about it.

"Not yet, hear me first. I'll say what I think this one means. I think we are not the highest creatures. I think our ancestors came from the ground. On the ground, we were different, more advanced than we are now. They were more advanced than we are now."

"Don't be stupid," a man said, "everyone knows we're tops. Answer me that."

Then why do the dragons make and we only take? It was odd that the man pressed his issue out of turn and the ladies let him. Jay, at a loss, ignored him.

"They, the oldest people worked metal themselves. More important, we are going backward if they used to be us. I have evidence. As time goes on, I think, the higher the trees grew the more stupid we became. We need to explore the deep and learn the truth of our history. We must regain our knowledge. I have an item—"

"Show us!" They all said at once.

He had no choice. This place was called the show-me tree for a reason.

Jay pulled a metal object from his sack and held it above his head. It was made from shiny metal. A silver stick with a shallow bowl on one end. When he found it the word 'spoon' jumped from his heart into his mouth.

He gave it to the nearest outstretched hand and it was passed around, women first as natural, then the men. When it came back to Jay, he asked for comments. The debate heated fast. Finally, the women agreed and the oldest spoke for the group.

"It must be dragon-make of a long-ago age. It is known that dragons work metal. There can be no other explanation."

"They work metals crudely and not like this," Jay retorted. "Yes, they work it but where do they get metal? I will tell you. My Gram had first foot witness of dragon life. They get metal the same as I got this. They find it. For sure they get it from mountain tops and rubble heaps but it's ready-made. They beat it into new shapes with fire. But it comes from the ground. Our history is on the ground!"

"History!" A voice cried.

The mayor himself stood on the outskirts.

"What are you a dragon friend?" The mayor said with a big voice.

People backed away from the stump.

"You are Jaybird Blue. Your Gram is a former dragon woman. An outlaw. History is the dragon's burden. It is not for us. Go near it and we'll all be cursed like they are. You have nothing to say."

People called out agreeing. The idea of history came out of the dragon's religion making it taboo. Dragons were compelled and obsessed with history although no one knew why. The stump shifted under his feet. Women cowered away as the mayor advanced. The men puffed themselves up.

Jay needed to pluck his words carefully. The women there won't defend him.

"I do not see any evidence that the dragon curse can become ours. I think—"

"This stump is over! Black-Wing, Bird-Tree, bring this outman to my office." The mayor jump-spun and walked to Main-Tree.

Two young men with big swinging tails came forward. Each man took one of his arms and yanked him off the perch and drug him to the mayor's door.

One guard swung open Main-Tree's huge plank door like it was a dead leaf. They tossed Jay inside but left the door open. He had never been inside such a large hollow before and this was only the waiting room. He took the bench along the front wall and sat facing an inner door. The bench was set away from the wall to accommodate tails.

He waited while pondering the nature of this hollow. Big hollows form when an irritant gets stuck before reaching the surface. That bark stream dies, festers, and rots. New conveyor paths go around it and budging the trunk. Knots push out small irritants. Hollows encapsulate bigger trapped infections.

Big ones are as rare as ice. When the rot is removed there is usually nothing left of the original sin but rust stains. *Whatever caused this hollow was huge.*

Hollows were too small to live in. This one was more than unusual, it was unnatural. *Whatever caused this one was nasty.* Was this carved out of the living tree? Jay shivered. Such an idea was horrible.

On closer examination, that wasn't the case. The walls were covered with faint marks like the script-like marks commonly found inside knot walls. He never tried polishing a knot wall. Doing so made the marks clear.

"It's writing, it's writing! Holy cow."

Jay jumped off the bench. Dragon letters were imprinted all over the exterior wall resembling faded ink tattoos. He had never considered what such marks represented. Dragon script didn't grow on trees but that was what it was. *No doubt. But why, how?* Tradition called the marks Dear John letters although it was thought to be natural. *This ain't natural.* Jay's tail stub twitched.

Gram said it was writing. He didn't believe it. What dragon writing he had seen was written on Gram's artifacts. Her hollow had such marks but he never studied them. This hollow was scraped smooth showing a library worth intensive study. Dragon text. No doubt. Jay's knees turned into bee-jelly.

How do they write inside trees? Going to the dragons may answer but that's still a bad idea.

He touched the wall and scratched it with a fingernail. The stub of his tail twitched uncontrollably. *More proof intelligence originated on the ground.* Conveyer knots only travel one way. This can't be the work of alien visitors.

But how was it done?

He swooned and swayed in deep thought and fell onto the bench like a drunk. He laid back marveling at the ceiling until the mayor's door opened.

"Jaybird, Mister Mayor will see you."

He rolled off the bench. The young male secretary who called waited at the door. At least that tradition held. Men were always secretaries. Females were too intimidating for the receptionist's duty. Jay took a step.

"Shoes off," the cub said.

"What?"

"No shoes. Mayor's a naturalist."

Jay slipped out of his moccasins and tiptoed clicking toenails on the hard floor which sounded like a cicada. Stiff hair along his spine pushed against his tunic. Cicada bites were terrible. He didn't give a leaf if the mayor was all-natural or not. He kept his tunic and pedal-pushers on.

Mr. Mayor's metal desk reflected a silver shine onto the man's fur-face making his hair glisten. He motioned Jay to take a seat but Jay couldn't move in his shock. *This is not normal.*

The desk and chairs could not have been dragon-made or made by his people. The furniture was double oversize huge and metal! Every part was big and thick, and slick-shiny like ironwood. Bee's wax lamps made the desk glow. It was like his lab table but huge and metal! Jay stood with his mouth agape mesmerized, swooning.

"Just don't stand there," the mayor said.

"Who, how?" Jay stammered.

"Sit, boy, it's alien make. It was given long before I acquired this office. If I could, I'd drag it outside and let it fall. I won't cut a bigger door into a living tree."

Jay faced the mayor's cold, dead stare which reminded him of the deep, black pools inside pitcher-flowers where bugs go to eat but die instead. Jay averted his eyes. The table's legs were embedded deep. *He lies. This made the hollow.* The words 'embalming table' filled his mouth but he did not say it.

"It's ancient," Jay spit out instead and immediately regretted voicing that dangerous idea. Jay's toes gripped at the floor but got no purchase.

The mayor laughed a long high screech inflating his cheeks. The elder man standing on the right shifted from foot-to-foot raking hardwood with his nails. The mayor's goodwill didn't last. The secretary and the other man had none in the first place. Mister Mayor positioned himself taller in the giant chair.

"I'll file your opinion as a joke." The boss said. "You can't take that idea seriously. And yet it seems you do. I hope this is not true. This brings me to why I asked you here."

The mayor sat back showing his teeth. He scratched his ass and sniffed his fingers before going on.

"I should kill you for heretical philosophy. However, you're a smart fellow and at times I need wisdom. Women don't share wisdom. You aren't in league with the women, are you?"

"No, of course not, I—"

"Good, good, good. When I call you will come?"

Jay was too afraid to speak. He wrinkled his brow in disagreement. He had shaved his forehead like a civilized man. The man dead-eye stared until Jay gave his bobblehead consent.

"Good, good, you go now, go home. Don't come stumping again unless I ask. Get out."

Jay flew through both doors dive-bug fast leaving his shoes behind. He stopped running at the stump. People on the wider platform weren't going to the stump but away from it.

Jay sniffed deep collecting his senses. He set out cross-country toward the Parkway ready for a meal, but fearful, he plowed on a long time. Eatable leaves and fruits were everywhere but he required protein. Cooked or not meat was a restorative food. Mammals suited best.

The first animal I see is history and the only kind of history Bricktown tolerates. I can do nothing for them.

The realization struck bitter as he snatched a winged rabbit off a branch and broke its neck.

"Raw meat for raw rebukes," he said.

With a traditional ironwood belt knife, he made a quick meal of its breasts. The rest he donated to the lower reaches as Women's Wisdom demanded. In a hundred thousand years someone will find its bones inside a knot and notice the knife marks and wonder. He had an odd idea that seemed right. In the future, knot-harvesters won't be people like him if human at all.

54

Mister Mayor

Mayor Morgan relaxed in his metal chair. His lawyer, standing aside, picked a mite off him and ate it. His counselor had something unpleasant on his mind. *If the old dragon woman was here, she'd take a switch to him for nit-picking.* Mayor chuckled. Nit-picking was an old taboo but he encouraged it—whatever breaks Women's Rule he pushed. Morgan let his lawyer pick knowing he was looking for an opening to speak and not a snack.

"What is it, Featherhead," Morgan said. "Speak plainly, I won't bite."

The lawyer rubbed the spot on his arm where Morgan had bitten him last week.

"Why did you let him go? He has them stirred up. See how the women chatter? If word of this goes to grapevine…" Featherhead touched the table. "They don't know we carved deeper and found this."

"You think I'm stupid?" Morgan said. "Fool. We know where he lives. He announced it at the stump."

"But I don't see how—"

"He's not the big danger. His Gram is the last dragon rider and that is the strong vine we must cut. She puts knots in our plans. People still follow her ways."

"I don't see—"

"I'm sending hunters after him. Jaybird will lead us to her and then he dies, too. Would you rather I have a spectacle here in the open? I won't give one reason for them to hate us. This must be done quietly away from Bricktown."

"Yes, I see it now. I'll stump that his artifact is dragon-make and that he is an agitator, nothing more. I'll stump those women who accept his words are dumbass."

"That's the idea. Women are not 'smarter in every way.' Get to work. Send hunters to me. Go."

Mayor Morgan dismissed him with a sneer. The man was not smart but he served the need. Featherbrain was a good talker and especially good at talking down the women. The women have little power left and with their moral leader gone, they will fall in. *Women's Rule will end once and for all.* Things were coming together. He only needed to wait a little longer and her influence will end. *Nothing will stop my war.* First, her and then Manhattan.

"The aliens will make a deal. There's no better place for them to land." He said to the secretary.

He thought to use the aliens for his advantage. Morgan poured himself a gourd of honey-brew and took a deep swallow. Getting drunk early was taboo, but he had a victory to celebrate and damn the taboos anyway.

He downed the liquor and poured another.

55

After Stump

Jaybird stacked layers of worry and not only because his stumping had failed. The farther northwest he traveled the greater his unease became. The common roads were too exposed and he didn't trust them. He continued cross country swinging blindly until he ran into Route Seventy running east to west near the Parkway. The offramps going toward the sea weren't used anymore. East was overgrown.

He sat at the intersection undecided smelling salt air. A desire for the ocean befell him. He proceeded without any experience of the country ahead. It was the long way back to Bergen County. Unpopulated, he assumed the old shore road would be safe if he could find it.

He hesitated. Fear fought desire and pricked his back hair.

"What am I afraid of? I can always cut west later."

He had never gone near enough to see the ocean up close. He had only spied the bay at a distance. The river he saw after the deadfall was his closest glimpse of open water. Over his life, he learned of waters beyond his experience. The wide water, strange as it was, sprang buds of curiosity against taboo. He enjoyed the smell of the ocean.

He lost the road within five miles. Another five and he entered the pines. *Nobody goes to the pines.* Gram's warning about that region dogged him, 'Keep hands on. Don't fall. There are spikes below like javelins. Falling will kill you.'

He should have turned back but he struggled on picking his way through towering needles.

After hours of hardship, he located a road of sorts, made of planks, going northbound. It was a weird sight. *The Boardwalk of tall tales?*

"Gram says it's brittle and unsafe if that is what this is."

Closer, he saw why it was feared. It was made of stone boards. He hung from a vine and touched it.

"Petrified wood—ironwood doesn't get this hard."

He had found stone wood inside knots before. But how can board construction absorb enough minerals to become rock up here?

"Because it's old, very, very old and it had pushed up from the ground."

The walkway had pitched and rolled. Some sections were on end while others were flat or altogether gone. Nothing grew on it. Foliage flowed around it as if the stones were cursed. How and when was it made? This was beyond all lore.

Dragon-make? Everything not understood was dragon-make. *This can't be that.* He followed a mile and gave up when his foot broke through a brittle plank for the tenth time. He climbed into the thicket above and tip-toed thin branches onward along and above the stone road.

The foliage was unusual consisting of slippery needles, thorn-brush, and spiderwebs holding mosses. Stopping to rest, tiny spiders were everywhere. Jay shivered. Small spiders scared him as much as the people-eating giants. His reservation was also an oddity. People ate them. Bugs are bugs. Gram taught that dragon riders hate spiders. He did too although he never met a dragon and only women ever rode upon dragons.

He spent many hours going around web fields rather than through them. Having no other way to move forward, the day ticking away, he plunged deep again and into a web field with gritted teeth. He soon lost his bearing. The sun was obscured. Above and below the stone plank road was tangled thick with webs and hemmed in pine needles.

Webs were less on the road as the road became more solid. The road was all he had. He dropped down onto it and proceeded. He regretted taking the boardwalk more with every step but went on as best he could for a time.

"I need direction, turn west. I can't take it."

Seeking passage up he came upon an oak branch between pine shocks. Weary and short of good footing he followed it. Lore spoke of an oak-way in the pines—rumored but not accepted fact. Gram dismissed the costal oak-way, but with a wink. *She doesn't gossip.* Dragon riders know things. She had seen what others cannot.

Gram won't speak of tall tales…or rider secrets.

A small branch led to a bigger one and the overhead soon improved with fewer needles and more oakleaf. Oaks reached and touched each other between pines. The going got easy. Jay smelled his home tree's main trunk which was miles on. He had never been so far east of his branch. He climbed to the very tip-top of the oak. As typical, lightning had flattened it. His home tree's leaves were unique like every tree. He had stumbled onto his home tree's home trunk.

He sat upon the oak's headless neck facing the sea with an unobstructed view. He smelled it all day. It was closer than he assumed. The Hudson opened into the ocean ten miles southeast and the bay was only a mile away. The sight was an unnatural comfort.

"I'm not like the others and that's my trouble."

He ignored Manhattan Mountain's gray stone. His interest was fixed on the sea. A sane man would turn away. Great birds held station in the air, bigger than any he had ever seen, bigger than condors and eagles. Puzzled, he watched closely. One banked nearer. It had arms and carried a stick.

"Oh, my tree! It caught a fish! It's huge."

He had eaten fish. Small, tasty things called sardines lived in tree-wells and cup-leaf ponds. Birds carry fish eggs stuck to their feet. Where birds drank from canopy pools, sardines and amphibians appeared. Fish were tiny, but apparently, not at sea.

"Intelligent birds! Nobody knows this. Why, because dragons aren't ridden and I won't listen to the last dragon rider. I've been so stupid."

His words tasted bitter. How often did he ignore Gram's teaching? As a scientist, he should have lifted his ears tall. *A seeker of facts? I'm a joke.* Shame filled him. The world was bigger than Mayor Morgan or he could admit. Wasn't understanding the world the point of his research? He had so narrowed his vision that he missed everything in sight. Regrets fell on him like dead leaves. Even as he watched round-eyed, he felt he was missing something important.

"What of these distant fisher birds? What bird uses tools? Birds do not have arms, only wings." The dots over the ocean turned as one and flew toward gray Manhattan. One creature carried a sack dangling from its feet.

"There's no such thing as a tool-making bird…Dragons. They are dragons! They're glorious."

Wonder shook fear from his heart. He lost foot grip and fell off the perch. He didn't fall far and scampered back although excitement made his grip weak.

I've missed so much.

Gram, long ago, had invited him to see dragons. She had asked when she was younger and still able. Afraid, he had refused and swore he would never visit dragons. He cowered whenever their massive shadows were cast upon high branches. Gram's dragon feather fan was as close to a dragon as he ever got.

"I'm an idiot."

The mayor's lies rinsed off like dust in the rain. He could no longer accept the common lore having seen them. Scorn for those majestic creatures was all he ever heard from townies. Gram was right.

She is not the crazy old woman they say she is.

"What a fool I've been."

From this height, he saw clearly. He saw more than the oaks between pines. The oak-way ran in a straight line—it was planted…that can only be done from the ground. A dragon rider would know. The way to thread these needles was clear from above. He set out toward his home sure of the direction. The oak-way was real and true and so was the wisdom of Sophie.

56

Return to Gram

Jaybird followed the coast for two days. The uninhabited zone was wild and unsafe, yet not one cat or raccoon, or snake came near him. He avoided them like a skilled wood-walker although he had not been trained for it. Or did they avoid him? He wasn't sure. His senses turned sharper on the oak-way. Innate skills he forgot blossomed. Thus, he saw them at a distance.

His raft was on one of Home Tree's main branches. His favorite perch for calling bugs stood six hundred yards across a leaf field. Hungry, he went to his food-call spot first.

He had a common condition called eagle-eyes but Jay never had a reason to use it. A glint of a blade flashed on his distant raft. He had left nothing metal out. He focused on magnifying his perception. The flicker of a tail going over the side sat him upright. His intuition thundered danger. He backed off the perch and ducked inside a blueberry bush.

Forbidden artifacts. They must have seen them.

He scanned until he found three of the mayor's men. Each sitting on a high branch. They were focused on his home like hunters after a big cat. They carried spears and knives.

They're hunters and I'm the prey!

He had to get out of there and tell Gram. Jaybird crept away and descended several hundred yards into the deep. He had never gone this low before and he had no fear of it.

Mayor's superstitious lackeys won't follow.

Reason fought convention as he went. He enjoyed the Down-Low environment dark as it was. It was new and interesting. What had compelled him to avoid the deep? *The fears of others.* Groupthink had captured his mind and he felt stupid for allowing it. The desires were always there and always self-repressed. Flying was his other secret desire and an opposite thing. Knowing them, he should not have stumped. So strange were his needs he thought something must be wrong within him. But he soon rejected that idea.

"Nothing's wrong with me. Society is sick."

The proof of that sickness hunted him with knives and spears.

"'And what's so funny about peace, love, and understanding?'" He said quoting old dragon rider wisdom.

His line had good night vision; night walking was no problem. Slimy as the vines and hanging roots were, he managed. The smell of rot was better than a spear in his back. And, oddly, in this strange place, he felt at home. He touched a spiral vine. *Am I so twisted?* Doubts piled on him but he had no doubt who the hunters were after.

Gram's tree was half a day west. He didn't need the sun to find it. The smell of her home tree was like no other—it was the only sugar-maple in western New Jersey. He went quietly until out of the hunters' ear-range. Thinking it safe, he climbed higher to find Gram's scent on the wind. From there he proceeded with less care.

Compared to hunters, he was a clod in the forest. But his days on the road brought back forgotten childhood skills—He was then unbeatable at hide-and-seek.

And how Gram used to laugh. He had not heard her laugh in years. A thought came as he neared her home. Sneak up on Gram. *She'll see I'm not so inept.*

Sneak crafting on Gram demanded great caution. He relaxed. Intuition carries deeper awareness. He made his heartbeat slower. His ears stood wide. He didn't trust his wood walker craft before running from Bricktown. Now he let his senses guide him.

Intuition serves dragons well. Visions were tied to the dragon's religion but natural intuition was not. Visions were taboo, uncivilized, yet dragons advance while his people falter.

Genetic memory must be intuitive as well.

His mind bent upon dragons as he waited with all ears in stillness. For two days on the road, he remembered her wisdom. What she said of dragons in the past, which he ignored, resurfaced forcing new realizations upon him. Dragon riders weren't like the others. Gram's saying came to his lips but he did not speak it.

'You and I march to the beat of a different drum.'

The hair on his spine hackled as he moved toward her place quite as death closing the distance. He stopped above her raft planning to jump down. To avoid vibrations, she could read, he had not touched any branches of her tree. It was good she wasn't home. Jay had an advantage.

He found a hidden place above in the wind which blew his sent away and there he waited. She wasn't on her boards. The sound of a great reeling of leaves soon came from below. Something crashed and ran in the forest. She chased game toward her nets.

Good, she is distracted.

It was not an animal, it was Gram. She leaped onto her raft, tumbled, and took up a sharp stick. She made to throw but a spear struck her chest. She fell backward. Two hunters landed, one from above, the other from the spear's direction. One hunter had only been fifteen feet below him. Jay didn't see, hear or smell him.

"Did you kill the little male?" The thrower said, a very large hunter.

"Lost him," the other said. "His must be an old scent. He's been here, his scent is everywhere."

The big hunter slapped the other.

"Stupid, you'll never find him now. You should know fresh scent a mile off, idiot. You wasted the trail, polluted it. We're going back to Bricktown."

"But Mister Mayor wants both dead."

The big one pulled his stick out of Gram, she moaned. Jay caught his breath.

"He wants this one. Let the others pick off the knot-seeker. It'll be soon enough. He doesn't matter anyway. Mayor wants to know soon as it's done."

"She's still alive."

The big one laughed. "That's a good one."

It was a joke. Blood wounds bring big cats and they like their meat still kicking. There was no easier way to be rid of a dead body other than to leave it for the bone crunchers. Toss it and it will hang up. Cats leave nothing behind.

"Let's scat before we're on the menu. It's feeding time."

The two made off with no attempt to hide their movements. The sound of their branch crashing travel echoed throughout the heights. Jay listened until only the sound of blood dripping through the floor splatting on her leaf hammock was heard. He slipped down to her raft trembling and not quiet.

"About time," she said. "I heard you up there. I planned to feign surprise."

She chuckled and choked on blood.

"Where's your medical sack," he said.

"No, I die now. Don't waste time. Come close." He bent to her lips. "The murder-man is not gone. Take my knife. He'll come head-on, do it. I taught you cat-killing, do it."

He slipped the knife out of her tunic under the cover of his body. Its long metal blade was made for stabbing big game. It was a tool of the dragon rider's lost trade. He gripped the bone handle hard.

"I'm ready." He breathed it so low he wasn't sure he spoke.

"Weep," she said in a faint whisper. "Bend closer to me."

He did. He lay over her body tensing his legs under him with his face close to hers. When the attack came, she choked, "Now."

Blindly Jay sprang and slashed as fast as a snake. The hunter took it in the neck mid-air. Momentum nearly severed his head. The killer tumbled and rolled onto and off the raft. Jay dropped the skewer. It happened lighting-bug fast.

He fell to her side. She raised a finger to her lips causing him to quiet. The spear hunter fell for a long time. His body bounced from impact to impact many times before silence came. Had there been another hunter, the racket would have drawn him.

"Dragons, go to them," she finally said.

Her voice was weak but her face shown peaceful. She touched his lips.

"I am proud of you. You have dragon skill, use it. There is…no place for you in this…"

She coughed up a clot of crimson blood and spat. Her splotched green skin had become like yellowed beeswax as her blood ran out.

"This world…is not for us…Go to them."

"I will."

He said it only to please her. Revenge stirred in his heart.

"Must not…go home…aliens…safer."

"What does that mean?"

He strained his ears to hear her last words but Gram's light winked out. He closed her eyes and could do no more for a long time but sit next to her in silence until the sound of a big cat roused him.

"Not today."

He took her leather sheath, jammed her knife into it, and tied it to his belt. He wrapped her body with all the cloth there: her tunics, blankets, and sashes. Her favorite item, a dragon feather fan, he placed over her face. Last, he covered her with dry leaves. He arranged all of her dragon-made possessions around her and poured hemp oil over all. The oil ran onto the boards and pooled. Left alone, the cats would scavenge a meal out of her if the vultures didn't arrive first.

"Sophie deserves better."

He quoted a Grateful Dead saying, "'Don't murder me, I beg you, please don't murder me,'" and kicked Gram's iron firepot over.

"Your stove wasn't dragon-made. It came from below."

If she had her way, this object would be acceptable. *Who would care? Mister Mayor?* Jaybird cared no more.

"Dragons, Gram, if only you had shut up about dragons."

The oil lit well. Jay stepped back and watched the flames grow.

"Who's at fault? The mayor, dragons, the world, the sky?"

Gram's dragon things caught flame and he was glad. He had his fill of dragon-made things.

"'Trouble ahead, trouble behind, Casey Jones you better watch your speed.'"

Jaybird dove, caught a good vine, and swung east toward New York.

57

Jaybird in Flight

He swung and ran branches frantic and didn't stop until the smoke of Gram's pyre was nothing but a distant wisp. He didn't run from the fire. It was the smell of her burning which drove him. Forests can't burn. Only mosses and dead leaves ever lite. Without fires, the forests would choke and rot. Fire controls unwanted plants and parasitic insects. Burning her body was fitting. Gram was a tick on Mayor Morgan's ass.

"May her ashes nourish the trees."

He climbed into an elm's upper reaches as lethargic as a sloth although he was eager for the wind and the pinnacle's sunlight. The lightning strike was fresh, still black and smoldering. He found a spot without live embers and sat on a burned knot ignoring the swirling soot. Perch fires were an opportunity for barbeque but he had no appetite. Ash blew on the wind and fell on his head. His mind went black with revenge. Even so, he couldn't bring himself to kill the mayor.

"'You don't kill what you can't eat, it is uncivilized.'" He spoke Grams words.

'I'm not an ape.' Gram had said, *'Peace is the way of the Grateful Dead. Peace is the way of dragon riders.*

"Rest with peace, Gram."

He stayed until the sun was low but still bright. He looked south over the canopy's crest wishing he had the insanity to pluck that sapsucker mayor out of Bricktown and snap his hairy neck. *It is a bad desire.* He could never accomplish it and if he did, how could he live with himself? If the mayor dies another like him will come after.

Gram's voice echoed in his heart and he voiced her teaching.

"'Killing begets killing. Such won't do.' What will do, Gram? No place is safe for me. You would have me go to Manhattan. That is a spiderweb. It is watched. I can't go there."

He had to go where the hunters won't follow but where? There were no havens he knew of to swing for. No other people lived within dragon's range. Dragons flew a thousand miles in every direction. All but a few villages had moved to Bricktown. Even Atlantic City was thin. Outlaying hoods were empty.

From this perch, trees covered the world. But their colors weren't right, many tops were brown. Northwards colors were red and yellow. South treetops were greener. But for how long?

"The world has changed and I can't ignore it any longer."

In the distance, a pie flyer zipped across the sky. Aliens flew in every generation but nobody knew why. Stumpers rumored that the mayor had talked with these sky creatures. For what purpose? *Why did they come now?*

"To watch our race die. They're zookeepers. Bricktown is a birdcage."

The heart of a taboo land was as good a place as any. He pressed northeast and farther away from dragons and mankind. He traveled two days, slow, quiet, and roundabout with hardly a bite to eat, so deep was his misery, and so lost his soul. He went wide around his old northern home range and found a line of healthy trees that grew along the riverway. Far above Bergen County, where the Parkway turned, he came to a place he heard about but had never seen called the Palisades.

He edged out onto a thin branch overlooking the river. The end had snapped off making an opening. His view was clear. He stood on the edge of his world swooning with fascination.

The trees ran straight down to the cliff's top. Below that was a rock-face leading to the wide Hudson River farther below. Water glinted between giant lily pads. The lower region was choked with water-plant life. Life was everywhere and on every level. *Life is more than the canopy.* The idea gave him comfort.

His eagle-eye did not provide long enough sight to see Mayor's bad intentions coming. Zoom perception doesn't provide social wisdom.

This was his first hard look at the lower regions since childhood and he was not afraid. His curiosity smothered grief for the moment. He had gone farther north than ever before. Yet Manhattan was still there in the south mists. East across the river were once treeless mountains which greened more every year. Something odd caught his attention. He shaded his eyes.

"It's a structure. That's crazy, it can't be natural. Rocks aren't square, those uprights aren't trees."

Jaybird's heart fluttered. His mind flexed. The word 'Temple' formed behind his teeth.

"Aliens? It must be them. Dragons don't build. Mass is held outside."

Looking on, he spotted more ruins in the jumble and a lot of it. It was evidence to support his theory and there was no one to tell. The old Good Friday saying came to his lips.

"'Just the facts Ma'am, just the facts.'"

Excitement surged but no branches crossed the river. The few that extended out past the cliffs were sick. There were no crossings north in the forbidden zone—only great gaps between sparse living trees were within sight.

The river runs wide one hundred days travel north.

Jay wasn't patient. The long trek north wasn't appealing. He decided to climb down against all reason instead. No one had ever crossed the Hudson except on the back of a dragon and no amount of reason could convince him to sit on a dragon's back. But it was either cross or go north.

"Let us see if hunters follow me there."

Fifty yards below the sun layer was as deep as anyone would go, and only to release waste. But here over the cliff, the sun reached far lower. The shear face lit a long way down as the sun passed from east to west. Hunters could follow. He had gone much deeper than the sun level himself before but his path invited others to do the same.

"Gram was for the sky and I for the lower regions. We were two broken birds pushed out of the nest."

At four hundred yards, the trees leaned out overhead so far, they shaded the face making it permanently dark and slimy. No treetops were within sight. Barks turned smooth with fewer handholds, vines became cold and wet, distances between trunks wider. There were few strong connections between weak, rotting branches except for spiderwebs. The sight of such thick webs chilled his soul.

"Might be easier inside." Jaybird shuttered.

Great spans of spiderwebs stretched between trunks as far in as he could see. Spiders big enough to spin such webs would eat a person. Many huge branches shot off main trees but slanted sharply up. Branches didn't spread horizontally for walking as usual. Nothing was normal in the Down-Low. The place reeked of cat piss and rot.

Keep the river in sight.

He had left his shoes in the mayor's hollow and that proved lucky. His foot-claws saved him from falling several times. Civilized implements were useless. It became dark as night nearer to the lowest reaches. Above the blue sky had turned pink and purple by the time he reached halfway.

Sundown was nest-time but he had nothing but slimy flora to work with. His fingers and toes hurt from digging for grip. He had no choice but to keep going. He reached trunk bottom and rested upon a tangle of roots in deep gloom. The river, at the cliff's bottom, was yet another eighty yards farther down. Slipping, he stabbed for a new hold and ripped a nail.

"Mother of the tree!"

In answer, a hiss. A great vine lashed out but it was not a vine.

A snakehead thrice his size stabbed the air just above him. Jay latched onto it and scrambled onto its back. The snake twisted away and slithered down the cliff with Jay clinging on. It stopped on the riverbank and raised its head. Jay slipped and dangled over the water with his fingers wedged under massive scales. Blood gushed from his injured cuticle but he did not let go.

A huge eye strained backward and searched for the irritant.

Jay had seen topside snakes flip pray into the air and snatch it. When the beast's muscles rippled to do just that, Jay let go. The monster shot up. It looped and rushed after him but it was too late.

Falling played like a dream. His life passed before his mind's eye until he crashed into a massive leaf floating on the river. It broke his fall but landing also shook him badly.

As Jay struggled to fill his empty lungs, the snake turned and disappeared into the root lands far above. Jay lay there unable to stop gasping. Bruised and sore he forced himself to be still fearing broken bones. His impact sent yellow spores the size of his thumb jetting upward from the giant flower he nearly crashed upon. The spores were twirl-wings. He caught the scent. Such spores bear acid. Like firebugs, they burn on contact. Watching one rise he noted a clear night sky above.

"Why are there no branches over the river."

The sound of slithering responded to his words and forced him to move for cover. He crawled across the pad fighting hurts until reaching a giant dried dead leaf that had curled forming a tube. His hideout rested upon the river's living blanket of lily-leaf. He wormed in and lay on his back. Spores don't burn their kindreds or so he hopped.

Jaybird, weak, tired, filthy, and glad of no broken bones, closed his eyes for the night not knowing what dangers surrounded him.

58

Jaybird on The River

He slept with unease. The rocking river beneath his shelter should have been a comfort like a nest in the wind but it was not. Tree branches high above swayed all night with the soothing sounds of home, but he couldn't ignore his strange surroundings. The sounds of night creatures he didn't know filled him with dread. *If this float breaks free, I'll wash out to sea.* Was it well anchored? Does deadfall float?

He dared not go out seeking food. Creatures there will think him table fare. His rest floated upon worries. He had dreamt the old dream, the one where he flew a dragon assailed by wild winds that pushed them along at an insane speed. There was no going back against that force. Fearful, he never asked Gram what flight was like. When morning came, he woke flying.

His hideaway moved.

"Hey, what gives?"

Through the opening, the back of a giant snake's head reflected sunlight. *We must be in the middle of the river…I'm on a snake's back!* Its scales were red and yellow diamonds. Each one outlined in black like the canopy's smaller poisonous snakes.

Is it aware of me?

Jay shimmied backward hoping to exit the other end and slip away but the curled leaf funneled smaller on that end. Dead leaves can't stretch. It was straight ahead or nothing.

Jay shivered; he dreaded snakes less than spiders but had never seen one so large. Big cats were easy to avoid while snakes were not. Jay's tail stub twitched out of control although snakes never bothered him before.

Inching forward, he stopped at the exit. The creature parted lilies swimming for the far shore dragging Jay's refuge. This monster was many times bigger than the one that had attacked him. His throat closed. Panic threatened to choke him.

Got to get out.

He bellied into the opening. The leaf had curled tighter overnight. He struggled to get out and got stuck.

"If I die, let it be in the open air!"

Forcing the air from his lungs, he pushed through kicking and squeezing. He wanted clear air, had to have it. He gulped and the sweet odors of flowers overpowered him. He sneezed. The snake stopped and twisted to see behind.

He curled into a ball and spread fingers to mimic foliage. Beyond Jay's fingers, its great tongue flickered. He clamped his ass tight trying not to shit. One great eye swept over him. Then quick as a buzz-bug, it turned and continued.

As the shore drew near, Jay saw his chance. A thin vine from a rare New York side tree hung low over the river. He burst forward, ran along the snake's back, over its head, and leaped. His momentum pushed him and the vine high. The snake twisted behind itself hissing. Excitement weakened Jay's grip strength. He fell crashing onto a wet lily pad adding fresh insult to his already bruised body.

The monster splashed down in the open water near him. The wave pitched him into the air. Jaybird flew sideways landing inside a giant bell-cup flower full of watery nectar. The snake provided a sticky but safe landing.

The giant's head hovered directly over him while Jay choked and spewed slimy water. Jay could have counted its jaw scales. The head sawed side to side with its tongue darting. *The flower's scent confuses it.* Jay already smelled of a lily leaf. The nectar and trapped bugs also covered his scent. It couldn't catch his drift.

Maybe, and maybe monkeys fly.

Jay knew nothing of such creatures. The canopy didn't support such large animals. When Gram mentioned giant snakes, he laughed. She recited many odd sayings besides Grateful Dead wisdom. Dead philosophy died before he was born. He didn't buy old sayings. They seldom made sense but one did. 'Out of sight, out of mind.'

And that's why I don't believe in giant serpents.

He'd kick himself if the snake wasn't near. The flower rocked with the monster's movements as it circled wide. When far away, Jay climbed for a peek but the bowl's sides were too slippery. Insects came for the nectar and slid down. Bellflowers were traps.

At least I have food. Or am I food?

He scooped a handful of bug-goop and sucked the jelly from his palm. Not cooked, but naturally fermented and better than the best honeysuckle candy. Dessert and a meal in one.

Is this snake flavoring me for fine dining?

The morning wore thin and more waves came and rocked him—snakes came in from every direction. He tested the sidewalls and found he could cut a slit in the flower and escape. He had Gram's knife, but he dared not let the contents rush out and give him away. It was better to wait but he didn't have that choice.

The sun had moved directly overhead, but shadows soon appeared blocking the light. Not one, but four snakes hovered sixty feet above him in a meeting of backlit triangle heads speaking with flickering tongues and a great hissing. Their voices released the stench of rotting meat from their teeth.

He imagined the activity above was a debate to decide which one got to eat him. He watched fascinated. Fear subsided. He felt a strange kinship with the creatures that were about to make a snack of him. To such giants, he was nothing but one bite so a debate made logical sense.

A faint horn sounded. The snakes turned and hesitated as if deciding what to do. They slid out of sight with each going in a different direction. The sound of great wings came on; an osprey, or giant eagle? A bird large enough to kill giants had scared them off. Splashing moved steadily away.

A candy-coated man is too delicious to pass up.

A great splat and thump. Whatever it was, it landed in shallow water very near him. He could have walked to shore. Jay was tired of waiting to die. The flower's top was a little above his head. He stood and drew Gram's knife.

"Here I am, come and eat me already, I don't give a shit," he yelled slashing at the flower without success. The peddles were tougher than he thought.

A serpent-like head ringed with feathers swung over his position very close. Jay couldn't make out who or what the backlit silhouette was.

"Dragon's give a shit, man. Sophie never told ya? You must be the dude."

A single claw tore the flower open. Waist-deep nectar rushed out and Jay with it. He landed in shallow water but slipped and fell many times before losing Gram's knife. Big, scaly hands scooped him up and set him on a dry boulder.

"Sorry, man, I didn't mean to freak you out. I'm Dave Bob Marley. I've been looking for ya."

Jay staggered back. Still slick with nectar, Jay fell ass over heels landing in a deep pool behind the perch. Jay floundered until the dragon grabbed him out and took three hopping strides. Dave set Jay down on a rocky but dry beach and stepped back.

He blinked and rubbed his eyes unsure of what he saw.

"The flower's toxic…I'm tripping!"

"No man, this is real. Take a good look."

The creature was many times his size but not big enough to take down a giant snake. The skin on its breast, face, and arms were leather. Tiny scales shone under feathers and down. Its wings and most of its body were feathered. Its face held human expressions. *It's smiling at me.* Gram had described them and he only half-listened. Her descriptions didn't meet this reality.

"Dragon," Jay said.

"No shit," Dave said. "Sophie's great grandkid, right? I smell her on you. Relax dude, I'm on your side."

Gram's loss flashed in his heart. His knees buckled, stomach churned, and acid gurgled into his throat. He fell back onto a rock miserable with grief.

"Gone, she's gone," Jay said sobbing.

"I know man, sucks. I'm sorry, man. She was a cool old lady. We figured she'd send you. We saw her funeral pyre."

Dave Bob Marley reached into the bag that hung from his neck and produced something resembling a rolled leaf. He used a little stick, struck a tiny fire on it by way of a flick of his thumb, and lit the thing. He took a big drag and exhaled the smoke.

"This will get ya right. You'll feel better, man. Here, hit this."

He tried to give it to Jay. Jay backed away.

"Oh, man I forgot, you dudes don't smoke anymore. That mayor asshole has got you guys all fucked up."

He took another drag.

"It's cool, try it. Sophie would bogart it, for sure, she dug weed." Dave extended a long skinny arm. "You gonna hit this or what?"

Jay took it with nothing to lose. Gram had smoked it. It was an old dragon rider tradition. She never smoked near townies but he had seen her doing it. He took two deep drags and felt as if he had smoked all of his life. He held the thing out and examined it before taking another hit. He passed it back.

"Far out," Dave said, "You're a natural, Mr. Natural. Hey, what's your name little dude? She told me man, but I forgot."

"Jaybird Blue."

"She had a dragon rider name for you, Hermes. Never told ya? OK, cool. So, Jay, let's get you outta here. Snakes are righteous but lots of shit around here ain't cool. Fucking spiders, man."

The dragon bent himself low.

"Get on my back, let's blow this joint."

Dave's weed had an instant effect. Jay in yesterday's mind would have run the other way. But, instead, he got on and found a hollow between the creature's vertebras that fit. He clung onto the long quills growing off the back of Dave's head. When Dave stood, extending his legs and wings, Jay remained secure. The dragon took a hit and snuffed the smokeable out between fingers before putting it back into his neck bag.

"Am I positioned correctly?" Jay asked.

"Right on. You're born for it. That's no shit. Let's go find Darleen. She's the Librarian."

You are born for it. Gram said that all his life and he never believed it. Dave ran down the rocky shore flapping and not far before going airborne.

Jay was stoned but it wasn't like alcohol. The smoke calmed his fear. None of this seemed strange. Flying was exactly like an old memory, familiar, visceral, safe. It was a desire and fear he always had but never faced. That conflict ended as Dave climbed.

"Mr. Natural, that's me."

"Right on dude."

High above the sky felt like home. His old recurring dream wasn't a nightmare after all. It was a premonition.

59

Meeting Darleen

"Hang tight little dude," Dave said as he climbed steeper. "I'm gonna loop-de-do to see if I see anyone. Time to get serious."

It was hard to hear in the wind but Dave explained he was looking for other dragons to call home on behalf of Darleen.

Jaybird relaxed and loosened his grip. He had made a mess of Dave's neck feathers. The dragon flew leisurely at first with the wind and tacked into counter-winds to make wide circles but it was slow going.

Dave reached a great height before looping. He repeated it over and over. Dave looped by folding his wing, diving, and reopening his wings at the bottom. They shot up at incredible speed. Each loop thrust them higher and covered more distance. Jay didn't care where they went or how long it took as the sensations and sights enthralled him.

A Dead saying came to mind. *'I may be going to hell in a bucket, but at least I'm enjoying the ride.'* It may have been the weed, but Jay felt content to watch the world pass. There was no one left on Earth like him.

"I am meant to be in the sky," Jay said in a moment of calm air.

"No shit, dude," Dave said.

Dave flew a wide circle many miles around and out farther from Manhattan on each lap. They flew so high only eagles could see details below. Jay's eagle-eye lent well. The boardwalk ran just inland along the ocean shore's white beaches. Huge sea creatures floated offshore which startled him. Gram's word, 'whale' resurfaced from his childhood. Firepots showed around Bricktown's outer platforms but not in the city proper.

People cooking in secret bespoke hope. Even so, he could never go back. *'Bad eggs spoil a good nest,' and I'm the bad egg.*

North of Manhattan were lands he only heard of in nest-time stories. It didn't resemble what was said about it. North Forest was sicker than tales told. Trees were laid down one on top of another strewn in every direction and dead. The landscape far north of Bergen resembled the game pickup sticks. This shocked him to his core. The difference between Bergen and Bricktown's foliage became plain. His home range was infested with disease worse than he had imagined. Places he thought were healthy were not. Tree death had spread wide and was closing on Bricktown.

Jay pressed his legs into Dave's flanks.

"My tree! Everything's dying!"

The dragon held station midair on Jay's reaction.

"Yeah man, this shit's all over. As far as we fly it's all the same. Trees are falling. Ocean, Monmouth, Cape May, everywhere around Bricktown's all fucked up."

Dave banked and flapped into a headwind. A big question burned and Jay shouted it into the wind.

"What's killing the trees?"

"Cosmic waves…Creation Wave, same shit. It's in the Book, man. I didn't see anybody anywhere…Must be at Library. Let's go home." Dave beat his wings hard.

"What's Creation Wave?" Jay asked but with speed came the wind. Dave didn't respond.

"Hold on little buddy," Dave yelled. "I'm gonna dive-tack."

The dragon dove at the ruined forest, twisted at the bottom and shot off at a steep angle in a new direction. Close to the ground the smell of tree rot nearly knocked Jay off the dragon. Dave repeated the move and Jay held his breath. The wind whirled. Hanging on was all he could do while Dave made a beeline for distant Manhattan. The top of each arc's air was frigid. Jay could hardly breathe. Dave paused before another dive.

"This is what I call a roller coaster. There used to be one on Coney Island, hotdogs, too."

"What," Jay said between chattering teeth. He hadn't heard that term before.

"Roller coaster, it's in the Book of Answers, man. Jersey Shore had them, too."

Jay blinked at Manhattan before Dave's dive. Great flat slabs were on the mountain's top pushing up at crazy angles. Unknowable forces over uncountable time must have caused the damages.

There were squares and rectangles and other contrived shapes below. As Dave glided in toward a gray flatland halfway up the mountain, the impossible became obvious. *This whole thing is a ruin.* It was a mountain made out of a ruined and unknown civilization. Jay nearly fell off of Dave.

Gram had shared about Manhattan but he didn't understand the gravity of it. She never called it a city. She had unwittingly sparked his interest in conveyor knots. Knots had provided evidence of a lost time, but he couldn't conceive of the immensity.

"This is impossible."

Dave came to a stop but Jay didn't dismount. His mind wouldn't take the scene in. His ideas were destroyed. He hadn't scratched the surface of this. People were more advanced in the past, no doubt, but their level of advancement was beyond human comprehension.

"Hey man, you getting off?"

"Sorry, of course."

Dave bent his neck low. Jay slipped off with unsteady legs. The ground was uneven, hard, and full of debris, and not what he thought the ground was like. He picked up a square rock. The word 'brick' popped into his head. Nothing in sight was smooth or graceful.

"What's that," Jay dropped the rock and pointed.

"New York Public Library, cool, right?" Dave pulled that rolled leaf out of his neck bag and lit it, took a deep pull, and said, "Dude hit this. You'll feel better."

Jay took it and smoked deeply. They stood side by side passing the smoke while facing the library. Jay became calmer. The strangeness of it settled.

Thoughts of home returned. He had killed a hunter. He had no home. He was on the ground and thereby marked for death. What could he say to his people? *Should I say anything?* Bricktown was no longer home. Yet his humanity urged him to save them. It wasn't the people's fault.

"I got to tell the people," Jay said, "The mayor can't refute what I've seen. I'll bring this back with me." Jay touched a toppled street sign. Its marks were the same type as on the mayor's walls. "I got to help them somehow."

"I'm afraid that's not possible."

A girl's voice came from behind. Jay turned. Another dragon and larger than Dave wearing an open white vest. Her feathers were soft blue and gray and displayed a familiar pattern. Her scales reminded him of an owl. She wore metal and glass before her eyes. Jay found one in a knot once but it was broken. He had called it glasses.

"Darleen, man, what's happening, K-pasta?" Dave Bob Marley said.

She ignored Marley and addressed Jaybird.

"Thank the Dead, we found you. You are Sophie's kin. I smell it. Your people want you dead, I am pleased you survive."

The big dragon hopped over Jay's head and landed facing the library. She twisted her neck back to face him.

"Come inside, as we Deadheads like to say, 'A picture's better than words.' In this case, I agree."

Darleen picked her way between rubble piles. Dave motioned for Jay to go, and he proceeded. Dave didn't follow. Jay caught up at the top of the library's tall steps. There may have been doors, now long gone, like the mayor's office. Inside was nothing like that hollow. There were stacks and stacks of books—millions of them—stacked everywhere. Light from upper windows illuminated the depts. The piles were high but neat. Gram had a dragon book. He recognized them but they were too big. No human could handle and make use of such large objects.

"I don't understand," Jay said. "What are they for?" Pointing at the dragons within he added, "What are they doing?"

Darleen explained. The younger girls were wiping clean the pages of old books. The boys, sitting on curled tails with quills in hand, were refilling blank books. Piles of them waited for new ink. Books required recopying as they decayed. Remade books were returned to the correct places.

"The work never ends." She pointed at shelves stacked in neat rows.

Paper rots so they transfer the message. Jay understood only because Gram taught that dragons write, and she showed him a red book, but Gram never said why or what it was that dragons wrote down.

"What's the point?" Jay said.

"Salvation," Darleen answered, "More so, survival. We're compelled to record the Source's memories. If we don't...It's not pretty...We become animals. As long as the work continues by representatives, 'of the people, for the people, by the people,' we are safe. We must write our visions as they come for the day of his coming."

"Forever!?" Jaybird asked.

"The Burden lasts only until we deliver the Book. It is, 'all one long song.' If we finish before the Source is found...We cannot be free or whole until we deliver. A rider's help is why I sent for Sophie...We were connected. She is gone, the connection falls on you. The Wave is coming. We must deliver before it gets here. Only recently did I understand the implications of our partnership."

This information was unfamiliar but Jay felt its truth in his bones. Scraps of his dreams and visions, Sophie's wisdom, and his artifacts collided pressing into his mind what he did not understand before. He staggered back falling into a seat of books.

Two species were made...designed for each other. We are symbiotic.

"How did I miss it?"

Darleen pulled a pipe from her vest pocket. Three dragons called out in one voice.

"No smoking in here!"

"What about my people." Jay said.

"Doomed, just as we are," she said.

Darleen finished stuffing her pipe and put it back into a pocket. The weed smelled of skunk bug but it wasn't that. He hadn't smelled this type of weed before. Smoking wasn't common but old people still did. Gram claimed the art came from dragons.

"Let's go outside," Darleen said, "We'll need a puff while I explain more about our situation."

Darleen spoke of many things that afternoon. He didn't understand everything. That the dragons were attempting to contact the aliens for help was clear. The aliens were monitoring Jay's people. Darleen assumed the spacers came to study the wave phenomenon. When energy comes from the center of the universe things change. Darleen had watched it happen.

"That's when trees began falling, that's why men and dragons fell out, that's when the sky changed," Darleen said.

That he accepted. But why he, Sophie, and the dragons were not affected was beyond his imagination. Dragons carry and keep the memories of the one they call The Source. Darleen thought the aliens could help determine if John Doe was still alive. The Head Librarian didn't know if they would cooperate. She reasoned that the aliens may have come for John Doe themselves ahead of the end.

"Doe and the aliens had a relationship in the deep past."

"How can you know this?" Jay asked.

"I have read the Books. Our alien visitors made a mistake. They approached the wrong species. Your people carry John Doe's DNA but we have his soul. They wasted their time. The next cosmic wave takes us all."

"Is there no hope?" Jay asked with a dismal voice.

"Somewhere down there is the Source." She pointed west. "If we find him… It may not be too late…for us."

Dave lifted his snout and sniffed in the direction of Bricktown.

"Not happening, man. The ground cover is too thick. Get stuck there and you're dead. Ain't no way a dragon can move around in that tangled shit."

"What happens if we find him?" Jaybird spoke quietly. "Won't the aliens help? They must."

"I don't know if they can, or will, but if we can't find John Doe…" Darleen made a cut sign across her long neck. "I rather die without the Burden."

"I looked a shit load," Dave said. "Jay, you carry the Ancestor Seed. You ain't scared of the ground like the rest. You're the dude, man. He's near, we feel it, he's on the ground."

"What about you?" Jaybird asked, "Can't you go?"

"There isn't a safe landing in the forest," Darleen said. "We want to be freed of the Burden, of course. Old wisdom says, 'live free or die.' I have never been free. I desire it if only for a day."

Born free Jay had lived free until getting caught pursuing history. Seeking the Dow-Low's mysteries was his death warrant. And the world was utterly failing. The only freedom left was choosing where to die. Gram's dragon saying came to mind. *'Born free, free as the wind blows. Follow your heart.'* Jay let his breaking heart speak.

"I will go. I will look for him," he said.

Dave quoted the lost philosopher Mr. Rogers.

"'I knew you could.'"

Jay didn't know if he could, but he will try.

Aliens

Surveying from orbit, Gabe zeroed in on a cluster of remnant DNA in what used to be called the east coast. Signals ranged from central New Jersey to New York City and that wasn't far from where they had the transport center in Connecticut ten million years before. He also picked up a tiny trace in north New Jersey.

As expected, the transport temple remained somewhat intact. The temple had a time-stop effect on local geology so he didn't anticipate such radical changes to Manhattan Island. Giant plants were predicted. He didn't expect Springfield's foliage to fail so soon. *Death is spreading ahead of the Wave.*

It was not a time temple effect. Something nasty had reduced Springfield into a pile of matchsticks. Gabe ordered the shuttle's AI to descend and circle the area.

"It's like a meteor airburst," Mike said from his observation screen. "I'm not showing bomb evidence. She screwed up again and sent a comet? That's what screwed her dinosaur project. I don't get it. How does She let shit get so far out of control? Intelligent designer my ass."

Gabe had the biological monitor running at his post.

"It's nothing like that. It's a genetic disease. The bail-out program kicked in and collapsed the environment. The last Mini-Wave triggered it. It won't stop."

Smaller waves precede big ones. Gabe recognized a new problem. Mini-Waves weren't supposed to kill living systems, only change them. *Either End Wave's leaking or She's crazy.* Life on Earth already had one wing in the sewer ejector.

"Shouldn't we do something," Gabe said thinking of all the new life forms. "Does it matter? I mean…in a couple of days End Wave." Gabe's wings shuttered.

Mike's perpetual smile faded. Both angels knew the answer. This planet's life systems were scheduled to be radically reset and there was nothing to be done about it. Nothing of old Earth will remain. Watching the place die sucked but they were obligated to collect the data. Planet Molders had never before witnessed an End Wave while onsite in real-time.

"I hate this," Mike said from his anthropology meter. "Hey...give me a second...I got a sentient lifeform that ain't human." He pointed at his screen. "They'll be wasted. What a crying shame. We gotta save some dinosaur samples."

"You know we can't. Get that out of your head." Gabe said. "No way am I bending the rules that far. Every time we go unorthodox, we get blasted."

"Christ, I hate this shit. Why's it got to be us?" Mike said.

Of course, Mike hates this.

Any decent Planet Molder must. Nobody wanted to see the end of an old race. Worse, that baby race just getting started...doesn't have a chance. Nothing but a good time shield stands against what was coming unless it was designed for it. The angels too must get off the planet before reset or they will be transmuted as well. Gabe didn't want to start life over as a snail.

Gabe wiped away a tear. Mike was so hurt Gabe felt it. Progress reports scrolled across Gabe's screen. Moon confirmed an Immortal in the vicinity. Gabe's equipment agreed but with so much life concentrated in one sector, it was impossible to zero in. John Doe's mark was everywhere.

"How do we find him in that mess?" Gabe's wings hit the deck.

John Doe left traces of himself for ten million years. The biomass around Manhattan was a gigantic plate of spaghetti. There was no hope of pinpointing John. His DNA had spread wide but also it had been diluted into uselessness for a Book of Answers. There was only one usable straw in that haystack. The last Immortal was still alive, but not for long.

"We'll never find him in time," Gabe said.

"What about the locals? Maybe we can hire homegrown help?" Mike said. "We got them sentient dinosaurs in Manhattan. What about those humans, or what's left of them, they're trashed but better than nothing...just saying?"

"Let me think about it."

Moon Base had sent another self-propelled AI a few weeks ahead of landing. The robot ship, using holo projections, had made contact with a degenerated human who was their leader. The AI's evaluation read him as untrustworthy. Bricktown had the same disease which leveled the northern forests but there it attacked their minds. John's ancestors were deemed too far gone to be useful.

The mayor had never even heard of John Doe. They had lost their mythologies and legends of the deep past as the social engineering department expected. But scraps of that fake religion he and Mike had created still remained.

"Devolved humans make shitty agents," Gabe said.

"We need locals," Mike said. "I'm telling you."

"Local hires? I don't think so. Besides, we fuck it up every time."

"No, no not John's distant relatives. What about the new sentient beings?" Mike said. His enthusiasm pushed out some of the glum.

"Local hires never work. Nonhuman? Never been done." Gabe said.

Every time Gabe tried a local…He didn't want to think about it. And the one guy he hired right was John Doe and they left him behind. Gabe had a Prime Seeder right there in his hands and then he went and dropped the key straight into a black hole. Gabe normally rejected Mike's ideas, but Mike was so depressed Gabe had to do something for moral support. Meeting new beings could perk them both up.

"We got nothing to lose."

"Shuttle," Gabe said, "put us in a dimensional shift. We're going down. Come on, Mike, let's check out them reptilian folks."

"Rodger that, Skippy, but they ain't reptiles. They're dinosaurs."

Mike took the manual controls and flew them out of orbit.

"Ship, what's geology look like in the target zone?" Gabe said.

"Update." The AI said. "Manhattan has been pushed upward three to four thousand feet plus or minus average, due to continental drift. Extensive ruins remain. A plateau suitable for landing is now on screen. Destination Lower Manhattan East Side. Press one to update navigation."

The spot came up on the screen. They also had a visual in the forward window.

"Good enough for government work," Mike said—his first wise-crack in weeks. Mike's white teeth reflected the console's light as he pushed the button.

They glided in slow. Gabe watched the landscape. *Remarkable anything is left.* It appeared that parts of Lower Manhattan had been excavated long ago. Much of the surface was too regular to be natural.

They're civilized.

They flew over a handful of huts close together made of stacked stone with smoke venting from roof pipes. There were a few hundred other dwellings spread around the area as well. They confirmed the locals were winged and feathered which reminded him of Earth's dinosaur age—another of Her good starts that failed. Nobody saw that asteroid coming. The dinosaurs were wiped out long before their time. *And oh boy, was She pissed about that one.* She was a big fan of that project. Earth was just another mud ball full of primitive salamanders before Her dinosaur Wave jumpstarted Earth's evolution.

"Got a decent spot. It's not far from the occupied area," Mike said, "I'm setting us down."

"This was the old First Church's graveyard," Gabe said.

"That's prophetic. This planet's about to die."

"Not everything," Gabe said, "just advanced life. Lower forms that are pre-programed remain. Remember trilobites? They survived three resets. That's why waves—"

"Whatever. Hey, I got a couple of big lizard-birds on the screen. That's our locals. Let's go."

While Mike shut down and opened the hatch, Gabe checked the bio screen. They weren't lizards, they were winged avian dinosaurs and weren't supposed to be there, no way, no how. They looked scary, too but Mike and Gabe had force shields and D-shift perception protection. Outside Gabe ran his handheld sensor. Mike didn't bother.

"Hey, Skippy, don't look now, but they see us."

Two dragon-like creatures, more feathers than scales, stood at the edge of the clearing. They wore vests and belts. The larger one had jewelry and glasses. Both were an odd mix of feathers and scales, long, articulated arms and crown feathers.

They appeared to be talking. The small one pointed directly at the ship. They headed right for the angels. Gabe activated his shield. It didn't work. His universal translator didn't start either.

"How the hell are we going to communicate," Gabe said in Earth English as the creatures arrived.

"With your mouth, I'd say," one of the dragons said. "I'm the Librarian. This is Dave, say hello Dave."

"Far out, man," the smaller one said. "What's up, dudes?"

"Don't tell me. You are Mike and Gabe. I am right, of course," the female said.

"How the hell do you speak English, I—"

"Shut up, Gabe. I'll tell you how." Mike bounced with excitement. His scanner blinked wildly. "Meet John's familiar race. He had a pet lizard. OK, so they evolved, shit happens. They must speak John's language, dumbass, same as the Earth hires on base."

"Son of a bitch," Gabe said.

"No, I'm a lady. Dave is not the son of a bitch either. His mother is a very fine person. When you meet her, you may judge that for yourself. Can I offer you a cup of tea? We do need to talk. We have a problem perhaps you…Well, after tea. Will you join us?"

Gabe couldn't help himself and blurt out, "You know John Doe!?"

"Not exactly," she said, "but we do know a relative of his. His last descendent or at least we think so. He is of the dragon rider line, no tail. One can't ride with a tail, can she? Let's have tea and perhaps a couple of joints. I'll tell you more over refreshments, is that alright?"

"Lead on," Mike said.

Gabe swallowed his annoyance. *I'm in charge, but then again, Mike's the anthropologist.*

The dragons turned down a wide path between rubble piles. Mike walked right with them like they were old pals. Gabe stood there having a hard time shaking off his reservations. Recovering, he ran after. Mike was in his element and chatting up a storm, laughing and making nice. This was no time for micromanagement. Gabe hung back and let the better qualified team member do his job.

The Librarian led them to a nicely constructed stacked stone structure.

"Please make yourself at home, sit where you like."

The roof was flat but high and made from massive stones. Several other dragons were already present. Although glassless, the window shutters were open. Candles burned with a pleasant scent.

This is not a primitive dwelling.

It was decorated with tasteful wood furnishings, textile drapes, lamps, and other signs of emerging technology. The big advancement were the books, books of bound paper. She had quills and ink. A young male served tea and left before conversations went deep. Gabe didn't feel like any one of the dragons was more equal than the others.

What a good start but…

Age generated rank, the oldest first. The dragons smoked pot like John. It was pretty good shit, too, better than what they grew on the moon. The tea and cupcakes beat ship stores. In another time, Gabe would have spent weeks getting to know them but the cosmic clock didn't stop ticking. He nudged Mike to shut up and get on with business.

"OK, so we're on the same page," Mike said. "You need to deliver your books, so you can get them out of your heads and off your backs, and we need to find the same guy if he is still alive. We think he is, at least the Eye thinks so. Is he, do you know?"

"We don't know," The Priestess said, Dave's mom. "Only progressively older visions come to us lately. It's understood that the Book will end when the visions stop at his awakening. That's the bottom. We are at the beginning of his life now. Nothing recent."

"Since dragon riders stopped coming late visions ceased altogether," Darleen said. "The newest visions are over ten thousand years old. We can't record him in real-time. My feeling is he yet lives or our compulsion would end."

"Why haven't you people gone looking for him?" Gabe said it hard. A few of them flinched.

The little bi-peddle mammal called Jaybird chattered like a chainsaw. Gabe had ignored it. The little monkey man was one of Mr. Mayor's people. Gabe didn't trust it. But it was trying to be heard. It spoke so rapidly Gabe needed the translator. Even so, the text scrolled too fast for Gabe to read.

Although it spoke English and understood the conversation, only Dave caught much of what it said. Dave reacted to the monkey's speech while everyone else ignored it.

"Hey, man, the little dude has got—"

Dave was cut off by the wave of his mother's hand.

Darleen continued, "We'd look for John if he wasn't on the ground. We are of the air and heights. The one thing we have in common with Jaybird's race is a fear of the ground. For them it's superstition. For us it's practical. We cannot navigate tangled forests. You have wings, you see our problem. Nothing lives on the ground except small mammals and over large reptilian predators and, I think, John Doe."

"How are we going to do this?" Mike said. "We don't have any jungle mobile robots ready. We got nothing that can move freely in that spaghetti pile."

Jaybird got more upset. He jumped up on a table and rattled off a speech no one understood.

"Slow down little buddy," Dave said. He understood Jaybird but even he was confused. "Wow, here man, take a hit, chill out. He's easier to register when he's stoned. Smoke up, little buddy, smoke up."

"I have him on the translator. I'll play it back in slow mode audio," Gabe said annoyed. He hated wasting time on the little beast.

"… you're telling me my ancestor, The Ancestor, is a giant like you aliens. How can that be—"

"Sorry, I'll fast forward," Gabe said.

"…why don't you listen, are you thick-headed? Not every one of my people is scared of the ground or dragons. By the way, Bricktown will attack you, but that doesn't…" Fast forward. "…He is my relative. I'll go. I'll find him. Where do I start? Can't anyone hear me…I'm not afraid…I'm a scientist…I'll go. I have nothing to lose…"

"Far out, man," Dave said.

"You will do this?" The Librarian said. Her head tilted 30 degrees.

"Read my lips. I will go. Wow, I'm stoned," Jaybird said at near normal speed.

"He's in Keansburg, New Jersey. It's got to be him," Mike said. "The strongest reading projects from there. I make it a mile off the beach but it's hard to say exactly. Biomass messes with sensors."

"I'll ride him over," Dave said. "Always wanted to try a beach landing. How cool is that?"

"If Jaybird doesn't find him and bring him back…at any rate," the Librarian said. "It's too late to start. First light tomorrow. Won't you stay for dinner?"

"Love to," Mike said. "Can I help?"

Gabe found a quiet place outside to wait while food cooked. It was not too late to save Her project. But the rest of them, the last of humankind must end. Jaybird won't survive. The dragons were finished. *Ironic if they deliver the Book of Answers now after ten million years of suffering the Burden.* Their reward for providing the Seeder's need in the final act was to die.

"I must do something for them."

Either the Designer has a fucked-up sense of humor or She doesn't know what She is doing. Some intelligent designer She is. This is all wrong, very, very wrong.

Last Wave changes everything, but maybe there was a way to save John Doe's familiars. Gabe didn't want to give them false hope. They didn't know how near they were to their doom and he was not allowed to tell them. Company policy. He didn't have the authority or stomach to buck that policy.

But at least they'll transmute and be free, right? Advanced planet molding was off the table, but he decided he would do what he could for them anyway, he just didn't know what or how…yet.

A radical idea sprung. Whether John was found or not, Gabe might play God and pay the price. *Damn rules.* Her Centerness owed dragon kind something. *She ain't going to like it. She won't pay my overtime either.*

The Creator was known to be a cheap bitch.

The cost of lost company equipment will come out of his retirement account no matter how it turned out. He only had one time shield in stock. Giving away the lifeboat before a storm didn't make a lot of sense.

"I hope my unemployment insurance is up to date. I think I get funeral benefits, too."

Mike was up by the house and waved at Gabe to come for dinner. Gabe's empty stomach didn't want food, but he got up and brushed off his wings anyway.

61

A Long Way Down

John Doe picked up a quill and considered his homemade hemp paper. It took a long time, and a lot of effort, to make that paper. He hated to waste it. He struggled with writing his will. He had to start over once again. He had killed himself many times before, but this time he had a new plan.

"Dead is gonna stick for sure. Right, little buddy."

He had figured out how to stay dead. Odd feelings and thoughts he never had before kept coming on like a freight train wreaking his concentration although he enjoyed the trips. Memories generated inside those tidal waves didn't match his reality. Living crazy didn't appeal to him.

"What a trip, man. Flashbacks."

The Formica and chrome table he wrote upon was freshly conjured and clearly out of place in his earthen home. He had resurrected this same table before. It was just like the one Mom had had when he was a child—if that had happened. The orange plastic pizza parlor chair he sat upon had long ago turned brown like everything always did.

John wrote:

I had a good life. I love the pine forest. It lets light reach the ground. Radio weed grows everywhere. Geckos and jumping lizards keep me company and they never complain. The house I reassembled from buried rubble is pretty cool. I grow weed on the roof. How cool is that? I raised an old Parkway off-ramp a million years back. I dug under it and made walls of brick, landscape ties, and other stuff to close it in. I raised plastic furniture. I used to love it, but now I hate wood. Big trees, you can't trust them...I don't remember why. But I remember a lot now, like Jerry and Abbie. You won't see me climbing a tree, fuck that. With all the weed and shrooms I do and all…

He put the pen down and crumpled the paper, tossed it into the pile. Off-track again.

"Man, I'm all fucked up here," he said to his main squeeze lizard. "I can't write for shit."

John picked up the bottle of snake venom he had collected and held it up to the light. The snakes gave it freely. The old bottle was hazy but it showed the yellow liquid inside. He had done this before but he added acids to the formula this time.

This shit will melt my head clean off.

"Man, I got no chicks. How many times can you jerk off?"

The lizard bobbed its head up and down and inflated the red sack under its chin. John didn't know if it understood him or not. Animals didn't act right around him.

Man, I'm tired of talking to lizards.

His memory was spotty until recently. What he latched onto wasn't dreams— it was past reality. *But it ain't possible, but I remember it.* Real-life became a blur. He forgot last week but things from way back, lives he lived before, came to mind even while awake and not stoned. There was a farm, a sister, parents, San Francisco, Betty bang-bang and so much more came up out of nowhere.

There was no escape from this madness. The more he smoked to get away from it, the more strangeness filled his head. It was all coming together and he couldn't take it. It was all coming back, everything he had lost, too much pain, too much sadness.

"Fucking Abbie."

The lizard boobed its head.

"Fantasy or insanity? It's all the same. I was crazy before but now I'm off the hook."

He put a hand down on the orange *Formica* top and let the small, green lizard he named Charlie Brown, climb up onto his shoulder.

"Man, are you for real?" He said to the lizard. "I don't trust my reality, man. Reality is for people without dope."

He squinted at his loaded glass bong. He hadn't lit up in weeks. He hadn't missed a smoke in centuries before that. He held the little bottle up to the window's light again. Bits of snake membrane swilled. Beyond the window, movement caught his eye. It was a dragon. He had seen them at a distance many times before. It spiraled around out by the beach and dipped below the brush line. *That never happens.* Dragons fly high. Next, he saw it banking offshore.

"Looks like it's got a monkey on its back."

He laughed like hell for a good five minutes slapping his *Levis.* The dragon and monkey were still there circling the beach when he stopped laughing.

"I got to stop eating shrooms, man." He watched more closely. The monkey wore clothes. "But I ain't tripping. Man, that's weird. Where's the organ grinder?"

A memory flashed. Human-like creatures. He had yelled at them. Then he remembered an organ-grinder hippie on Asbury Street. That chimpanzee from the *Lost in Space* TV show came to mind. They had glued rubber drumsticks to its ears to make it look alien.

"'Bloop, bloop,' man."

He climbed onto the earthen roof of his place for a better look. The dragon dipped below the brush line again.

"Yup that sucker's landing. Man, that's not good. Crockagaters will eat the shit out of them."

He put his hand out and another small lizard crawled onto his palm. John held it close to his face and examined it closely.

"What do you think little dude, go to the beach?"

The lizard inflated its neck pouch.

"I'll take that as a yes. You know dragons used to scare the shit out of me."

Tolkien's book, which he had resurrected, had a nasty dragon in it which freaked him out. But that was fiction, it wasn't real and he knew the difference. Real dragons don't act like Smaug. Doubts filled him.

"Just stories, right? I know, don't be a pussy. What can it do? Kill me?"

His memory mixed good dragons with bad ones, fake and real. In the past, he couldn't tell what was what. Lately, it was all real memories. The difference between books and movies and real cleared but he couldn't believe half of it or wrap his mind around it.

"I'm losing my shit, man. Time to stop the crazy train."

The lizard bobbed its head. He put it down.

John had no reason to fear dragons but he wasn't immune to fear. He had freaked out last week when an orb floated down toward Bricktown. He had never seen anything like it and it scared him. *Spaceship?* John stuffed the 19th-century morphine bottle into his pocket and went inside.

"Let's smoke up some courage first, then we'll go see the dragon. Right, little buddy."

The bong needed water. He pointed at the table next to his water bed and floated a joint over to him. The Power used to fade right after waking and stay off but it came back on recently for no reason.

He lit his finger, lit the joint, and took a deep drag. He enjoyed the embers' glow a second or two before taking a few more pulls. He set it in an ashtray and forgot why he broke his fast. Smoke used to help him remember, mostly things he didn't understand. He forgot how smoke also wiped his short-term memory. He couldn't motivate himself without it. He went outside and faced the sea. In the distance, a dragon flew up over the hedge tops heading for Manhattan.

"Far out. Hey, wasn't there a monkey? I shouldn't have lit up."

His main lizard jumped on John's head—something needed attention. Having no clue what the little guy wanted, he hit the joint. Sometimes pot sprang a memory. The image of an early twentieth-century organ-grinder with a monkey wearing a red vest and fez popped into mind. John had a feeling he should go down to the beach. But the last time he went to the beach, a shit load of crocs followed him home. It took a week to get rid of them. They kept eating his dope and pets.

It took a lot of time for him to do anything. He had time, time was all he had, that and pets and a bottle of deadly poison. He had an odd feeling that his time was running out.

"Poison ain't got a freshness date. What's the hurry?"

He stepped out and sat on a plastic lawn chair to consider the dragon winging away northeast. It progressed slowly against the prevailing winds.

He registered time like never before; it was running out and running together in a loop. That sensation started when his memory sorted out. It was all true, and too far out to live with. *I can't relate.* He watched until the dragon disappeared and he doubted he saw anything at all.

"Man, I got to stop shrooming. But I didn't do any mushrooms today. Weird."

He sat there until the crocs' barking escalated. He cocked an ear to the beach. It felt like something was calling for a resurrection like that time he dug up a 1962 Ford Falcon van. Things close to his heart called him all the time. He often dreamt about the time he spent a night under an overpass while hitchhiking which inspired his first overpass house.

The things he saw while zonked didn't exist unless he materialized them. Were they from his imagination or real items from out of time? *What's reality anyway? Maybe I make this shit up? Maybe I'm God.*

He set out to see what the barking was about. John picked his way through the scrublands with a lizard clinging on his back.

"Damn it, I forgot my towel." An image of a cartoon towel came up, saying, *'Does anybody want to get high?'* It was a good suggestion but he forgot his dope, too.

"'No Towelly, we don't want to get high.'" He pressed on.

Beach sand only supported palm trees, scraggly vines, and dune grasses. Around one such tree in the distance, three crocs milled sniffing the ground between yelps.

"What's wrong with this picture?"

Crocs were scaly mammals with long snouts, short legs, and gator tails. They reminded him of dogs. They were dog-like but not exactly dogs That bothered him. Dogs weren't supposed to look like alligators. He stopped on top of a tall grassy dune. Along the water's edge, something big had torn up the sand.

"Sea turtles laying eggs? That ain't it."

The crocs didn't see him as they were occupied with what was in the palm tree. Crocs were a pain in the ass when they wanted something. There was some kind of critter up in the tree. *It's Rocky the Flying Squirrel.* He laughed and dug into his front pocket for a pipe but didn't find it. Rather, he pulled out the bottle of venom.

"Fuck me."

He turned for home to get a pipe to help him remember but then he remembered he forgot why he was there. He rolled the bottle between fingers. *I could drink it here? Crocs love carrion. No, my body will poison whatever eats me.*

"Dead is better in bed."

He decided to stick with the plan. The urge to protect his dead body was felt but his concern was more for the scavengers. He had planned to take it and lay down at home. He had done it that same way many times before. His Book of Answers said he woke each time. *Not this time.* Facing home, he was convinced his next death will be the last one and forever. He started down the backside of the dune.

A chattering voice called out, "Wait don't go."

The crocs went nuts jumping around and barking. A small hairy hand appeared over the foliage top and waved.

"That's not a squirrel, it's a talking monkey."

John ran down the dune yelling, "Fido, Spot, get out-a-here! Git, git!"

The crocs backed away with heads down and tails swinging. John marched up to the palm.

"Thank the tree somebody came. I've never seen such creatures in all…"

Monkey man chattered so fast John lost what it said.

"Oh hey, little dude. What's happening, K-pasta? I might be tripping but I don't have to be an asshole."

"Is it safe to come down?" The monkey man said with a long string of words John didn't catch.

"Yeah, it's cool, but dude, talk slow you're losing me, man. Get off the reds man, that shit's worse than crack."

Before John finished speaking, the little guy was down. It was a dude for sure but less than half John's size. Pretty hairy, too. He wore clam digger pants, a hemp shirt, and no shoes. Take the hair off, and its face would pass for human.

John had seen all kinds of critters above and below the trees but nothing like this. A TV documentary about Doctor Leaky in Africa flashed in his head. The bi-pedal animal Leakey had found resembled Monkey Man. A Beatles song played in his head but he couldn't remember why bugs sang, 'Lucy in the sky with diamonds.' Another out-of-sync memory rushed in and out.

"Allow me to introduce myself, I'm Jaybird Blue from—"

"Far out, man. I'm John," he pointed at the crocs. "Let's get the flock out of here before they grow balls."

John headed back the way he had come. The little dude followed but was unsteady on the sand. Monkey Man did better in the underbrush by walking on dead logs.

This little dude ain't built for the flat earth, then again, maybe he's a flashback.

John rejected the idea. The barking was real and delusions don't make footprints.

62

Monkey Business

After hours of trying Jay's frustration peaked. John Doe's stupidity wore him down. Jay had to talk like an idiot. His nonverbal expressions weren't understood either. Intelligent conversation was wasted on this strange creature who only heard half and understood less. Most of all, Jaybird didn't like being called monkey man. *That's beyond stupid. Monkeys don't talk.*

Either John Doe was high beyond treetop or as thick as a burly knot.

Nothing got accomplished. The Ancestor, if that was who this odd-knot was, wasn't going anywhere. John Doe just didn't get it. And, Jay was out of time. With the noon sun, Jay had to leave or miss his ride. It took four hours to get to the mouth of the Hudson opposite Manhattan where Dave was to pick him up. A younger stone boardwalk, closer to the ground than the one he had found, ran near John Doe's nest and Jay planned to use it.

This person can't possibly be the Ancestor.

"I'm not getting anywhere."

Noises of giant predators all around disconcerted Jay so much he could not relax. As fears grew, he pontificated faster. Jay was about to say goodbye when a giant lizard crashed out of the underbrush. Jay jumped up and landed atop Doe's head.

"Hey man, don't do that! You're fucking up my hair."

John grabbed Jay by the shirt and put him down. Jay froze in terror as the monster came right at them with its huge head swinging flicking its tongue.

"Trigger's excitable," John said. "He'd run you down nothing flat if you took off. Just chill. He's mostly a vegetarian but he'll snake on monkey now and then so don't act monkey-ish."

Doe addressed the animal. He loosened the leather thong tied around the beast's neck. Doe pulled a candy out of his top pocket and put it in the monster's mouth. Put it right in its mouth. John patted its neck.

"There, there, that's a good horsey. Now you go on and get."

John turned it around and slapped it on its rear quarter. It took off crashing through the brush knocking down everything in its path.

"A pet, a woman-eating pet, I don't believe it."

"Old Trigger's cool, a little crazy sometimes, but don't worry, he won't be back for a while."

That's the last twig. There was no getting this stranger to understand. Jay doubted everything he was told about the Ancestor. Surely, this person was not who the aliens sought.

"How can you be related to me? You have made friends with the creatures that eat people—people are food for the company you keep. Am I food?"

"Food man, wow. Did you say food? Food's a groove. I got the munchies. I never ate with my imagination before. I gotta table inside."

"What imagination?" Jay asked, his curiosity granted another minute.

John didn't answer but pointed into his house. They sat at Doe's hearth outside before the attack. It may have been safer inside, but Jay refused to go underground. Doe's place wasn't open and light like Darleen's airy house. Dirty lizards and snakes went in and out of that hole all the while and Doe never even blinked. Doe got up and walked around his little clearing with a hand out palm down.

What's he doing now?

Doe stopped, got on his knees, and chatted, "om, om, om." A fog appeared. He reached into the ground, rocked back, and stood with something wrapped in paper. Not paper made of woven hemp, but it was slick and solid and white like a beetle's shell. It had dragon writing on it.

"*White Castle* man, can't beat it for the munchies."

Doe handed Jaybird a bundle. There was meat and bread inside the package, very strange but it smelled eatable. He bit. It was a burger-bug on wheat leaf. Pretty good, too, but the sun shifted straight overhead. The timing device which Gabe had lent him sounded before Jay swallowed.

"I'm going," Jay said convinced the effort was wasted. He handed the food back to John. "Look, I must leave. Gabe and Mike need me back." Jay spoke slower and louder. "They have to leave and they will take me. I will inform them I invited you and you refused. Sorry, I couldn't convince you, but I'm going back to Manhattan. This is goodbye."

Jay took two steps and stopped.

"I'll let Mike and Gabe know. Goodbye."

John Doe didn't understand. Jay leaped onto a low branch and climbed fast. His luck held. The only low branch in a sea of pole pines was the oak he needed. John Doe's home was under the oak way branch which led to Sandy Hook. Jay didn't expect to find a lucky low branch. The lower stone boardwalk was just above and he ignored it. Jay was a hundred yards up-tree before John's shouted farewell reached his ears.

"Hey Monkey Man, don't go. I got different food. What about a *Jersey Mike's* hoagie?"

"Monkey Man?" Jay repeated. He stopped and called back. "Fuck you," and continued on his way.

He had arranged to meet Dave where Dave could land without danger, dragons get along with most creatures, but Dave feared for Jay's safety. The best landing was across the bay from lower Manhattan on a sandbar called Sandy Hook. Dave had had a bad time landing on Doe's thin beach. Sandy Hook's beach was wider and treeless, but a big inland tree had fallen and bridged the lagoon providing a path for predators. The sands shifted too much for anything green to take root, and woman-eaters avoided open space. Warm-blooded reptiles overheat fast in the sun. Jay's chances of survival were good.

He trusted Dave. But crocs didn't mind the sand as he had seen that morning. Jay felt certain Doe's pets wouldn't mind eating Dave either if given a chance. Jay had done what he could and it wasn't enough.

***

John lost sight of the little guy. "That dude's quick. What a nervous little shit."

Weird his friends didn't like Monkey Man. They scattered or hid in the house. Even Trigger was wound up. Why would a diplodocus fear one monkey but eat another kind? Monkey Man didn't like his pets either. John stood smoking and watching the treetops until a little pine lizard jumped on his head which snapped him out of it.

"Oh hey," John pulled it out of his hair and held it out in his hand. "So, man, did you catch that shit?"

The lizard inflated its neck sack.

"Did that monkey talk or am I tripping?"

The lizard bobbed rapidly.

"Yeah man, I see your point, you think it talked, too. Did you make anything out? I didn't think so. Fucked up my schedule. Man, I got venom from the big suckers. This shit will kill me for sure. I figured it out. This shit will do the trick."

John pulled the little bottle out of his front pocket. That part was real. *If the poison is real, too, maybe the talking monkey's real.* He tapped the vial on his lips.

"Man, I could swear that monkey said Gabe and Mike are here, them fuckers. I remember them. Come to think of it. I'm remembering a lot of shit. It's crazy shit, but… I don't know man. You think I should go up to the city?"

The lizard bobbed frantically.

"Oh wow, chill. OK, I'll go. Fuck it. I'll kill myself tomorrow."

He held the bottle up to the sun and shook it. Particles whizzed around. He had an overpowering urge to rip the cork out with his teeth and drink it.

"Bring it along, what if I get thirsty?" The lizard froze. "Alright, alright." He put it back in his pocket.

Once he stopped laughing, he put two fingers in his mouth and whistled. Trigger started crashing his way back. John felt pretty sure he was insane before today. All that stuff in his head was nuts. Then again, the more he remembered the more it was right on. Memories had been coming back in big waves since the sky turned blue. But that spaceship over Manhattan blew the stop-gate wide open. His mind had been flying since. A new memory wave came on as Trigger slid to a halt.

He as a boy and the books he had read, his parents, Margo, and that first dying day crashed upon him. The day he became aware bubbled into focus. Dad was talking about immortals and he was one. Only death ever stopped this kind of wild shit from filling his head. Suicide was his only relief. He had killed himself and his memories over and over but he always came back and the search started all over again. It was all one long song. He pulled out the vial.

"This will stop my crazy train once and for all." He pulled the cork and put the little bottle to his lips.

But what if it was all real? He had never tried to find out. If the shit in his head was real then Monkey Man was real, too.

"I should figure it out." He dumped the bottle and tossed it into the firepit.

"Come on Trigger, let's go find Roy Rogers and his faithful sidekick, Toto."

John mounted his stead laughing like an idiot. His animal was the size of a draft horse, and John rode him often, but it wasn't anything like a horse. It was more like a tractor. He grabbed its mane to hang on. Neck hair was its only horse-like quality. The rest was 100% dinosaur.

"Hi-ho, Silver, away!"

His steed didn't move.

"OK, fine." He stuffed candy into its mouth. "Gitty-up."

John steered north along the edge of the scrub forest. Trigger trotted much faster than the original Trigger could run. Roy Rodgers' horse would have had to go around what John's ride plowed under.

63

Making Ready

Gabe moved the shuttle to westside Manhattan facing Jersey where Darleen said there was a flat spot with room for everyone. The Wave will come from the east and meeting below the peak gained a few seconds. He stood near the ship's door counting the minutes. It was sundown, but End Wave projected visible light ahead of itself making dusk a strange blue. The dinosaurs were fidgety and for good reason. Gabe was too, he had removed a key safety device from his ship.

Gabe adjusted his mind to better understand Jay's quick speech. It didn't take but a few minutes to get Jay's story. What he reported amounted to John Doe was barking-frog mad. Upon Jay's return, Moon Base had sent a sacrificial AI flyer to John Doe's camp as Jay provided the location. Gabe ordered it fast, but too late. Doe's live readings weren't detected.

The AI had projected its analysis into Gabe's handheld. Moon rechecked and confirmed it. John Doe was dead. He must have swallowed that venom and wandered off to die. An empty vial was found with enough toxic residue remaining to kill a dozen dragons. There was no way to find his body in that tangled jungle.

"Yeah, he killed himself," Mike said reading his handheld.

"Why do humans do that?" Gabe lamented. "He's dead for good now."

"Human," Jay said, "I'm human. That creature's not human. He's insane. That's why. You can't fix crazy."

"He'll never reconstitute again. There isn't anything more to do." Gabe said.

"What about the body?" Darleen said.

"We don't have time," Mike answered. "Wave's almost on us. We got to go. Darleen, you pulled in your people, right?"

"We are here. Why did you ask this? We are done with Mass."

"Tell her, Gabe," Mike said. "You're the boss. This one's all on you. I still say we shouldn't."

"What, what should he not do? What is worse than the Wave?" Darleen said.

"I put a shield around here," Gabe said. "It'll fade after the Wave passes. You and yours' are protected. You won't be affected. I'm not allowed to do that."

He could not help but drop his wings. His good deed should be joyful. But, breaking First Directive will get him more than a demotion. It will be jail time. Stealing company equipment meant hard time.

"Your world won't be the same," Gabe said. "But you'll stay as you are now, barring natural evolution. The ones left out there—"

Gabe pointed inland. Dinosaurs, intelligent and not, were everywhere and there was no way to gather them in.

"Noah's ark never happened. They won't make it."

"Some will," Mike said. "Base models don't suffer Wave effects, Waves made them. The advanced ones get screwed."

"It's better if we die," Darleen said. "We can't deliver the Book. We will become insane. We are linked. Don't you see? We will become what we fear."

"We don't know that," Gabe said. "It's worth a try. He's gone forever. The Burden died with him."

Gabe got to know Darleen and her people and he saw great promise in them. They were the first nonhumans he met who deserved Center's protection. That shield was going to cost him dearly. *Fine, there's nothing left for me with the Planet Molders anyway.*

He felt The Galactic Trade Organization wouldn't touch him with a ten-foot thruster rod after this bonehead move. He had failed Her Centerness in all things and he will take his lumps like an angel. But he won't fail Darleen and her people, too. That much he got right.

Go out in flames.

"Gabe, it's time. We gotta go," Mike said with no sign of his usual good humor.

"He's right, we can't be on the ground when it comes. I'm sorry, Jay. We can't shield your tribe. Come with us?" Gabe said.

"There's nothing for me here," Jay said.

"Gabe, you can't do that!"

"Shut up, Mike, just shut up. I'm doing it."

"Where you guys been, Jesus tap-dancing Christ!" John Doe said coming around a boulder. "You fuckers better have a good story."

"You remember!" Gabe cried as alarms rang.

"Man, I remember everything, weird right?"

"No time. Get in the shuttle! Quick, it's here," Mike cried.

Mike ran up the ramp with Jay close behind. Gabe took John by the arm and drug him through the shuttle's door. The sky lit like a rainbow. Doe grabbed the open door's jamb to hold it open. Gabe slapped his hand down.

"What about the Book?" Darleen called as the door slid shut.

Mike was at the controls. The ship lifted off. Gabe picked up the intercom. "Consider it delivered."

***

They flew to Far Side Moon Base, out of the Wave's reach, and just in time. Gabe's team stayed three days until the Wave cleared. Gabe thought to send a remote back to pick up the volumes Darleen had made but there was no point in it. Left there, the books will crumble like everything else that remained of the old world. Gabe had to get going anyway.

The recall signal had beckoned. After medical had worked him over, John was put into stasis. Twenty light-years outbound and well clear of Waves, Gabe woke John. It was to be a long trip to Center Station. There was no reason to keep him on ice. John was fun back in their temple days together. The old hippie had adapted to ship life with ease.

Gabe was in his office when John walked in with a lit joint.

"Hey no, smoking," Gabe said, "Don't you know the rules?"

Of course, he did. He knew everything. The tank infuses information. The upload took in both directions. Control got its DNA prize, and John's Book of Answers for social construction. By executive decision with no explanation, Gabe didn't get fired although he had broken every rule in the book.

"Rules, John, Planet Molders go by the rules…"

"Fuck that," John said, blowing smoke. "Since when did you dudes follow rules? Rules are for The Man, man, the establishment, not dudes like us. Fuck the Man."

"She at the Center is not a man," Gabe said.

"The chamber, where you put all my people, it's what, like five years ago ship-time, right?"

"That's correct."

"And the Tribes I sent to temple, they still cool?"

"Yes of course, to them only a few months have passed," Gabe said.

"That hot chick Bertha made it, right? That's the one I sent to Springfield on a dragon." John said taking a hit. Gabe gave a thumbs-up. "Far out, I'm going in. See you suckers later."

John took off toward the multi-dimensional transfer containment vessel.

Gabe should have stopped him. He should have put a lock-out on the containment controller. Real-time visiting a subject race in holding was against the rules. John was crew now. *If he goes in, he can't come out until planet-fall. That'll take years in ship-time.*

She might put them on ice permanently for all Gabe knew. He had no idea if that planet where they had chased off the Grays was ready. Gabe didn't have new orders. He picked up the intercom.

"John, wait, I'm coming with you. Mike, I'm going inside the D-tank, you're in charge."

Gabe ran down the hall dropping feathers. He didn't care. He caught up with

John at the port entry. John wore a backpack stuffed with weed. He had ripped off the Earth hires stash.

Stealing's prohibited. That's Mike's problem now.

"Did you get seeds?" Gabe asked.

"Do hippies shit in Golden Gate Park? Yeah man, papers, too. Here you go."

John handed Gabe a lit joint. He never smoked while on duty before, but Gabe took a big hit. Together they entered the multidimensional transport containment field and arrived in the Garden of Eden properly stoned.

***

The Librarian rested easy drinking tea at table. Manhattan had greened outside of her kitchen's window. They used to kill any plant that grew to prevent the migration of dangers, but now Darleen welcomed it. Little of New York City remained.

The giant forests had laid down. New environments had sprung from the rot. New species appeared out of nothing. The Creation Wave filled its namesake. Animals did not venture into rock-bear New York before but now it was full of the sounds and sights of life.

Let the flora crack stones. Let time, roots, and rot eat old New York.

"Fitting," she said of the branch that scraped her new glass window in the breeze.

The New York Public Library itself remained, thanks to Gabe's force shield. It could stand for generations if allowed. Darleen struggled with it. The Librarian didn't see the Priestess coming until she nearly arrived. The path had overgrown. Darleen opened her door.

"Leave your monkey outside, please," Darleen said.

The Librarian had nothing against pets but this one resembled the mayor. Humans became animals. That creature may have been Mayor Morgan for all she knew. The Priestess tied her monkey's leash to a sapling.

The usual official pleasantries were exchanged. *That too will soon end.* There was no longer a need for a Priestess or a Librarian. New leadership titles were being considered. The youth were excited to take a role in governance. The elders rather preferred the library to be gone and forgotten.

"How goes the book burning?" Darleen asked serving tea. Having spent so much time overseeing the books made her unable to watch them burn.

"That is why I'm here. The young don't like it. They want to save them. They're making waves. They want the books."

"No, we can't allow it. They must go or we'll have a religion on our hands. You heard what Mike said."

"Of course. These kids don't know John Doe but he is worth knowing. Should we give them a break and save a few Red Books? They are curious."

"That's what I fear," Darleen said. "Let nothing of the past bleed on their future."

She had hung on too long. Giving up her life's work was hard. She spent a thousand years organizing those stacks, filling in the blank pages, making sense of it all. But, still, it must be done. She had them burned outside because she could not bring herself to torch the library. This failure exposed youngsters to the Burden. That was a mistake.

"The burning will take years at this rate. It's a lot of work," the Priestess said.

"How many left inside?"

"Half and that's a shit load. It'll take a year just to bring them out."

"Torch it, the library, set it to flame before the kids can sneak in there."

The Priestess did a double-take.

"Are you sure?"

"Does John Doe shit in space?"

***

"Come on," Ralf Corvair Nader said. "It's going up in flames, there's a hole in the back wall. Let's go."

"Are you nuts?" Mick Jagger Stone said.

Mick was a big dragon for eleven years old and he wasn't able to fit through the hole in the library's back wall. Ralf was always making Mick do stuff Ralf didn't want to do, but not this time.

"I'm not getting burnt feathers for some dumb old books," Mick said. "You want them, you get them."

"Fine, I'll do it myself!"

Ralf was small and skinny for fifteen years old. He was an egg when the library was closed. Mick figured he better tag along in case Ralf got stuck. Ralf was skinny but that hole was pretty small.

The boys made it to the back of the library unseen. Smoke poured out of that hole. Still, Ralf reached in and managed to grab a couple of red books. The boys backed away and checked them out.

"Shit on a cracker! I almost got burned for this." Ralf said handing three skinny books to Mick. "Dragon diaries, boring!"

Mick separated a few wet pages. "Smell that mold. It's all stuck together."

"No shit, Sherlock." Ralf grabbed the books back. "I bet the good stuff got burned first."

Smoke poured out worse. Ralf tossed all put one book toward the hole. With so much smoke, Mick didn't know if they reached the hole or not. *Whatever.* Nobody wanted to read a grownup's diary but Ralf kept the best condition one.

"The girls might find it interesting but so what?" Mick said pointing at the book. "You better toss it or they'll follow you everywhere."

"You're right," Ralf said chucking it into the hole.

"Only old farts care about the before-time. Boring!"

"And Girls!"

The boys decided to go fishing at Sandy Hook. The library didn't hold Mick's interest long. He understood the world was new with much to discover.

Why waste time?

EPILOGUE:

At Center, everything is an avatar. The human mind cannot conceive of Her true nature or surroundings. She created places to communicate directly with the people She hired. That was how She had explained it to Zinno. Zinno was called to give Her a summery reading of the Earth report.

She had other realms for other beings. This room was a cube of bright white energy hanging in space made for the angel race. She appeared in forms her beings could understand. She took her best guess anyway, and not always with good results.

"People don't get how far out of the way I go for them." She said over Zinno who was reading aloud.

Zinno stopped. She visited Her creations in their local form and tried to help them along from time to time. Her direct involvement usually produced bad results. He was reading Her that part again. She shouldn't have gone to Earth in the guise of Shiva. India never recovered. That was a mistake. He finished that chapter.

"I'm not perfect, so shoot me," she said.

She insisted that Zinno read the bad parts along with the good and then She made him read the bad parts again. She didn't like it but She had him do it anyway.

He ignored Her comments for the most part and read on. It was a long book. Zinno, the highest of angels, finished. He laid the Book of John down on a white-on-white table—the only furniture present.

"That's it. The whole story. The important part is we have the DNA. The rest of it…I don't know if the social engineering took."

He put a hand on the Book. While he read, She paced the cube. At times during the ordeal, he could barely sense Her unless She stopped.

"I told you I had to go. You see why right?"

He saw Her avatar but not Her point. It was difficult to take Her seriously.

She was in the form of a 14-year-old Earth girl who was too skinny. The unruly page-boy haircut was ugly. Her teeth were too big for Her mouth. The tutu and a blue T-shirt with a big metallic star on Her flat chest fit the motif, he granted. But She forgot the boobs again.

"I'll search the footnotes and appendices. Our files are—"

"That's how it works, see. You don't get it, do you?"

"…are in the mainframe. I have whatever the recorders witnessed. There are holes, of course, but—"

"You want to know or what?" She said.

It was best to play along when She was in this mood. He gave up reading.

"Please explain."

"Someone has to die, duh. Nothing changes if nobody dies, see?"

"Well…I'm sorry but—"

"I had to die again. Just ask Jesus, he knows, right."

Jesus appeared.

"Hey Ma, you called. Why are you doing, Margo?"

"I'm not. I'm Pope Joan, see." She spun around holding out her tutu. "Tell him somebody had to die. That's how it works. Tell him."

Jesus repeated what She had just said and in the same way. But Jesus added his touch by rolling his avatar eyes along with the words.

"OK, Ma? I have to get back to the transport pod. It's about to dock. An empty pod won't do. It's your plan remember? We'll talk later. OK, Zinny?"

"Whatever dismissed," She said with a flip of her hand. She turned back to Zinno the scribe. "You get it now, right. Gawwwed, I hope so. Get back to Central Control. Bust Gabe and Mike back to labor. They deserve a promotion. I'm hungry."

"I understand," Zinno said. "Gabe's already on the job. He's inside the seed containment vessel with John Doe and—"

"They got good burgers on Nefertiti Two. Real cows," She said and disappeared.

Zinno didn't get it. What he did get was an evolved Earth-human group ready to seed a new planet. He also received a new intelligent species to watch over on a recycled planet.

It may be that this arrangement was what She intended all along. The work never ends. It dawned on him that the Earth was reset back to the original plan. The dinosaurs who were supposed to rule finally got their day. She had taken the long way around to get the original project back on track but managed it just the same.

"The reset worked. If only She had seen that asteroid, all of this could have been avoided. Or did She send it? God only knows, if there is one."

Her Centerness got two for the price of one. Was it an accident? The Milky Way's intelligent designer wasn't perfect. However, the side effects of Her mistakes—if that is what they are—were extremely creative.

THE END

ABOUT THE AUTHOR:

Rachel C. Thompson, writing as R.C. Thom, began her writing career in journalism after surviving a near-death motorcycle accident in 2003. She has published nonfiction pieces and cartoons in newspapers, magazines, and materials for nonprofit organizations. Her short stories have appeared in various anthologies. *Book of Answers* is her fifth novel. *The Adventures of Tom Conley*, her sixth novel, will follow soon along with her next anthology of quirky sci-fi.

Thompson—writer, painter and musician—worked in construction for 25 years before going on to write full time. Keep an eye out for her nonfiction title about the home improvements industry, *Construction Confidential*.

ACKNOWLEDGEMENTS:

Many thanks to everyone that provided expertise and support on this book and in the past on other projects which led to this one.

In random order:

Thank you, Angel Ackerman, my former news editor and mentor, who helped proof this book and did far more than I expected. I asked Angel for a little help and she gave a lot; Lisa Cross my life mate, main reader and story critic; the Greater Lehigh Valley Writers Group and its network of supporters and critique partners.

Thank you, Gayle F. Hendricks, my book formatting guru and book designer who always does more than I ask. Finally, that college professor who told me in 1979, regarding a story I wrote for a college class, "Hey, that's pretty good." This book was based on that story and his encouragement lit my desire to write.

"Any sufficiently advanced technology is indistinguishable from magic."
— Arthur C. Clarke: *The Third Law Of Robotics 1962*

www.ingramcontent.com/pod-product-compliance
Lightning Source LLC
Chambersburg PA
CBHW011927300726
48970CB00008B/2599